The Breath of Woman's Nature

The Nameless Series Book Three

by Christina L. Barr

www.NinjaDustPublishing.com

Table of Contents

Chapter One

I like to believe women have the power to become anything they desire, and it was my intention to create a world where such possibilities could flourish. But becoming whatever your heart desires isn't always an admirable ambition. After all, the heart is deceitful above all things. The truth, as I have often observed, is that women do not become who they wish to be. They evolve into what the world needs from them.

I was told I could be a queen or a god. Whatever I desired, I could have. The most powerful man in the world could make it so.

But all I wanted was to be his wife and a mother. All I wanted was to enjoy the morning stillness when I could sense the sun's presence and not feel the burden of its sting. There, I would lie in my bed, fashioned by my beloved's hands, and rest between the love shared that night and the future we had yet to make in the morning.

I felt his eyes on me. My chemise was on the floor. I recalled tossing it over my head during our previous passionate encounter. A blanket was draped over the front of my body, but my back was exposed. "You're staring again."

"Sorry…" John mumbled and sat on my sheets. I turned to scold him. His skin smelled like frosted wind, and his face and chest possessed a good sheen. If not for his miserable smile, I would have fussed. "I don't mean to stare, I only wish I could have healed your wounds."

"If my wounds weren't healed, you wouldn't see the scars. Just because I'm imperfect—"

"Oh, you could never be 'imperfect,' my dear. You are pure perfection." He was so handsome as his lips curled and pulled into my body. His tender kisses felt like a dream. Sometimes, I expected Miss Ruth to snatch my hair and pull me back into my old life on the plantation, but the dream kept on. If not for John's nose feeling cold and wet like a dog, we would have made some more fantasies together.

"How far did you run today? Ten miles? Twenty?" I leaned over and picked the chemise off the floor. The fire was getting low and needed another log. One thing I missed about the South was the warmth. At least, that's how I felt in the winter.

"No. I only ran a few miles to the general store. I thought I'd surprise you with a nice breakfast."

"Breakfast?" My voice cracked as I sat up against the bedframe. "That's rather different of you."

"I wanted to do something extraordinary for my beloved. Come and eat."

"I'm not hungry. At least, not for food." I raised my brow, hoping to entice him. I could tolerate his cold body and sweaty trousers if it meant avoiding whatever concoction he whipped up.

"You know I can't resist a good proposition…" It was a deception well worth the sacrifice. The Lord crafted John's lips for mine. It was a wonder that he found the will to mumble, "…but if we get distracted in bed, your food will get cold."

John peeled away. Surely, he heard my elevated heart with his superior hearing. Unfortunately for me, he could tell when I was excited merely by his touch and when I was being deceitful. "Are you avoiding my breakfast?"

"Well…"

"Woman, you are going to eat my breakfast." He scooped me into his arms. I kicked and pleaded, but he held on tightly and blinked through the doorway, down the stairs, and into the dining room. The table had already been set. There was a newspaper, a fresh bouquet of flowers in a vase—a daily gesture from my romantic husband—and a pot of tea that smelled of peaches. It was my favorite, but we ran out the night before. Though the possibilities of his creations mortified me, I slumped my shoulders in defeat. I owed him a nibble or two.

"What did you make?"

John grinned and rushed to the kitchen. While I anxiously waited for my last meal, my eyes fell on the paper.

He returned with two plates and set one in front of me. The fried potatoes were a bit oily, but they had onions and parsley. Visually, I didn't suspect I'd die. There were also some roasted tomatoes. They were lovely. But I didn't recognize whatever the yellow slop was supposed to be on top of my bread. "Eggs and potatoes."

"Who taught you how to make eggs like this? It certainly wasn't me."

"Adam taught me."

"Adam?" I scoffed. "He's British and clearly still bitter about the Revolution."

"Charlotte, you don't have to be that way. You know he's one of us." He laughed, but his impatience seeped through.

"John, I have poached, fried, and scrambled your eggs for years, and you have never witnessed a monstrosity like this. As much as I appreciate your kind gesture—"

"Woman, you will eat my eggs." John used his foot to pull the leg of my chair forward, then burned his eyes into mine. They weren't shining gold, but he hardly needed his "sway" after adding that gravel in his voice.

"Alright." I cut a piece with the edge of my fork. John wasn't eyeing me like a doe-eyed hopeful child whose whole world would be crushed if I didn't approve. He was smiling like he already knew what I was going to say.

"Well?"

I narrowed my eyes and chewed slowly. "It could use a little bit more salt, but you did fairly well."

"Honestly?" There was the doe-eyed hopeful! It always flattered me that he cared so much about my opinion. I dove into his lips.

"What was that for?"

“I love it when a man can cook,” I smirked while my arms were still around his neck. “It’s rather attractive.”

“I suppose I’ll have to keep at it then.”

It didn’t take much to set us off into bouts of intimacy. We were young, very much in love, and making up for lost time. Our food did get cold, but it was tolerable after sprinkling some salt on it. John warmed the tea as I smelled my flowers. That day, they were roses. The day before, he brought me daisies. I could only imagine what he’d bring me tomorrow. Even if he had to travel far, John still brought me gifts. After he set the tea down on the table, John grabbed hold of my waist and sniffed my neck.

“Again, John?”

“I’m sorry, my dear, but you smell divine. Something about your scent has changed.”

I gently pushed away from John. “Changed how?”

“I don’t know how to describe it, but I can’t stand the thought of being away from you. I think I’d go mad.”

“Well, you’ll get no argument from me on that.” As much as I wanted John to keep me prisoner all day, we had things to do and people to see. Besides, the newspaper killed my excitement.

Lincoln’s War Divides Union, Reelection Bid in Jeopardy.

The Union had grown weary of the prolonged war, and General Robert E. Lee seemed invincible. Lincoln recently hired a new general, Ulysses S. Grant, who was said to be a hero in the Mexican-American War, but he was also rumored to be an alcoholic. Many Unionists were furious that Lincoln fired George McClellan, despite his losses. McClellan was a vocal critic and gained traction as a potential contender to unseat Lincoln. If he defeated Lincoln, I feared the end of the war wouldn’t lead to abolition. And if the end of the war were to result in the country becoming more intolerant, John would surely unleash his wrath.

“What do you make of all this, John? Do you think Lincoln will lose his reelection?"

"Why does it matter? It’s rumored he’ll put a Democrat on the ballot to gain power. Sooner or later, the Democrats will be in charge.”

“They’re aligned in winning the war against the South.”

"But they're not aligned in what to make of slaves." John placed his finger under my chin and guided me into his eyes. "Don't put your faith in these humans, Charlotte. I'd hate to see you disappointed."

I could take being disappointed. When you extended your faith in anyone, they were bound to let you down eventually. I could stand a little heartache. I couldn't bear to spend the rest of my life without hope. But John didn't understand my need to grant grace to humans. He never had the benefit of someone like Joseph Cooper to showcase the best of humanity, so I nodded to hush him up. "Have there been any letters?"

"Not since Mary Anne's update on the hotel, and she only assured me the bills were paid." A sly smirk formed on John's lips. "If you miss her, you should go see her. Perhaps we can persuade her to join us."

A shiver went down my spine. I didn't speak my concerns about Mary Anne out loud, but he must have sensed her killer instinct. I much preferred her living a domestic life at the Crimson Hotel with Cooper, helping colored people in New York. "No, it's not the right time." Besides, I couldn't see Mary Anne without seeing Cooper, and the wounds between us were deep. I wasn't ready to pick at those scabs.

And I knew John. He wouldn't like it either.

"I'll change into something warm and meet you outside for our training."

A solemn expression overtook John, and he nodded. John respected me as a warrior, but he was gentler than Cooper. When we sparred together, I never truly felt like we were fighting. John would move so fast, I could never lay a hand on him. And John would never consider laying a hand on me. I might as well have been sparring with a gnat.

Eventually, I'd get frustrated and try blinking behind John, but he'd ever-so-slightly move his head and catch my wrist. "Come on, Charlotte. If you always depend on your powers, you won't get faster." Then his other hand latched onto my arm, and he hurled me over his shoulder.

My hands and feet landed in the soft snow. I loved that John was faster and more powerful than any other man, but I hated that I could never beat him. If I blinked, he could sometimes sense where I reappeared. It was a wasted advantage, so I resumed with my punches.

Cooper viewed pain as a teacher that needed to be surpassed. John viewed pain as an admission of failure and weakness. Even when I did manage to hit his face, it hurt me more than it damaged him. And after I quickly winced from the pain, I saw the brunt of the sting in his eyes. "I'm sorry."

"If you were truly sorry, you'd lose!" I wanted to beat him so badly. I tried to knee him in the gut and some fancy combinations, but he'd block, bob, and weave every time. My last trick was to look up and blink real high in the sky. John gazed with a stupor as he waited for me to come back down. But I didn't mean to be at the mercy of gravity. I balled up my right fist, pulled back my elbow, and threw my whole arm forward just as I blinked in front of his face.

But my whole body rippled after my knuckles cracked against the palm of his hand. "Interesting attack. I'm sure that'll work on someone other than me."

I growled like an angry dog and jumped on John's back. He thought it was funny, but I was trying to choke him. I didn't expect him to let me win, but I certainly hated losing. "One of these days—"

"If you could ever manage to defeat me, that would mean I suffered a dramatic decline in ability, Charlotte. Most women would be happy to have such a superior man as their spouse."

"I'm not like most women!" I only tried to choke him for a little while longer. Besides, he was strong enough to pull me over his shoulders, carry me in his arms, and kiss my cheek and neck. From then on, my anger erupted into infectious giggles. I found John's strength to be rather alluring. There was so much we could accomplish together. With his nearly indestructible hands, we would build a future for our people and whoever else came from our union.

But I wasn't indestructible, and there was only so much my brass knuckle gloves could accomplish. For that reason, John also had a firing range in the backyard. Learning how to load and fire a rifle and a pistol was part of our morning training. After a while, I could clear a can from sixty yards, but John said it was more important that I worked on consistently firing back-to-back. John didn't care too much for guns, but he was good at shooting. I'd blink across the field and throw out targets, and John would rarely miss with his Colt. It made me glad to know we were such capable individuals, but I had a horrible feeling that I couldn't shake. Sooner or later, I was afraid our perfect little life would be torn from us.

John seemed completely unbothered. He was either militantly focused on the future or diligently present in our marital bliss. I didn't have the heart to burden him with my fears, so I tried to drown my worries in a warm bath. I liked to spoil myself with special soaps and tonics to make my skin soft and fragrant. I liked reading different magazines to see what sort of advice there was for women's skincare.

John always thought I spent far too much time in my copper bath, so I was never surprised when he interrupted my relaxation time. "Is that oatmeal on your face?"

I was in the midst of rinsing when he came in. He didn't even let me get a chance to speak before his spoon dove into the bowl. "Charlotte, this needs more sugar." And that simple fool took another two bites before furrowing his face in disgust.

"That wasn't for you to consume, John!"

"You know, the experts say cold baths are better for you."

"Those experts don't have to deal with you every morning." A cold bath would have been good for bruises, but I wanted to soothe my body. "John, if you come in here, you'll smell like a woman."

"No, I'll smell like *my* woman, and I'm going to smell like you anyway." Well, I didn't mind when he put it like that. John stripped bare and dove in to kiss my neck. I would have been annoyed about him spilling water on my floors, but his touch was euphoric. It wasn't long before his tender and ticklish lips stirred a bout of insatiable passion within me.

"I thought we didn't have time…" John had a handsome curl on his lips. I had pinned him against the copper frame, so our tardiness would have been on me.

I cupped the face of my beloved, grazing the sharp lines of his jaw with my thumbs. "We can always make time for our world, John. Always." I received no more objections. There was just enough space for me to wrap myself around my husband and pleasure him once more.

When we finished our bath, John's eyes were still on me as I dried and clothed my body. It made me wonder how long he'd be under my spell. My fingers were pruned from water, but one day, they would wrinkle with time. I had many years to worry about such things, and living that long would be a blessing. "Do you think you'll still love me as an old woman?"

John's head propped up from the task of tightening the laces on my black corset. "What sort of nonsense question is that?"

As I turned to face him, his eyes briefly wandered to my chest. "What happens when you can't cup my breasts, and you have to scoop them off the floor?"

John released a bellowing laugh. I asked my question with a smile, but his delayed response grated on my patience. "And will you love me when my belly resembles a barrel more than a board?"

"You are not growing a belly, John. Not on my watch!" I tried to pinch him, but he was too quick and lean for me to grab.

"Oh, but you will!" His hands snaked from behind and hugged my waist. "I will love you when you are plump after years of birthing our ten children."

"Excuse me?" I practically twirled in the air. "We have never spoken about ten children, and I will not agree to that many unless they can blink out of my womb."

"It'll be your fault, woman. You can't keep your hands off of me." Oh, he blamed me, yet John was the one who rushed me with ticklish kisses upon my neck and chest. I withered in his grasp, completely unable to resist.

I imagined a growing belly in the mirror as John smothered me with affection. "You know, if we keep up this pace, I'll be pregnant very soon. If not, I would assume something is wrong—"

"Nothing is wrong, Charlotte. God just knows we're not ready yet. We need time."

"Time?" I had already waited too long for him to be my husband. "Time for what, John?"

"To build a new world. If we had a child right now..." John's voice trailed as his gaze wandered down a dark and distant path. His grip on me loosened, but his hands and eyes rested on my womb. John's head was down, but his reflection was dimly lit.

"Are you afraid of your sway?"

His chin dug into my chest as his head went limp. "I know the kind of man I am to keep you safe, and you haven't always liked that man. I don't know what I'd become to keep my children from harm."

John could persuade others, but he was the greatest victim of that terrible power. Once his sway was activated, it was nearly impossible to weaken his resolve—whether right or wrong.

I pulled away enough to turn and face my husband's golden eyes, but they flickered and faded into beautiful blue rivers, eager to pull me into their rapid current. I placed my hands on his shoulders, hoping to steady us both. "I haven't always approved of your methods, John, but I've always loved you."

John swallowed a lump in his throat. Sixteen years faded from my husband's face, but even as a child, I had never witnessed such an expression from my beloved. "And are you happy, Mrs. Cohen?"

I chuckled at that helpless fool for even thinking he had to ask such a thing. "Unbearably."

I closed my eyes and leaned in to display my affection, but they popped open when he latched onto my arms. "John, what's wrong?"

A thud followed, and John rushed to the foyer. I chased after him and gasped at the quivering black body, covered in dust and blood. His face was pressed into the floor, shielded by his bruised and scraped arms, but I recognized that bare body. The scars on his back were given to me by John. "Steven!"

I dropped to my knees and rolled him over, prompting a fierce hiss. His body was warm, especially around his seared flesh, embedded with grains of dirt and tiny pebbles. A cool shadow swept over us as John's jacket descended onto Steven's body. He clutched onto it and kept his eyes on the floor as he shook.

"Where is Tillie?" John's jaw was tight, and his fingers were clenched even tighter. The longer Steven whimpered, the more his eyes burned with fury. John didn't raise his voice. It was filled with a wolfish timber that even rattled my spine. "Answer me."

Steven slowly raised his head, and the shame in his eyes exploded into a sharp sob. "The zealots took her."

"You mean you left her behind?"

"John!" I had to push against his chest. I had seen John's fury. I had even earned some of it before, but he rarely frightened me.

John lowered his voice in tone and pitch, rattling my bones once again. "If you weren't wearing her face, I'd knock your head clean off your shoulders."

"John…" I eased between the two of them to draw John's rage. "Will you please step outside until you simmer down?"

John tried to get another good glare at Steven, but I shielded him. My husband marched through the front door and slammed it shut, prompting a shake from Steven's shoulders.

I had grown used to seeing Steven take my form and wear my face, but I hadn't grown accustomed to watching him overwhelmed with emotion. The last time I had such shame in those eyes was when we held a beautiful child, as radiant and pale as a full moon's glow, lying dead with a bullet in her head. I lost another child to the cruelty of mankind. And as the faux Charlotte doubled over in tears, the aching suspicion that my world was on the other end of a lit fuse became more real to me.

Chapter Two

"I've disappointed him." It ached my whole soul to see my mirror image shaking like a leaf in a storm. Steven managed to sit up, but he was still hunched over and clutching onto John's coat for dear life. As I watched him sob with my husband's garment, my mind traveled to when I was a little girl in pain. John made me confess that I was strong.

"Is Tillie still alive?"

His lips trembled. "I think so…"

"Then stop crying! It won't do anything, so grit your teeth." Steven immediately ceased whimpering and straightened up. I'm certain he recalled my memories of Miss Ruth hovering over me and fussing. Even when I was a child, no one would allow me to be one. When there was work to be done, the work came first. "Good. Now, heal yourself."

Steven wiped his face with hands that began to lighten. I envied how his hair lengthened and straightened, though I preferred the softness of my stubborn curls to Zhang's coarse strands. The feminine curves on his body tightened and flattened into muscular bulges. I was grateful his mustache came in after his face took a masculine form. I certainly didn't want to see my face wearing whiskers. Steven didn't usually grunt and wince while transforming, but I suspected he may have had a broken bone or two. His right shoulder was a little too pointy, and when

Steven closed his eyes and took a deep breath, there was a wheeziness in his tone. He closed his eyes and opened the palms of his hands. As warm light bathed Steven's body, his wounds began to heal. The dirt and pebbles that dug into his skin fell as he wiped them away. There was even a pop as his shoulder went back into place.

"Good. Now, go and change into some of John's clothes. Hurry, then explain what happened."

"Yes, Lady Charlotte." He peeled off John's coat, and I averted my eyes as he walked upstairs. I didn't expect he'd take long, given the sensitive issue we had with time.

While we waited for Steven to join us, I went to the kitchen. I met him when the zealots captured me. He and John saved me, but I was too weak and wounded to blink home. They fed me and replenished my energy, so I wanted to return the favor. I didn't have time for anything fancy. I sliced an apple pie, cut a loaf of bread, and then started on a pot of peach tea. John came as I set a steaming cup on the dining table next to his plate.

"He left Tillie alone with those demons, and now you're giving him my pie?"

"He was busted up real bad. His wounds may be healed, but that doesn't mean he's not exhausted. Why are you being so unreasonable?"

"I trusted Steven. He's not supposed to let something like this happen." John liked to do things himself, but we'd never have personal time without delegating responsibilities. John felt guilty that we were mating like rabbits while Tillie and Steven risked their lives.

"Even if you were by Tillie's side instead of Steven, that doesn't mean you wouldn't have been captured with her or dead."

"I can't be killed."

I sighed at his stubborn and inaccurate declaration. If John were still in the circus business with his parents, his specialty could have been escaping death. He was spared when his parents were murdered. When the zealots tied us to stakes, John copied Mary Anne's powers in time to save his life, but I would have saved him if he hadn't. Of course, John wouldn't have inherited Mary Anne's powers if we hadn't come to rescue him. "This is dangerous work that we do. You can do everything right and still lose people. There are things you can't account for, like that slave who immobilized you and your mother."

John sneered. Ever since he became the "Ghost" persona, I'm sure he felt invincible, but recovering quickly from a wound didn't mean he couldn't be hurt. As long as he was a man, he'd always have a weakness. His heart was fearsome for his people, but it was also tinder. "Tillie is a true believer, and she's been loyal to me. If they have her, they'll interrogate her. Then, they'll burn her."

"We won't let that happen," Steven said while entering the dining room. John's shirt and pants fit him rather well. They were about the same height and build. They were close to the same shade, but Steven had more yellow undertones. Their eyes were similar as well, beyond being radiantly blue. They possessed the same traumatic glare, as if their past was looped in an infinite motion. I suppose they both had memories of John's mother being burned alive.

Steven clutched onto the back of a chair and pleaded, "I'll do anything to get her back, John. I swear."

I stared at John, and though he wouldn't return my gaze, I knew that he felt me firing my nags like a Gatling gun. A few seconds of silence passed before he finally relented and motioned for Steven to take a seat. "How did you lose her in the first place?"

Steven obeyed, and John and I sat down as well. "We were following the lead about the zealots' new weapon. They were transporting it to their base of operations, as we expected. It was in one of their prisoner wagons; there must have been twenty men on horseback surrounding it."

"You should have retreated," John scolded, but not too forcefully.

"We needed more information. If we couldn't gather intelligence, we would have been going in blind on our next raid. I'd rather risk my life than endanger the rest of yours."

"It wasn't only your life. Tillie was also at risk."

"And she was willing to make the sacrifice for our vision, John. All of us are."

John's body was tense. I wouldn't have been surprised if he still wanted to knock Steven's head off, but he kept his mouth shut.

"What happened to her?" I asked.

"I'm not certain. Tillie flew in close to see if she could peek inside the carriage, but she lost her bird form and fell to the ground as a woman."

My eyes met with John, and though he tried to remain calm, his brow certainly wrinkled. "And she survived the fall?"

"From what I could tell, but she was hurt." It was awful thinking about Tillie soaring through the sky, with her golden eyes focused on achieving her task for us. Then, suddenly, her reddish feathers receded, and she became too large and heavy to keep herself up. It took a lot to scare that fearsome woman, but I imagined she screamed when her eyes made contact with the ground.

"And the same happened to you?"

"I crashed and skipped like a stone. Once I realized I couldn't transform, there was nothing I could do for Tillie. They had already swooped her up." I imagined Steven as he presently was, hitting the ground so fast that he skidded and got scraped up. Steven must have been so panicked that they saw his real face. "I hobbled to my feet and ran to escape the horses. They almost got me, but then I felt my power return. I took Charlotte's form, and then I blinked out of there."

"That means you could blink us to her right now," John eagerly said. "Maybe we could catch her."

I swear, men had a talent for only hearing what they wanted. "You can't take on twenty men with no powers, John."

"The weapon has a range. They didn't lose their powers until they got close to the wagon."

"It's hard to say what the range is," Steven said. "It could be fifty yards. Maybe a hundred. Everything happened so fast, and I was running for my life."

"Then I'll have to attack from a long distance."

I glared at my beloved fool. "What if the range extends? Lady Cohen isn't around to sniff you out if you're captured again. Or even worse, they could put a bullet in your head if they decide your soul can't be cleansed. We have to be careful. You can't do this alone, and I won't allow it."

John returned my glare. I wasn't trying to doubt him as a capable man, but there was no point in being reckless. If John died, we would all be lost. He must have understood that, since he gave me a little growl. "You have no idea what made you lose your powers?"

"No, sir."

John slouched back in his chair and sighed. "Well, they know one of you escaped. They know we'll be back. We've lost the element of surprise. The Overseers won't waste time with Tillie. They'll try purifying her soul tonight with their other prisoners. We have to make a move on them today."

"Then tell me what I need to do. I'll do anything, John." Steven's eyes were already radiant, but the gleam of desperation had them shining like cut gems. His tone and expression were just like a child begging for a parent's words of affirmation, but John still had a sliver of annoyance in his eyes.

I pushed the plate of bread and pie in front of Steven before John could make him jump into battle. "Eat. Take a breath. Then come back to base. John and I will begin preparing the others."

Steven looked past me and at John before he dared to touch anything. John, reluctantly, nodded. The poor boy tore into that pie like a good ham. I wanted him to regain his strength, but Steven also needed time to regain himself. The others didn't need to see Steven shaken before going into battle.

"Come on, John. We've got work to do." I stood and finished putting on my new coat and boots. I made a decision to marry John and stand by his vision, but I was uneasy about Runaway making consistent appearances with Ghost. Runaway led slaves to freedom, and Cooper called her a hero. To the public, Ghost was a thief and a murderer.

I thought John's persona would have gained a more favorable opinion after pacifying the mob during the Draft Riots, but the papers were divided. *The New York Times* wrote about a mob and sightings of Ghost and his crew, but they wrote as though we were part of the calamity. They mentioned brawls in the streets, fires, and explosions that took lives, but they didn't hint at any supernatural or extraordinary explanations. *The New*

York Evening Post reported on sightings of the Runaway and Ghost saving black folks in the Harbor. *The New York World* made it seem as though we were beating up working-class Democrats for no good reason.

To protect Runaway from harm, I made a new getup to match my husband. I had a dark leather coat with a hood, pants, a shirt, a scarf, and goggles. I still wore a pair of gloves with brass knuckles. It was similar to my style as the Runaway, but I blinked so fast, who could tell? I also styled the rest of our gang in similar dark fashions that hid their faces. A day would come when none of us had to hide or live a double life, but that time was not upon us yet.

My husband put on a jacket, then stuffed a pair of goggles in his pocket. He grinned as I wrapped him in his scarf, and I blushed. John was always dashing, but black certainly was his color.

I caught Steven staring out of the corner of my eye as we kissed. His eyes dove into his tea once he had been found out. There was no sense in Steven being embarrassed. He was always staring, and I wasn't certain what to make of it.

"Do you know where we need to go?" My husband asked as our fingers wove together.

"Of course."

I took a breath and thought of great stone walls, reaching about thirty feet in the air. While I lived on the plantation, John and I read books about the fascinating achievements of mankind, such as the Great Wall of China. It took thousands of years to build and spanned over twelve thousand miles. It took much for humans to impress John, but he had spoken about wanting to see it one day. Just as the Chinese had built their wall to protect themselves against invaders, John did the same to protect his massive plot of land.

The government desired for explorers and families to expand out West and develop the land. The Homestead Act offered settlers a chance to acquire 160 acres, but John had a much grander vision. After selling his father's property, he presented himself to the government as an aspiring land baron and managed to buy ten thousand acres in the Dakota Territories.

It was mostly open plains to raise cattle and farm, but we had also begun to build homes for our first citizens. In the center was a large mansion cut from marble. The outside was lovely with tall columns and large windows, like many of the plantations in the South, but the inside was still a work in progress. Most nights when we could relax, John and I liked to sleep and cook in our private home. If there were an emergency, Steven would fetch us.

I thought of the backyard. It was rather plain and too cold for flowers, but there were slabs of marble waiting to be cut by the main occupier. Once I could picture the swirls in the marble, we were off.

We appeared behind a woman with long dark hair, as black as a raven and as shiny as silk. Her braid reached down to her bottom. She wore a leather coat and a plain red dress, but her boots were neatly tucked to the side, next to a folded navy blanket. The lovely stone face of the woman she carved was pointed upward toward a brighter future. "What do you think of my latest masterpiece?"

I should have known that she could sense us. That's one of the reasons she liked keeping her shoes off, even though the ground was mushy and wet from melted snow. It helped her connect with the land better and with all who were around her. "It's wonderful, Kachina."

It was strange watching her carve pieces of stone in her statue's headdress while she made feathers. She seemed to be controlling it all with her mind, but she raised her hands a lot as she worked. John would do the same. Perhaps it helped them think, like talking with your hands. "I call her the 'Spirit of Freedom.'"

Her marble woman had high cheekbones, like most Native women, but her jaw line was much sharper, while Kachina's face was rounder. Her woman was also more mature in the face, perhaps in her 30s. The stone was still rough around her arms, but she seemed to be prepping to shoot an arrow. The arrowhead itself was shaped like a star found on the US flag. "You know, there's already a statue of a woman on top of the Capitol. It's supposed to represent freedom."

"And yet men under her care forced my people off their lands, and they continue enslaving your kind. Perhaps we'll replace their statue with mine once we conquer the nation." Kachina smiled with such optimism, and John also had an amused smirk.

I wasn't sold on their dream of conquering the country, and even if I were, it was certainly further away than any of them hoped. We didn't have the numbers to fight a united America, and certainly not if they obtained aid from foreign partners. "Indians have slaves as well. I've heard some tribes are crueler than white men."

Kachina's eyes narrowed slightly. "Freemen also have slaves. It's human nature, I'm afraid. How fortunate for us that we aren't burdened with humanity." A burst of dust exploded in her statue and blew away in a gust of wind. I covered my mouth and eyes while a cloud of debris passed. A few seconds later, the Spirit's arms were free and ready for war, and her beautiful headdress was completed.

John gasped and rushed up the stone steps Kachina had created. He touched the tip of her arrow, then gazed at his student with amazement. "Your control is impeccable. It's incredible how much you've progressed."

"Well, you were an inspiring teacher." She was almost bashful to receive his praise, but it was praiseworthy. John discovered her not too long after I took Mary Anne and left him. He heard of a terrible earthquake that devastated the Indian Territory. About a hundred lives were lost, and John had a hunch that something unnatural had occurred. Kachina's father tried to instill hatred and bitterness toward the white man in his daughter by telling her tales of the Trail of Tears. He lost his parents and many friends on the road of exile. Instead, he imparted anxiety, which caused a powerful night terror that took his life. Kachina was driven out of her tribe and into the arms of John. With her abilities, John was able to quickly grow his fortune.

"I need your assistance."

"For the raid?" Her eyes brightly beamed. "You don't normally ask me to join in battle."

"These are special circumstances, and your particular set of skills is necessary." John took a hard swallow, knowing how his words would affect her. "Tillie has been taken."

After I left John, he returned to the Overseer's hideout to retrieve his mother's body for a proper burial. He went deeper into the caves and found a few more Overseers to kill and interrogate. It's also where he found Tillie pinned up and squawking. John thought it was a cruel thing to do to a beautiful hawk, so he freed Tillie, and then his sway activated. He sensed something special about the bird and nursed her back to health. He was surprised when he woke up to find a naked woman hovering over him.

After they became acquainted, Tillie and John sought me out. They found me in a couple of days, and John was furious when he saw that I was being cared for by Cooper. But instead of barging into the gym and demanding I join him, he decided to keep building his army. Tillie kept an eye on me while he traveled home to handle some affairs. He meant to sell his father's land to a wealthy plantation owner, but his prospective partner didn't want to do business with a deserter and a suspected demon. But the man's son happened to be Steven, who hated his father tremendously and sought to free his slaves. John helped Steven stage a coup, and Steven became his loyal companion ever since.

He purchased John's land and then sold both properties. Steven gave his fortune to John, and then they began building up John's persona of a land baron in the North and the territories. They were careful in the South because John was wanted for his desertion, but he grew in favor with Republican politicians by speaking about the evils of the Confederacy. The Democrats were fond of his money.

Tillie spied on me for months before John came to retrieve her. Then, they found Kachina and rapidly expanded his fortune and their empire. The four of them were extremely close. Steven was John's right hand, Tillie was his master spy, and Kachina was entrusted with our growing nation.

She only allowed a flash of panic to manifest in her eyes before calming. "Should we get the others?"

"I want everyone."

"Even the humans?"

"Only the representatives. They need to be ready to defend our home in case of an attack, but I don't plan on bringing any of them along. They'll only slow us down."

"Understood. I'll have everyone gathered in Communion Circle within thirty minutes." Kachina rushed away, mounted one of the horses in the closest steeple, and went to find Henry and his best friend, Arthur. They were likely at the tavern because Henry was always eating if he wasn't running. Once she told them we were having a meeting, everyone would press their way.

John continued admiring the statue of the lovely Indian warrior. She was smooth and polished as if Michelangelo had spent months crafting her. If John inherited Kachina's increased power upon her death, would he be able to create cities with a thought? And would he keep such a power? He let go of Asha's power, and now, there was nothing left of her besides the doll meant for our future children. "There is something we haven't discussed."

"I wasn't going to keep you from the battle, Charlotte. I didn't plan on wasting my breath."

"No, it's not that." I hated to even broach the subject. It churned my stomach even contemplating the words, especially while standing in the shadow of Kachina's masterpiece. "When Mary Anne's father gave her up to the zealots, he didn't know they were going to kill her. He claimed they were going to cleanse her."

"The zealots cleanse by fire."

"That's what they usually do or have done in the past, but now we know they can take away our powers."

"Only in proximity to the weapon."

"That's what we assume, John. That's what we *want* to assume…" It was Cooper who first mentioned the possibility to me, and I wouldn't entertain it then. But even though Mary Anne's father was a prejudiced man, he didn't strike me as a man incapable of loving his daughter. "They were transporting her somewhere. What if they didn't plan to burn her? What if they were going to cure her?"

"We're not sick, Charlotte. We don't need a cure."

"I know, John…" The way he snapped made me want to retreat into momentary silence, but I had to press through. "I love what I can do. But what if there is a way to permanently remove our powers?"

John sneered as he allowed the thought to permeate. I saw my ability as a gift from God. It gave me freedom, offered freedom to others, and connected me to the people I loved most in the world. To John, we were God's gift to mankind. We were his superior creation meant to dominate the fallen world. To the zealots, we were abominations and the products of a fallen, sinful nature. John, of course, believed God agreed with his view. But how could there be a cure for the divine? "Then we need to destroy whatever is causing this to happen. Whether it's a machine, a potion, or even a person, it needs to be eradicated."

"A person?" I hadn't considered it, and I wasn't ready to affirm murder.

"The zealots used that slave to try to kill us, Charlotte. He's the reason I was captured and why my mother was killed. Anyone who sides with the zealots is a traitor and needs to be destroyed." He jumped from the stone platform and grabbed my arms. "Are you with me?"

I'm certain that if John could see his reflection in my eyes, he would have interpreted his steely gaze as determination to do what was necessary to survive. To me, my beloved appeared desperate, and that startled me. I questioned whether he was truly trapped in marital bliss or if he shared the same uneasiness I did about the future. "I'm always with you, John."

I wrapped my arms around him tightly. It took him a few seconds to press his hands into my back and give me a good rub. "I won't allow anyone to jeopardize our future, Charlotte. I promised when I took you as my bride that you would be unshackled from the insecure frailties of this world. We will be free to be as God made us, and no one will take that away."

No doubt, John felt my heart pounding. It was embarrassing to be afraid, but we were about to hit the last known stronghold of the zealots. There was always the chance we could die, but I rated that rather low. We were all too powerful, especially John. After the zealots were defeated, we would continue to build our world of freedom. And after the Americans no longer had an enemy to fight, they would turn their eyes toward us.

John made a promise to me when we were wed, and I also made a promise to my husband. Part of me dreaded it, but I accepted that my freedom was contingent on my willingness to fulfill it. “Come on. Let’s go prepare our people for battle.”

John smirked as I peeled away from his body and took his hand. Communion Circle was part of our town square. Kachina made it by digging semi-circular layers into the ground, similar to a fan. It was a descending auditorium that could fit a couple of hundred people inside, and there was a stone platform in the center for our stage. I wanted John and some of the men to build a pavilion. I imagined that one day, children would be gathered for plays and puppet shows. Perhaps I’d put some of John’s circus blood to good use.

Our people trickled in. Adam, the British man who dared to teach my husband how to cook soggy eggs, came in swaggering first. “Did she enjoy breakfast?”

I folded my arms and glared, but John gave it away with a nod. I elbowed my beloved, and he had the audacity to laugh. “What? You liked it!”

He was a handsome fellow with long curly hair that bounced in the wind, which he happened to control. It was the perfect power for a sailor. His father was a scoundrel, but his grandfather was an abolitionist. When it was time for Adam to decide what sort of man he wanted to be, he chose to follow in his grandfather’s pursuit of righteousness. That led him to the United States to preach against the evils of slavery in the hardened South. Needless to say, he got into some trouble and revealed his power to get out of it. The zealots found him. He was one of the captives held in sweatboxes down in Texas.

“Lady Charlotte!” Emma abandoned her chaperone, Goldie, and ran straight into my chest. I knew she meant to be gentle, but she cracked my back in three different places.

“Not too tight,” John nudged her off of me. “You’re going to squeeze all her insides out.”

“Sorry, Master John.” Emma jumped off the stage and ran to take her seat. Goldie was acting as Emma’s adoptive mother, and she was raising the girl to be a scrapper like herself. When I learned her powers were to generate sparks of lightning from her fingers, I was grateful I had quickly knocked her out during the robbery of National Trust Bank.

Other children came to swarm us with hugs. I helped John rescue eight children from captivity. A few of their parents had abilities as well, and the zealots butchered them for it. Some of them had perfectly normal human parents, and the zealots killed them anyway. The country was so focused on war that it turned a blind eye to the injustice under its nose. Their misfortune saddened me, but it overjoyed my heart to see John kneeling before the children and making conversation. I assumed by his gentle way with them that he'd be a kind and attentive father to any child I bore.

"Mister Cohen, can you take us fishing like you did with Arthur?"

"Oo! I want to go, too!" They jumped and pulled on him and each other.

"Of course," he assured, and roughed up the hair of two of the boys. "It's not a proper childhood without hunting, fishing, and—"

"School," I reminded. A few of them couldn't even read yet.

"We'll do that as well," John said with a mischievous smile. "What would the world be like if the women couldn't read their asinine love novels?"

I gasped and gave him a good shove. "Says the man who pined after me his whole life! Your exploits for me put Jane Austen to shame."

"It's all in jest, Charlotte. No need for violence." He laughed, but I knew John enjoyed my books for reasons other than snuggling beside me in bed.

"I want to learn how to make pretty dresses," Scarlett, a blonde child with rapturously gorgeous locks, told me. "Will you please show me?"

"Yes, please!" Another child pleaded, this one about my complexion. She was no bigger than me when I was purchased by Lady Cohen.

"I promise, Effie. As soon as I have the time, I'll make you a master seamstress." It was difficult looking into their bright and beautiful eyes at times. I was grateful to be in their lives, but my heart couldn't help but wander to the day I lost Abby. Sometimes, when I dreamed, I saw her chewed up and wheezing from the Cohens' hellhounds. I couldn't bear the thought of all their bright eyes shining from horrific flames. I would never allow it. I'd rather die than have zealots or anyone else harm those precious babes.

We ushered the children off the stage, but they sat on the ground to be close to John. They chatted and played with one another, but I trusted they would come to a hush once John began his address.

Edith, Peter, Hoshi, and Zhang came in next, followed by Caroline and Tony. The latter was a brother and sister duo, who controlled light and shadows. They were both pale with pinkened pointed noses, thin lips, and a dash of color on their cheeks. She had long, blonde hair that was bone straight like an Indian; it was nearly white. His hair was pitch black, cut short, and curly. Their sunken eyes were ethereal, as if they held the stars in them. He was the elder, the same age as me, but they were barely a year apart.

When Caroline absorbed light, she could become warm. She was partly responsible for the lack of snow. Adam was also good at directing falling snow away from us or shoveling a path through what made it on the ground. Nathaniel, who was busy lighting torches and fire pits with his hands, was also another reason why our winters weren't so harsh.

The humans arrived shortly after. John convinced about a hundred Indians to excommunicate from their tribe and join in his vision. The United States had great tension with the Indians. Settlers forced them off their lands and competed for resources. Reservations constantly dwindled, leading to starvation and few resources to keep them warm in the bitter winter. Settlers also brought diseases. John knew he wouldn't be able to properly tend to his land while fighting, traveling, and warring with the zealots, so he offered a deal to the Natives. The land would always belong to John, but they were welcome to the resources. John would also keep them safe from illnesses, make the winters bearable, and they would work together to protect each other. Many elders had no interest in abandoning their traditions and beliefs, but once Kachina demonstrated her power, John received volunteers from strapping young men and hopeful women.

Sadly, not too long after John's offer, warriors led a brutal uprising against settlers in Minnesota due to improper living conditions. Hundreds were killed, and their leader fled. The United States military proved to be too powerful, and mass executions and internment followed. For those who survived, a perilous journey to far reservations led to even more casualties.

We also had a few dozen colored men and women among our ranks. They were liberated from the captivity of slavery and were looking to make a life for themselves. They were hard workers, knowledgeable in their trades, polite, and grateful. It warmed my heart to know that while I was liberating slaves, John was doing the same. Though he mostly did it to bankrupt zealot plantation owners, I chose to believe his heart was secretly thinking of me.

In total, eight Indians and four black men came to sit in our meeting. Nathaniel and Kachina sat with them. She didn't take much pride in being an Indian after her tribe cast her out, but she was fair to the humans and mostly dealt with them. She never intended to be as unwelcoming to them as the US government happened to be. And since Nathaniel was more passive than most of us, he spent much of his time partnered with Kachina and protecting our people.

"Steven isn't here yet," John mumbled with his arms crossed.

"He'll be here soon enough. He wouldn't run out on you, John."

Suddenly, a dust cloud came from the west and blew above us. The debris mostly hit those in the top seats, but I shielded my eyes and mouth. John stood unfazed until a young man emerged. "Am I late?"

"How many times do we have to tell you, Henry?"

"Sorry, sir!" He sat down and slumped his shoulders.

Arthur was approaching from the sky. He had a fascinating story, known as "the floating negro." When Arthur's power activated, he was sent to town on behalf of his mistress. Little did he know, flying is more than levitating off the ground. He hovered above the forest, screaming and scooting away. Arthur was fortunate no one shot him down before he figured out how to land. His exploits were a wild rumor among abolition circles. I didn't quite believe it (nonsensical rumors were abundant, especially after the Runaway's exploits), but I did investigate. John found him before I could verify anything, and I chalked it up to tall tales. John taught Arthur how to control his hovering and add speed to it. He barely spent any time on the ground. He was floating with his legs folded like an Indian.

A few more of our people trickled in. In total, we had sixty-two powered beings. John had a theory that we were drawn to each other, and the more we congregated, the more of us would awaken and come. I also theorized that John drew us to him, similar to how Lady Cohen could call animals to her side. There were only thirty-nine of us when I first joined John. In a few years, our firepower would be unbeatable by a human army. I questioned whether a human army could defeat us now. John was alarmingly powerful, and so were his lieutenants.

Thirty-two minutes after Kachina promised to gather the people, Steven made his approach down the stairs. He traded John's clothes for black drawstring trousers and lace-up ankle boots. For his shirt, he wore a black tunic under an oilcloth cape. Despite his personal arsenal, he wore shoulder holsters that carried two pistols. On his hip, Steven had a knife. "I do hope you all weren't delaying on my behalf."

"Of course, we were." John stretched his hand toward a spot next to him. I'd say his mood was stern, but his fury had subsided.

Steven breathed a sigh of relief, letting go of his internal shame for abandoning Tillie. Then, like a flash of lightning dancing across the sky, his focus intensified like his master's.

"Thank you for gathering on such short notice," John said to them all. "We expected to conduct a raid on the Savannah location two days from now, but we can no longer afford to wait. Thanks to our reconnaissance team, we know the Overseers have anywhere from thirty to fifty captives. It will be our largest rescue operation with the most to gain. However, our enemy anticipated our infiltration and staged a weapon that disrupts our abilities. Tillie was, unfortunately, captured as a result."

The crowd was already captivated by John, but an even greater hush covered them all. It was Emma who gulped and gathered the courage to ask. “Is she still alive?”

“From what we know.”

The same horror and disgust that John and I experienced must have been in them as well, but the fear was also obvious. If I lost my abilities, I wouldn’t know what I’d be. Adam handled the news stoically and didn’t internalize the pain. “If the Overseers can stop our powers, how will we defeat them?”

“We have our wits, our wills, and we have weapons. We’ll utilize everyone with long-range attacks, but others of you will have to fight without powers.” Most of their expressions were subtle, but the fear rising from their bodies was thick enough to choke a lesser man to death. Fortunately, John was no such thing. He took two steps forward as his eyes filled with a golden haze. “This will be a dangerous mission, perhaps the deadliest one yet. We’ve all lost someone to the evils of the Overseers’ superstitions and their fear, and I refuse to procure any casualties due to my own. If we don’t rescue Tillie and the others, they may be burned alive and shot like my parents. I cannot allow such a grim fate to occur—not for Tillie and our future brothers and sisters. The enemy we face may look like men and have the limitations of mortal men, but they are not so. We may go into battle with no biological or supernatural advantage, ordained by the divine, yet we are not mere mortal men and women. They are monsters, and we are slayers. We have a moral obligation to rid our world of their hate and to build a better one for our children.”

I should have watched our people’s reactions, but I was firmly captivated by my husband. He had a presence that filled any space, and his voice was smooth and intoxicating. I stepped forward, took my husband’s hand, and his face curled into the most handsome grin.

It was no shock to me that the first to rise to their feet and express vigorous affirmations was a woman. “We’re with you, John. Tell us exactly what we need to do.” Of course, Kachina would stand beside him. I doubted she was merely flushed with excitement for battle.

Adam, Peter, and others jumped to their feet in approval. There was applause and rowdy cheers, but it was all distant noise to me. All that existed was the space between our bodies, filled with optimism and desire for one another. I loved going into battle with John, but that paled in comparison to the joy I found while imagining endless possibilities of our lives after victory. Perhaps I would bear ten of his children.

Steven slowly came into my vision as he stepped directly next to my husband. He was steadily staring again, but he didn't possess the same thrill as the others. He attempted to mask it with a confident grin, but I had grown accustomed to his performances. Steven was shaken.

"The humans will stay behind to guard the property. With the exception of Henry, Javier, and Nathaniel, every man above the age of seventeen and below forty will accompany me."

"Seventeen?" Arthur asked while pointing to his chest. "I'm seventeen."

"With Tillie captured, you'll be our eyes in the sky. Once we establish the perimeter, you should be fine as long as you don't fly into the neutralizing zone."

Henry grabbed his friend's shoulders and gave them a good squeeze. "You can do it! Everyone is depending on you!"

"Sure, sure. I can…" His head bobbed, and we took that as compliance. It would be his first official raid, but he had been trained by Adam, who had gotten into many scraps before committing himself to the abolitionist cause. Arthur could shoot, and he could throw a punch if need be. If we were fortunate, we wouldn't require him to do physical violence.

"As far as the women, Kachina, Caroline, Edith, and Hoshi will join us. The rest of you capable warriors will guard our home and protect our children."

"We can fight, too!" Alfie threw a raised fist in the air. He was an odd and attentive child, like John. He had a fire inside of him, which was a contrast to what he could do. He huffed out blasts of chilled air, filled with resolve. Some of the children held their arms and shivered as a result of his involuntary display.

When John's eyes fell on the boy, the rest of the children's eyes filled with terror. I had never seen John put his hands on any of them, but he had a fearsome look that intimidated even the adults. Though the boy's arm slowly lowered into his lap, he kept his eyes focused on John as he left the stage and knelt beside him. "I know you can, but protecting our home is important. When we rescue more of our people, we need to make sure this place is secure for them. Don't they deserve a good home?"

Alfie hesitantly nodded, buying time before he recalled how to speak. "Yes, sir."

"Then, I'm entrusting our future to you." John rested his heavy hand on the boy's tiny shoulders, and for some reason, possessing that burden was satisfactory. The two exchanged hardy smiles, then John continued addressing the crowd.

"Nathaniel will give instructions on security measures while we are absent. If you were summoned for battle, see Peter, Steven, and Charlotte in the armory. I expect everyone to be prepped and ready to jump within the hour. Nathaniel and Henry, see me before I leave for further instruction."

I wasn't a weapons expert, but I knew how to style men and women. Many of our people had no alternate life to go back to and no reason to hide their identity, but I liked going into town to buy sweet potatoes and other things. If everyone knew I was the Runaway, I wouldn't be able to slip in and out, and my life would be in considerably greater danger. After the war with the South ended and the zealots were defeated, perhaps there'd be no need for masks. Until then, I wanted to protect our people.

It was all mostly dark garb to mimic John's persona. I covered their faces with scarves, bandanas, hoods, and goggles. I also tailored their clothes to their powers. Hotah was an Indian who could adapt his body to mimic different substances, so I gave him a leather belt with pouches to carry samples. Henry was a challenge because his constant running wore out just about anything I made. I experimented with wool, cotton treated in borax, cotton duck, and leather. With him, every success was temporary. I taught Henry how to sew his own clothes, so I wouldn't be condemned to eternally mend his pants. Steven was also a challenge because his form shifted so much. I had to think of things that he could adjust while in battle. Hopefully, he didn't have to turn into someone as small as Emma, but he certainly enjoyed taking my form. We all carried pistols and knives, and I made certain they had holsters and backup ammunition.

John and Steven were the last ones to grab their weapons, and they were suspiciously quiet. Steven stared at a saber as if he expected it to come to life and talk to him. "Is something bothering you?"

Steven looked up at Adam, who was waiting by the door. "Do you mind granting us some privacy?"

Adam left without a fuss, but Steven's mood didn't improve. If anything, his mouth quivered as if he was struggling not to swallow his tongue. It was rather annoying since he knew we were short on time.

"Speak, boy."

He took one deep and final breath of courage. "I believe I would be best utilized fighting outside the nullified zone."

John's preoccupied mind snapped into focus, and his eyes became like a furnace. I figured I'd better nag Steven before John burned him to ash. "You're one of our best fighters, and you have the memories of one of the guards. You know the property and likely where Tillie is being kept. We need you."

"Charlotte, I want you to consider staying outside of the nullified perimeter."

My whole body stiffened like a railroad spike, and I turned ninety degrees to drive my rage right into my husband. "You know I can fight as good as any man."

"With your powers, you're better than almost any man. Without your powers, you'll be better than many men, but they're still men, Charlotte. And even if your fists are faster, you can't outrun bullets."

"Neither can you!" My mind conjured so many mischievous words to infuriate him. For starters, John was kidnapped by the Overseers after he defected from the Confederacy, even though he had two powers at the time. He had overestimated himself and underestimated his enemy, creating the need for three women to rescue him. "You've had your mother's powers since you were a little boy. You have the least experience fighting as a normal man than any of us."

John pointed to his chest, and his brows rose as he made the most arrogant smirk I had ever seen. "But I'm still a man."

"Oh, don't give me that, John—"

"I'm not trying to discriminate against you, sweetheart..." He dared to grab my arms as if that would calm me. "...but the fact is, we won't be fighting normal men. They're killers who want to kill you. I already have to fight without my powers. Knowing how vulnerable you'll be is a distraction."

"Then that's your issue to overcome. Don't blame an impending failure on me."

"I won't fail."

"And neither will I!" John had a will of fire, and I respected that, but I did as well. He knew that about me. He thought it was an endearing—even arousing—quality of mine, but I wanted to be more than admired. I wanted to be respected. "You told me that I could be your queen. Better yet, you told me that I was your equal. We cannot ask our people to risk their lives and not be willing to do the same."

"I am risking my life."

"You have to be willing to risk mine, John, if you're willing to risk theirs."

John was not an unreasonable man, but it was painful watching his heart wrestle with his brain. His eyes even flashed gold. John claimed that most of the time when he used his sway, it was involuntary. I wanted to believe my beloved, but some moments were a little too convenient. But his powers never swayed me against my better instincts. Perhaps he couldn't use his powers against me because he secretly knew that my counsel was far too important to alter.

He turned to Steven, who had been quiet like the dead throughout our fight. "My wife is willing to risk her life, and you have the nerve to tell me you're afraid?"

"I'm not afraid, John. I would die for you and our cause a hundred times over, but I would be better suited just outside the perimeter, offering support." I didn't know what to make of Steven. He and John fought beside each other plenty of times. As long as they were together, even if it were just the two of them, they were invincible. He certainly wasn't a coward. I didn't suspect he was afraid to die, but he was afraid of something. "This is about strategy. They station the most guards in the center near the manor."

"That's in normal circumstances. They'll know we're coming to rescue their captives, so they'll protect them in the underground cellar. That's also where they'll store their weapon."

"Do you think they'll have more men than usual?" I asked John.

"No. We aren't giving them enough time, and the South is stretched thin due to the war. Managing to have fifty men guarding their base is a testament to the Overseers' wealth and connections. They also won't expect our numbers. We've never taken this many on a raid before."

The fifteen of us could certainly take on that many men, especially if we had our powers. John and Steven could handle them all, if not for the weapon. "What if we take out everyone on the outside and all go in together?"

"Zhang's power is too valuable to risk, and I need him protected."

"Steven can do that better than I can. And I could easily make the case that you're too valuable to risk going in without your powers, but there's no sense in arguing with you about it." Steven's eyes widened. I don't know why. I often vouched for him. But I had another motive. Steven was clearly shaken by losing his powers earlier, and if his head wasn't clear, he'd be a liability in those tunnels. "This is one instance where keeping you both separate is probably the right call. Steven is the second most powerful. In case something happened to you—"

"Nothing is going to happen to me, woman."

"Even if it did…" I took my husband's hand and held it to my chest. I wanted him to know that it beat for him and our future together. Those eyes of cold steel melted for me. He truly possessed the utmost confidence in his abilities, and John expected to return to me. I could never doubt him. Somehow, someway, my love would survive. But as a mere mortal, I had to leave a sliver of a possibility for the worst outcome. "I want to be by your side. If something happened to me, I'd want you by mine. We conquer together, we rule together, and we die together."

John struggled with the thought of losing someone he loved again, but he managed to mask the unpleasantness with a handsome grin. "I assume we're still in the conquering phase."

"But of course, John." I returned his smile and pulled him into me for a kiss. Steven rolled his eyes and turned away. He was such a child. It was a burst of passion, but it only went on for a few seconds.

As soon as it was over, John glowered at him, and he straightened up. "I'll grant your request, but you and I are due for a long conversation when this is all over."

"Yes, sir…" Steven slightly bowed his head, then walked out of the armory. John's stern eye followed him out the door.

"You know…" I said, ever-so-sweetly, "We could ask some of the humans to fight with you."

"I don't trust them."

"You trust them enough to leave them on your property while you go off to make war."

"I don't *trust* them, but I don't *fear* them either. If they're moronic enough to stage a rebellion in our brief absence, there's enough of our people behind to take care of them. Emma and Alfie have been itching for a fight."

I scoffed, even though the playful shift in his tone suggested his comment was in jest. "Hopefully, we'll do all of the heavy lifting. This war isn't for children."

"The zealots are almost defeated, and we're growing faster than I ever imagined. It won't take but a couple of years. And once we've made our own nation, you'll start on my ten children." John managed to dig underneath my scarf and lay ticklish kisses on me. I nearly collapsed on his chest.

"We've got to go, John. Don't distract me." I pushed him off and readjusted my scarf. "There will be plenty of time for that afterward."

John cocked his brow, probably to tease me, but then we walked out to meet the others.

"This is everyone," Adam announced. I glanced around the group to be certain. Arthur kept bouncing on his feet and flexing his fingers. Edith rubbed his back to comfort him. Caroline and Tony were perfectly calm. Most of them were. Adam, Peter, Christopher, James, and Hotah had all been through this song and dance before. I could also attest Hoshi and all of her demon spawns were ready to brawl. Kachina was glowing. John trained her personally, but he never took her on a raid. She hadn't been on a robbery either. As a powerful and true believer in his cause, she was suited to manage and protect his property. I assumed Kachina wanted to be the future Lady Cohen until John and I reunited.

The only seasoned warrior who seemed a bit uneasy was Steven, which became more evident when he transformed into my likeness. Steven was decent at the art of deception, but I recognized the glimmer of fear in his eyes. He, too, believed the world we had created was about to be forever changed.

Chapter Three

"Alright, most of you know your tasks, but since we've made adjustments, I'll go over them once more." John ran through a description of the plantation, the manor, the guards, their posts, the cellars, and our responsibilities. Once he was finished, he asked if we all understood. We all gave verbal confirmation.

Christopher had the first task. Arthur looked at his hands and feet and became more nervous. "Are you certain we're invisible right now?"

"Yes, I'm certain," he said, annoyed. "What good would it do to make us all invisible to each other?"

"No, that makes sense…" Maybe his clothes were warm, but I think Arthur was sweating out of nervousness.

"It'll be alright." I gave the boy a kind smile to comfort him. "You'll do us proud." I was up next, so I stretched my hand to the center of our circle. One by one, they stacked their arms on top until we had all connected. I hadn't been to where we were going, so I was only helping to carry the load. It was Steven who had to direct John and me.

"Ready?" Steven looked at our fearless leader for confirmation.

"Let the operation commence."

I didn't like blinking and not being in charge. It was a bit like being tossed into the air. Some children enjoyed the thrill of flying, but some were terrified of being thrust into the unknown while depending on another person to stop them from hurling into the ground. John always had the utmost trust in me, but I didn't have the same confidence in Steven. He might have possessed my power, but I managed it better. I was grateful the journey was quick.

A golden haze swept over us as the bright sun approached noon. The air was humid and heavy with the scent of swampy water. The silence was filled with the croaks of bullfrogs and buzzing cicadas. The marsh acted as a natural guard to protect the villainy and secrets of the Overseers. We blinked beyond that, to an area cleared and structured for rice paddies. Colored faces were pointed down at the rice shoots protruding from the mud. My heart cried out for them, and John's gentle hand on my shoulder reminded me that I had pledged loyalty to another cause.

I restrained myself. Once our battle commenced, the Overseers presiding over the slaves would be dealt with. No longer would they have to fear the lash of their master's whip. My heart was stirred just thinking about their first breaths of true freedom, like when I crossed the Ohio River after leaving the Cohens' plantation.

Steven's skin lightened to a ruddy complexion, and his body filled out until his clothes were tight. Christopher was an inch shorter than Steven, but he was stocky. He carried rocks and logs all day to build his muscular physique. It tickled me that his power was invisibility since his red hair and beard made him easy to pick out from a crowd.

Christopher had the task of keeping everyone else undetectable while John and I blinked across the property, cloaked by the powers Steven copied. I had to let John pull us around. That was more tolerable than Steven carrying us such a far distance, but I still didn't like it. It felt as though I had a rope tugging at my waist.

The plantation's property started from a swamp, dense with cypress trees protruding from the murky waters, transitioned into a marsh, and then into rice paddies. Together, they made up 260 acres of the property. The rest was cut and groomed for living, besides another ten acres of oak trees surrounding the back end as a natural line of defense. A white fence and an iron gate established a barrier between the work of the enslaved and high society. The only road leading to the manor had a focal point of a cracked, naked cherub with a bone-dry basin. The red brick manor itself stood in the center of the thirty acres, two stories high. It was similar to many great homes in the South, with large windows and tall white columns stacked like elegant prison bars.

Five oak watchtowers were erected around those thirty acres, all equipped with a giant brass bell and one gunman. A naïve outsider may have questioned why the watchtowers were positioned to surround the manor instead of having some of them focused on the rice fields, but I doubted the Overseers prioritized their slaving. Their true passion was capturing and killing us, yet they had no idea that we were right under their noses.

The plantation had other typical features. There was a well pumping water, a stable for horses, and slave cabins. The scent of cured meat flowed to my nostrils when we passed the smokehouse, and I cursed myself for not eating a bigger breakfast. That smell was quickly overwhelmed when we came upon a small barn, doors open wide. A man carrying a plate of chicken bones threw them to some mean-looking bloodhounds. Those dogs immediately sniffed us out and caused a commotion, running and banging on their wooden cages. The man looked right toward us, bewildered. He couldn't see anything, but he trusted the superior senses of the beasts and began to reach for a holstered pistol. John smirked, and he blinked behind the man. His body dropped to the ground with a twisted and broken neck before he could even touch the gun.

A small gasp escaped both Steven and me. I understood the need for brutality, but I hadn't quite gotten used to John's visceral nature. Steven, on the other hand, was in awe. I swear, his eyes were glittering.

The dogs sat quietly while their new master opened the gates. "Come on." He motioned for us, and I reluctantly obeyed. I never enjoyed the company of dogs, and I certainly wouldn't after witnessing how torn up Abby was. If it weren't for John's golden eyes, I would have blinked out of there. "Transform into Tillie."

Steven tightened his pants as he knelt next to John and significantly shrank in stature. Tillie was about my height but thinner. Steven was swallowed in fabric, but he wasn't wearing gloves. He let the dogs smell his hands and pulled down his scarf as well. When the mongrels slobbered all over his face, a flutter of magic escaped his mouth. Tillie was always so serious, and we never became close friends. I didn't hear her laugh that often, which was a shame. It was a bright melody that floated like a lullaby.

"These creatures are going to do me a favor." John held the head of one of the dogs until his golden sheen reflected inside of them. It sent a shiver down my spine like lightning splitting a tree. I was hurled into a memory of Lady Cohen in the woods, taking control of a silver wolf. "Tillie is here. I can smell her blood in the air."

The more he breathed through his nostrils, the more they flared with rage. He gritted his teeth, baring sharpened canines like the beasts he controlled. As he growled in fury, they mimicked their master. "Charlotte, try to blink to the manor."

"Alright." From my estimate, we were about a hundred-twenty yards from the house. We were on the side, facing east. I focused on the brick and imagined rubbing its grainy surface, but when I tried to blink, a sudden shock came to me like a door slamming in my face. I felt cold, as if a blanket had been ripped off my body. Whatever substance that lingered on my skin from the place I traveled through was gone. I was closer to the bricks, but I was still thirty to fifty yards away.

There seemed to be only air between me and the house. I wondered if I should reach out my hand and see for certain if my powers would be stripped away, but my hand trembled as soon as I raised it. Steven wasn't shaken for no reason. He didn't want to be without his powers, and I deeply sympathized with that. If I had never awakened my abilities, would I have ever run from the Cohens? Better yet, would I have ever found John? Lady Cohen purchased me because they suspected I would have powers. John wouldn't have courted me, even if I were on that property. He probably would have married Mary Anne and convinced her to bear ten combustion babies. So much of the good in my life came because of my powers. I wasn't ready to give that up.

I blinked back to the barn, grateful to be fully myself. "I can't. I'm stopped by the weapon."

"That's what I expected." John walked past me to a few feet in front of the barn's entrance, stomped his foot, and then bent his knees. The ground rumbled while he raised his hands, as if he were trying to lift a cart. A ring of disturbed dirt formed around the manor, representing the perimeter of where we dare not cross or risk losing our powers. It stretched about a hundred yards, but the manor did not sit perfectly inside the ring. Most of it was in the backyard.

"Reunite us with the others, Charlotte." Steven took my form again while we both clutched onto him. We were back with our crew just as bells from the towers began to ring. "Take your positions! Do not go inside the ring surrounding the manor."

Tony flapped his oilcloth cape, expanding the length of his shadow. The white in his eyes filled like spilled ink on a page, and then he dropped into the dark as if he had fallen into a well. When he reemerged into this world of mortals, it was through the shadow cast by a swinging bell. The man in the tower had his eyes and a weapon pointed at the ground, searching for intruders. He missed the silent shadow floating in like a leaf caught by the wind. By the time the guard had barely turned around, Tony's saber had plunged into his backside and out through his heart.

For others who didn't have any otherworldly means of transportation, it was my job to blink them to the towers. Adam took a deep breath and hurled a gust of wind like a discus at the guard before he could aim his musket. He fired a shot off in the air as he twirled from thirty feet. To his credit, he survived the fall, but the last thing he saw was the barrel of Adam's gun. One of the patrollers tried his luck, but Peter yanked the musket out of his hands from afar. He wasn't good at lifting heavy things with his thoughts yet, but it was enough to distract his foe. He was still gazing at his empty hands, bewildered, when Adam fired a bullet into his skull.

James had a fearsome power that reminded me much of Mary Anne. He released a stream of red power from his hands.

It didn't lead to combustion, but he destroyed most things. Unlike Mary Anne, he could also soften the blow so the opponent would only be stunned. The more he concentrated on destruction, the deadlier the attack became. James's power blasted the tower like a stick of dynamite, and there wasn't much of anything left but a charred corpse and rubble.

John handled the next tower by uprooting its solid foundation. It couldn't handle the tremors and collapsed in on itself. The guard leaped for his life. Unfortunately for him, Kachina was paired with John and eager to prove herself as an adept killer. She stomped her foot and clawed up at the earth to summon an angled stone as tall as she was. There was a terrible crack, a sharp and brief scream that was choked right out of him, and then he fell limply to the ground.

Kachina was granted John's smile of approval, and it filled her with a fire to continue. A patroller came at her, quick at the draw. She raised her arm to shield herself, and the ground beneath her feet obeyed. The bullets from his pistols could not pierce her wall. Kachina permitted herself to panic silently as debris blew off her stone shield. John had moved on to kill another patroller; he blinked right in front of the man and slit his throat with a bowie knife. I blinked behind the patroller shooting at Kachina, and he was quick to turn around and aim his pistols at me. I blinked and shifted to the side, enough for him to miss and close enough to ram my brass knuckles straight into his upper teeth. The awful ringing in my ear drowned out the crunch of his bones. I despised how noisy firearms were. I could hear Kachina yelling for me to move, but I spotted the flying rock wall and blinked out of the way just before it smashed me to pieces. I wasn't certain if the man was alive after she smashed him, but the blood from his head was squished on the rock like a bug.

The final tower guard met a simple and terrible fate. Steven blinked to the top of the tower, then jumped on the zealot from behind. He was, undoubtedly, stronger than Steven while in my form. He was stocky and a few inches taller than John. I bet when he peeled Steven's arms from around his neck, he never expected to toss him off into a graying sky. I told myself never to have sympathy for the zealots, but it was a terrible sight. He flailed his arms and legs while screaming for help. Steven aimed for the man to fall into the well, but his height was greater than the well's diameter. I had to turn away when his head hit the stones. I was told he cracked like an egg before what was left of him bounced down like a billiard ball. Steven landed perfectly on the well's rim to watch his handiwork.

The sky continued to darken but never blackened. Bright and vivid colors were muted to pale pastels, and crisp shadows blurred. Tony had safely exited the shadow realm and awaited further instruction with his saber near the backyard perimeter. While he and many others secured the area around the manor, the rest of the team laid waste to the twenty men overseeing the slaves.

A blast of black smoke gushed from Hoshi's mouth and flooded the rice fields. The uncertainty caused the slaves to panic and run. Their piercing screams and scrambling startled the horses. Some of the slaves even ran into a few of them. One of the slavers was toppled and trampled underneath human feet and hooves.

The smoke twisted and compacted into tiny pillars, and those pillars formed exact duplicates of their master, from the crease in her pants to the bullets chambered in her gun. She was less intimidating than a swirling pit of black smoke, standing tall at 5'3" and barely 100 pounds, but she was quick—and there were twenty of her.

She preferred hand-to-hand combat to firearms, but she was precise with throwing daggers. Once one of the duplicates was mortally wounded or knocked unconscious, they dissolved into puffs of smoke and were reabsorbed into the original host. The opponents weren't likely to find her. The real Hoshi was tucked behind a wall of black smoke that surrounded the zealots from all sides—an illusion created by Edith.

The zealots must have thought they were battling through Hell, and I could only imagine the righteous vindication that surged through their bodies when the sky began to gray, and a bright light pierced the dark fog. Those uppity fools probably thought the floating golden woman was an angel of the Lord, radiating God's grace and righteous judgment. How horrible it must have been when the angel carried the wrath of Sodom and unleashed God's fury upon them with blasts of hot light.

The last patroller tried to shoot at Hotah as he sprinted for the house, but our friend had fashioned his body into steel. Even if the bullet hadn't bounced off his shoulder, it certainly wasn't a fatal shot. Hotah wasn't skilled with a gun, so he came armed with a bow and a quiver full of arrows. Hotah shot the man in his Achilles heel just as he sprinted across the perimeter line. He dropped to the ground after a good scream, but his fear gave him enough strength to stand and quickly hobble onto the back porch. That arrogant fool smugly grinned, tempting any of us to come forward.

I knew my husband well enough to know he should have been horribly annoyed, yet he smiled. "Steven, come here…"

Steven blinked from the well and to John's side. "Yes?"

"You touched the guard you just killed. Do you know where our people are being held and how many guards are in the house?"

"There are four underground bunkers. There should be five guards in the one closest to us, and it doesn't have any of our people in it. The other three should have three guards in each, and they all hold hostages. Most are in the left bunker. Tillie is in the one on the right. Nine men are hiding in the house. They expect us to begin our raid inside. A trap door in the pantry leads down to the tunnels, and there's also a hidden exit attached to the left bunker. It's within the perimeter."

"And what about the weapon? Where is it? What is it?"

"Fifty meters in from the pantry entrance is the center bunker. There, you'll find the weapon sitting in a cage." Steven released a small sigh, and in that tiny huff of air was a whirlwind of frustration. "It's a little black boy."

"A boy?" I looked at my husband, whose brows had raised just a smidgen. I envied his composure because my heart was racing. "John, if it's a boy—"

"If none of our people are in the house, then we have no need of it." The curve of John's lips deepened mischievously.

I was certain John heard what Steven said and chose to ignore it, especially since he refused to look at me. I had to walk directly in front of his face. "John—"

"Kachina," John turned his whole body away from me, "do you sense the bunker?"

"Part of it." Her eyes shifted between the two of us. "Some of it must be in the perimeter."

"Then we'll enter from underground. Take cover."

I didn't want to fight him in front of the others, but my stomach was in knots. A small black boy was causing so much trouble? A child was responsible for Tillie's peril? Why couldn't it have been an ancient artifact or a witch's brew? If it had to be a person, why not an older person with a mature mind that could distinguish right from wrong? I could have told myself that John snatching their life was justifiable. But a child…? "John…"

"I said, 'Take cover,' Charlotte."

We took a few steps away from John, then huddled together as Kachina stomped her foot and raised her arms. The ground trembled a bit as she erected a seven-foot wall in front of us. I stood on the edge so I could peek over at my husband while he worked.

The stone well was outside the perimeter, so John focused on pulling about ten of them, all about the size of his hands. With only the power of his mind, he drew the stones close and circled his body. Then he took in a couple of breaths and closed his eyes, gathering his strength for the next part. The patroller couldn't have known what was about to happen, but he had enough good sense to go inside the house and hide. Good sense couldn't save him from John, though.

My beloved extended his arm and spun in a circle as if he were David flinging smooth stones toward Goliath. Some were aimed high toward the roof, some were bound to crash through the windows, and a few were on a collision course with the brick walls. Once they crossed the threshold of the perimeter, John could no longer control their trajectory. He also couldn't put a stop to whatever Mary Anne could do. The stones had already begun to brighten before John ran and took cover beside me.

John's golden eyes were especially fearsome as the earth trembled beneath our feet and the explosion echoed across the sky. A bright burst of light managed to pierce through the dull haze forced by Caroline, and it intensified as the columns and furniture caught fire. As a few horrific screams emerged over the crackling fire, John's face was perfectly still, reminiscent of when Mr. Cohen threatened to kill every slave on our plantation if he didn't whip me. I tried not to think of Maddison's brown eyes hollowing out as her soul ascended or the piercing of Abigail's scream. If I hadn't sobbed on John's leg and begged, he would have stood there and watched all of the slaves die, even poor little Abby, to spare me the lash of his father's whip. In the end, I bore the burden of those scars, and John wielded the weapon that split my flesh apart. He did it to spare my sanity; I couldn't bear to watch Mr. Cohen shoot Abby. It had always been clear that John would do anything for me, and he hadn't changed.

Not one bit.

"John, please…" There were a million things I wanted to say, but it wasn't appropriate to argue in front of our subordinates. Even worse, Arthur was coming in from a distance, hollering. I only hoped that as John stared into my eyes, he felt my convictions deeply. He knew, better than anyone, that I had no desire to have another child's death on my conscience.

"Charlotte!" Arthur's voice was shrill as he came down from on high, clutching his rifle. "Charlotte, there's something wrong with the slaves. They're all fighting against us."

My heart must have stopped. I don't remember breathing either. Liberating the slaves would have been a kind and noble deed, but John and I had an understanding. Rescuing our people and ensuring their safety was the priority.

"You should go, Charlotte."

I was taken aback. "No, I'm fighting with you in the cellars."

"Would you prefer if Steven handled this matter in whatever way he sees fit?"

Steven was still wearing my face. He could blink to the slaves and then take Asha's form. But lulling them to sleep wouldn't have been his first instinct. I recalled what it was like to face Steven's sadistic wrath. He nearly killed Cooper, which was unauthorized by John. "No, I don't want that."

"Then both of you should go. We'll be fine." John whistled so loudly, you would have thought he used an instrument. It wasn't long before the beasts he befriended made their way to us, happily barking.

Kachina also made her move, sensing the closest underground cellar and splitting the earth like Moses parted the Red Sea. She made a perfect ramp descending to a stone and clay wall. After they punched through it, all hell would break loose.

"Can you wait for me?"

"No. The smoke will begin seeping through the tunnels. We've got to go now."

The manor wasn't completely destroyed, but the smoke and flames were quickly rising. I thought the flames were counteracting Caroline's light absorption, because our world brightened and the contrast of colors increased. But the bluer the sky became, the more I feared for my friends.

"Lady Charlotte," Arthur pleaded, "we need help!"

I cursed myself, then quickly pecked John on the lips. I wished I had time for a sweeter goodbye, but I had no intention of that being our final moment together. "Be careful."

"Oh," he smiled handsomely, "I wouldn't dare dream of it."

I managed to roll my eyes before blinking near the gate, close to where I had left the rest of our crew. I wanted to find a grateful bunch of slaves, thanking Hoshi and the others. Instead, they ran to Hoshi like a swarm of bees. Our golden gal had lost her glow. Caroline was sliced open, and blood poured like a fountain. She was in the arms of Zhang, who had lost his protector. Edith was by his side, applying pressure to the wound in her own shoulder. Christopher had taken his axe into battle with Hoshi against the slaves in the rice fields.

"What happened?" Steven blinked in and hovered over my shoulder after I knelt to Caroline's side. The poor girl was wheezing and shaking. If they hadn't gotten her to Zhang in time, we would have lost her.

"We killed their masters, and these ungrateful mongrels turned on us," Edith said with furious tears. "They said we were demons, and then they picked up their weapons and attacked us. Some of them had knives, and when I was stabbed, I couldn't use my powers."

I looked up at Steven, confused. "You said it was a boy limiting our powers."

"It is the boy," Steven said as his eyes blackened deeper than any night sky, "and they're using his blood." Steven's complexion rapidly lightened, and his features refined into the sharper edges of a young man, though his stature hardly changed.

"Steven, no! Change to Asha. You don't have to hurt them!"

I'm uncertain if the intensity in Steven's face was due to his possession of Tony's memories and seeing his sister wounded, or if it was due to his earlier scare of briefly losing his powers. There was much I didn't know about him, but the contempt on his face was a reflection of John after Asha was killed. "They're zealots," he seethed. "All zealots must die."

I desperately reached for him, but all I managed to grab was Steven's oilcloth cape before he slipped into his shadow. I didn't know if I could follow him, nor was I eager to make such a discovery. The brief moment I took to contemplate the matter was enough for his shadow to vanish.

I only had seconds to observe the fighting crowd of slaves and determine if any of them could be saved. The rice fields were littered with bodies. There were two dozen slaves left standing. Hoshi and Christopher were both huffing and puffing, but they stabbed and hacked every foe who dared to face them. I took Christopher's visibility and the cut across his chest as evidence of infection with the boy's blood. I didn't see any children among the slaves. Most of them were men of fighting age, but there were two women. Perhaps I could save them. Perhaps…

"Charlotte…" Caroline grabbed hold of my wrist before I could blink to the crowd. Her lovely and glittering eyes were normally filled with such magnificent light, but that light had diminished. They were still lovely eyes, brown with hues of green and hints of gold, but even that was a dull sight in comparison. "They took my light away…" Tears flowed down her cheeks. I meant to blink to the female slaves while I had a chance, but she pulled me close and sobbed on my sleeve.

I wanted them to be free of their bonds and to have a chance at a life full of love, just as I did, but my freedom was never solely predicated on escaping my captors. My powers were a part of me, and I desired to use them without fear of persecution. I wasn't bound by the normal rules of man or nature, and Caroline wasn't either. Knowing that those slaves had the power to place chains back on my feet made me pause.

Not all slaves were desperate for liberty. I had run across many who enjoyed the security of singing in a locked cage rather than the freedom of soaring into the unknown. Agency demands accountability, and not everyone can live by the choices they make. Many humans are too afraid to try. Perhaps they desired to be the zealots' slaves. Perhaps they believed in the cause and wanted to kill us. Perhaps they were threatened and forced to attack us. Or perhaps they were horrified when Caroline emerged glowing from a pillar of black smoke. She may have been our angel of vengeance, but to them, the Angel of Light was another name for Lucifer.

They were afraid. They weren't warriors. Individually, they were no match for Christopher swinging his axe or Hoshi's high-flying kicks. Yet, they tried. They threw rocks, bit, and stabbed Hoshi's duplicates until they dwindled to a handful. The slaves could have run to their freedom while we battled the Overseers. What did it say about us that they were willing to risk everything to put us down?

They were fighting for their lives, perhaps they even believed they were fighting for the world. I didn't believe they should die for that.

I set my sights on one of the female slaves, who wielded a knife and had her eyes focused on the real Hoshi. I began to imagine myself beside the slave with my hand wrapped around her wrist. As my skin grazed hers, she was jolted back and knocked off her feet. Blood blew out of her backside as the echo of the gun rippled across the battlefield. Her grip loosened, and she surrendered the knife to gravity. It fell in front of my feet, and the fresh blood on the blade lit up to me like a flickering star.

I picked it up before the water washed away what I presumed to be the boy's blood. John said it would have been difficult to find more men to guard their base, with the war taking so many. We never considered that they would recruit and equip their slaves.

Arthur hovered over me, trembling at the sight of the slave woman's blood in the reddened marsh. I didn't want him to bear the guilt of an impossible decision, so I gave him a nod of appreciation. He continued to shake, but he nodded in return.

The shadows from the bodies, living and dead, began to merge into a giant crisp circle. By then, I knew there was nothing that I could do. I blinked to Hoshi's back, and after I carried her safely to Zhang and the others, I did the same for Christopher. Arthur was wise enough to fly toward us quickly.

Steven's face peered through the shadows like a gator gliding to new prey. The shadows raised and wiggled as if they were tentacles from an octopus. The slaves circled and murmured in terror, unprepared for what was to come. I assumed the zealots told the slaves all sorts of stories about our horrific powers: we could disappear and reappear like ghosts, wield the fires of hell, and shake the foundations of the earth. But they certainly weren't told about a man who bent shadows. Any mission Tony went on never left any survivors to spread the tales.

By the time Steven's arms and torso emerged from the pool of shadows, the survivors sprinted for their lives. But they couldn't outrun their own shadows, which took the form of javelins and materialized through their chests. In one fell swoop, Steven was the only man standing in a sea of corpses. John was a force all on his own, powerful enough to take on an army by himself if properly equipped. We all respected him. We all had enough sense to fear his capabilities, and there was no question that while Steven was no longer his second-in-command, he was certainly his second in power.

Steven only admired his handiwork for a moment, then turned toward us. His face wasn't clear from a distance, but I felt as though he was aiming his blackened eyes at me in defiance. I kept my eyes on Steven as he fell into his pit of shadows, and while he rose again, up through my own. After the black in his eyes receded, it was clear to me that Steven wasn't overcome with a burst of fear. He wasn't acting out of desperation, like many of those slaves. He made a choice as clear as the sunny sky that defined his shadows.

"You didn't have to kill them all. You could have put them down like Asha."

"And risk being put down like Asha?" He scoffed and narrowed his eyes. "They were trying to kill us, Charlotte. No mercy."

I felt all of their eyes on us. Steven had never blatantly defied me since I joined their group. Everyone didn't necessarily like that I was second to John, but I thought they respected it. "John sent me over here to avoid this scenario."

"No, John gave you the option to come because he wanted to stop you from going in the tunnels. He knew that I'd do whatever it took to keep us all safe, just like he always has, and he *always* will."

The others had no idea what Steven was hinting at, but his implication was clear. "He won't do it."

"Don't underestimate him." Steven had such confidence in his words, but my voice was a bit shaken. I knew John, but he had taken his form and seen all of his memories. Steven was his confidant who had killed dozens of zealots by John's side, spending days and even weeks with him. There was no doubt Steven knew John's mind, but we both knew that I was his heart.

As I stepped forward to stare him down harder, a shockwave rushed through my body and grounded my feet in a way I had never felt before. I was heavy, as if every piece of me was tied down. I was nearly knocked over and looked at my feet. There was nothing on me, but I was unmistakably changed.

My eyes gazed upward to the figure in front of me. His stature hadn't changed much, but instead of gangly muscles attempting to fill out his tunic and pants, there were slender curves. The curves on the figure's chest were unmistakably female. The edges of his face smoothed while it darkened into a cool light brown. Tony's dark curls lightened and lengthened until they draped over her shoulders and down her back. The dainty fingers felt her face as if it were unrecognizable, but I recognized those eyes just fine. They were glittering blue, just like Steven's.

"This is your true face?"

Seeing her, it was so much more evident that Steven was a black man passing for white. The texture of their hair, their noses, and their eyes were similar. She must have been kin to the real Steven. I glanced around to make sure everyone else was surprised by the revelation. The master impersonator was, suddenly, a stranger to us all.

The stranger inhaled a few gasps of panicked breaths as she absorbed our questions and converted them to judgment. “We don’t have time for this. If they found a way to expand the barrier, then the zealots were desperate. John must be in trouble.”

I took off running, concentrating on the back of the yard and trying to blink. The unfortunate reality of human limitations still weighed heavily on me, but I wouldn’t stop. Even if I had to trek through mud, marsh, swamp, or hellfire, I would return to John. Powers or no powers, I was prepared for the sprint of my life to find my beloved and make certain that he came home with me alive.

Chapter Four

When I was a child, a group of slave boys verbally harassed me with words too insignificant to recall, but at the time, it was enough to make me run in sorrow. Blinded with tears, I collided with a horse and was nearly trampled to death. If not for my powers activating, I would have been killed or doomed to live the rest of my life as a crippled slave. Instead, I ended up on the Cohens' plantation. One day, I was chased by one of their savage dogs. Hell was on my heels, but I understood that if I reached Lady Cohen, she would protect me from the beast. That clear understanding of the danger and a focused goal turned me into a miracle. I couldn't fathom what I had done or the power dwelling inside of me, but I did know that I could run.

I would have fun with Abby, climbing trees and running across the plantation. I never imagined that Mr. Cohen would free me, so I dreamed of running from the plantation with John by my side. And when I needed to run away from Lady Cohen, I ran and blinked until my stomach was ravenous with hunger, my feet were covered in blisters, and my chest burned. I ran from Mississippi to Tennessee, and then I ran to my new life after meeting Cooper in Ohio.

I moved to New York and began to train. My body was already durable and agile, and my endurance impressed Cooper.

We'd run through the streets of Manhattan early in the morning, just before the sunrise lit our precious city in a warm haze of amber. Cooper had no love for it, but he was diligent, competitive, and he knew what it took to create a champion. Besides, we were training for more than bloody matches in his gym.

I had to be faster than the slavecatcher's hounds, or else they'd tear my flesh apart like they did young Abby. It was easy to evade captors and outpace their horses with my abilities, but I never could have succeeded without building stamina. Everything I did in life prepared me to be the Runaway, and my legs and heart were molded for that moment to save John. If all I could be was an ordinary woman, then an ordinary woman would have to be enough.

The others couldn't keep up with me. Christopher's natural strength would have been an asset, and he was quick for his size, but his stamina was already stretched from battle. Hoshi was also winded, but she'd push herself. Edith was not a runner, and Caroline wasn't faster than the average woman. Zhang couldn't have been too far behind me, as long as he could keep up a good stride. As far as Steven…I had no idea what that imposter could do with the body of a strange woman.

The air smelled of smoke and intensified as I ran through the yard back to the tunnels. There were also coherent hollers from voices I didn't recognize. Kachina used her powers to cut diagonally through the earth and bust a hole through the back cellar wall. Two of the zealots must not have realized they were standing within Kachina's reach, and she swallowed them up, leaving nothing but their heads visible. Speckles of blood covered them, the product of an explosion that took the arm of the man holding a gun. Metal shrapnel and soot were scattered across the walls. The shock of the savagery served as a distraction well enough for John to rush in, blazing his guns. Three bodies were dropped, and the others exasperatedly yelled profanities and slurs with their limited air supply as I rushed by.

I didn't bother taking the time to gaze at their corpses and splattered guts. Nor did I have sympathy or the stomach for it. I had to keep moving forward.

Three *guards* must have rushed down the tunnels to aid their comrades, but they were close enough for James to aim from just outside the nullified perimeter and fire streams of red power. Their corpses were singed and lying on the ground.

John must have sent the dogs ahead of them afterwards. His last directives held a firm grip on their animal instincts, even though John's influence had ceased. One of their bodies lay dead in the tunnel, and then another. But the second managed to bloody his teeth. The zealot he attacked lay dead—his arm pierced and torn with two bullet wounds in his chest. Another zealot also lay a few feet in front of him, but there was more blood on those walls of clay that had yet to be accounted for.

The stale air was getting warmer, but the lack of light meant the fires hadn't spread down to the tunnels yet. Oil lamps hovered above me, connected by cable wires. There were dim and even dark patches, and the tunnel curved. I hated that I didn't just see John up ahead waiting for me, but I heard voices in the distance, and they were growing louder. I didn't hear any gunshots, so I assumed their brawl was over.

Then, the moment of truth came. I rounded a corner and saw light pouring out from an open door. "John!"

My anxiety certainly clouded my vision. I don't recall anything else until I entered the room. There was a cage, no bigger than what you'd put a dog in, and a blown lock on the floor. John was holding a little black boy around five years of age, and he was bleeding on his leg and on his side.

"John, are you alright?"

I tried to clutch onto him, but he handed the boy to me instead. "You have to get him away from us before it's too late."

John was sweaty and huffing a lot, but his wounds appeared to be from gunshots. There was a chance he could heal on his own, but his body trembled, and it frightened me. "Zhang is on his way."

"And he needs to be able to heal the others when he gets here." Some of the bodies on the ground were from the zealots, and some were ours. Tony was on the floor, holding his bloodied stomach, and his face was as red as a tomato. He didn't have long without a miracle.

"Charlotte, you run."

"How far?"

"Until you can't run anymore."

Though I was pressed for time, I quickly slammed my lips against my husband's. I didn't think of it as a kiss goodbye. It was fuel for the fire under my feet and a reason for John to hold on a bit longer.

I rushed back through the tunnels. I wasn't surprised to see Zhang coming in as I was headed out. There was no time for an explanation. I told him, "Keep moving forward," and kept on running. He obeyed. By the time I returned to the first bunker, female Steven was standing in the middle of it, wide-eyed and deranged. I think she was surprised to see me clutching onto the child. She almost reached for him as I rushed by, but I shrugged her off and kept moving.

I was glad that he was such an agreeable child. Once I was outside, I moved him to my back, and he held onto me as if he were my own kin. He was about as heavy as a bushel of sweet potatoes. I caught a glimpse of some of my allies attacking stray zealots who attempted to run through a secret exit. Christopher, Hoshi, and Caroline joined Kachina in fending them off. I trusted they'd be able to handle it. I had to keep moving to the tree line, and even further.

Sometime after bobbing and weaving through the trees, my chest started to burn, and my legs began to shake. I tried to trust that John would be alright, but I didn't know how powerful that child was. What if Zhang were still without his powers while I steadily slowed down? What if I wasn't by John's side as he said goodbye to this world? What if it was all for nothing?

My foot slipped on a tree root, and I fell to my hands and knees. That child suddenly felt like a hundred bushels of potatoes, and I wheezed for air and sobbed. He slid off my back and watched me quiver in fear and heartache, with big brown eyes. He was a beautiful boy, and I hadn't noticed all of the little scars on his arms until then. I pulled up his pants leg and saw they had poked and stabbed him there as well.

I was horrified. There was only so much blood they could draw from him, but they had clearly been doing it for a while. "Where are your mother and father? Do you know?"

He shook his head.

"What about your name? You must have a name."

He shrugged his shoulders.

I remember being that small and afraid. "Well, I'll have to give you a good name then. I have to call you something, and I promise to protect you."

I had been pondering baby names for months. It was a given what I wanted to name John's first (and only) son, but I had thought of other names. "How about Moses?"

He shrugged his shoulders again. He certainly reminded me of myself. "Well, if you remember the name your mother gave you, you can tell me. Until then, we're going to call you Moses. Let's keep moving."

I stood on my feet and held onto his hand. I needed him to walk a little bit until I regained my strength. Then, I would run to the other side of the world if I had to. I would do anything to keep John safe. Anything.

"Charlotte!"

"John?" I whispered to myself. I turned around. He was somewhere in the trees with me. "John!"

"Charlotte!" That time, his voice was much closer, as if he had blinked toward me.

"John!" I was certain I was still without my powers, so I let Moses's hand go and ran toward the voice. Moses's power must have weakened significantly. John must have blinked within a hundred feet of me. I jumped on top of him, kissing his lips and cheeks while soaking him with fresh tears. "I was so worried about you."

"It's alright. I told you that I would survive. Most of us made it."

"Most of us…?" I slid off of him and braced myself. "Who did we lose?"

"Peter and Hotah." He took a hard swallow. "James, Edith, Caroline, and Christopher lost their powers, but Tony was fine once Zhang healed him."

I fell into his chest and trembled for a few seconds. There was still so much to do, and we could mourn for them at an appropriate time. "Tillie? Is she alright?"

"Her powers are also gone. All of the prisoners were injected with the boy's blood. According to Dinah, the suppressant should last about four months."

"Dinah…?" Her name sounded too comfortable on his tongue.

"That's Steven's real name." John seemed remarkably calm.

"Did you know?"

"I would have told you if I did," he said, mildly annoyed. "I should have, though. Dinah was Steven's sister. I didn't think she survived her father's plantation. We buried her together, but I suppose that body belonged to her brother. The last thing he offered her was a fresh start."

There was no point in being jealous. John never paid attention to other women, but I'd be lying if I said I wasn't bothered. I knew where I stood with Tillie and Kachina, and I understood their affections. I had to rethink every interaction I ever had with Steven, now that I knew I was looking into the eyes of a woman.

"You know she wants you to kill the boy. She thought you would."

"A few of them want me to. They're too ashamed to admit it, but they're afraid."

My lips trembled before I summoned the courage to ask. "And what are you going to do?"

"It would be the safest thing for us, so I understand their position. It's not only our safety we have to consider. We have the children back home, and we can't protect them if the boy is with us. And we also can't be safe if the boy is out in the world, unsupervised."

"I understand that, but he's just a boy!"

"Charlotte…" John gently grabbed onto my arms and wrinkled his brows. "I will not harm him. But he can't stay with us, and everyone I trust is right here."

Trust wasn't his specialty. Even if he could trust one of our own, they'd be no better than a good human fighter. "What about someone I trust?"

"Cooper is the first person Dinah would suspect."

"You believe Dinah is a danger to the boy?"

"I think Dinah is terribly conflicted, and I'd rather not press our luck."

"But Coop would keep him safe if he knew the stakes. He would do that for me."

John's neck jerked back. "He'd have to leave New York and disappear. Do you truly think he'd do that for you now? After everything?"

John's questions felt like an interrogation. My love affair with Joseph Cooper was long over, but part of me believed he would always love me. But Cooper was kind enough to give me extraordinary care before he fell for me, and even after he knew my heart belonged to John. "I do. I can convince him."

John took a breath, and I braced myself for his rebuttal. "You can go to New York and convince him, but I need to take the boy elsewhere. Cooper can meet me somewhere else, somewhere Dinah wouldn't think of."

I perked up in shock. "Well, Dinah has both of our memories, so it has to be a place neither of us has been or someplace we'd never return."

"And if it's a place you've never been, you can't blink there."

Even if I hadn't been there, if I could think it up, wouldn't that mean Dinah could figure it out? "Pick a letter."

"C."

I pondered for a few seconds. "How about Chicago?"

"Doesn't Cooper have brothers in Chicago?"

I folded my arms and cocked my brow. "How do you know that?"

John smirked. Of course, his spies learned all they could about Joseph Cooper while I was under his care. "How about Cincinnati?"

Ohio seemed like a safe enough place. It held significance to me, so Dinah would likely guess it, but it was so large that we could hide anywhere. My main concern was John's travel. It was going to be difficult for John to navigate his way through the South, especially if people found out he was a deserter. "How long will it take you to get there?"

"Without my powers and avoiding the Confederate army…" He raised his head toward the sky as he thought, then sighed. "It could take weeks. Probably a month."

"A month?"

"That's what has to happen if you want to keep the boy safe. I'll bring him to Cincinnati. You get our recruits home, then go convince Cooper to take the boy to safety."

"And you're leaving now?"

"I have to, Charlotte. I need to get the boy out of Confederate territory as quickly as possible, and before the others start voicing their darker desires."

I tried not to get emotional, but my eyes welled. We had such a beautiful morning together, and not even three hours later, our world was upside down.

"It's only one month. We've been apart longer than that…"

"Not since we've been wed." I hadn't even spent a night without him. We were always together, and that's how I always wanted us to be.

"It'll be alright." He kissed me on the forehead while I fiddled with his black coat. Leather garments weren't out of the ordinary, but black ones were.

"You can't go out like this. Let me grab you a change of clothes, some food, and money. And some blankets. It'll be cold in Cincinnati. You'll want to keep the boy warm."

"Of course, dear. You're right."

If Dinah was truly a danger, there was always a chance she could discover the boy's location and show up as Cooper. Of course, she couldn't get too close without getting exposed, but John didn't know him like I did. "You need a code word that only the two of you will know."

John chuckled. "I'll ask him how many of my children you'll bear."

"Uh!" I rolled my eyes. "Can you be serious?"

He glared. "That sound of revulsion will be the perfect code. I'm certain Dinah wouldn't utter such disgust at the thought of bearing my ten children."

"And Coop won't forget it either." I wondered what it would be like for the two of them to see each other once again.

I wouldn't be able to play the role of mediator. "How will Coop find you?"

He paused for a moment. "Why don't you think of two letters?"

"How about G and W?"

"That's fine. There's no reason Cooper wouldn't arrive in Cincinnati before me, so tell him to find a hotel that starts with a G and check in under the name 'Mr. Winebeck.'"

"Where did that name come from?"

"I made it up." He grinned, far too proud of himself. "I'll be careful, and I trust Cooper will also exercise tremendous caution. The zealots can't ever find him, or it could mean the end of us."

"I know." I took John's hand and led him back to the boy. He was quietly sitting on the roots of a tree with his back pressed against it. His heavy head was nodding off. Perhaps he was so docile because he was exhausted. When John hovered over him, his head sprang straight up, and he reached for me, whimpering. I was tired myself, but I picked the boy up and gently rocked him. "It's alright, Moses."

"Moses?" John tried to pat the boy on the back, but he shifted his body away and moaned.

"He didn't tell me a name, so I gave him one." Moses and the Exodus was the first Bible story John taught me. It was such a powerful tale that plantation owners edited it out of Bibles distributed among slaves. Deep in our bones, slaves knew that subjugation was not God's desired plan, and they couldn't afford for us to be inspired by the power of God unleashing mighty wonders to free the Israelites. "I reckon you can lead him to the Promised Land."

"If he'll let me." I didn't know what was so intimidating about John. His powers were suppressed, and so were his animal characteristics. We were both wearing dark clothes. John was a tall man, but he wasn't enormous. Maybe it was his color. "You don't have to be afraid. John may not look like us, but we're the same. He'll see you to a safe place. I promise you."

I rubbed the boy's back and rocked him gently. There was a good chance I could give birth to a lighter child, but there was always a chance my mulatto would resemble my shade. John would always look radically different than his son. But he was so gentle as he reached for the boy. Moses moaned a little, but I shushed him and rubbed his back until he quieted in John's arms. "I promise, John will make you safe."

"You have my word." He would do whatever was necessary to ensure the safety of that child. I couldn't bear to lose another one. I just couldn't.

"I'll be right back." I walked out of the boy's reach, blinked back to our home in New York, then immediately grabbed some essentials for John and packed them in a carpet bag. I also grabbed another bag and filled it with food—bread, a jar of honey, crackers, apples, pears, raspberries, jerky, and half of an apple pie. When I returned, John was sitting on the ground, and Moses was sleeping on his coat.

"Did you bring the pie?"

"Of course, I brought your pie." John had to change out of his bloody clothes, in case any stray zealots or military men found him. No one was around to see his beautiful body besides his wife. John couldn't bring any notable items Ghost would wear, like his coat and boots. I brought a light gray wool coat that I had made for him. It was too warm for it now, but he'd be grateful for it later.

"I'm more accustomed to sneaking around in the South. Are we certain I shouldn't be the one to take the boy?"

"You would do a fine job, my dear, but if I bat my eyelashes at Cooper, I don't think it'll have the same effect."

"Is that what you think I do? Bat my eyelashes?"

"Well, you have other notable weapons in your inventory, but they're not appropriate for a married woman." John snatched my waist. That animal aura might have been suppressed, but there was a natural predator in him who wished to devour me. The way his eyes smoldered and his lips curled, melted the strength in my knees. If not for the sound of approaching horse hooves, I would have lost myself in him for a little while.

John let me loose and stepped in front of me, prepared to fight, but it was only Dinah. The horse was unfamiliar, so I assumed it belonged to the zealots. It was wearing a saddle with large leather pouches. Her face was a bit tense, and her eyes were watery. I didn't know what to make of her, but she certainly did look pretty with those long spiral curls down her back. "There's no way to talk you out of your decision, so I might as well help you."

John's silence was like a thick molasses pulling her to the ground. I recognized her expression from earlier in the day. I wondered if she was simply terrified of disappointing her leader or if her affections ran deeper than that.

"That's awfully kind of you." I nudged John, but he still wouldn't speak to the girl.

I thought Dinah was prettier than Steven was handsome. Her almond-shaped eyes were sparkling blue like her brother's, and her skin was smooth like caramel. She had a square face with a strong jawline and sharp angles. Her full brows furrowed the longer he kept quiet, and after a few excruciating seconds, she exploded. "John, I'm sorry for deceiving you all this time. I never meant any harm by it, and—"

"We don't have time to discuss it now." He didn't raise his voice, but John was firm enough to hush her. "I need to leave with the boy, and you all need to get out of here before the authorities come and investigate."

It was too strange watching the two of them stare at one another. John was angry, even a bit sad, but he didn't have time for either emotion. He attached the bags I brought with leather straps and snaps. I checked the pouches. There were canteens of water, matches, ammunition, and things like that.

I grabbed the boy after John mounted the horse. He stayed asleep, even when I transferred him over to John's care. He must have been tuckered out. There was no way to know all of the horrors the zealots inflicted on him.

Dinah frowned as she petted the horse's face, too timid to look John in the eye. "I don't suppose you'll tell me where you're going."

"It's better if you don't know. The boy has to disappear. Trust me, Dinah."

She reached for the boy's hand and rubbed her thumb against him. I think she pressed her luck to see if it was possible to learn about his life while he slept. But his power hadn't lifted. I couldn't blink, and she couldn't take on his life experiences and his powers. He would always remain a mystery to her. "Of course, John. I trust you." She gathered enough courage to glance into his eyes.

He bid me farewell with a nod, then was off. It was too bad John wouldn't have the cloak of night to protect him, but he was a smart man. If he said Moses was his slave, who would bother to even question him? As long as John wasn't recognized in the South, he'd make it safely to Cincinnati.

Dinah didn't share my optimism. She clutched her chest and was near tears. "I hope you can understand that I have many questions for you."

The glossy shine remained, but a sharpness quickly emerged and pierced through me. "We can settle up once we get home, Lady Charlotte. Until then, we have much to do."

Chapter Five

We were mostly quiet on the walk back to the manor. When I felt my powers return, I grabbed hold of Dinah's arm and blinked to the entrance of the tunnels. The liberated were lined up in four rows. There were a little more than forty people, a mix of different ages. They must have stuffed them in those cages. Even animals had more dignity.

I was relieved to see Tillie alive and well. She approached us, wearing Caroline's coat. Adam and Kachina were by her side. "John took the boy?"

"He'll be safe," I promised her. "And we'll be safe as well. This is the best thing for us."

"Well, I'm glad," Adam said. Based on the airy relief in his breath, I figured he was one of the few who wanted to keep the boy alive. "I just hope that John can keep himself safe."

"And where is John headed?" Tillie asked.

"He didn't say," Dinah said. "If it's safe to tell us, I'm certain John will once he returns."

"Nobody asked you," she said sharply, and Dinah held her tongue. Tillie then looked directly into my eyes. "Did he tell you?"

I did my best to keep a stoic expression. If they knew that I knew, I wouldn't have any peace about it. "I don't know where the boy will end up. All I know is John will connect with me, and we'll see him in about a month." That was true enough for them. "He'll find his way back to me. He always does."

"That's enough chatter," Dinah said. "We have work to do." I wasn't surprised Dinah wanted to keep busy. All eyes seemed to be drawn to her. I took it that no one knew about her true form, not even her closest friends.

Peter's and Hotah's bodies had already been removed from the cave. Peter's fatal wound was a shot in the neck, but he had also been shot in the chest and stabbed in the leg. Hotah had so many holes in his body; I couldn't begin to imagine what the final blow might have been. It was no wonder Zhang couldn't get to him in time. He had no reason to mope around with his head low.

"You did your best, and you saved many lives today." I rubbed his back, hoping that it would bring him comfort.

"Hotah was a true warrior," Adam said to me. "He voluntarily took on many of the blows, so we wouldn't have to. If he hadn't protected John, he'd be without his powers."

Wherever John was, I'm certain he was punishing himself over it in his mind. "And would he be alive if he hadn't protected my husband?"

"No. He was shot up even before we got to the cellars. I don't understand how he persisted for so long."

"He was too stubborn to die," Kachina tearfully stated. "I can't believe he's gone…" I believed he fancied Kachina, but she was still very much in love with my husband. Even if she could have moved on, it wouldn't have been for a long while.

We collected every weapon that had the blood of Moses on it, and we incinerated them in a metal foundry. We gathered notes from the tunnels and kept those. The zealots who tried to escape during the attack had vials of blood on them. We burned those as well.

The two zealots who were buried alive were still screaming hoarsely whenever we walked by. Dinah touched one of their heads, and he furiously tried to bite her. Once the zealot was no longer of any use to us, Dinah took out her pistol and blew his head off. Then, she did the same to the second survivor.

I did my best not to give away how I truly felt, but I was alarmed by Dinah's cold and calm demeanor. Even if she were still a man, I'd still think it was unnatural. "That's a fine trick, remembering everything someone has ever said or done."

"Sometimes. Most of the time? You don't want to know what goes on in these humans' heads."

No, I certainly didn't. She was invaluable to us and did a service no one else wanted to. Even John hated her power and having all that knowledge. He had only used it accidentally. John already had enough demons rattling around in his brain.

Normally, John would address our new recruits, but that duty fell to me. I was relieved to see so many men among them, men of fighting age. "My name is Charlotte. My husband is the leader of our group. We can offer you a haven, free from the tyranny of the zealots and other bigoted humans, or we can release you back into the wild. We cannot guarantee your safety if you refuse us, but if you join us, we will teach you how to use your powers. I know you have temporarily lost your abilities, but they will return. And once they do, you will be free to use them as you please. The choice is completely up to you, but you have to decide now."

They were very quiet. They all looked around to judge each other, but nobody else was brave enough to move. "No defectors? Good."

Dinah stepped forward to the first person in line. She had blonde curly hair with tints of red. It was frizzy and a bit tangled. She was shaking in Dinah's presence, even though she was a bit taller. "I'm going to evaluate you."

"You're what?" The girl trembled and squeaked when Dinah's hands clasped her cheeks. It didn't hurt Dinah, and it only took a few seconds for her to relive their entire life.

"This is Evelyn Baker from Florida." Dinah removed her hands and smiled. "She's twenty-five and can control plants."

"That's fascinating," Adam mumbled, almost as if he were mesmerized.

"That is a useful power. She could help grow our food supply…" I turned around and realized our honorary reverend was a bit flushed. I chuckled and turned to Dinah to get her attention, but her brows had furrowed, and she was frowning. "What is it?"

"I can't mimic her powers because they're suppressed. I'll never be able to mimic these people if I touch them."

I didn't know what to make of that. I liked that Steven was a powerful force of nature, but Dinah was a deceiver who had just butchered a bunch of slaves and contemplated murdering a child. Limiting her power seemed like a good thing to me. "If that's fine with you, that's fine with me. We need to know who they are before we take them in."

Dinah sighed and continued, hopefully without sensing my relief. She was power hungry, but she was also loyal to our mission. We couldn't wait four months to know whether these people were safe. "This is Benjamin Johnson. He's from Georgia. He was plucked right out of the army by the zealots after they discovered he had enhanced speed and agility."

He must have been barely twenty and was in good fighting shape. "The zealots took John after his stint in the Confederacy as well. It seems the war is a common way they prey on extraordinary men. We'll be far more loyal to you." I only meant to touch his arm, but I got a good squeeze of his biceps. Benjamin would be a great warrior, indeed.

"Do you have time for this?" An impatient man in his early thirties barked. He was standing at the end of the first row. "We should go back to your home, then sort all of this out."

Adam had extinguished the fires in the manor, and we were too secluded to think anyone outside of the plantation heard the battle. We had time, unless reinforcements were coming. That was a possibility, but he struck me as a little too anxious. "And what's your name, sir?"

Dinah's eyes latched onto him like a hawk. He tried to step away, but one of her hands gripped onto his wrist, and the other aimed a pistol right under his chin. An awful scream ripped through the crowd, especially the second row, which was coated in his blood and brain matter. Some of it managed to splatter on Dinah, but she was too furious to care. "That was

Frank Davenport. He was a zealot spy with no powers, meant to infiltrate our home and destroy it, and he's not alone."

The others were too obvious. There was an older woman and four other men. A flash of panic shone through their eyes. Dinah made eye contact with them all, which prompted them to run away. It was useless, though. Adam could have blown a wind so powerful that it knocked them into the air high and fast enough to kill them. Kachina could have buried them alive with a thought. But those possibilities were better than what Tony had in store for them after his eyes turned black. The shadows that ran with them got closer and closer, until they were right on their heels. Tony reached out his hand, then closed his fingers tightly. They all fell in unison, screaming as their shadows pulled on their legs and dragged them down into the dark portals. I had never seen what it was like in the world of the shadow, but once Tony slipped into his own to meet them there, it was evident that they'd never return.

Honestly, the whole ordeal was a little too familiar. My stomach was in knots, but I had to remind myself that we were not killing innocents like Mr. Cohen. The zealots were murderous fanatics who wouldn't stop until we were all dead. John needed me to be strong, and I promised him that I would. "That's why we need to evaluate here."

I marched up and down the row, so they could see the fiery conviction in my eyes. "I won't jeopardize the safety of our people. Some of you may not be spies, but that doesn't mean you're not a danger. Again, if you want to stay and salvage whatever is left of your human lives, you're more than welcome to do that. But if you're ready for something more, you're welcome to join us. Our leader can show you your full potential, as he did for Tony and the others."

I pointed to Tony, who had just begun to emerge from his shadow. His face was peppered with blood, and his saber was stained red. There were murmurs from the crowd, but they mostly contained themselves. As terrible as our abilities might have been, there was a natural curiosity within them. They needed to know how far they could go. "Stay and be prey. Come and abandon your limitations."

I waited in silence. I hadn't given many speeches, and I didn't have John's sway, but I felt as though I had done a fine job. My heart was pounding fiercely, though.

I heard footsteps behind me and turned around. It was Benjamin, with a smirk that mirrored many of John's men before going off to battle. "I'll gladly join you. I didn't want to fight for their cause anyway."

Evelyn rushed beside him as well. "I have nothing to go back to. My family thought I was mad for talking to plants."

Others began to raise their hands and volunteer, until they all did. They couldn't leave their spots until they were properly evaluated. There were no more spies among them, and Dinah deemed them safe enough to travel. Once five were cleared, I blinked them home. Then I did another batch, then another. Dinah took my form and then took two batches of her own. She was a little tired, so Tony offered to take his sister home, and the bodies of Hotah and Peter. To no surprise, no one else wanted to join him. I was a bit tired myself, but with our combined power, we were able to get the rest of our group home.

We added forty-two recruits to our cause, rescued Tillie, took two casualties, and removed an invaluable weapon from the hands of the zealots. All things considered, it was a successful mission.

When we returned home, Nathaniel and Javier took care of wrangling our liberated friends and placing them into temporary living arrangements. We planned to build nice homes for our people, but in the meantime, it was easier to keep most of them together in apartments. Kachina wanted to help, but I ordered the raid team to rest and prepare for the funeral later that evening. The only one who wouldn't obey was Tillie. Since she was captured, she felt it was her responsibility to make arrangements for the funeral. I asked Henry and Goldie to assist her.

As for me, I couldn't rest yet. I changed into something more comfortable, then went to the tavern and had myself a juicy turkey sandwich with boiled potatoes. Afterward, I gathered a blank book, ink, and pens, and made myself comfortable in a private room in the complex. Nathaniel was tasked with sending in our new guests, one at a time.

The first to come in was a young girl. She had bone-straight raven hair and was a skinny thing. When I stood to greet her, she panicked and bowed her head. "Good afternoon, Lady Charlotte."

"It's just Charlotte, for now. Please, have a seat." As she sat across from me, I noticed tiny dark spots on her arms, along with healed cuts, like the boy. "Your name was Margaret?"

"Yes, ma'am." She pulled down her sleeves once she realized I was staring.

"Do you like that blouse? I sewed it myself."

"You did?" The sleeves were a bit puffy, and frills trailed down the center. It wasn't complicated to make. I designed it for Emma, who was two years her junior. She was small enough to fit it, but her arms were a tad too long.

"Yes. I was forced to learn many skills in my life of slavery, and after freeing myself from bondage, I put those skills to good use and enriched myself. I'd like to teach you to be a capable and respectable woman, if you'd allow me."

Margaret tightened her lips and nodded.

"And in return, I'm hoping you'll use your abilities to help us develop our land. Can you tell me more about what you do?"

"Well…" Her eyes hid in the skirt's ruffles. "When I get sad, it rains, and when I'm scared, there's loud thunder, and it makes me more afraid." She clung to the fabric, wrinkling it more as her sweet voice softened. "My grandmother was said to be a witch. They thought my mother might be the same."

"And what happened to your father?"

She shrugged. "I don't know. He tried to stop them from taking me. That was a while ago."

"In Massachusetts?"

She nodded and hunched deeper toward her legs. I wrote the details of her sad story down. It was likely that her father was killed while trying to protect his daughter and wife, but he might have survived. The zealots weren't above killing the "innocent," but they didn't go out of their way to harm them. It depended on whether her father could expose them.

"Would you…" She swallowed a lump in her throat while battling oncoming tears. "Would you help me find my father?"

She exploded after that. I knelt by her side and took the girl's hands. I hadn't honestly put much thought into whether my parents were alive. I accepted that I was alone until John came along. I was more than willing to be her new family, but she might have needed something more. "I promise that I'll try. If he's still alive, we'll find him. And in the meantime, my husband can teach you how to use your powers properly."

She leaned on my chest and cried for a little while longer. Margaret wasn't certain how long she had been with the Overseers, but after talking with more of the liberated, I estimated it was about three years. Once her powers began manifesting more frequently, they decreased her rations and even bled her. Once they began injecting her with the blood of Moses, they could feed her more without fear of her sending a storm to wash the world away. She hadn't been able to feel her powers in over a year.

The others also had sad stories. Most had lost their families and had no hope of reunification, but a handful asked if it was possible to find their loved ones. I could only promise to try, but if their mothers, fathers, and spouses weren't gifted, they weren't guaranteed acceptance into our community. They would need to be evaluated, pledge loyalty, and leave the rest of the world behind. Then there was the question about how many humans we were willing to accept at all. I didn't mind if we could live in peace, but John still didn't care for humans.

By the time I had met everyone, I was tuckered out. But the night couldn't end without laying Peter and Hotah to rest. After Asha died, we set some land aside for burials. Kachina sculpted a beautiful angel to guard over their resting place. I wished it were spring, so the flowers could bloom for them, but Dinah came and laid fresh flowers at their grave. She probably blinked somewhere warm to get them.

I noticed she tried to converse with Tillie and Kachina, but they shut her down. I wasn't close enough to hear their argument, but I gathered what it was about when Dinah walked away to stand by herself. John wasn't the only one she deceived.

There were many kind words spoken about Peter and Hotah. Tillie meant to speak of their brave exploits and how thankful she was, but she only managed a few words before tears overtook her. It was the most emotional I had ever seen her, and Dinah wasn't allowed to comfort her closest friend. Even when they had a minor reception with drinks, Dinah left to be alone.

I joined them in the tavern so I could eat again. A few of our new citizens joined us. Evelyn was sitting at a table, entertaining dozens of questions from Henry and Arthur. I noticed Adam standing by the entryway, pretending he wasn't looking. I stood right next to him, intending to pay him back for breakfast. "You ought to wait at least four months, rev."

"Four months?" He chuckled while thinking real hard. "For what?"

I leaned over and spoke quietly enough for only his ears. "Before you invite her to your bed chamber. I assume a nice church boy would at least wait until marriage."

Oh, I loved embarrassing white men and watching them turn as red as a tomato. "Did you hate the eggs that much?"

I giggled and latched onto his arm. "I noticed you seem to fancy her, and she is pretty. However, creating more of our kind is a priority for John. I think we should wait until their powers come back before any intercourse is had."

Adam's history as a charismatic abolitionist made him the closest thing to a minister that we had. If something blossomed between the two of them, I expected him to make an honest woman out of her. I couldn't guarantee that to be the case for other gentlemen. "Can I trust you to encourage everyone to hold off their passions?"

"Yes, but…" His bashful smile slowly fell. "What if their powers don't return?"

That would be a terrible fate, and it made my stomach queasy just thinking about it. I was more optimistic about poor Caroline's powers returning, but someone like Margaret had been suppressed for so long. But I also couldn't believe Moses, even unknowingly, could hurt them like that. He was such a sweet boy, and I didn't believe God would want that legacy for him. "They will. I know they will."

Arthur must have said something humorous because Evelyn and Henry exploded into laughter. She had such a charming voice, soft like flower petals. Adam's eyes lit up, and he grinned once more. "Four months, you say?"

"Behave yourself, reverend." I elbowed his side before leaving the tavern.

I blinked inside the manor. Most of the structure had been crafted, but it lacked the finer details that made it feel like home. My bedroom and a few other rooms were decorated, but most of the mansion lacked drapes, carpet, and lighting. There was no kitchen yet. Since hardly anyone stayed inside, it was freezing. There was only one fire in that whole building, and it was inside the room I was standing in front of. "Dinah?" I knocked on the wooden door. She had carved and installed it herself. Carpentry was one of the many skills she had acquired from our talented former slaves. "Dinah, may I come in?"

Just before my fingers grasped the handle, the door pulled open. "Lady Charlotte," she raised a glass of bourbon for me. "What a lovely surprise."

Dinah's room was bare, but she did have a bed, a few pieces of furniture, and acquired a collection of liquor. She downed the glass and set it on a table, trading it for a lit cigar that was resting on an ashtray. She was only dressed in a black tunic, which was long enough to look like a scandalous dress, and it became even more so once she sat and spread out as if she were still a man.

"You're a very odd woman to me."

"Oh?" She took a puff of her cigar. I hated the smell of them. I'd have to wash to get the stench of it out of my hair and clothes. "What's so particularly odd now? You don't believe a woman can enjoy a good cigar?"

I took a seat across from Dinah and crossed my legs. "I don't understand why you would impersonate a man for all of this time."

Even as she blew a puff of smoke and tapped her ashes into the glass tray, she still appeared remarkably feminine. Perhaps it was the way she pursed her lips, the daintiness of her wrists and fingers, or the way she exaggerated her sluggish posture. “If you could be anyone in the whole world, you’re telling me you wouldn’t be a man?”

“I would never choose to be anyone other than myself.”

Dinah released a bellowing laugh. “Scars and all?”

“Scars and all.”

She pressed a hard grin on her face, then smiled widely. “That’s what makes you so special, Charlotte. You’re honestly telling the truth, even though you know there are many benefits to being a man. There’s obviously more power in it, and it’s safer.”

“Do the men drafted in war feel safer?”

“I’d rather be drafted into war than drafted into the life I used to live.” She took another puff of her cigar, this time with her eyes on the end as it slowly destroyed itself. “You’re fortunate, Charlotte, lucky even.”

I swear, every hair on the back of my neck stood straight up. “Lucky?”

Dinah eased off her seat and hunched over the table, so she could smash the butt of the cigar until the lit ember diminished. Then, she raised her empty glass and stared into the few fragments of light. “Reality runs through a prism, and that prism is the perspective of men. You might have been a slave on the Cohens’ plantation, but you had the heart of John. You were educated, well-fed, adored, and got away with what other slaves would have been beaten or killed for. You benefited from a man’s love and affection. I, on the other hand, suffered from the affections of men, but I never had love. The only men who ever did anything good for me were my brother and John.”

As she poured herself another glass of bourbon, I resisted the urge to slap it from her hands. “I don’t know your life story, but you certainly know mine. I was beaten.”

“That was one time, Charlotte.”

“It was ten lashes from the man I love!” I quieted myself. I didn’t mean to raise my voice, and based on her slight smug smile, that’s exactly what she wanted.

“You got those lashes because you defied the natural order of the plantation. You challenged Lady Cohen, threatened to run away with her son. And for what? You and John could have run away and left the world behind. Instead, you both took up her vision and built a haven for our kind, and you built it on blood. You're the new Lady Cohen! Or…should I say 'Lady Charlotte?'" Dinah smirked as she took a swig of her drink; this time, it was deliberately obvious. "I'm sorry. Did I offend you?"

"Clearly, I offended you."

"What? When you judged me for impersonating my dead brother? You think that bothered me?" She set her drink down and slid back into her chair, seemingly unamused.

"I assume many things about myself bother you." Tillie was in love with my husband. Kachina was in love with my husband. I had begun to wonder if Steven's eyes were always wandering in my direction because I had stirred feelings in him, but perhaps he was never looking at me. "I can only judge you based on what I know, but what I know is that you've deceived us all, even John and Tillie."

I always knew there was more to Steven's story. What I did know for certain was that he was devoted to John's vision of destroying the zealots and supremacy; he was ruthless and twisted, and he very much hated losing. Dinah was dangerous, and I needed to know that I could trust her. "Would you mind finally telling me the truth about who and what you are?"

"It isn't for the faint of heart."

"My heart's strong."

There was a gleam in her eye and then a slight glare as if she didn't believe me. "Then prepare yourself, Charlotte."

Chapter Six

I'll begin my tale at the beginning of my creation...

A pair of brown eyes intensely watched me tremble from the pain of being torn wide open. There was a mild look of alarm on her face as she stared at my blood-soaked chemise. As she knelt beside me and stroked my hot and reddened, tear-stained cheek, I wished for her to take the pain away. I couldn't ask. My voice was reduced to a hoarse whisper, and even swallowing burned. All I could do was sniff, moan, and murmur.

"Dinah..." My mother's voice was sweet like a music box, and she smelled of perfume. Her fingers were soft like the pillows smeared with snot and face paint. She brushed a few sweated strands of curly hair from my face and spoke so matter-of-factly, "You shouldn't resist. It will be easier if you play along with what they want."

My mother had brown skin, like the bark of a tree, yet her hands had never toughened from days of hard labor or even suffered burns from accidents in the kitchen. She was a refined beauty, thin yet shapely like an hourglass. I thought I was justified in wanting to be like her, but that changed once I realized why she was unblemished. I was also a sacrifice for her lifestyle.

I gritted my teeth and bore the pain. I accepted that no other words of comfort would be given to me. The amount of blood did concern her enough to call for a doctor. They spoke about me, but never to me. My client was too rough, and the damage done would likely result in barrenness. I was barely old enough to dream of a family, and as a slave, there was little hope for one anyhow. Yet, I found the strength within myself to sob once more.

My mother shed no tears for me. If anything, her sigh was born of relief. Madam's products would be better if they weren't slowed down by producing a child. I felt as though my future was snatched right out of me. I would never be more than what I was, and I would never create anything greater to live beyond myself. My whole world was reduced to that harem. I decided to suffocate my innocence on that filthy pillow. At fourteen, I was officially a woman.

Madam and the other girls taught me how to dress, how to walk, and how to entertain the master's visitors. Many times, we were treated as accessories to a room, meant to add ambiance and be pretty while men talked business or played cards. If they needed a little bit more whiskey or champagne, I'd fill their glass and smile. Most men thought I was worth visually feasting, but too forbidden to touch. Only the vilest of them wanted me for themselves, and they were difficult to please. It seemed as though they wanted me to be afraid for my life, but I refused to beg or cry, even if they hurt me.

If I were to die in that place, why would it matter? There was nothing beyond those walls, anyhow. And as I stared back at them, completely apathetic about my fate, they were unsettled and eased their assault.

Madam expressed more annoyance than concern when my face ended up busted and bruised. I recall her words after observing the discoloration on my neck. "You're too light-skinned, Dinah. Don't provoke them. You have to figure out what the client wants and fulfill his fantasies."

My throat was sore, so I didn't spout the obvious answer. Some men took pleasure in inflicting pain on others. That was the thrill they paid for. I wouldn't bother fighting, and I certainly wasn't about to scream for them.

At least, they kept me inside our living quarters while I healed. I took the time to learn card games. I wanted to learn how to read, but only Madam knew how, and she didn't have the time or care to teach me. Madam was the most requested and most recommended by our Master. She was not only an expert at pleasing our clients but also at gathering secrets. For that, she received favor. Madam had the finest clothes, beauty tonics, and even jewelry.

Master didn't mind flaunting Madam around like a prize. He had no wife to appease; she died years ago in childbirth. He assumed his insatiable lust was hereditary and worth encouraging, so when his son turned sixteen, he took him to our harem to lose his virtue. He moved at a turtle's pace, too shy to look most of the women in the eye. His father never entertained Madam as an option. She stood behind Master, flapping a fancy frilled fan.

The girls were posing in ways to emphasize their hips and breasts. Perhaps they believed pleasing the Master's son would elevate their position, or they could be heirs to Madam's glory just as he was the heir to the Master's 2,500 acres. Their womanly bodies intimidated him. But what was a skinny boy, barely taller than me, supposed to do with that much woman? He continued shuffling down the line until he got to me. He hesitantly raised his head. He was handsome, much more handsome than his father. I recall his eyes being so bright and strikingly similar to mine.

"Not that one!" His father practically snatched him away from me and back toward the previous girl.

"Why?"

"Just obey me, boy. Not that one."

His son's eyes darted back at me, just before he pointed to the woman standing next to me. She excitedly placed her hands on his shoulder and escorted him away. His father also glanced at me, but Madam stared a little too long. She tried to cover her nervousness with her fan, but I was perceptive enough to ask myself the relevant questions.

He didn't visit the harem again to call upon our flesh, but I did see him more frequently with his father and his acquaintances. He avoided eye contact with me, even as I poured him a drink. He nearly gagged it up, which prompted a roar of laughter from his father's peers. The same nearly happened when he smoked his first cigar. He tried his best, though, to fit into his father's world, but he was always a beat behind every laugh and didn't contribute much to any conversation. And when one of the friends decided to grab my wrist and lead me away from their parlor, the yellow tints in his skin faded into pale white.

That night, I waited for Madam to return to her room after she finished pleasing Master. She was the only one of us to have her own room in the harem, and her face fumed when she saw me sitting on her throne. "What are you doing in here?"

"He's my father, isn't he?"

"Of course, he is." She didn't hesitate in the slightest, and her tone was so condescending. Perhaps I should have pieced it together sooner. I was lighter than my mother, but I was too brown to pass for a white child. But I hadn't even heard my kinship whispered as gossip.

"Then why is this my life? How come I don't live in the big house with my brother?" My father witnessed grown men take my hand and lead me into spare bedrooms. I couldn't recall even the faintest sign of remorse on his face. "Is it because I'm yours?"

"It's because you're a woman." Her eyes slightly narrowed at my dumbfounded face. "Don't blame your lot in life on me. You take your woes up with your Creator, if there even is such a thing. But if the Creator is a man, I wouldn't expect much from him. The purpose of all women is to pleasure men. Your life isn't especially tragic because your role is more obvious. Your father's wife had no more will than you and me, so don't complain. The best you can do with your life is to learn your role and play it well."

I didn't even remember the master's wife. I was a very small child when she passed away, sickened after delivering a stillborn child. Most men in his position would have remarried, but he did not. No one even spoke of her. There were no paintings or photographs. Perhaps all he needed was a warm body, and Madam certainly filled that description.

"I deserved to know."

She cruelly chuckled. "What does it change?"

I stared her down for a few seconds, contemplating my life. There was always a possibility that my father was another one of Madam's clients, but he protected his son from me for a reason. He knew. He knew the entire time, yet I was still a slave and a whore.

"Get out."

I left her room with a quiet rage. Both Madam and Master deserved to be punished. I had no observable representation of love within humans, but I had seen dogs care for their pups. If animals had enough sense to care for their kin, humans should have been able to do the same. I found myself wishing that something horrible would happen to both of them for their betrayal.

As life continued, Master acquired a new group of friends who frequented the plantation. They didn't indulge in the other girls and me, but they didn't judge Master for his particular vices. They spoke of destiny, God's divine plan, and Master's purpose in the world. Master already had a big head, and plenty of empty space to fill it with their boasting. It would have sickened me, but I was grateful for a pleasant evening that didn't require the removal of my clothes. When it was time to bid them goodnight, the leader took Madam's hand and kissed it. No one else seemed to notice, but her eyes were wide open from fright, and she was shaking.

I didn't ask Madam what had her so frightened because I wouldn't expect an answer. When Master's new spiritual friends returned, Madam tried to stay in the harem. The rest of us were more than capable of pouring liquor and giggling in their ears, but Master liked keeping Madam close. He sent one of the girls to fetch her, and she arrived a few minutes later with a forced grin. She clung to Master and kept her breasts firmly pressed against him, as if she were trying to make a first impression all over again. It was odd. Even if her attention was on Master, she was still dutiful toward visitors. She tried to ignore his friends, but their eyes often fell on her. It wasn't in a lustful way, but it was certainly…unbecoming.

When we returned to our quarters to sleep, Madam's steps were cumbersome, and she didn't speak a word. Her proud head was lowered, and she sank into her dainty shoulders. The others were worried and urged me to talk to her, but I didn't care enough to knock on her bedroom door. She had shut me out my whole life. Why should I care if she was upset or unwell?

I went to sleep, and in the morning, she was gone. The girls were worried, but I assumed she left late in the night to be with Master. It had happened many times before. I bet they were having bourbon and eggs in bed together, and I left it at that. I got dressed, made myself some breakfast, and waited to be summoned or for some clients to come by.

When it got late into the afternoon, I planned to go to the Big House myself, but one of the patrollers rushed toward me with a shotgun in hand. "You can't wander today. Stay in your harem." He was stern, but not ready to shoot me.

"Is something wrong? Did something happen?"

"It's not your concern. Go back."

I had an eerie feeling that whatever was going on had something to do with Madam. Even if she had slept with Master, she would have returned by then to freshen up and change into new clothes.

I decided to watch the plantation from the porch in a white rocking chair, sipping on a glass of lemonade. It was peaceful for such a terrible place. The slaves who worked in the fields were far off in the distance, and their cabins weren't close to ours. I hardly ever saw them. We often worked with the house slaves, but only when we served Master and his visitors. They all probably thought I lived the high life. I wondered if they could put up with my type of labor. Picking cotton in the hot sun couldn't have been worse than peeling off pieces of my soul. The rest of the girls thought we were fortunate to give our bodies to vile men. Some of them even found pleasure in it. I could fake a smile while with a client, but I couldn't recall ever experiencing true happiness, not even with the most experienced of men.

By the time the last bit of my ice had melted, Steven came from the Big House. I glanced around for patrollers before making my way toward him. I had no intention of provoking Master's fury. "What are you doing here?"

His arms latched onto mine, which startled me. I didn't want any onlookers to think we were engaging in an abominable relationship. Steven's eyes danced around, and then he leaned in and spoke real quiet. "I don't know how to tell you this, but your mother tried to run away last night."

My neck jolted back, and my eyes narrowed. "No, that doesn't make sense. She loves this place and her power. She would never run. Run where?"

"I don't know, but she did try to run, and she was caught. She never made it off the plantation."

Had the Lord answered my silent prayer for revenge? Out of the things I passively asked over the years, had he finally revealed his hand? "So, where is she? In a sweatbox? Whipping post?"

"No, Dinah. I don't know how to tell you this, but..." Steven's brows continued to furrow, and his bright eyes dimmed as if a shadow had fallen over his face. "...they burned her last night."

An involuntary, amused snort pushed through me, loudly. "Burned her? Alive?" He didn't change his posture or his furrowed brows, yet I giggled at the absurdity. "They burned Madam? For running away?"

"I'm afraid so."

I took a step back and slipped from his grasp. "That doesn't make any sense." Memories of Madam sitting beside Master at dinner or hovering over his desk while he worked came to mind. He never raised his hand to her or said a harsh word. It was the closest thing to love I had ever witnessed. "She's Master's favorite. She's worth far more alive than dead. He'd never do that. You're lying!"

"Why would I lie to you?" His eyes had a shine in them that I didn't understand. Did he sympathize with me? I didn't care if that woman was dead. I despised her. Truly. I had no reason to miss or mourn her, yet...

My heart rattled like a rat in a cage. "Get out of here."

I tried to walk away, but his hand latched onto my wrist. "Dinah—"

"Let go of me..."

When his skin collided with mine, my senses were overloaded with colors, noises, scents, and feelings. The sweet and watery taste of breast milk on his lips and tongue as the hunger in his belly subsided. The cool sweep of darkness blanketed his body in a dark hallway, while his curious eye peeked inside his father's bedroom. Tears ran down a white woman's face as she screamed curses at his father. The scent of violets intoxicated his nostrils as his lips trailed a soft and delicate brown neck. Shame gnawed at his stomach as he watched his sister ease into the lap of a man twice her age, rubbing his chest. The hot smack of his father's hand across his face, and a powerful sting that followed. And lastly, blood-curdling screams pierced his ears as he watched his mother's brown skin blacken from the blast of fire beneath her feet.

I tried to push out the invading memories and sensations from my mind, but several of his memories and thoughts lingered. Once my vision returned to me, and I stared at his face, it became all too clear to me. Our eyes were the same. We inherited them from the same man, but the texture of our hair was similar, even though he tried to mask it with tonics. His nose was also wider than the average white man's. Even his skin had an undertone of yellow. I was such a fool. "You're not my half-brother. You're her son."

His eyes were strange, as if he were watching train cars pass by while he squeezed my wrist tighter. I hissed and pulled my hand away. As I cradled it, his eyes met mine once more. "You have it, too. Don't you?"

"I have what?"

"Her curse. That's why she tried to run away. That's why they killed her."

The flashes were all from his perspective. He stood beside his father, watching him grimace as Madam screamed. Eight of his spiritual friends surrounded him, cloaked in white garments. They chanted and lifted praises to God as she begged her lover, but Master continued to harden his face. Steven couldn't bear to look at Madam once her skin blackened. He raised his eyes above her, watching the smoke and embers rise, praying that her suffering would end quickly.

"You stood there and did nothing!"

"What else was I supposed to do?" Even from what I observed from afar, I knew Steven had a weak stomach. He mostly tried to live his life alone, away from his father's clients and the enslaved. If he had to work and watch them, he was too kind to them. He stood in the way of disciplining a slave once and ended up with a smack across his face. If they came for me, I had no confidence that he would stand against Master.

"And they'll kill me, too?"

"Both of us, I suspect, if they find out we have it."

I realized why Madam was afraid before she was murdered. She must have seen that they would kill her. Perhaps she had seen that they had done it before. If I wanted to survive, no one else could know. "This is a trick. I've never done this before. It must be your fault! There's nothing wrong with me."

He huffed out a frustrated sigh. "By all means, pretend as though you're normal because these zealots have gotten inside of our father's head, and if they discover your curse, they'll kill you as well. They'll be watching you because you're her daughter."

"And they don't know she's your mother?" Life was unfair. He could get away with so much, just because of that white skin.

"Our father knows, and we shouldn't give him a reason to tell them." Steven was strong in his own way. His voice was a little shaky, but he mostly controlled his emotions.

"If you knew that I was your sister, why haven't you done more for me?" He asked his father in private why he couldn't choose me, and he was as blunt as Madam was with me. He was shocked, but too timid to question how a father could stand to treat his own daughter like a whore. He suffered through the years with guilt in silence.

"What would you have me do?"

I shrugged, then tensed up my face. "Kill him."

He scoffed and shook his head while laughing in disbelief. "I can't kill our father."

No, he wouldn't. He didn't have it in him. But I was certain if I were a man, I'd be able to kill anyone. "Then we don't have anything else to talk about."

I returned to the harem and didn't speak a word to the girls about what I had discovered. That evening, all of the slaves on the plantation gathered together. Master announced that Madam had tried to run away and had died in the pursuit. The girls covered their mouths and sobbed silently. I allowed one of them to lean on me while I stoically rubbed her back. I hated that he lied to us, and even more than the girls fell for his deception. But it did instill a new fear within their ranks. No one had successfully fled from our plantation, and no one ever would.

The zealots didn't return for a while, and I was grateful. With Madam gone, my familiar face was a comfort to her regulars, who were fearful and angry about the current politics. I might not have been as shapely as Madam, but my womanly curves and lengthy limbs were more than enough to take their mind off their woes. Some slaves whispered prayers of hope that war would bring freedom to our doorstep, but I had no such hopes. I was going to die in that place, and I'd rather it be on my back than roasted on a pyre.

The only dreams I had were of Master dying horribly. My arms were too skinny to choke him to death, and I lacked grip strength. I could stab him or slit his throat, but I was hardly ever around him. He wasn't quite depraved enough to allow me to seduce him, and even pondering the idea made me ill. Poison would ease suspicion of me, but someone was bound to figure it out. I wasn't in a hurry to be whipped to death. I had no way of pulling it off, but I liked to imagine as I poured a cup of wine, that he'd soon gag on the floor. Sadly, he'd go on entertaining his guests.

A group of brothers began to visit us. The first night, there were four of them. The eldest among them, William, was pale and sickly. He would gander at the girls, but he didn't have the will to bed any of us. A chubby and short one didn't pay us any mind. He even sneered when one of the girls gave him a wink. The brothers mostly enjoyed the liquor and gambling, but the youngest brother kept his eyes on me like a prowling animal. His paws would reach and pull me into his lap. His hand rested on my inner thigh, very close to merchandise he was supposed to pay for. I smiled as if I enjoyed it, and that was thrilling enough. They left happy customers, and no one had to take their clothes off.

When they returned again, they were not so cheerful. Their eldest brother was not with them. He was too sick to travel. They grumbled in Master's leather chairs while smoking his cigars. "This is madness," George said as he tapped his foot on the floor.

He was the second eldest, but he was the largest among them. "We're being completely shut out of our brother's will. All of his land will pass onto his imposter of a son."

Master took a long puff of his cigar, eyeing across the room at Steven, hunched over in his chair. "He is still his father's son. It's only right that he leaves the boy with something, even if he isn't blood."

"You don't understand." Thomas sneered. "He's in love with one of the slave girls. He hates the plantation. When he returns from war, he'll sell our land—our father's land."

Master's eyes fell inside his glass while he tried to hide the budding smile on his lips. "And would you rather sell it?"

George's brow slightly rose. "Would you be willing to make an offer?"

"No sense in discussing the matter with you lot." Master's smile fully bloomed, but he hid it with a sip of bourbon. "But if the boy is willing to sell, I can make him an offer and hire you gentlemen out."

"I'd rather it stay in our name," George grumbled. Landon and Thomas consulted each other with looks. Perhaps they considered Master's proposal, but George began to simmer. "This wouldn't be happening if William hadn't met that witch."

A curious glimmer appeared in Master's eye. "A witch?"

"Lillian." George tried to squeeze venom from every syllable in that beautiful name. "William proposed to her on the day of their first meeting. He hardly knew anything about her, her son, or her former husband, but that didn't stop him from pushing us out. No doubt, that was her doing."

"That doesn't mean she's a witch. Women have natural ways to be persuasive, and I have heard of Lillian's beauty."

"No," Landon shook his head as George's words settled in his mind. "She's strange. She has an odd presence about her, and her son is odd, too."

"He's as strong as an ox," George said, "I whipped him at the behest of his father—to teach him a valuable lesson—and I did it hard enough to kill a slave. John barely winced."

"And he hit George so hard; he went blind for a few seconds."

"Hush up!" George's face reddened with bashful rage. That explained his crooked nose.

"It's the truth anyhow!" Landon yelled back at his brother. "It's nothing to be ashamed of if the boy is touched by the devil."

"They sound like an interesting pair…" Master thought deeply as he swirled the last bit of liquor in his glass. "And you say he's leaving for war?"

"Yes, the 18th Mississippi," George told him. "Hopefully, he'll kill a host of Lincoln's men before they manage to kill him."

"Indeed." I refilled Master's drink, then walked over to Steven and topped off his barely touched glass. His eyes briefly met mine. He was stoic, except for the intensity of his eyes. I didn't know how to be so uncaring, knowing Master was capable of burning another woman alive for his beliefs. Madam's screams were terrible enough. I doubted he wanted to hear it again.

But I wasn't supposed to know such things, and I felt myself beginning to tremble. I hid it by forcing a smile on my face and continued pouring drinks for the brothers. Landon set his glass on the table before I could get to him, then pulled me into his lap. I appeased his ego with a giggle, even though his grip was low on my belly.

"How about a game of cards?" Steven asked Landon with a cigar in his hand. "I'll give you a chance to win some of my father's money."

"Oh, I can think of a better use of my time. Isn't that right, dear?" If Steven wanted to stop Landon from ravaging me, he would need to be more aggressive. There was a hunger in his eyes, and he had already begun kissing my arm. With Master in the room, I had to pretend as if his touch was enticing.

Thomas frowned his face until he exploded into a loud scoff. "Landon, surely you can find a white whore elsewhere."

"A woman is a woman while she's on her back." Landon nudged me off his lap so that he could stand. I quickly looked at Steven to see if he would make a move or voice his disapproval.

"She's not cheap," Master said with a prideful smile. "Dinah's one of my best girls, and she's well worth the investment." He also looked at his son to see what he would do.

Steven continued smoking his cigar, hardening his mind as the smoke filled his lungs.

"We won't be long," Landon promised his brothers. "I've had a lot on my mind. Dinah will alleviate those burdens, I'm sure."

I never expected Steven to stand up for me. Honestly? Landon was nowhere near the worst of my clients. He wasn't handsome, but at least he was plain. At least he wasn't chubby like Thomas. He wasn't as muscular as George, but his muscles were firm. He was older, but he wasn't old enough to be my father. I also didn't sense that he wanted to hurt me, as long as I fully invested in the illusion of wanting him.

He was a selfish lover, but decent enough to get my heart going. It was then that Landon's memories flooded into my mind. His mother had a sharp tongue that never ceased, and his father loved to drink. His father died shortly after his mother, and William practically raised him. He was treated very much like a child until he proved he could gamble and charm women. They were all very close until William happened upon a beautiful blonde woman and her son.

Landon saw the woman as a threat, but he didn't mind her son. As the youngest, he thought he'd bond with the boy. However, Lillian believed the Cohens were a negative influence on John and convinced William to put them out. He was outwardly friendly with the boy on occasions when they would interact, but a seed of jealousy was firmly planted.

John grew into a handsome young man who was clever and strong. He was obedient to his parents, but it was clear that he fancied one of his father's slaves. To Landon, she was a black beauty who became a forbidden fruit. She was precious to John, and he desperately wished to defile her. John fought for you, was bold enough to kiss you in front of everyone, and even took a beating for you. Every grand gesture fueled the desire that Landon shared for you, and it became apparent to me that while I was on my back, he wasn't making love to me. He was making love to the idea of Charlotte.

I had hoped the curse of seeing one's memories was a one-time occurrence or something Steven forced on me at the moment, but John was as clear as day. Landon saw such defiance in John's eyes as he held onto the bloodied body of his beloved. That defiance magnified Landon's insecurities, so he masked it with an even greater hatred for his nephew. But not even the intensity of his hatred could skew how John's defiant eyes burned through my mind and straight to my soul.

All I could think about was how I knew if he were in Steven's position, John would have protected me. He would possess the courage and conviction to kill Master. I wasn't certain whether he or Lady Cohen possessed special power, but I was certain that John was incredibly special.

And if Landon could pretend that I was Charlotte, I reckoned there was no harm in pretending his hard and deep kisses were John's.

I'll be honest. I expected to see Landon again. He was nearly tripping over his feet when he left the bedroom. He was local, so I thought he'd be back within a week. But a week came and went, and then another.

My curiosity was eventually satisfied when Steven paid me a visit on the porch one afternoon. "I thought you should know that the Cohens won't be bothering you anymore."

"I know I didn't scare Landon off."

"No, they're dead." Steven nearly had a grin on his face. "The eldest brother succumbed to his illness, and the other three were killed shortly after the funeral. Lady Cohen survived. She claimed a bear killed them all."

"A bear killed all three of them?" All three of them always carried pistols. Even if the bear got George or Thomas, Landon was certainly fast enough to run away while they were being mauled to death. "No one else escaped?"

Steven's mood quickly soured, and a chill shot through me. "If you don't believe that, neither will Father."

I wasn't certain of Lady Cohen's abilities, but there was no doubt in my mind that she was responsible. Government officials came to the manor often. If the authorities found anything unusual about their corpses, my father would hear about it.

"You have to warn them."

"Lady Cohen can take care of herself. Besides, if she did kill the Cohens, she's a cold-blooded murderer."

“And what of John?” My heart raced, and my stomach was knotted so much that I thought I’d vomit up breakfast. “He’s at war. He has nothing to do with the murders.”

“As far as you know.” He knitted his brows as if disappointed in me. “The Cohens weren’t good men, but they weren’t monsters, at least, not compared to the monsters I’ve seen.”

That was easy for him to say. He hadn’t experienced the eyes of lustful men through the perspective of a woman. You were something to possess, by force if necessary. “Are you saying Lady Cohen deserves to be burned alive?”

“I am saying that I will not risk our lives for theirs.”

I tamed the bubbling rage I had for him to a simmer. “How could you be born with no courage? What sort of man are you?”

Steven’s hands tightened into fists, and his jaw stiffened. Anger cast over his face like a dark cloud, and he resembled his father. Master had never laid a hand on me, and neither had Steven, but I was concerned. Perhaps I had gone too far, but he never moved to strike me. He huffed through his nostrils for a few more seconds, then went off on his own.

The days that followed were full of local young men preparing to enlist. Many were poor and could hardly afford a good tumble with me, but they were determined to experience pleasure before risking their lives in the Confederacy. Many of the men eager to fight had no slaves; they were encouraged by their relatives and friends to fight for the pride of their states and against the tyranny of the new Republican president. Looking back, they weren’t nearly afraid enough. They were too idealistic and thought they’d return home as hailed heroes and form families. I imagine most of those young men were cannon fodder.

There was a burst of business, followed by a period of calm. In that time, I rested my body and my mind. There were so many memories living inside of me by then, and I was mystified by the strength of my vessel. I carried their hopes, fears, greed, and sins. But just as memories fade in humans, they became background noise. There were only a few that I chose to hold onto and cherish, like the moment John enraged his family by planting his lips on a crying slave girl, unafraid and unashamed to reveal his heart, regardless of the consequences.

I had long lost my belief in God, especially not a benevolent one who believed in mercy and justice, but I did hope in something. I wished that somehow, someway, such a man would come into my life.

Then, one day, I was summoned to the manor for supper and told to dress for the occasion. I wore a blood-red dress and a pair of dangling silver earrings, found in Madam's things. I expected to entertain a prominent man of war, perhaps a lieutenant. When I got to the drawing room door, I took a deep breath. If I controlled my emotions, perhaps I wouldn't have to see a battlefield of dead men. While I was still gathering myself, one of the servant girls opened the door.

Steven and Master were seated and facing the door, but their guest was polite enough to stand in the presence of a woman. He was tall, had broad shoulders, and filled out his suit well. I had to tell my heart to calm down. I didn't want to see his memories, and I certainly didn't want an audience.

Master removed the cigar from his mouth as the visitor turned to face me. "Dinah. This is John Cohen. He'll be staying overnight while I mull over a business proposition."

"John Cohen…" Perhaps I was wrong. There could have been a benevolent God somewhere in the heavens, waiting for such a time as this. Perhaps there was a touch of God shining in his golden eyes.

Chapter Seven

"How do you do, sir?" I tried to smile in a steamy manner, but I was a bashful mess. Landon's memories didn't do his handsome face justice. My voice was shaky, and he had clearly begun to reach for my hand, but I opted to grab my dress and curtsey. My heart was racing far too much to risk touching him. I had to calm down and act as though I hadn't seen a golden glimmer in his eyes. There was always a possibility that my mind was playing tricks on me, but I felt so odd in his presence, as if I had known him my whole life.

John bowed his head. "I'm pleased to make your acquaintance."

"A gentleman. How rare!" I hoped Steven felt every bit of my quick glare. His face didn't change, but I trusted the message was received.

"Supper has been prepared." Master shoved what was left of his cigar in a glass ashtray, then stood to his feet. "Why don't we go on to the dining room?"

John motioned for me to make my way out first, and he followed close behind. Steven placed his hand on his shoulder, and the two chatted a bit. John mentioned his parents were both gone, and so were his ties to the Cohens' land.

I was in my own head, telling myself to continue playing a seductress instead of an enchanted child. Master brought me there for a purpose, and I couldn't abandon that until it was safe. But it was difficult to keep my composure when John pulled my chair, then chose to sit beside me. Steven chose to sit on his other side, while Master sat at the head.

I wondered if John truly had extraordinary strength and endurance. Seeing him up close and personal made me believe his muscles were filled with strength, but that didn't make it uncommon. Another strong man could have knocked down George and withstood a lashing.

"My condolences." I felt his eyes on me, but I was still a little too shy to return his gaze. "I heard of your mother's passing."

"I appreciate that." His shoulders dropped, and John's grief filled the room. John had a small smile inspired by her memory, but the pain behind it tore my heart. "It's still surreal to me that she's gone. My mother was a remarkable woman."

"At least you have Charlotte. I imagine she's been a comfort to you."

John's brows rose subtly, but just enough for me to realize my error. "How do you know about Charlotte?"

I was desperate to lift his spirits; those horrid words fell right out of my mouth. Steven gawked at me, waiting for me to clean up my mess. "Your Uncle Landon. He fancied her."

John's brow curiously rose higher. "He had an interesting way of showing it."

Steven breathed quietly and a bit more easily. It shouldn't have been difficult to believe that Landon would visit our establishment, but Master's eyes narrowed as if annoyed. He wanted me to distract John. There was a chance he wouldn't be interested in me if he knew Landon had me first.

I quietly punished myself as the servants brought the first course, a bowl of pea soup. When John's bowl arrived, his eyes shifted to Master, and he didn't remove them. It was rather rude, and particularly noticeable that Master avoided John by staring into his own bowl.

"There's a hair in my soup."

Master looked up at John, who hadn't observed the bowl at all. "Are you certain?"

"Positive." A handsome smirk emerged. "Would you mind if we trade?"

"You can have mine, John! We don't need to cause a stir." Steven quickly exchanged their bowls, but he never set John's down on his saucer. He handed it to a slave girl standing near the kitchen door, who was wide-eyed and trembling. She was trapped within Master's snarl. Steven had to physically pull her face toward him. "Will you take this back to the kitchen? Only bring Mr. Cohen the highest quality food. Do you understand?"

She couldn't move her head, but her eyes were dancing in Master's direction. She waited for his hesitant nod before answering in a trembling voice. "Yes, sir."

I wasn't a fool, nor was anybody else at that table. If John suspected his soup was poisoned, why did he continue eating as if nothing had happened? And why be so blatant about it? Was he so powerful that he didn't fear death? I suppose he was arrogant, how he flaunted you around the plantation. He knew it was against the rules, but John thought he was above them. To meet a man worthy of such arrogance was stimulating, to say the least.

Master was furious, but he kept quiet through the first course. The tension and the silence were unbearable. "Mr. Cohen, you're here for a business proposition?"

"Why, yes, Dinah. I'd like to sell my father's land, but your father is haggling with me on the price."

"Father?" I laughed with such disbelief; I almost convinced myself. How wonderful it would have been if I could remake the truth by wishing it to be. "He's not my—"

"I apologize." John's blue eyes danced between us all. "The three of you look remarkably alike. It seemed obvious."

Master took a moment, then sank a little bit into his seat. "She's mine." He almost shrugged. Never a single day in my life did he acknowledge my parentage, and then he had the audacity to act as though it meant nothing. "I'm certain your father had mulattos as well."

"Only one, to my knowledge, and she was conceived before my mother came into his life."

"Yes," he chuckled, "I heard Lady Cohen kept him on a tight leash."

"She was a woman worth being faithful toward."

Master frowned. He couldn't break John's spirits with tales of William Cohen's escapades. He kept his hands to himself and even seemed disinterested. I attributed that to his illness at the time. "It's unfortunate your father's loyalty didn't pass on to his adopted son. You did defect from the Confederate Army. I don't suspect you'll have many offers as generous as mine."

"I wouldn't underestimate me."

"Oh, I wouldn't dream of it, Mr. Cohen."

They ceased speaking until our meal was completed. I thought of asking John whether he enjoyed his cherry pie. He mostly poked it, only nibbled once or twice, then stared at it despondently. Landon had a memory of Charlotte preparing John an apple pie, and it was perfectly sweet.

Master cleared his plate, then wiped his mouth. He had the look of a man contemplating the fate of the world. I believe he considered abandoning his evil plans, fearing John's suspicion would derail his hard work. But that stubborn fool stood and addressed John one final time. "I have some other matters to attend to. My children will keep you company. I'll give you my final offer in the morning, Mr. Cohen."

Master didn't need me to explain what was expected of me. I had done it many times, but I had never looked forward to being alone with one of my clients before. "I'll show you to your room, Mr. Cohen."

The wrinkle in his brow spoke to his distaste. It wounded me a bit. John looked at Steven for a cue, and with a nod of permission, he got up to follow me upstairs.

I had a designated bedroom in the manor. It was a large room with a bed big enough for four, and it also had a mahogany table designated for cards, and the bar was always fully stocked. The room used to belong to Madam. "Is this to your liking, Mr. Cohen?"

"It's pleasant." He took a turn about the room, and by the time he faced the door again, I slammed it shut with my back.

"And am I to your liking?" I had put the bashfulness aside and hunched in a way to accentuate my breasts and hips.

John's mouth hung open for a moment before he shook his head and chuckled. "Your father is a real prince. He expects me to sleep with you?"

I locked in my position, expecting him to succumb to my body like every other man, but the longer my bosoms dangled in front of him, the more absurd I felt. "If you don't, he'll be angry. I usually fetch a high price."

John smiled and began his march. I straightened my posture and prepared to receive his succulent lips. He stopped a few inches before colliding with my skin. "You're supposed to be a distraction. There are other ways."

I followed his eyes to the card table, and a quick and boisterous laugh escaped me. I genuinely didn't understand him, but I was determined to figure him out.

The easiest answer to why he didn't indulge in me was that Master was planning something, and John had no reason to trust me. Perhaps he detested my profession, but I found that difficult to believe for a man who found pleasure in his father's property. A woman bought and paid for is no less shameful than any other slave. Certainly, he could have been uneasy about the number of bodies that had touched mine. You were exclusively his to touch, and he was wise enough to speculate that I had pleasured his uncle.

Whatever his reasons, I concluded they were sufficient not to take personally. Master didn't need to know we didn't sleep together. Beating John in Poker all night would have to be enough. My skill excelled once I observed it so many times in the memories of my clients. John was decent and good at restraining his face, but he had trouble reading mine. Tiny smiles and shifty eyes were his undoing.

"How are you so good at this?"

"God made me to be an excellent liar." I was kind enough to play for marbles instead of money, and I bankrupted him.

"Well, I'm not too bad myself, and I can usually sniff out a lie."

"Well, deception goes with the territory." We had been playing for hours, and John was still in high spirits. He was so perplexing. He must have known the danger was increasing. "What are you really doing here, John?"

"I am genuinely trying to sell my land to your father."

"And why are you staying here? Do you believe he tried to poison you during dinner?"

"I know he did. I could smell the poison." That was curious. I didn't smell anything but peas, and I was right beside him.

"Why stay?"

"Because your father thinks he's luring me into a trap, but he doesn't know that I'm not the type of being who can be hunted." My heart raced again, spurred by the masculine presence practically glowing from John as he smirked and leaned back in his seat. I gathered he must have been powerful to be so arrogant, but there must have been something more to it.

"Did Steven warn you?"

"He did."

A ray of hope began to spread throughout my chest. Steven finally showed a lick of courage. "And do you know what he is?"

"I do."

"And what did he say about me?"

"Nothing, but I can sense it. You're special."

I tried not to blush, but his golden eyes stirred something in me that I often inspired in others but never reciprocated. But John had me practically trembling. "And you can kill my father?"

The curve on his lips leveled, and his eyes became stunningly cold. "Your father's life is no longer an option on the table. I hope you're alright with that."

"I'm thrilled." It was embarrassing how smitten I was. I could barely speak, as if I were salivating over a good meal.

"Well, if you don't mind, I have mischief to attend to. I must bid you goodnight." He stood and reached for my hand. We had yet to make skin-to-skin contact, and I was certain that if I touched him then, all of John's secrets would be revealed to me. I was curious about his powers, his mother's untimely death, and his gruesome plans for Master, but I was also mostly curious about the affairs of his heart and where I could stand.

I rose to my feet, provided the gentleman with my hand, and allowed John's memories to pour into me. I saw the brief love and wonder of his childhood before it was burned away by the evils of the zealots. I discovered Lillian saved him from another encounter with the zealots, then took him in as her own. Together, they conned their way into the Cohens' family and inheritance. Most importantly, I came to realize you weren't a lovely trinket to possess or a phase of rebellion. John genuinely loved you with his whole soul.

And when John promised to make you a queen or a god among men, you returned his golden gaze for one filled with sorrow and fear. You looked at John not as the love of his life. You looked at John like a human would. And then, you blinked away from him with Mary Anne, leaving him alone to mourn his beloved and murdered mother. You tore a hole through his chest and pulled out everything that gave his world any meaning.

The despair in his heart was more potent than anything I had ever felt. I had never known such love and had never mourned a loss. He didn't deserve to carry around such pain, and I desired nothing more than to heal us both.

"What are you doing?" John valiantly ducked away as I closed in on his lips.

"I want to please you." John was so sweet, and he knew me better than I realized. He could have defeated me in a few of the games, but he enjoyed my happiness. His eyes could always see through me, straight to my soul.

"No." He gently took my hands and pleaded. "You don't need to do this for your father."

I smiled. I had forgotten about what I was and my fate. He didn't see me as a whore or a slave. John saw me as a superior being, destined to sit above the humans. For that, John demanded more than my respect. He earned my total devotion. "For the first time in my life, I'm doing something for myself."

The golden haze in his eyes dimmed as I caressed the sides of his face. I wondered if the oceans were as crystal clear as his blue eyes. I hoped that one day he might take me to the endless waters so that I could see for myself. Isn't that a silly thing to think about at a time like that? In our sacred time together, all I could think about was what was next, even as our bodies collided like water hitting the shore, rocking back and forth—

***

"Stop."

Dinah faked a look of surprise, but an irresistible curl formed on her lips. "You don't want to hear the rest of it? As you know, John's a very thorough lover—"

"This isn't real." I tried my best to tame my heart, but it was racing. I didn't believe her vile tongue, but if I didn't resist the urge to leap to her neck and choke her, I would have appeared like a jealous woman. "John never slept with you. He would never."

She slightly tilted her head and pursed her lips. "After you broke his heart and left to rejoin Cooper, a man you deeply considered marrying? You don't think John rightfully tasted another piece of forbidden fruit?" She laughed, far too amused by the rage brimming from my body. "Oh, I'm sorry. Did you think you were his first? Did you think you were his only?"

I quickly wiped my face. I didn't believe her. I refused, but she was certain to interpret those tears as me being deeply wounded, rather than the last bit of peace leaking through my eyeballs. "You're lying because you're angry with me, and I don't appreciate it."

"If you say so, but John isn't here to correct the record. You sent him away with a weapon that strips him of what makes us special. We could have eliminated the threat." She snarled, as if my righteous indignation was a revolting stench.

"All of these theatrics because you're afraid of a little boy?"

"I haven't felt weak and helpless or ordinary in a very long time, Charlotte. And now John is completely vulnerable in enemy territory. He could already be dead, for all we know, and then you'll never know the truth." She spoke as if her words were a spear meant to fatally pierce me. She even smiled a little, expecting that it did.

I took a deep breath. I could absolutely take her in a scrap if she remained in her true form. If she took my form, she'd also lose. Dinah could only be as powerful as the version she copied at the Crimson Hotel. Her Charlotte would never age or change. I, on the other hand, had dramatically improved while training with John. But if she truly wanted to brawl and defeat me, she would utilize her arsenal of abilities, and she transformed so quickly that it was nearly impossible to stop her. Dinah was only second to John in power, and as much as she was asking for a beating, I couldn't succeed unless she allowed it. Perhaps that was reason enough to punch Dinah in the face, to see if she was still willing to submit to my authority, but she reeked of liquor and was admittedly afraid. It wasn't fair of me to make such an assessment about our future when she was having such a mental crisis.

I stood to my feet after I was calm enough to be certain that I wouldn't attack, even if she provoked me further. "I know the truth, and if you think John is weak, helpless, or ordinary just because he's without his abilities, then you don't know him as well as you pretend."

Dinah's anger softened, and her smug smirk inverted into a trembling frown. Perhaps she felt guilty for underestimating John, but I hoped some of it was for her abhorrent behavior. I waited a few seconds for an apology or a revision to her story, but she stayed silent. The only peep I heard from her was the last slurp of bourbon. I thought it best to leave her to get some sleep, since she'd be vomiting it up in the morning.

I was too riled up to sleep, and it didn't help knowing John wasn't waiting for me. I decided to sweep the property to ensure everything was in order. It was mostly quiet, and our night watchers were at their posts on the border and patrolling the interior. On nights like this, Tillie might have been flying overhead. Instead, she was perched on the top of the wall, watching an unchanged world that would never be the same.

"Are you mad, woman?" I called out to her, so she wouldn't be too surprised when I blinked next to her. The top of the wall was thick enough to walk and sit on, but it was easy to fall off if you lost your balance. "How'd you even get up here?"

"Arthur. I told him I needed to be up someplace high so I could gather my thoughts."

"And is he supposed to come back for you?"

"In a few hours." Tillie had a coat, but the wind was still pushing that frigid air on her cheeks. I was already cold, so she must have been freezing. She didn't have any food to eat or a fire to keep her warm. She had slept on top of the wall before, but never as a woman. "What are you doing up here?"

"I'm checking up on you." A day ago, Tillie was itching to join Steven on that scouting mission. We didn't question their capabilities, and they were only meant to observe. I would have never expected that vibrant fire in Tillie's eyes to burn out a day later.

"That's very kind of you, Charlotte, but that's not necessary. We've never been friends."

"No, we're closer than that. We're sisters in arms, fighting for a brand-new future. You've meant so much to John and me, and you still do." Tillie watched over me while I stayed in New York. She let John know that I was safe. She was almost like a resentful guardian angel. "Besides, it's never too late to become friends."

Tillie lifted her head to the sky, where I'm certain she wanted to escape to, and sighed. "Well, I do have an opening."

Losing her powers was devastating, and so was the loss of Peter and Hotah, but I hadn't considered how deeply it might have wounded her to lose another friend. "You and Steven were close…" I would never forget the day the two of them came to Cooper's exhibition. Tillie's features were always striking, but she didn't often wear fancy dresses. She was so lovely. Steven, while disguised as John, clearly brought her to make me envious. "Did the two of you ever—?"

"I tried," she admitted irritably. "We were such great friends, and he gave the impression he was interested. He enjoyed his flirtations. But every time a physical altercation seemed inevitable, he pulled away or made excuses. I thought the issue was with me." I had revisited moments with Steven to see if I had missed the signs, so I assume Tillie had been doing that consistently and laughed at her own stupidity. "At least I have clarification now."

"Yes, it's clear Dinah loves John like the rest of us." Was Steven more afraid of losing his powers, or was Steven more terrified of John figuring out that he had been sleeping under the stars with a woman who tried to seduce him? "You've known John longer than the others. Did you hear him ever mention her?"

Tillie's sharp brows pressed on her eyes. "What did she say?"

I threw my head up and sighed. I felt like a fool for even broaching the subject. "Dinah claimed they slept together on her father's plantation."

Tillie's eyes widened for a few seconds before she burst into laughter. She hunched over and slapped her leg. I pushed her back into place, in fear that she'd tumble right over the wall.

"What is so hilarious about what I just said?"

Tillie covered her mouth, but her shoulders shook. Eventually, her body calmed, but a smile remained. "If there's anything I know in this world, it's two things. John absolutely never, nor will he ever, be with another woman besides you. As long as there's breath in your body, he will only love you."

A load lifted from my chest. I already knew her words were true, but they meant more coming from her. "And what's the second thing you know?"

"That you're not worthy of the devotion you've inspired." She laughed again, this time at my glare. "Don't be offended, Charlotte. No woman can match that sort of love. It's unique to him."

"John is unique." I couldn't be offended by her words. I had witnessed John being cold in the heat of battle, even ruthless to his enemies. But I was privy to a gentler side of him, so tender and caring. What I wouldn't give for another morning of his lips tickling my neck while being wrapped in his arms! "I can't even begin to explain what he means to me."

I felt myself on the verge of an explosion of tears and frustration, but a surprising rub on my backside confused and soothed me. "He'll be alright. John has gotten out of tougher situations than this." Tillie swayed her head while she contemplated swallowing her tongue. "And…I'm glad that he has someone to come home to. You've made him happier than I've ever seen him, and…you're not too bad of a leader."

I blinked a few times in stunned silence. I certainly wasn't used to Tillie being so kind to me, and her new trust and appreciation for me were appropriately timed. "I do need to leave in the morning. John needs me to go on a mission of my own. I can't say much about it, but I need you, Kachina, and Nathaniel, to take care of things while I'm gone."

"And what are we supposed to do about Dinah?"

Without John, what could be done about Dinah? I didn't want to cause a war with her for multiple reasons. "She's still the same person who built all of this with you, and I have no reason to suspect that she's not committed to John's vision. Dinah will have to rebuild the trust she earned in the past, and I think she understands that. Whether you forgive her for the deception is up to you."

Tillie pressed a frown onto her lips but nodded. I didn't love the fact that John surrounded himself with so many beautiful women, but at least they were wise and capable. I trusted that Tillie and others could keep order in my absence.

"Come on. It's too cold to stay up here."

"No, I want to wait for the sunrise."

I quickly counted the hours in my head. "No, that's far too long. You'll freeze to death."

"I need to see it!" She pleaded, while her eyes sadly twinkled like the stars above. "I need to be certain that this isn't a terrible dream."

"Your powers will come back."

"But Hotah and Peter won't." Tillie collapsed and cried on my chest.

"It's not your fault, Tillie." I doubted my words would ease her guilt. I hadn't forgiven myself for allowing Asha to fight the mob of humans during the Draft Riots. I wish I could have told her that time heals all wounds, but the most time did was prepare you for the reality that your life was different, and you had to get used to the changes or die. Asha, Peter, and Hotah were no longer a part of our struggle, and we had to persist without them. "As long as we remember our fallen, they're never truly gone. They died to save you and the others. They didn't die with regrets, so honor their sacrifice."

I felt her nod against my chest, but she cried on me for a little while longer. I couldn't allow Tillie to stay up on that wall and freeze for another four hours, but I promised to return her to the wall just before sunrise. We went to the tavern, and I baked to pass the time. A sweet potato pie couldn't solve all the world's problems, but it could soothe heartache. We traded stories about our fallen friends and spoke about our ideas to make our land a home to all of our kind. If not for my tiredness, the time would have flown by. But true to my word, I returned Tillie to the wall just before sunrise.

No, the loss we felt for our fallen brethren was not a dream, and Tillie still had no wings to use to soar past the horizon. But as the sky filled with a golden aura and blanketed our secluded paradise, we became more determined to protect our land and our loved ones. I knew that John, wherever he was, would get Moses to Cincinnati in one piece. It now fell on my shoulders to convince my dearest friend to abandon his life and be that child's guardian. It was either that or death, and I was too stubborn to lose another to that fiend.

It was finally time to reunite with Mary Anne and Cooper.

Chapter Eight

Nathaniel used to live on a farm and was used to rising with the sun. I gave him the same vague explanation of my mission and passed the responsibility to our growing nation onto his capable shoulders. “Is it wise to keep everything so close to the chest? How will we know if you need assistance or a rescue?”

“Oh, I’m capable of handling my task. You just make certain there’s a home for me to return to, or else John will blow up like a volcano.”

“Understood.” His face brought me comfort. I once told John that I thought Nathaniel favored him a bit from the brim of his brows to his nose. On account of that and Nathaniel’s fiery powers, I questioned if he might have been related to John’s real father. John was dismissive of the idea, but I liked to silently hope for it.

“Farewell.” I blinked to my home in New York, just so I could sleep for a little while before seeing Mary Anne, Cooper, and Mick. I only meant to rest my eyes for a few hours, but it was almost noon by the time I peeled away from my covers. I was saddened by John’s side of the bed being so cold, but I would grant John a warm welcome once he returned.

I dressed myself in a blue cotton dress, nothing too fancy. I didn't know what sort of mood Mary Anne might be in after taking so long to check in on her. If all was forgiven, she'd want to go out dancing to celebrate, so I put on a comfortable pair of boots. Mick was a sweetheart, and I suspected he'd be happy to see me. Cooper was difficult to anticipate. It was clear that my heart belonged to John by the time I left, but Cooper's heart lingered for me. Hopefully, my absence allowed him to move on.

I also packed my Runaway getup in a bag. I didn't expect to do any heroics while I was gone. To be honest, John wouldn't want me to, but I did need to be prepared. Once the Runaway was safely packed on my hip, I was good and ready to go.

I first thought of blinking to the lobby of the Crimson Hotel, but when I thought of the location, I could only think of Mary Anne nearly dying while waiting for Zhang to heal her, or it being crowded with chaos from the Draft Riots. Another room stood out in my mind like a sore thumb. I remembered the green wallpaper, the fine cushioned chair that Steven sat in when I first saw what I believed to be his true face, and the bar where Cooper broke down after Dave was murdered. I easily appeared in that space, facing where Dave's body used to be. The long card table was gone, traded for a smaller round one. I wasn't surprised. The old one was soaked in blood and carried terrible memories.

"Charlotte!"

My heart leaped at the familiar voice. "Mick?"

Before I could turn around, he jumped clear over the bar and wrapped his arms around me tightly. "Oh, Charlotte! It's been ages."

"I know. I've missed you all." He looked nice, dressed in black trousers and a burgundy shirt. His hair was cut neat and short, and I swear he was a little taller and filled out. I squeezed his arms in disbelief at how much his muscles had enlarged. He wasn't big like Dave, but Mick had become quite the young man. "You've changed."

"I had a growth spurt, and I've been training hard. With Cooper gone, I had to step up for Mary Anne and protect this place…not that she can't take care of herself."

"I'm sorry, did you say Cooper is gone?"

His face paused as if his brain was stuck in the mud. "You didn't know?"

"Know what?" My heart took off like a startled horse, especially when Mick took my hand and led me to the couch to sit down as if he were going to break horrible news. I didn't want to speculate in my head. I'd jump to the worst conclusions if I did, but even blanking my mind made me panic. "Go on and spit it out. I can't take the wait."

Mick took a deep breath and practically winced at my anticipated outburst. "Cooper joined the Union Army. He left right after his birthday."

A profound rage exploded inside my body, but I contained it to a dragon's breath, released through my nostrils. "That stubborn fool. Mary Anne didn't talk him out of it?"

"They discussed it, but Cooper didn't want to be talked out of it. He said you shouldn't have talked him out of it in the past either."

That made me even more upset, especially because I couldn't give Cooper a piece of my mind. Who did he think he was? Arguing against me while I wasn't even present to defend myself! "He could get himself killed."

"Well, so could you. You've been putting yourself in danger for as long as I've known you, and you and Cooper kept it a big secret from me." The intensity in my body slipped out like water spilled on the floor. I could argue with Cooper all day long, but Mick was my sweet boy. It pained me to think that I may have hurt him.

"Mick, I'm sorry."

"You both did what you thought was right. I can accept that, but you're not the only one who gets to make life and death decisions or put yourself in harm's way. You're fighting for your people, just like he's fighting for ours." There was a glimmer in Mick's eyes, a sign of his admiration for Cooper. It made me reflect on my pride in him and our other friends who fought for the Union.

"I suppose I can't be mad at him for that." I believed they'd all be fine soldiers. Cooper was strong, fast for his size, and a wise fighter. I had to trust that he would make it back home alive. "But I needed Cooper's help."

Mick cocked his brow. "You came, after all this time, to ask Cooper a favor?"

"Mick, please don't be angry with me!" My heart couldn't take it. I had to be completely open with Mick. He was owed an explanation. "John and I have loved each other since we were children. I knew in my soul that we were supposed to be together, but our paths and beliefs weren't always aligned. I felt like I had to leave him, and I grew close with all of you during our separation. Cooper and I never consummated anything, but we grew closer than I ever meant to. In the end, we couldn't make it work because I never truly let go of my first love. I decided that John was worth the disagreements and debates; he was even worth holding my tongue sometimes."

Mick chuckled. "Oh, he must be special."

I smiled. I hoped, more than anything, that Mick would experience great love. "What we have is powerful, but it was broken and fragile. I couldn't keep coming back here to a man who deeply loved me and who deserved my love in return. I couldn't do that to John, or Cooper, and especially Mary Anne. I always intended to visit. I just needed some time. It was the right decision for me, and I hope it was the right thing for him…"

"I understand, Charlotte." Mick patted my knee and offered a small grin. He was always more understanding than the rest of the boys. "And I think Mary Anne would appreciate the reason if she knew. I only assumed you might have come to see her, given her condition."

My whole world abruptly stopped like a derailed train. "What condition?"

Mick's eyes widened, and his voice quivered. "I thought she wrote to you."

"She only relays information about the hotel. What is happening? What's wrong with Mary Anne?"

He heavily sighed, rested on his feet, and offered his hand to me. "It'll be easier if I show you."

I took his hand and anxiously followed him out of the parlor, down the hall, and toward the lobby. I began to get a terrible sense that history might be repeating itself. I had such terrible dread in me, like the moment when Dave's body was waiting for me, along with Cooper's grief. There was nothing I could do to change what happened. All I could do was be there for my friend and pray I could bring comfort.

There were two doors behind the front desk, and one of them had a sign indicating it belonged to the manager. Mick knocked on it twice, and her soft voice permitted us to enter. Mick looked me in the eye, and I took that as a sign to brace myself. When he opened the door, Mary Anne's bright blue eyes rose from her paperwork to greet us. She was just as beautiful as ever, with raven locks cascading down her back and chest. When Mary Anne smiled, it was like dawn pulled a blanket of darkness off the whole world.

"Charlotte?" She pressed her hands into the desk and pushed herself up. My mind and body went completely numb, and I couldn't prepare myself for her waddling over and giving me a good squeeze. "It's so good to see you!"

I couldn't be certain of what I saw. I might have been losing my mind, but I swore the bottom half of her poofy dress extended out more than it should have. I also swore that something rotund was poking me. Then, Mary Anne pulled away enough to get a good look at me, but my eyes were completely drawn to the roundness of her stomach that was too perfectly curved to be anything other than the obvious. Once I found the courage to look back up into Mary Anne's face and saw her smiling like everything was normal, my mind snapped back into place. "Whose baby is in your belly?"

Mary Anne took a step back and rubbed her gigantic stomach. The shape became painfully undeniable then. "Who else would it be?"

"I haven't the faintest idea!" I knew good and well who she wanted it to be, but it couldn't be true. The man who waited two years to even kiss me certainly did not put a baby inside Mary Anne.

I turned to Mick for an explanation, but all he did was snicker. "It's not mine!"

"Come on, Charlotte," Mary Anne whined, and her brows wrinkled. Even that gesture was adorable. "I think it's obvious that I've got a little Cooper in my belly." Mary Anne gleefully rubbed her stomach as if it were perfectly acceptable.

“Wow, alright…” My legs were about to give out on me, so I took a few uneasy steps and landed on a chair. Mick rubbed my back, giggling at my bewilderment. It was hard to accept. Could she be running a game on me? Her stomach appeared real enough, and her breasts were suspiciously larger, but how could her face be the same? Was the baby sucking fat and appropriately distributing it in attractive places? How was that even possible or fair?

“I know it’s a bit scandalous. We’re not married in the eyes of man or God, but we got carried away in a wild night of passion.” Mary Anne’s cheeks reddened, and on account of how she swooned at the memory of the entanglement, I reckoned she was being honest. “I promise, I am capable of loving and taking care of his child.”

When Mick picked up a stack of papers and fanned my face, I figured I had exaggerated my stupor. I sat up straight and tried my best to sort it all out in my head. “Of course, Coop is the father, Mary Anne, but I don’t understand. Joseph Aaron Cooper impregnated you, then left for war…?”

“Not exactly.” She blushed harder. “I mean, yes, but it happened the night before he left…”

***

After you left, Joseph talked about joining the military almost immediately. I was opposed, and he didn’t want to leave me, and many who were saved the night of the Draft Riots. He helped Mick and me establish this place, and it kept him busy for a while. You know how good Joseph is with children. The orphans love him dearly.

However, Joseph wasn’t the same after losing his gym and Dave. I think he wanted to join the Union because he believed it was the right thing to do, but he also needed to escape from all he had lost. I understood his pain, and I wanted to ease it. I wouldn’t fight him any longer about his pursuits, but I insisted he had a proper send-off.

Joseph wasn’t in the mood for much dancing, but he was in the mood to drink. Mick couldn’t keep up with him, and I paced myself. When everyone else had gone off to bed, Joseph and I were alone at the bar in the green parlor finishing off another bottle of whiskey.

I wanted to be strong for him, but I eventually saw my reflection in the empty glass, and I looked like the most miserable woman in the world. "I can't believe you're leaving me in the morning. What if you die, Joseph?"

"Can't you be a little more optimistic? After all we've been through, you think that's going to be my end?"

"This is different, sir. This is war." I couldn't comprehend why he was taking the situation so lightly. I wanted to assume he was doing it for my benefit, but a small yet powerful part of me feared that Joseph had given up on life and wasn't merely willing to die for his country, but was rather willing to die in general.

"You worry too much, Mary Anne." As he stared into my eyes, and I gazed back into his, I felt nothing but coldness. He used to have such warmth in his eyes. He brought me more joy than I could ever express, and I was desperate to return the favor.

"Joseph!" I jumped off the barstool, took his hand, and placed it on top of my heart. He gazed at our hands, baffled, then lifted his eyes to mine. "You are my heart. I hope you know that. And I may not be the greatest love of your life now, but I know that I can be."

Joseph stood silently with his mouth slightly hanging low. I imagined the words he had to say were difficult to express.

"The last time I confessed my feelings, you didn't feel the same way. If your feelings haven't changed, then so be it. But I couldn't let you go without telling you, Joseph. I couldn't..." Tears poured from my eyes, and he was gentlemanly enough to use his free hand to step a little closer and wipe my cheeks. I wanted him to ease my torment and kiss my lips, so I leaned in a little closer, intending to pray to God that he would knit my heart closer to the man I loved.

Before I could even think the words, Joseph tenderly held my face and pulled my waist into his body. When Joseph Cooper tasted me, I almost lost all the strength in my knees. The first time I kissed Joseph, he only indulged me a little before I pulled away. This time, he fully embraced me. I trembled, but he was powerful enough to raise me off my feet and onto the bar.

From there—

***

"You did not have intercourse on that bar!" Mary Anne's whole head was as red as a cherry. I could sympathize. I kissed Cooper before, and he was exceptional. My whole world felt like it was spinning, so I could only imagine how powerful Cooper's kiss felt to Mary Anne. I worried how he had become so experienced, but perhaps it was a natural gift.

"We were only on the bar for a little while. There's other furniture in that room."

I scrunched up my face. "You live in a hotel, yet you couldn't find one bed for you two to soil?"

"Honestly, between the alcohol and Joseph's kiss, I wasn't thinking straight enough to find another bed. Are you going to keep interrupting my romantic story?"

"It doesn't sound romantic…" I wondered how drunk Cooper must have been to lower his inhibitions enough to do that to Mary Anne. I have no doubt she wanted him to pleasure her, but it seemed so unlike him. He was no fool. The wars were taking the lives of hundreds of thousands of men. Why take Mary Anne's virtue when there was a decent chance they'd never see each other again? "And what did he say in his letters once you broke the news?"

"Well…" Her shoulders shrugged, and her eyes began to wander. "I haven't exactly…"

"Mary Anne!" I swear, every hair that wasn't on top of my head was pushed up by exploding rage. "Are you telling me that this baby could spill out of you at any moment, yet this child's father has no idea they exist?"

"No, of course not. I'm not saying that!" Her eyes wandered to the side again, and she mumbled, "I at least have two months to go."

My mouth hung wide open, and my eyes tried to jump out of their sockets. I looked at Mick. I couldn't believe he would allow her to keep such a secret, and all he did was shrug. To be fair, what could he do? He could have written Cooper himself, but he wouldn't have thought that to be his place. I'm certain he encouraged Mary Anne to do the right thing. “This is inconceivable. Coop deserves to know.”

“I know, but I…” The way Mary Anne whined and squirmed didn’t fill me with confidence. There was a living, growing human in her belly, and it was going to be birthed from a giant child. “I didn’t know what to say.”

I hopped on my feet. “Oh, gee! I don’t know. How about, ‘Dear Joseph. How’s the war? Oh, I’m marvelous. Your spawn’s been kicking my spine and bladder, but nothing else to report. Yes, that’s right. I’m pregnant with your little bastard baby!’”

“You don’t understand!” The whiny pitch turned into a hoarse mess as she teared up. “His letters were so cordial. There weren’t any poems or flirtations. There wasn’t anything on those pages communicating that Joseph still wanted to be with me. I couldn’t bear to tell him.” I was enraged on Cooper’s behalf. The last thing he’d ever want to do was abandon a child, and he certainly wouldn’t want to die without ever knowing he had one. But it was difficult to stay furious, especially to such a high degree, while Mary Anne trembled and sobbed. She was a woman, but still a young one. Even if she had another ten years on her, pregnancy was a wonderful terror.

I took a deep breath to calm down, then guided her onto the chair. I knelt in front of her, took her hands, and pleaded as softly as I could. “Coop deserves to know, and there is absolutely no chance that he would abandon you and your child. He’s going to marry you.”

I hoped to get a smile out of her, but Mary Anne only sobbed harder. “I never wanted to trap him into a loveless marriage. I want him to be with me because he loves me, not out of obligation to our child.”

I thought that was noble of her, but terribly naïve. I didn’t know how to express my next thoughts without calling her ungrateful. Thankfully, Mick sat beside Mary Anne and rubbed her back. “You aren’t the only one in the picture, so you have to think of more than your relationship with Coop. Besides, he would be an amazing father, and you two have an undeniable connection.”

They certainly did. Even when Cooper was still chasing me, she had an eye for him. He was attracted to her, like every other man with eyes. They flirted, and they touched each other all the time. They trained, they danced, and found other occasions to touch a shoulder, nudge an arm, and so on. They also lived upstairs together, so she had more private time with Cooper than I did. While I was out trying to free every slave, they were at home strengthening their bond. "It's fitting, Mary Anne. Truly."

"But I want more for Joseph than that. I didn't mean to do this. You have to believe me, Charlotte."

"I do believe you, but Coop needs to know."

Her head sank into her shoulders, and she whimpered and sniffed a bit. After she gathered enough breath to speak, she relented. "I'll send off a letter."

"A letter?" Cooper was going to absolutely lose it, and he didn't need to make a fool out of himself in front of his peers and commanding officers. Besides, how long would it take for the news to truly reach him? What if he were sent to another battle before then? "No, I will find Joseph and tell him myself."

"Charlotte, you don't have to—"

"It needs to get done, so I will do it." I gave her a real stern look, and her brows furrowed. She shut her mouth tight, though. I wasn't asking for permission. "Do we know where he is?"

"He should be in South Carolina near Beaufort. He couldn't get more specific than that." Mary Anne pointed to a wooden box on her desk. Mick fetched it for her and placed it in my hands. It was carrying several letters, which I assumed to be Cooper's. There might have been at least twenty.

"You want me to read these?"

"I don't mind, Charlotte. If it'll help you find the father of my child, that's all that matters."

I had been to South Carolina many times before. It was the first state to secede from the Union and offered tremendous military support to the Confederacy. However, the Union maintained strongholds. The Underground Railroad and the Union devastated many plantations, and I played a role as well. South Carolina was full of wanted posters of the Runaway. John wouldn't want me sneaking around without any help, but I was confident that I could accomplish my task. "Before I hunt Cooper down, I must confess that I came here to ask a favor, and it is massive. I wouldn't ask if it weren't a matter of life and death."

"Whose life and death?" Mick asked with a hint of nervousness.

"Mine. John and the others, perhaps Mary Anne as well." Even still, I set her box on the floor and considered whether I should stop there. With Cooper gone, who was going to help Mary Anne with her delivery and newborn?

But I had already frightened her. Mary Anne was holding her belly like she expected someone to snatch the life out of her child. "Go on, Charlotte."

"We've been fighting zealots, liberating others like us, and growing our budding nation. It's exciting, but the zealots get more desperate the weaker they become. We discovered they had a secret weapon, a boy who can remove our powers if we're close or if his blood gets in our bodies. He's too dangerous to keep with us. We would be no more useful than ordinary humans, and the zealots will want him back. John and I decided we needed someone we could trust to take the boy and disappear."

Mary Anne had become very accustomed to her abilities and the benefits of her raw power, so I expected her to be offended or terrified about the news. Instead, she focused on what mattered most to her. "And you wanted to ask Joseph to do this?"

"It's so important, and I didn't know about the baby then." I touched her hand, and she flinched.

"No, but you knew that I loved him."

"Mary Anne, I don't want to ask this of anyone, but the boy's power is a danger to us. Coop would understand." I would never do anything to purposely hurt Mary Anne, and neither would Cooper. It would take some convincing, but he'd want to protect us. Perhaps he'd even want a fresh start.

Mick understood. His eyes were filled with worry. "These zealots almost killed you, Mary Anne, twice. We cannot allow them to wield that power." Then, his eyes shifted toward me. "There's a man who came by asking questions."

I didn't enjoy being afraid, and I often wasn't when it came to my safety. I wouldn't even be that concerned about Mary

Anne in normal circumstances. She had tremendous power, and she wasn't afraid to use it. But I had no idea how much stress her body might be under while pregnant, and if it was healthy for the baby. "Was he a reporter?"

"I don't know. He had a lot of questions but wouldn't reciprocate any answers. He asked about the riots and if we had seen Runaway. He wanted to talk to some of our tenants, but we shooed him off."

"And you think this man is dangerous?"

"I think you and Mary Anne are always in danger, and I understand why you left." Mick stood to his feet, with his chest puffed out like a bird, and his head held high. "If you need someone to protect the boy, I can do it."

I wanted to hug and kiss him; it was such a relief. But I suppressed that flicker of joy for Mary Anne's sake. "I need you to do this, but I don't want Mary Anne to be alone."

"I'm not alone." Mary Anne smiled and rubbed her belly again. "No matter what happens with Joseph, I won't ever be alone." I envied Mary Anne. It wasn't for the privilege and wealth she was born into, or her unrivaled beauty, or how easy her pregnancy seemed to be on her body. I envied how simple she believed love and life to be. There was such profound love in her eyes that I knew all she truly needed in this world was to hold and kiss that child. I don't mean that Mary Anne didn't find value in anything or anyone else, or that she wouldn't find joy or worth outside of motherhood, but being a mother to that child was the pinnacle of meaning.

I instinctively touched my stomach, hoping that motherhood would someday simplify my world. "I'll keep you safe as well."

She nearly gasped. "You will?" Her eyes were wide and hopeful like a majestic doe.

"Of course." I threw my arms around Mary Anne, one of the most powerful among us. Even if her child were half-human, such a power could not be snuffed out or hidden away. I refused to believe Cooper would dilute her powerful line of heirs. John would be pleased to hear she had reproduced, and it was a priority to make certain the next generation was protected. "I won't ever be apart from my sister again, and I'm so very sorry that I was."

"Well, I was a little upset with you, but maybe it was for the best. If you were here, I don't know if I'd have this bundle of joy in me." With that confession, I allowed my guilt to dissolve. There was no point in reliving the past. Our obligation was to protect our future.

I offered more details to Mick and Mary Anne about our mission and how we happened upon Moses. They were mortified to learn that some of my people considered eliminating the boy. They agreed to secrecy and expediency, due to the zealot's desperation. But I couldn't explain all the details to Mary Anne, in case Dinah blinked to the hotel and acquired her power and memories. She went to her room to rest, while I explained the secret details to Mick.

My brave adventurer quickly packed, and he made certain to carry a pistol. He didn't go anywhere without one after the riots. Mick had money, but I gave him plenty for his trouble. His eyes nearly jumped out of his head when I gave him a billfold with a thousand dollars in it. "White men would kill for this type of money."

"Then don't get caught. Be smart. I know you're resourceful."

"And how will John know to expect me?"

"He won't. Once you're in Cincinnati, find a hotel that begins with the letter G. Reserve your room under the name 'Winebeck,' and wait for John to arrive."

"And why would he hand Moses over to me if he were expecting Coop?"

"Because you'll know this secret phrase." I tried to reenact my disgust and body language properly. "Uh! Can you be serious?"

Mick blinked a few times and looked at me, dumbfounded. "Surely, there's a better way to verify our arrangement. If I do that, I feel like this man will kill me."

"He will not. John had Tillie spying on us. He probably knows more about you than he'd care to admit. After you give John your answer, ask him to tell you what the question was. I promise, it will make sense. You'll probably even chuckle. If what he says seems out of place, you might be talking to an impostor."

"And has John changed much since the riots?"

"Not physically. You'll recognize him. You'll know the boy by his scars, healed pinpricks, and cuts."

"Those zealots are cruel…" Mick had a fierce determination in his eyes and a stunning lack of fear. It made me regret not sharing my secret earlier with him. He would have certainly done his best to protect me. "Don't worry. I'll find Moses and bring him somewhere safe. I'll get some land and raise him for as long as I need to. When the time is right, we'll reunite." There was a hint of sadness in his voice, but the thrill of adventure shone in his eyes. I would miss Mick, but exploring the West was always his dream.

It should have only taken Mick about a week to reach Cincinnati, yet John would need at least three times that to travel. "Keep to yourself, but make up a good story."

"Perhaps I'll be a novelist like you, Miss Charlotte." His flattering smile embarrassed me.

"I haven't had time to write yet, but that would make a nice cover. You'll have to pick up some journals for your travels, to make the story seem legitimate."

I sent for Mary Anne when Mick was ready to depart. We didn't make too big a spectacle. Mick thought there would be too many questions if their tenants got wind of his adventure. Saying goodbye to the orphans would have been especially difficult, so Mary Anne promised to tell them he had special business to attend to.

"Keep little Mick safe," he said with a final good squeeze of Mary Anne.

"Joseph will never agree to that."

"He doesn't have to know." Mick chuckled, prompting a punch to the shoulder.

"You be careful out there."

"I'll send word if there's trouble I can't handle." Mick was handsome and confident. He reminded me of all our other friends that I hadn't seen in such a long time. Then, there was Dave. What I wouldn't give to see that big fool smile one more time…

I rushed into Mick's chest for a final hug. There was a chance I would never see him again. Even if exploring the world was his dream, being separated from his friends was never part of it. He was doing it for us. I was fortunate to have such wonderful men in my life, and that joy offered a vibrant contrast to Dinah's grim story. She was partly the reason why Mick had to quietly rush away, yet I felt pity for her. "Thank you for being such a good friend."

Mick firmly returned the embrace. "I know you've been living life with your husband, but don't forget who you are, Runaway." He kissed my cheek as the warmth of his words radiated through me. We locked eyes as he pulled away, and I sensed he wouldn't leave unless I agreed. I grinned and nodded to him, and he smiled back. Mick was so proud when he found out my secret, but he always admired me. I was honored by that. It was one thing to know I was special, but my friends made me feel it.

"I won't." As I watched Mick walk down the steps of the Crimson Hotel and climb into a carriage, I was filled with a steely resolve. My friends would do anything for me, and I had to be willing to do the same. I would find Cooper, tell him about his child, and he was going to build a family with Mary Anne out of love.

I went back to Mary Anne's office and read through her letters while she was busy working. After he left the hotel, Cooper reported for duty on Riker's with the United States Colored Troops. With his superior fighting skills and leadership qualities, he was quickly promoted to the rank of corporal. He was in South Carolina by March. He didn't talk much about his demeanor, but I imagined training was a good way to keep his mind occupied. As far as his relationship with Mary Anne, no one would know the two of them had a wild night of passion right before he left, but he did inquire about her well-being and the daily affairs of the hotel. There might not have been a King Solomon type of sonnet about her bosoms, but that didn't mean he wasn't thinking about her. There were more than thirty letters. He must have written to her about every week. A man that thoughtful must have been in love.

After I gathered enough information, I went to the dining room. I was starving, and it was dinner time for the children. After they finished, the rest of the occupants trickled down to eat. Their caretakers mostly watched them, but Mary Anne helped. She did look motherly, offering friendly smiles to well-behaved girls and scolding naughty behavior, like when a boy threw a fistful of peas at his peer. She was positively glowing from her maternal prowess; there was no way Cooper wasn't going to drop to his knees once he saw her again.

I wandered into the kitchen, recognizing the familiar scent of seasonings. Bess and Loretta were dressing a few plates, and I remembered the cooks from Harvey's restaurant. Big Willie was even stirring a pot. "May I offer my compliments to the chef?"

The girls rushed at me and nearly squeezed me to death. Willie was big enough to wrap his arms around all of us and squish me further. Their excitement resulted in inaudible squeals until they released me.

"You are so beautiful!" Loretta said.

"Absolutely stunning!" Bess looked me over, from the back to the front. "You're glowing like Mary Anne. Are you expecting as well?"

"No!" I covered my cheeks, though I was too dark to redden. "John and I aren't with child yet. It's a little too early for us." I figured once I became pregnant, my husband wouldn't want me to go anywhere. His sway could have a powerful effect on others, but he was the greatest slave to it. Fatherhood would significantly challenge and change him, for better or worse.

"Well, the girls are right. You do look lovely, Charlotte. It's good to see you."

"You as well…" It was difficult to see Willie and not relive what happened that night. I had a thousand times, but I always tried to redirect my focus to what happened after John found me on the roof. I thought of us fighting together, saving people. I recalled the thrill of my increasing power when we rescued the orphans, and John's sweet kiss afterward. I remembered Asha's sacrifice and my new resolve and goals, which led me to give John my hand and stand beside him.

But Harvey was a reminder of my failure. I remembered the lines around Harvey's reddening face as his neck bulged. His feet dangled five feet off the ground from a telegraph pole. His wet fingers struggled to loosen the rope as the mob cursed and beat him. It was difficult to focus through the fear of what they were doing to him and what they were willing to do to me. What disturbed me, even more than Harvey hollering in pain or writhing in agony as his body went up in flames, was the light from the fire illuminating the familiar faces of men, women, and children in the crowd. They were like gargoyle statues preying in the dusk. The only consolation to having a brick thrown at my head was that I didn't have to see more of their devilish faces or the destruction Mary Anne caused afterward.

When I thought of the crowd pressing in on me as I failed to save Harvey, it was a little hard to breathe. It was like their feet were stomping on my chest.

"What's the matter?" Bess asked, immediately full of dread. "Is something wrong?"

"No, it's…" I would burst into tears if I explained, and I didn't want to cry in front of the girls. They'd expect me to explain more, and I would never have been able to get through it. "I'm fine. Don't worry."

Willie's brows slowly began to furrow. "Come on, ladies. We can catch up with Charlotte later. We have to finish for the dinner rush." He nudged them away, though they were concerned and confused. I gave Willie a nod of appreciation and walked into the hallway to catch my breath.

How could anyone set a man on fire? Why would anyone behave that way in front of children? And why were children cheering it on? The zealots were twisted fanatics, and I rationalized their evils by thinking of them as monsters seduced by the devil's false doctrine. But what was the excuse of these so-called normal humans? Did they not attend sermons in cathedrals and churches? Did they not hear sermons from priests and ministers, telling them that all men are made in the image of God?

Mary Anne came looking for me, still so bright and beautiful as if she had been untouched by the cruelty of the world. Even her hair was shinier and bouncier. "Charlotte, did you finish eating?"

I tried to speak, but my heart felt like it was trying to shrivel up and die.

"You're shaking!" She held my arms and rubbed them to steady me. I wondered how Mary Anne could appear so unaffected. When I passed out, she used her powers to tear apart the telegraph pole and other weapons in their hands. There were at least a hundred injured and a dozen dead, though it could have been much worse.

"It's the memories."

"I know. There are a lot of sad ones here…" She frowned and gave me a few seconds of silence to fight through oncoming tears, but a few leaked out. I quickly wiped my eyes and focused on my breathing, so I didn't become a blubbering mess. "We've also built a lot of good ones."

"Clearly." An awkward laugh burst out of me as I pointed to her belly.

"We'll make more memories, Charlotte, happy ones." It was a relief seeing Mary Anne embrace her maternal instincts. There was a time when her budding power frightened me. Perhaps it was a good thing that she stayed behind with Cooper instead of killing zealots.

"We will." I took a deep breath and rooted myself in protecting her smiling face. I wanted to preserve that version of Mary Anne. I didn't want to need the one eager to fight and comfortable with killing. And for that to happen, Cooper needed to remain by her side. "I will make certain of it."

Chapter Nine

A handful of people in the hotel knew about my powers, like Big Willie and the girls, but we didn't want the rest of the residents to know. I wanted somewhere private to come back to, so Mary Anne took me to her suite on the second floor. It was spacious. Besides her luxurious bed, there was a sitting area. The table and chairs were covered in white fabric and tiny clothes. "I apologize for the mess."

"It's fine, Mary Anne. You are a working mother." It was something I would normally scold her for, but my heart was drawn to one of the infant gowns sitting on a chair. Infant clothing was generally the same for boys and girls until the child was mobile. It was a simple gown without any of Mary Anne's normal extravagancies, and that was fine. I might have been holding the gown for a little prince. When I thought of a little Joseph Cooper in my arms, I was overwhelmed with affection and pretended to hug the imaginary boy.

I caught Mary Anne staring at me with the strangest grin. "Charlotte, you would tell me if you were expecting, wouldn't you?"

"Expecting what?" I knew what she meant, and my face erupted into a bashful smile.

“Charlotte!” She shook me. “You must tell me if our children will be nearly twins!”

“I’m not expecting anything or anyone!” I told myself it was a good thing. The thought of John’s fatherly instincts was frightening, but I did have a maternal desire to have a child or two. It did seem a little unfair, though. John and I engaged in intercourse nearly every day, yet Mary Anne was pregnant after one drunken encounter with Cooper.

“Well, it’ll happen soon enough.” Mary Anne made herself comfortable in a rocking chair. “Are you certain you can find Joseph?”

“Finding and moving people used to be my specialty, if you recall.” I glanced around the rest of the suite. I knew the Crimson Hotel was high-end when John purchased it, but I didn’t know it was fancy enough for water closets. I wanted him to put one in our home in upstate New York, but he had no talent for plumbing. I also wasn’t surprised to find she had a tub to soak in, since she was accustomed to Cooper having one in the gym.

I walked out to Mary Anne’s balcony. It wasn’t much of a view, since we were only on the second floor, but that was probably a blessing for a pregnant woman. It was hard to believe she had another two months to go. I suspected she was carrying a big baby and that she’d be in labor for days. If she were in significant pain, her powers might activate. How much damage could she cause? A few exploded and fiery plants, or could she take out a few buildings?

“Charlotte, is everything alright?”

“Yes, I’m fine.” I pushed those fears down. Cooper and I would have to figure out something together. Even though he didn’t have any powers, he had a gift for training Mary Anne. She didn’t appear to have any worries, though. After I was gone, she was going to knit tiny baby shoes. “You be sure to make a pair of those in my size.”

“Don’t tempt me. I’m quite good at this now.”

A pair of slippers would have been nice. The floor in our house could get so cold in the middle of the night. “You have your task, now I have mine.”

I blinked to a general store. It was painted white and had a row of rocking chairs on the front porch. I did miss the bright charm of the South, compared to the harsh colors and textures of northern cities. It was a quaint town with a few hundred people in it. No one took notice that I appeared out of nowhere, but a bell rang above me as I opened the door, alerting all to my presence. A negro smiled and nodded in acknowledgment. He wore an apron over his black vest. I returned his gesture, and he continued attending a group of white women who had questions about the merchandise. There was a variety of dried and salted meat, crackers, alcohol, candles, socks, buttons, etc. Near the counter, I found a stack of thin atlases, and next to those, there was a stack of wanted posters with a masculine portrayal of Runaway. I got a good chuckle out of it.

I waited patiently for an employee to assist me. The colored man walked behind the counter, and I stepped to the side so that he could finish up with the white women. Once they had gone, he caught me eyeing the posters again. "Would you like to purchase a Runaway poster?"

I laughed through my nose, which sounded terribly unladylike. "You sell these? Why? I thought this was Union territory."

"There are still Confederates who would like to string the Runaway up, but that's not why people buy the posters. Some folks like hanging posters on their walls like a portrait. Union soldiers, freedmen, and children are all mad for her."

"Her?" I tapped on the picture. "This is a man. I've never heard anyone call Runaway a woman before."

"Well, most people haven't met her." I can't say his face was particularly familiar. He had dark eyes hidden behind a pair of glasses. They bulged a bit, like a bullfrog. He wasn't much taller than me, but he filled out his clothes well. Our complexions were also similar, so I doubted he was a house slave. His hands were also rough and scarred, as if they had lived twice as much life as the rest of him.

"Did she liberate you?"

"Not exactly, but I owe her, nonetheless. A young woman from our plantation came here for supplies and met a woman asking questions. She said an angel would arrive that night to set her free, and then Runaway came."

I had seen so many faces over the years, and I couldn't place him, but I did recall the young woman. She had a yellow tint to her light brown skin, and her hair was completely wrapped. I saw her in the general store, unable to read the list provided to her. I gathered that she was a slave sent on a mission from her masters. I caught up with her and asked a few questions as a curious stranger, making conversation. By the time she began pushing back, I already knew enough about how many were on the plantation and the layout. When she asked me who I was, I told her to be ready for a visitation from a guardian angel. There were about one hundred slaves on that plantation. I only got about ten out. I didn't have a conductor to pass them off to, but I managed to get them to the Union soldiers. I went back the next night for another ten, and then another five.

"She came three times, I believe. She couldn't take many on the third night because the master had men guarding us with guns. I understand why people believe she's a man. She's an invincible fighter."

An involuntary smirk emerged. I was impressive that night. When men came with guns and tried to shoot, I blinked out of the way and reappeared through swirling smoke to bust their faces wide open. There were five of them, but they were so disoriented from my constant blinking. One of them shot two of his friends. I knocked out Mr. Trigger-Finger after hitting the back of his head. Once they sent for more men and dogs, I retreated with two men, then came back for a mother holding her child and another man. I was tuckered out then and didn't want to risk going back.

"Union soldiers had learned enough information from the freed slaves to liberate the rest of us. They ransacked the plantation for supplies, then torched the rest of it to the ground. My master was killed when he tried to retaliate."

It was an ugly part of the war. I didn't believe it was moral for soldiers to kill and rob civilians, but some Union soldiers believed sedition needed to be cleansed from the nation with the wrath of God. The great and obvious issue was that too many men wrongly believed they were granted such a divine task. If they were truly in proximity to God, they would know his wrath was not without mercy.

I had heard that the Union liberated the plantation and did the same to others in the area. I decided to move on to other desperate souls far removed from the Union's grasp. They needed me more. "I suppose if Harriet Tubman can liberate slaves, another woman might be able to take up such a mantle. I can hardly imagine it, but it's inspiring."

"She certainly is…" The way the man's lips curled, and his eyes twinkled, made me concerned that he knew more than he was willing to say.

"I don't need a poster, sir, but I'd like to purchase one of your atlas books."

"It's on me," he insisted, with his eyes focused directly on my own.

"No, sir, I couldn't—"

"I insist." I could certainly pay for it, but it would have been rude to refuse him. I couldn't admit the truth to him, but I didn't have the heart to think of some masterful lie to push him off my scent. Perhaps I should have, but it seemed the most respectful to accept his gift as an acknowledgement of the truth and a debt of gratitude. "Thank you for stopping by."

"There's no need to thank me. Ever." I took my book and smiled widely. I was grateful to see a former slave exercising his free will to earn a wage. The world had changed in such a short amount of time. I prayed to God that the Union would prove to be successful in the war, so they could share in his bountiful pride.

Beaufort was southeast of my location. Traveling about twenty miles wouldn't be difficult for me. If I were more familiar with the area, I would have made the trip in about six or so jumps, especially if my eyesight were unobstructed. I decided more blinks were better, since shorter distances were less taxing. I walked down the dirt road for about a mile. After that, I was far enough from prying eyes to blink in a chain of movements. My journey took me across marshy lands, rice fields, and pine groves. There were a few bodies of water I had to blink across, but I cleared those easily. If not for the time it took to figure out which direction to blink toward, I'd say the entire trip from the time I left the general store was about twenty minutes.

Beaufort was hot and humid, surrounded by marshes and tidal rivers. I walked the sandy streets in search of much-needed privacy. I was certainly close to Cooper. There were men in blue coats patrolling the streets, and there were plenty of freedmen everywhere. Beaufort was part of the Port Royal Experiment, which was designed to prepare former slaves for freedom and citizenship. I found a boarding house, abandoned by a Confederate family, to stay in for the night. It was only supposed to be fifty cents, but I requested my own room. The freedwoman working at the front desk granted my request, but only after I paid a full two dollars for the night. The room was simple: four small beds in one room, a small desk and chair, and hooks to hang clothes. It would suffice for my purposes.

I went back downstairs to the dining area, where the freedwoman was serving tea to some of the guests. If anyone knew anything about the town, I assumed someone like her would. I took a seat in the corner of the room and waited for her to pour me a cup. "I noticed there were a lot of Union soldiers nearby. Would you happen to know if the USCT is stationed near here?"

Her posture straightened. "May I ask why you're curious about such things?"

"I'm looking for a friend. We were close, but I haven't seen him in a while."

She stared at me real hard. Confederate spies rolled through town, on occasion. She was probably doing her best to protect our brave soldiers. I got the feeling that I wasn't going to be able to fake a story well enough to soften her.

"His name is Joseph Cooper. He took me in after I escaped from a Mississippi plantation. I only just heard that he joined the army. I don't want him to die in battle like Fort Wagner without ever truly expressing my gratitude." I laughed softly and directed my embarrassed eyes to my twiddling thumbs. "Who am I fooling? I don't have the time to express how important his kindness was to me. The best I can do is say goodbye in case the worst comes."

The brows that pressed down on her sharp eyes relaxed, and she eased into a chair across from me. "Fort Wagner changed so much around here. Loads of black men were recruited, thanks to

Colonel Shaw's sacrifice. That's why they named the camp after him."

"Camp Shaw?"

She nodded, and her eyes shone with a recognizable pain. Something terrible had split her wide open and poured her soul out. "Do you love this man?"

"I do, but he's only a dear friend." I wiped an escaped tear. I must have felt the pain on her face and feared that I would become acquainted with it once more. "I've married another, but my bond with Coop is deep and well worth a proper goodbye. I also have important news that I must deliver in person."

A somber smile formed on her lips, and she spoke barely enough to hear. "I loved a man in the 54th Regiment..."

The 54th was a volunteer regiment from Massachusetts with colored men. I distinctly recalled reading in the paper about their unequal pay to their white counterparts, and John used it as another example of the Union's corruption. It was a pitiful stain on the Union's soul, especially since their regiment bravely led the assault on Fort Wagner, knowing the casualties would be extraordinary. The papers called them "heroic," and the world's eyes were open to the true capabilities of black soldiers. The assault on Wagner happened shortly after the riot in New York. I knew within myself that Cooper would be convicted after hearing such a tale, and I selfishly prayed that he didn't. "I'm so very sorry."

"He did his duty. I do not mourn a man who's been reunited with his savior, but I do miss him every day." She was fair-skinned with a tint of yellow. In spite of her tight spiral curls, she could have passed. Even in her sadness, she was lovely like Mary Anne, but I certainly didn't want them to have such tragedy in common.

"How might I find Coop?"

"Camp Shaw is about two miles from here, but they won't let you in. However, it is possible for Cooper to be granted a day pass. Do you believe he is in favor with his superiors?"

"He's got quite a tongue on him, but since he's a corporal, Coop must have wisely worked his charms."

"Then I may be able to help you, but it will take time."

"How much time?"

"What's your hurry?"

I contemplated sneaking onto the base. I was prepared to blink around in the dead of night until I found his tent, but there was no guarantee he'd be alone. Perhaps a human approach was better. "Please, keep this between the two of us."

She nodded, and I trusted her.

"Coop is soon to be a father, and he has no idea. I want him to know that he has a child to fight for, to come home to, and to love. I believe he needs the motivation."

She nearly gasped. "You're not carrying his child, are you?"

"No, the mother is my dearest friend. She didn't have the heart to tell him through a letter, and she's too far along to travel all this way. It's best if I tell him face-to-face."

"I completely understand." She reached across the table and placed her hand on top of mine. They weren't the rough hands of a field slave, but they had calluses. She also had a burn scar near the base of her right thumb. I reckon it was a kitchen accident. I had a few of those myself. "I'll press my contacts and see what I can do, Charlotte. Lord willing, you'll see Joseph Cooper in the morning."

"Thank you, Miss…?"

"Rogers."

"Miss Rogers. I sure would appreciate it."

"Don't travel too far from the boarding house. I'll bring you word tonight. I can't make any guarantees, but I promise I will try my best." She left me to attend to her other guests. John would have thought I was being foolish for trusting a human with such an important task, but she understood better than most what was at stake. Besides, I could always blink back home if she turned out to be some sort of spy.

I wandered around town, peeking inside various shops. I didn't know whether or not I'd have a niece or nephew, but I was obligated as the child's aunt to purchase gifts for them. There were toys in one of the shops: ugly wooden dolls, a rocking horse, and other things that wouldn't be age-appropriate for a newborn. Eventually, I found the most adorable baby rattle. It was a silver duck attached to two bells. Knowing the child's parents, I assumed they would love making noise.

My stomach was in disarray, thinking about Cooper and Mary Anne. On one hand, I felt fluttering when I thought about how beautiful their child would be. They were an attractive couple who took tremendous care of their bodies. Mary Anne would dress a girl in such extravagant gowns, and Cooper would likely make a son just as stylish. No doubt, Cooper would teach his child how to fight. I imagined he would be a supportive father, since he resented his own.

I also had moments when my stomach was all in knots. I knew Cooper wasn't going to react well to the news. I'm certain he'd be happy to be a father, but he would have been embarrassed to have a child out of wedlock. He'd also be furious once he learned Mary Anne kept it from him for so long. He was bound to have steam coming out of his ears like a kettle. I bet I'd have to bear the brunt of his fury. I wasn't going to let a man shout at a pregnant woman.

I needed food to calm my rumbling belly and mind, so I picked the first tavern that enticed my nostrils. The scent of cornbread flooded the streets and practically carried me in. There was a crowd of men inside, some were in uniform. It was impossible to sit alone, but I found a place on the edge of a long table, containing multiple parties.

I didn't eat much fish, but the man across from me was tearing up a fried redfish. It didn't smell fishy, especially when the earthy scent of collard greens overwhelmed the room. He mixed his greens in with his boiled potatoes and cornbread. When a woman came to take my order, I pointed to his plate. "I'll have what he's having, and a cup of buttermilk."

The man in front of me smirked through his chewing. He had only glanced at me before, but now he had found reason to stare. "What's a beautiful woman like you doing traveling alone?"

"I'm eating alone. That doesn't mean I'm traveling alone. I'm a married woman."

He tilted his head and squinted his eyes. My blank face was impenetrable, but his smirk grew in mischievousness. "And where's your husband?"

"That isn't your business, sir, and I doubt you'd want to make it so."

"An' how you figure that?" He licked his juicy lips, as if I were supposed to be enticed by such a thing. He still had meat in his teeth.

"He's a man of great importance, power, and strength, but I can take care of myself." I was bored with him and pulled a book out of my bag. You could never read Mr. Darcy's spectacularly awful proposal to Elizabeth Bennet too many times. I sensed the man's anger, like heat rising from a fire, but I kept my eyes on the pages.

His embarrassment eventually ended with his hands slapped on the table and hunching toward me. "You uppity harlot! You think you're too good for me?"

I sighed and turned the page, purposefully denying him the dignity of eye contact. "That isn't even a question on the table. I told you, I'm a married woman."

I imagined from his grumbling that he was sneering at me, but I was having too much fun ignoring him to make certain of it. I sensed he was becoming dangerously perturbed. Perhaps I'd hit him with my book if he lunged? No. I didn't want to risk damaging the binding. It was already worn from several readings. Perhaps I'd borrow the piping hot teacup in front of the woman beside me. I could scald his face, then punch him dead in the eye. That would stun him for a bit.

He growled some more. I assumed it was a reaction to my involuntary smirk. I wasn't dying to fight him, but I might have had a tiny itch.

"That's enough." A white man came over, dressed in Union blue, and placed his hand on the colored man's shoulder. I raised my eyes to watch his stiffened lip of defiance fall. There were other soldiers, black and white, who were in the midst of rising to defend their friend and my honor. The agitator knew he was outnumbered, and though his breath stank of beer, he wasn't drunk enough to get thrown out. "Pay your bill and leave."

He grumbled and gave me a final glare, but that was all the defiance left in him. He pulled some money out of his pocket and set it on the table. Some of the other soldiers escorted him out without making physical contact. The white man stayed steady, hovering over me. "I'm sorry about that, Miss."

"I'm a Mrs., sir, and you don't have to apologize. You didn't cause the ruckus." I aimed to get back to my reading, but he was still hovering.

"You enjoy reading?"

"Ever since I was a child."

He had a round face that made him look like a boy, but he was a fit man. His coat was tight around his arms and chest. I was grateful to have such a strapping lad come to my aid. "There's a church up the road. The abolitionists and missionaries brought books from up North and built a small library. You might find something to your liking."

My heart melted. "Thank you, sir."

He slightly bowed his head and rejoined his friends. He was a sweet young man, and no doubt very brave to have joined the army. He laughed and smiled with his friends, and I wondered about their loved ones back home, waiting for their valiant return. Were they praying for the best, yet expecting to bury them in a wooden box? The likelihood of them all making it home was slim. I had quite enough of death. Even though John didn't want me to think of the human war as my problem, I couldn't help but be troubled. After all, my friends were mixed up in it.

A few minutes into my sulking, my plate was brought to me. The fish sang a gravelly tune when I scraped my fork across its crispy skin. The inside of it glistened like pearly white teeth, and it was perfectly flaky. It had just enough spice that cooled from the creamy milk. The potatoes were a little bland, but it didn't matter when I mixed them with greens and cornbread. I made certain to pay extra for the cooks and my server. They more than deserved it.

The walk to the church was a good way to work off my meal. It was considerably cooler, and a nice breeze swayed Spanish moss on the oak trees. The purple and golden haze in the sky would soon become gorgeous blue speckles against a black canvas. I hurried along to the white church down the street before it closed its doors for the night.

The door quietly creaked as I slowly pushed it open. The air was heavily scented with candle wax and wood. Two double doors blocked the entrance into the sanctuary, but it could be seen through the glass windows. There was a small congregation inside, humbly bowing their heads in prayer.

An elderly woman sat in the vestibule, as if she were guarding the entrance. She was dressed in all white, rocking in a chair and cooling herself with a lacey fan painted with blue flowers. "Are you here for the prayer service?" Her voice was so sweet and fragile.

I felt like a heathen. "No, ma'am. I wasn't aware of it. I'm just passing through town and was told you had books here."

"Yes, we sure do!" She sprang out of her chair and opened the door to the right side of me. There was, indeed, a small room with shelves packed to the brim with books. I practically ran to it like a sinner rushing to a river to be baptized.

There wasn't any particular organization to it, so I took my time. I grazed the spines, cracked open the glorious works, and smelled the pages. Most of the works were Bibles, hymnals, and religious writings. There were also several writings from abolitionists that had stirred many hearts into fighting for the cause. Frederick Douglass's autobiography was present, and so was a copy of *My Bondage and My Freedom*. There was also a copy of *Uncle Tom's Cabin*, which I had read in New York after I saw the production in Barnum's theater. Next to it was a companion book that Harriet Beecher Stowe produced to prove the cruelties in her work. It was incredible that humans had such a blind eye to the evils they allowed, and how offended they were when the truth was written plainly in black and white.

"Have you read many of these?"

"Yes. Reading is what I love to do in my spare time. I used to spend my income on books, but I had the good sense to find a husband to do that for me now."

She giggled. "Yes, that would be a worthy benefit." She began to aid my search. I hadn't read everything in the library, but I wanted a new novel to distract me. Otherwise, I would have worried about Cooper all night and morning. "Oh, how about *Ivanhoe*?"

"*Ivanhoe*?" The cloth was sun-bleached and frayed along the edges, but the gold-leaf title shimmered in the candlelight. It had a decent weight to it, as if all my troubles were bound to its spine. It was thicker than *Pride and Prejudice*, but certainly shorter than *The Count of Monte Cristo*. I ran my thumb across the faded lettering, intrigued. "What's it about?"

"A knight, his unwavering love, and a great woman of dignity who was never loved in return."

"That sounds sad." Even still, my intrigue only grew.

"Not all heroes are rewarded in the ways we hope, but that doesn't mean their rewards are any less meaningful."

Well, I certainly couldn't ignore that sort of tease. "How much?"

"A dime."

I gratefully paid her a dollar. "Give the rest to the church. I appreciate what you're doing here." I felt a bit convicted. Once I exited the tiny library, a straggler entered the sanctuary. A child looked back to assess the noise. She couldn't have been older than I was when Lady Cohen first took me to meet John. I didn't think I was old enough to hope for anything, but I knew deep within myself that I was owed more out of life. "What are you all praying for?"

"An end to the war."

"Of course…" I felt embarrassed for even asking such a simple thing. "What do you think will end it?"

"Well, men of God have preached and prayed until the hearts of men were softened. The sacrifice of brave men has inspired thousands to fight for a just cause. Now, all we need are extraordinary feats to secure victory!"

"Extraordinary feats, huh?" I liked her spark. I wished I had a grandmother growing up and hoped I'd live a long life with such vigor. "I bet you could teach our boys in blue a thing or two."

"Oh, I could teach them at least twelve or thirteen!"

I had to cover my mouth. I didn't mean to burst into laughter. The little girl in the sanctuary looked back once more, and I turned away. "Thank you for the book."

"It was my pleasure. You be careful walking home."

She opened the door for me, and I clung to the massive block of words on my chest. It was over 500 pages, probably just shy of 200,000 words. If it were any good, I reckoned I'd blast through it in about eight to nine hours. I was practically skipping back to the boarding house.

Miss Rogers was on the porch with a few other workers, enjoying a glass of lemonade. Her eyes lit up once she spotted me, so I assumed it was good news. "Were you able to do that favor for me?"

"I was. Assuming all goes well, your friend might be here by the afternoon or evening."

I breathed a sigh of relief. I wouldn't need to sneak onto the base and could instead dive into my book. "Thank you so much! I don't know what I can do to repay you."

"It's a little too early for assuredness, Charlotte, but you are welcome."

Oh, I loved that little town! When I got to my room, I opened my window to let in the salty ocean air. It was prominent as the optimism I sensed and experienced since setting foot in Beaufort. It was inconceivable that in other portions of the state, people were still enslaved, and war was raging on. But in that little town on that starry night, all was calm, and hope persevered.

The story took place after the Third Crusade in England, amid cultural tensions between the ruling Normans and the oppressed Saxons. Wilfred of Ivanhoe was a Saxon knight who pledged loyalty to King Richard the Lionheart. He was also deeply in love with Lady Rowena, a noblewoman who was his father's ward and destined to marry a Saxon lord for political advantage.

Ivanhoe returned from war to compete in a jousting tournament where he defeated several Norman knights, but he was gravely injured in the process.

From there, the story shifted.

He was taken into hiding by Isaac of York, a wealthy Jewish man, and cared for by Isaac's daughter, Rebecca. Skilled in medicine, she nursed him in secret as he recovered.

The narrative escalated into the abduction of Ivanhoe, Rebecca, her father, and Lady Rowena. The story reminded me of tales of Robin Hood, and I was not surprised when the "Locksley" character was revealed to be the famed archer himself. Locksley and his men staged a daring rescue, though Rebecca was separated from the others and taken by Brian de Bois-Guilbert, a Templar knight who had become dangerously fixated on her. He offered her protection and an escape from her circumstances, but she refused him and condemned him for abandoning his vows.

Eventually, she was placed in the custody of the Templar Grand Master and falsely accused of witchcraft—an accusation fueled by prejudice against her faith and independence.

Rebecca demanded trial by combat. Ivanhoe fought on her behalf against Brian de Bois-Guilbert. During the duel, Bois-Guilbert collapsed and died, undone by his own conflict and collapse of will.

In the end, Ivanhoe still loved Lady Rowena. Rebecca understood their worlds were too different for any life together and accepted that they would never be united. She left without marriage or a place in his world, but she retained her dignity.

Ivanhoe marries the lovely Lady Rowena and is restored to King Richard's service, as England moves toward reconciliation between Saxons and Normans under Richard's rule.

I read until I passed out on the pages. Then, I woke up and dove right back into it. Once I finished, I collapsed on the bed and reflected on the lovely Rebecca. She wouldn't compromise her heritage to save her life or avoid persecution, and the people who mistreated her claimed to be religious. If she had ended up on a pyre, her tale would have been too eerily similar to mine.

It was a bittersweet ending. She may have left without a man, but she began a journey to find a place where she could live freely as herself. She had such courage and conviction.

When everything is stripped away, and we're left bare, all we'll have are the choices we've made. Eventually, everyone has to stand alone and live with who they've made themselves to be.

Three gentle knocks shook my door, and I sat up in bed. Time had completely gotten away from me, and I was only dressed in a chemise. "Who is it?"

"Who do you think?"

I was like a hungry child summoned for dinner after a long day in the field. My fingers were so fidgety, I struggled to unlatch the lock. But once I opened the door, Cooper's handsome smile was a whirlwind that soothed my heart. I nearly burst into tears, and I jumped on him.

"Charlotte!" He carried me through the doorway. "You sent for me, and you're completely unprepared. Why aren't you dressed? It's the middle of the day."

He set me down and closed the door behind him. After not feeling him on me, it was apparent that I had gotten a little too excited. There was only a thin piece of fabric separating my skin from his uniform, which he looked strikingly handsome in. "I apologize." I covered my embarrassed face, then I was even more embarrassed once I felt its warmth. If I weren't black, I would have been a tomato. "I got lost in a good book and I—"

Cooper chuckled, and it was so comforting, like humming a good hymn. "You haven't changed at all, Miss Charlotte." Our interaction felt a little too familiar. When we met in Ripley, I pretended to be his wife for my safety, and Cooper took me to a hotel room. He told me I was beautiful, and we'd paint the town green with envy in a new dress. I dreaded that he was making little moments to build a great love with, because I was already madly in love with someone else.

"Well, I'm Mrs. Cohen now, so I've changed a little bit."

"Of course…" Cooper continued to smile, but there was a tiredness to his voice and a dimness in his brown eyes. They usually held such life and an inspiring optimism. I didn't witness those constants as I gazed into his eyes. I sensed a longing—which wasn't new—but I didn't sense it was for me.

Thankfully, our awkward silence was disrupted by a rumbling in my tummy. I covered it and blushed profusely. "I'm sorry. I haven't eaten yet today."

"Wow. That must have been some book."

I fumed and tried to hit Cooper in his shoulder, but my knuckles landed in his palm so perfectly, you'd think I aimed right for it. I forgot how fast he was, and his hand seemed even more powerful. "You can't ever let me win anything!"

"You threw that punch mighty fast, Charlotte. It didn't seem like you were playing around."

"I knew a big soldier boy like you could take it." It was amusing sparring physically and verbally with Cooper, but I was genuinely annoyed that I could never get the best of him or John. "Please, wait for me downstairs. I will get dressed as soon as possible. I promise. Once again, I'm sorry."

"Alright, alright…" He left without any more fuss.

I hurried to the communal washing room. It was shameful to start so late in the day, but I had the area to myself. I quickly changed into my spare dress. I kept my dirty clothes in the inn with my books, but I brought my satchel along and went downstairs to greet Cooper.

"Why are you carrying that bag around with you?"

I threaded my arm around Cooper's and waited until we had walked off the porch and away from prying ears. "It's carrying a particular getup, and in case someone searches my room, I don't want anyone to find it."

"I see." Cooper lifted the strap from around my shoulder and placed it on his own. Once he was done, I cozied up to him once more. "And do you expect a certain heroine to be working on this little trip of yours?"

"No, but she's got to be prepared. Besides, hardly anyone believes her to be a heroine."

"Lots of people believe Runaway is a woman. Nearly everyone in camp does."

"A freedman told me that soldiers have my poster, but I didn't fathom that I made such interesting conversation."

"Charlotte…" Cooper's tone was amused and perhaps a bit dumbfounded. "Runaway is a legend. I've met at least three men who were either saved by you or had a loved one freed by your heroics."

My surprise barely left breath in me. "Really?"

"Yes, and I may have shared some of your heroics during the riots…"

I pulled on his arm and shook that fool. "What if someone connects me to you?"

"They can, because I told them you saved many lives during the riots, but one of those people was my good friend, Charlotte, who decided to leave the city like many other blacks. I'm not a moron, Charlotte. Everyone knows I'm from New York, and you're in the papers. It wouldn't be natural if I didn't talk about you."

"Well, I want you to be careful."

"I appreciate the concern, but I can take care of myself." If I didn't know him so well, maybe I wouldn't have picked up on anything. I couldn't quite put my finger on it, but he seemed down, like there was an underlying sigh in his voice.

Otherwise, it truly did feel like the two of us were transported back in time to Ripley. I loved being in an abolitionist town, surrounded by black and brown faces. And this time around, I wasn't afraid of anything.

Well, I wasn't afraid of being captured by slavers. I was terrified of how Cooper might react to Mary Anne's pregnancy. Should I blurt it out while his mouth was full of food? It would be rude to talk, and he wouldn't want to make a scene. Should I have waited until we were back in the boarding house? If he yelled, everyone would hear our business. A nice stroll after filling our bellies might have been the way. Maybe he'd be too relaxed to explode.

We went to the same tavern. It was early dinner time, so it wasn't too crowded yet. Cooper and I were seated at a private table for two. The same barmaid from the prior night served us, and she was all smiles once she laid eyes on Cooper. "Good to see you again, Corporal."

"It's good to be back." Cooper returned the smiling gesture, and I didn't like it one bit. I didn't take notice of her impressive bosoms the night before, but her drawstrings were suddenly undone.

"I'll have a cup of milk, the duck stew, and a heaping of sweet potatoes to share with Charlotte."

"And you, darlin'?"

I tried not to glare. I cannot recall if I was successful. "I'll have a cup of tea and the chicken and rice."

"Certainly." I did not imagine her boldly winking at Cooper as she walked away, and I certainly didn't imagine his smirk.

"You been here before?"

Cooper leaned in close, but he certainly wouldn't have if he had known how close I was to smacking him. "I snuck out of camp once to get a good meal."

"Are you insane, corporal? What if you were caught?" That fool could have been whipped or shot.

"Charlotte, the food is terrible! The meat is so salted! And the hardtack is thicker than your books. You've got to soak it in coffee for thirty minutes before you can even chew through it. I was losing my mind."

"Mary Anne's cooking didn't prepare you for Union cuisine?"

He laughed through a smile wide enough to showcase his pearly whites. "I hate to disappoint you, Charlotte, but Mary Anne can cook now."

I nearly leapt out of my seat. "She cannot!"

Cooper grinned as if the devil himself possessed him. "Apparently, Bess and Loretta are far better teachers than you are."

He would have suspected a punch or a slap, so I settled for a kick to the shin. Cooper grunted, and we both glared at one another.

"You're an incredible student, but you're too hard on yourself. Because you're hard on yourself, you see your students' failings as your own. So, in times when they need grace and encouragement, you scold them because you're frustrated with yourself. That's why you never properly taught Mary Anne how to cook and why she always preferred my training. You're too impatient."

"Or perhaps Mary Anne preferred your teaching because she enjoyed your sweaty bodies rubbing up against one another." I folded my arms and leaned back into my seat with a raised brow. "From what I hear, you didn't mind it too much either."

Cooper hung his head back and sighed toward the ceiling. I'm not sure why he looked to the heavens for help. God knew he was a heathen. "Mary Anne told you."

"Mary Anne is my sister. Why wouldn't she tell me?"

The barmaid came back to the table, swaying her hips more than she had before. "Here are your drinks. The food will be out shortly." The amount of bending she did was excessive toward Cooper. I swear, her drawstrings were even looser than before. If I were the manager, I'd ship her off to a pirate bar where she could properly prostitute herself.

Cooper tried not to notice for my sake, but nothing is more obvious than a man trying not to notice. He did make a valiant effort to keep his eyes focused on her face, but Lucifer's grin was still on his lips. "Thank you. We'll let you know if we need anything else."

"His girl, Mary Anne, will love to hear about this place. Everyone is so attentive…"

Cooper's eyes cut me like a dagger, but she scooped her breast right back into her blouse where they belonged, then went on her merry way. "Charlotte—"

"You're a scoundrel for flirting with other women after you swept Mary Anne up in a romantic whirlwind!" My blood was boiling; I wouldn't have been surprised if he reported that I had steam coming out of my ears. Even without knowing Mary Anne was carrying his baby, he still witnessed her heartbreak after she confessed her love and received nothing but silence. "Honestly, Coop—"

"You're disappointed in me." His words doused me like a sudden rainstorm. His tone of voice was almost monotone, but I knew him well enough to recognize something he rarely—if ever—carried. Cooper was ashamed, and I couldn't retain my fury. If anything, I was practically shivering from making a central foundation of my life and identity feel so horrible.

"I don't know if disappointed is the right word. But I don't understand how this happened. How could the man who waited two years to even kiss me take Mary Anne's virtue the night before he left for war?"

"Well, a lot has happened, and I wasn't my best." He muttered the tail end of that sentence into his cup. It was jarring knowing how patient Cooper was as he silently courted me. He was the perfect friend, never giving me any indication that he would prematurely or inappropriately cross a line. He might have been the most respectful man I had ever met.

We had gone through a traumatic experience. Cooper believed I hadn't changed, but that wasn't true. Too much had happened, especially after Dave was murdered and Asha was killed while trying to soothe a mob of cowards. I wanted him to stay the same. I needed him to be the same optimistic dreamer, but it wasn't fair to expect that of him. It wasn't even fair to ask.

"I don't mean to judge you."

"But you do it so well…"

I clenched my jaw to block my initial choice of words. He was hurt. I needed to be patient. "I only want to understand. How did the two of you end up making love?"

***

After Dave died and you left, things were hard. Mary Anne, Mick, and I mourned him and others who were taken from us—like Harvey—and we couldn't forget what had been done to us by our neighbors. An exodus of black families and entrepreneurs began. My father told me I should collect the insurance money, leave, and move near him. "You may not be a medicine man like your brothers, but you can learn a skill and do honest work."

The gym was unsalvageable, and I didn't have the heart to rebuild. I needed time, and there was also a real possibility that my clientele was gone. But I also couldn't stand the thought of running from the city. I was forced to do it once, and I wouldn't as a grown man. So, Mary Anne and I decided to turn the Crimson Hotel into a haven for black faces who lost too much on that day.

Mary Anne believed we needed to keep busy. We took care of orphans and families. We required able-bodied men and women to work so we could afford the hotel. To John's credit, he wasn't concerned. It was only right that we pulled our weight. We had to evict vagabonds and troublemakers, but most people were willing to do their part to help everyone. I thought that would be my new mission, but everything changed after the failed siege on Fort Wagner.

Steve had such a powerful conviction about joining the war effort and ending slavery. He wasn't technically allowed by Lincoln to do it, yet he found a group to join. He convinced Danny to go. Sam thought it was an asinine idea. "Why should we make such an effort to die for a government that wouldn't even respect our sacrifice? They don't even think we're capable or worthy of it." But leaving was the only way to protect his brother.

I was torn. It wasn't an organized idea. It was more like a defiant raised fist, and I had other ways to contribute. And, of course, I had you in my life to look after.

But I was convicted.

After the Emancipation Proclamation was signed, the Union officially allowed colored troops to fight. I watched young men voluntarily put their lives on the line, while you did the same as Runaway. You begged me not to go on more than one occasion. You said that you needed me, and maybe that was true. But I was looking forward to the day when you wanted me.

I was naïve enough to believe that you'd, one day, put your feelings for John aside and accept my proposal. I would be your husband, and we would build a family. That day never came, and you left with John. Two years of my life pining for a woman, and I had nothing to show for it.

I had nothing but a gnawing obligation that you had distracted me from, and it tore me apart after reading about the 54th Regiment. They bravely put their lives on the line, and their sacrifice wasn't in vain. They weren't coddled children who needed to be rescued by white men. They, themselves, were proud men willing to die for their liberty.

All my life, I worked for a better future. I've fought for it, through blood, sweat, and tears, but I needed to be willing to die for my cause.

I wasn't certain how Mary Anne would take it, so I took her for a stroll in Central Park after supper. I realized my error when Mary Anne took my arm and giddily gazed at the sunset. I had to set her down on a bench, and she breathlessly stared at me with awe. "Mary Anne, I've been considering something for a long time."

"Oh?" Looking back on it, she might have believed that I was going to make a romantic confession when I held her hands.

"Yes, I've decided to enlist in the army."

Her face fell, but she quickly managed to make an understanding smile. "Joseph, you're the bravest man I've ever known, and you always do what's right. If you think this is for the best, I'll support you."

"I should never have allowed Charlotte to convince me not to go, so I hope you won't attempt to persuade me either. You can't. This is what's best for everyone. I have to fight to free my people and save this country. It may not love us, but it's still ours."

"I understand. Don't worry about me. I'll be alright." It was a brave face, but it wasn't only for my sake. Mary Anne had grown stronger since the day she arrived at my gym, in every way imaginable.

"I do feel guilty for leaving you alone."

Her fingers gently squeezed my hand. "It's alright if you need to do this for yourself. You've always done what's right for me, Charlotte, and the whole community. You don't need my permission to put yourself first. You've more than earned that right."

She surprised me, and with her blessing came a mandate. "Then I'll get my affairs in order and go."

"I hope you'll allow me to plan a going-away celebration! We can make it the same day as your birthday."

"I wouldn't have it any other way, Mary Anne."

She planned to throw a party in the grand ballroom of the hotel. Many of the grateful residents were invited, and she paid for a band to play. She made herself a new dress for the occasion, studded with sparkly purple beads. She wanted to dance, but I wasn't in much of a mood. Mick could move well enough, so he held her off for most of the night. She pulled me up out of my chair once, and I tried to appease her, but I wasn't much of a partner.

I wanted to leave. I needed to, but I didn't expect to make it back home alive. I read about the battles in the paper, counted the casualties, and read their names. There were so many young men, my age or even younger, who never got the chance to experience life.

My business was gone. I didn't have the time to accomplish anything memorable. And those sorts of feats pass away anyhow. Family is how you keep a legacy alive. But I kept thinking that I'd never get the chance to have a wife or children of my own, like Dave…

You know, he started seeing a girl. I hadn't met her yet, but he was smitten…

I have a high tolerance for liquor, but I drank a lot. At the end of the night, Mick and Mary Anne took me to the green parlor for privacy. We talked and laughed. Much of it is honestly a blur. Mick finally had enough and stumbled to his room.

Mary Anne had been an excellent hostess the entire night. Truly, she had been since Dave had passed. She performed her necessary duties with a smile on her face, but she finally allowed fear and desperation to take hold. “I can’t believe you’re leaving. What if you die, Joseph?”

“You think those white boys can kill me?” I guzzled the last bit of liquor in my glass. I couldn’t confess to her the truth. I expected that to be our final night together. “You worry too much, woman.”

“Joseph!” She leapt off her stool, and I thought I was in for a Charlotte-level tongue lashing. I expected that she would go back on her word and try to convince me to stay. Instead, she took my hand and placed it on top of her breast. “You still have my heart. I want you to know that.”

I know she said other words, but my head was cloudy. After she leaned into me, I finally indulged in Mary Anne…

***

“Please, stop.”

He shamelessly smirked. “You don’t want to hear the rest?”

“Do you even recall the rest?”

“Bits and pieces.” He took a swig of his drink. Drunk or not, Cooper was cognizant enough when he propped Mary Anne up on that bar and took her clothes off. I wondered which one of their versions was more accurate. I didn’t doubt Mary Anne’s noble romantics, but she wasn’t a stranger to seduction.

“Anyway, Mary Anne was practically floating off the couch in the morning, and I was a vomiting mess. She nursed me back to health and helped me get my things together. We didn’t end up talking about what we had done, and she never mentioned it in our letters.”

“You never brought it up either.”

“Well, our letters are checked by the military. Why would I want them to know our business?”

I sighed. His dryness seemed to be a misunderstanding. He did write all those letters to Mary Anne, not to Mick. That must have meant something. Perhaps that was the proper time to tell

Cooper he was going to be a father. After all, that's what he wanted out of life.

"I am glad that you're here, Charlotte. There was something I've been meaning to tell our friends, but I didn't think it was proper news to read in a letter." Cooper was somber, all of a sudden, and the sadness I sensed in his eyes earlier was unmistakable.

I braced myself, fearing he wanted me to tell Mary Anne that his feelings for her weren't the same or that he was in love with someone else. "What is it?"

"Sam, Steve, and Danny were at the Battle of Olustee last month. Their regiment suffered many casualties, and I feared their lives may have been lost. Now, we believe they've been captured by the Confederates. They're being held in an encampment near Baldwin, Florida, but probably not for much longer."

I thought about the day we all traveled from Ripley. The boys had such wonderful dreams, except for Danny. He wanted to live in the moment, and that's what he did. Steve and Danny were often my partners, following me around the city to plays and other attractions before Mary Anne came along. "And what will they do with them?"

"Confederates don't see black men as legitimate combatants. They're insurrectionists or runaway slaves. They may be imprisoned. Worst-case scenario, they sell our friends into slavery or execute them."

Steve and Sam had escaped that horrid life, but the boys dreamed of reuniting with their lost family. Cooper and I tried to find out where their sister and brother were sold, but I never did. "I have to save them."

"Charlotte—"

"I have to!" I didn't mean to raise my voice and cause a commotion. I didn't make it better by covering my face and blubbering, but I hadn't felt a rush of dread that powerful since the zealots took John. It was my genuine nightmare for them. If any master would bother buying a Union soldier, expecting to break them, they weren't going to be like the Cohens. Their master would have been brutal and bloodthirsty. They weren't worth that sort of trouble, not Cooper's boys. They were likely to be whipped to death—if not shot.

"I didn't bring this up to mount a rescue. This isn't like before. I only wanted you to know. I'm sorry to make you cry."

The barmaid came with our food, and she didn't say a peep. That was for the best. I wiped my eyes and moped through a few nibbles. Then, I toughened up. The chicken was already moist and properly salted; it certainly didn't need my tears. Food was good for the soul anyhow. It gave me much-needed strength, and I had a lot of work to do. I didn't care what Cooper said. I was going to rescue my friends, with or without his help.

We were quiet for the rest of our meal, except when Cooper got a little annoyed with how many sweet potatoes I ate. "Oh, you must be paying the bill."

"I'm surprised a gentleman like you would even suggest such a thing."

"Well, I'm a black soldier making ten dollars a month, and you married a bank robber."

I shot my leg out and kicked him in the shin again. He grunted, but not even his pain dissolved my annoyance. "Some things we shouldn't jest about in public, Coop."

"I was only kidding. Of course, I'll pay." Cooper had plenty of money in the bank during the riots, as well as some in a steel lockbox at the gym. Some of his spending money was destroyed, but he was better off than most soldiers. If Cooper truly needed me to pay, I would have done it. Of course, he never would have put me in such a position.

We left the tavern and had ourselves a little stroll. There were other couples, arms locked, enjoying the budding spring. The sun wasn't too harsh at that time of year, and a cool breeze carried my dress in the wind. I bet we'd look like the perfect couple in a portrait, underneath the draped Spanish moss of an oak tree.

"And how is your criminal? Is he treating you right?"

I tensed and looked up at Cooper. He wasn't smiling, so I didn't think he was teasing me. That's just how he saw John. "Please, don't speak poorly of my husband."

He huffed out a short and uncomfortable laugh. "Come on, we're friends. Can't friends be honest with one another?"

I unlatched my arm and stood firmly in front of him. "We are friends, but John and I are one flesh. If you talk badly about my husband, you talk badly about me."

I wasn't expecting an apology. I, at the very least, expected an understanding. But he seemed genuinely baffled by my stance, and the firmer I was, the more offended he became. "Charlotte, you didn't marry a good man."

"I know."

A flash of confusion danced in one of his brown eyes, through his empty skull, and out the other one. I hadn't knocked my head and lost the memory of when I read about John's butchery on the train. Cooper had to console me in private for a good forty minutes before I could manage to tell Mary Anne without bursting into tears. I had seen what he was capable of and vomited at the sight of it.

"I didn't marry my husband because he's a good man. I married him because he's a great man. If I wanted to marry someone good and aspirational, I could have. But what I want out of life is impossible, so I married a man strong enough to break the world in two and forge it into my image."

"So, you didn't marry for love?"

"I married John because I love him, *and* I can tame him. If he didn't have power and we didn't have love, he wouldn't be worth the trouble."

Cooper's chest rose and fell as he breathed in the words and let them cut him up like shards of glass. "I was wrong, Charlotte. You have changed." I thought it would have been shattering to watch his vision of me break into a million pieces, but I had made a choice long ago that I wasn't broken, and he couldn't tell me different.

"I'm not as naïve as I used to be. The war you're fighting is for liberty. The war I'm fighting is about survival. If I lose, I can't sue for peace. Everyone I know will be burned. I can't afford to have fairytale ethics like a child lost in a good book. I'm a leader, and my people depend on me to make a better world. We've grown beyond this old one."

"And have you grown beyond humans?" His eyes were heavy, more burdened with premeditated heartbreak. "Do you look at us the way he does?"

"Of course, not." I was a bit offended. John didn't have the privilege of knowing him, Mick, Dave, and the others. "I've traveled around this country, and I've seen miracles and horrors. This world is dark, but men like you demonstrate that humanity can be redeemed."

"But even still," he raised his head, defiantly, "I'm only a good man."

"You're the best of mankind!"

"And yet, that wasn't enough for the mighty Charlotte…" He masked his pain with a chuckle. I had hoped that with nearly a year of separation, Cooper would have healed from our doomed love affair. I felt a bit ill, knowing I might have been the snag in his relationship with Mary Anne, while she depended on me to knit them back together.

"Well, I don't matter. We've both moved on. I married John, and you're with Mary Anne."

He sighed a little too long and shook his head. "I know you didn't come here for gossip. What finally brought you home? If you had visited before, she would have written about it."

I noticed a tree stump about twenty feet off the path. Cooper followed me. It was shaved down by a saw and wide enough for both of us, but he motioned me to sit. Then, he set my bag down on the ground and sat beside it with his legs folded.

I suppose that would have been a good moment to mention the baby, but there was enormous tension between us. He would have blown up at me. Besides, it wouldn't have truthfully answered his question. "I needed a favor from you, but Mick volunteered."

"What kind of favor?"

"We did a raid on an Overseers' lair. We rescued a lot of our people and took two casualties. There was a boy there who could block our powers when we were close to him. If his blood mixes with ours, our powers will be gone for months."

"And what did John decide to do with the boy?"

Rage hit the back of my neck like a pinprick. "*We* decided, *together*, to get the boy somewhere safe. No one knows where he's going, besides me, John, and Mick. And once Mick takes the boy, not even John and I will know where they'll be."

I didn't enjoy the intensity in his eyes, and his jaw was stiff. I expected to get an earful for sending Mick off to only God knows where, or that I expected him to do the same. But he sat in silence until he softened. "That is certainly a big enough reason to finally bring you back home."

There was more hurt in him than he had confessed, more than he'd ever be willing to say. Grief was an endless match. You take the punches, throw a few, get knocked down, and get back up. It's never over unless you choose to stay down, but there's no winning. It tore me up that I wasn't in his corner when he needed me the most. "Coop, I'm sorry for being away for so long. I figured you and Mary Anne could get on without me, and I had just married John—"

"You don't have to explain." He leaned back on his hands and sank into his shoulders. "I completely understand."

"You do?"

He cocked his brow, and he looked mighty handsome. His rich, dark eyes sparked with enchanting confidence, reminiscent of the first time I saw him in that cream vest. He was much more mature, though. His face was fuller, his body more refined. He probably looked like a machine under his uniform. "After I broke things off with you, there were moments when my resolve weakened. I'd say to myself, 'Just go humble yourself and kiss her. It's only pride.'"

I wish I could say that having a husband made all other men unattractive. The best I can say is that it dulled our connection. He wasn't what I craved anymore.

But back then…?

"Why didn't you?"

"Because you could have never done that to Mary Anne, not after she came back."

Cooper was right. I couldn't betray our friendship, even if Mary Anne had supported it. Besides, by that time, John had his hooks in me too deep. He carved his initials on more than just his Odysseus tree. "Well, everything worked out for the best. I'm happily married, and you're with Mary Anne."

I hoped to see his pearly whites in a wide and dazzling smile, but he almost frowned.

"What's that face for?"

He was stone cold like a statue, except for his eyes. They were running a million miles per minute, begging me to move on. I couldn't. I cocked my neck forward, and then he cocked his to the side. "You know that I've always wanted to marry a black woman."

My heart fell right out of me and to the very depths of hell. The only thing keeping me from growing demon claws and wringing his neck was my sheer disbelief. "You're not prejudiced, Coop."

"Preference isn't prejudice." I had caught him eyeing her too many times to buy into that nonsense. Mary Anne would be any sane man's exception.

"You took her virtue!"

"It was a mutual taking, and that doesn't mean we have to get married."

"In the eyes of God, you already are, you dirty heathen!" I bet Mary Anne didn't get a wink of sleep since I left. Or even worse, she was well-rested and giddy because she didn't believe that I could fail her. "I genuinely don't understand."

"And you wouldn't." His tone was sharp. He shifted like an irritated child, desperate to end the conversation.

"If John and I can make it work—"

"We are not like you and John." He chuckled, in a cruel and mocking sort of way, and with more than a hint of disgust.

"And what's that supposed to mean?"

"It means he's a white man and I'm black. It's different."

"How?"

Cooper's eyes wandered to the side, and I wanted to snatch those chocolate orbs right out of his skull. Then, he had the audacity to stand and grab my satchel as if we were done talking. "You won't be able to take it, Charlotte."

"You started. Now, you finish."

Cooper intensely stared, mouth tightly shut. He begged with his eyes to move on, but I folded my arms and crossed my legs in defiance. Then, he chuckled once more. "When people look at you and John, they believe you belong to him."

A visceral rage gushed out of me, and I sprang forth into his chest. "No!" I hadn't been that angry with him since he mentioned my whipping, but this was worse. I pushed him, but he barely moved. I tried to punch him, but he caught my hand and held me close.

"It may be strange to them—a little exotic for their taste—but you belong to him."

"We are partners in a holy covenant designed by God!"

"He's a man. You're a woman. I didn't say you were his chattel. I didn't say that I personally believe this, but in the eyes of the world, you belong to him." He shoved me back and braced himself for another attack. I stumbled a few paces but regained my footing.

I wanted to hit him again, but I couldn't beat Cooper unless I used my powers and genuinely wanted to hurt him. I didn't want to, even though he tore me open, and I was crying like a dang fool. It was evident as he watched me sob that he had already been hurt enough.

"If people looked at Mary Anne and me together, they wouldn't think she belonged to me or that we belonged together. They would look at me like I stole something. She isn't just some woman or even some white woman. She's one of the most beautiful women I've ever seen. I could be lynched for walking down the street, for holding hands with my wife. The covetousness of men isn't just dangerous, Charlotte, it's lethal."

I didn't doubt his words, not even a little bit. But memories flashed in my head of a daring man who talked back to bounty hunters, who meant to drag me back over the Mason-Dixon line. I remembered a fearless business owner who told a corrupt policeman that he was going to change the country with his will and effort. Mary Anne's father made it his mission to track me down, yet Cooper faced him, so we could bring her home. "You're the one who's changed. You've never been afraid before, not too afraid to fight for what you want."

"Yeah, well, maybe I'm tired…" He attempted to shrug it all off, but that's when the burden of the world collapsed on his shoulders. "I've had to fight for normal things—rights and opportunities that all humans should be entitled to—my whole life. I lost my home in Seneca, I lost my gym, and I'm prepared to lose my life because these bigoted hypocrites don't have enough decency to see all human beings as equal and worthy of

'God-given' rights. And even that sacrifice is worth three dollars less than every white man's. I. Am. Exhausted."

Each echo of his words stripped a new layer away from me. Once it had passed, the woods were too quiet, like every bird and cricket was keen on listening to my sobs. Perhaps it wasn't fair to expect so much out of him. The riots changed me. They changed everything. Even so, Mary Anne was still worth fighting for. "But you love her. I know you do."

He took a short yet deep breath. "I don't love her like I loved you."

"You don't have to love her like you loved me. You only have to love her like you ain't letting go. That's all she needs. That's all she wants." I hadn't cried that hard in front of Cooper since I left John. Cooper could have made me happy if I let him. I was just a stubborn fool who couldn't let go of a ghost. But I wasn't as difficult as the two of them, and I refused to be the reason why my sister couldn't find her happy ending.

Cooper's brows furrowed, and his lips trembled. "Charlotte…" He rubbed my shoulders with his thumbs, while his eyes ached and reflected a fraction of my anguish. "I know I've made a mess of things, and I want to make this right. I just…"

"Hush." I pressed a finger against his lips. I would protect Mary Anne and her child, and I would protect that fool from himself. "You confess to me right now. Don't overthink it. Just be honest. Search the pit of your soul, Cooper, and tell me the truth."

I wiped my eyes, hoping to look more presentable. "Do you love this woman?"

A few grueling seconds of silence scraped by. The next words uttered would determine the fate of his family. He couldn't possibly understand the weight, but I was trembling and ready to collapse. Cooper swallowed a dry lump in his throat, then breathed with a quiver. "Of course, I love Mary Anne, but—"

"That's good enough for me!" I latched onto his arms and thought of the pile of clothes laid out for his child in Mary Anne's room. I was facing where the rocking chair should have been, but it was gone. Cooper jerked his arms loose and took a step back. He was frazzled, even a little red in the face. He might have been prepping himself for a good yell, but her soft voice cut through his anger.

“Joseph?” She was gently rocking on the balcony, taking advantage of the golden rays raining from the heavens. Mary Anne was normally fair-skinned, but motherhood had given her a radiant glow. She was like an angel, with white frills draped over her toes.

Cooper had the look of a man standing in a dark tunnel, unable to grasp that the oncoming light was a train. She stood to her feet and wobbled, making the shape of her belly more obvious. He must have heard the chugging of six tons of responsibility heading his way.

Mary Anne was unaware of his mental crisis and lovingly rubbed her stomach. Cooper stumbled back, and I had to catch him. It was then she ascertained that her beloved was mortified and a few seconds away from exploding.

My dear sister withered into her hands and unleashed a harrowing whimper. Cooper was disarmed and disquieted. If I could have gutted him with my eyes, he would have been laid out on the floor. He didn’t pay me any attention. She was his whole world, and she was breaking.

“Hush, now. It’s alright.” He threw his arms around Mary Anne and flooded her with kisses.

“I’m so sorry. I was afraid to tell you…”

“It’s fine, Mary Anne.” Cooper had to remove her hands. She was bright red, her eyes glittering blue. He continued drying her tears with tender kisses between his soft words. “I was surprised at first, but it’s alright. This is a blessing.”

“Really?” Mary Anne sniffed and shook, squeaking and convulsing in spasms as she struggled to normalize her breathing. She hid in Cooper’s chest, gently bouncing every few seconds.

“Everything is perfect.” His voice trembled, but it was chipper. Mary Anne couldn’t see his face, but Cooper had his eyes on me. They were filled to the brim with shame, but I wouldn’t judge him. I wanted him to do right by my sister, and he would.

A gray slipper with a missing heel lay flat on the floor, along with her knitting needles and yarn. The other was resting on a small glass table, waiting for me.

"Charlotte, can you give us some privacy?" Cooper asked, but his eyes were begging.

"Of course!" I was desperate to give them privacy and blinked to the first place my thoughts would take me. I thought of feet shuffling across the floor, the snap of rope bouncing, and the smack of leather against flesh and bone. The scent of sweat wasn't powerful enough to overcome the aroma of a freshly baked sweet potato pie. It was bustling with people throughout the day, and they were cheerful and optimistic. Cooper's entrepreneurial spirit inhabited everyone who stepped through our doors.

Those doors were gone now. The floors where Mary Anne and I used to practice dancing had collapsed and splintered onto the lower level. The brick walls were blackened, windows shattered. The clothes that Mary Anne and I spent months making were scorched, and my bookcase was a pile of ash.

The charred frame of the ring survived. I climbed up onto the platform. There was no rope to duck between. That had all been burned away. My footsteps were accompanied by a creak, but it was steady enough to endure the blunt force of when I dropped to my knees.

Cooper had lost too much, and for what? For the crime of having too many dreams while living as a black man? He helped everyone and anyone. He sowed optimism and kindness into the world, and he reaped ash and sorrow for his trouble.

Even if the Union prevailed, the nation reunited, and slavery was abolished, the nature of mankind wouldn't change. Cooper was the type of man who could win a race fifty paces behind the starting line. Plenty of men would come to respect such a man, but too many would resent his success and fear his resolve.

I wondered if Cooper or John was worse for the egos of ordinary men. Would they despise John more because his power was unattainable, or would they despise Cooper more because his achievements were possible and proved their lack of will?

Chapter Ten

I figured about twenty minutes or so was enough private time for Cooper and Mary Anne to talk. I blinked to the front of her hotel room, but before I could knock, I heard noises that I'll discreetly describe as "wilding." Even as a married woman, I blushed.

I blinked down to Mary Anne's office. I had noticed a bookshelf, but I didn't have time to see what she had collected. She had a few Jane Austen books. It had been a spell since I gave *Emma* any attention. I felt a bit like her, matchmaking my friends. Hopefully, I didn't make a mess of things.

I read for about two hours, made myself a sandwich for supper, then walked upstairs to Mary Anne's door. Their voices appeared to be engaged in a normal conversation, so I knocked.

Mary Anne opened the door, and she was beaming. "Come on in, Charlotte. I must tell you the news!" I didn't have much of a choice, since she snatched my wrist.

Cooper had his pants on, but he was in the midst of putting his shirt back on. He was still built like a brick house.

"Well, I hope it's a marriage announcement, since you two are doing married folk business. A baby doesn't give you a license to sin."

"We'll get that taken care of." Cooper wrapped one arm around Mary Anne's chest and placed the other on her belly. She uncontrollably laughed as his kisses tickled her neck. Her laugh was magical, like a swarm of butterflies. Each flutter carried away a piece of his sadness.

"Joseph, stop. My bladder isn't what it used to be."

He kissed her a few more times and chuckled at her squeals. "I'm going to request to go on leave as soon as I can. When my request is granted, I'll come back to New York and have a proper wedding."

She held his arm, which was firmly wrapped around her chest, and bit her bottom lip. It was a bit uncomfortable watching the two of them act as though they were about to eat each other. "I want a beautiful white wedding gown like Queen Victoria. I'm going to look so beautiful for you."

"Not as handsome as I'll be for you."

"Are you getting married in Union blue?" I spoke quickly, before he smothered her with his lips. The question was enough to sour his mood and sneer. "Relax. I was mostly teasing. I figured you'd want a new suit."

"I'll handle that myself. You focus on helping Mary Anne with the rest of the details."

Her eyes were so bright and big like an innocent pup. If she had a tail, she'd be wagging it. A girl like Mary Anne had probably been dreaming about her wedding her whole life. I had many other obligations, but I could plan such a good party. "What are sisters for?"

Cooper landed another big one on his wife-to-be's cheek. "Charlotte does need to take me back. I promise, I'll be home as soon as I can."

He tried to ease away toward me, but she latched onto his arm again. "Wait! We should ask her before you leave."

My heart sped up. "Ask me what?" Whatever it was, it had her jumpier than a hare.

"If we have a son, I want to name him after his father. Joseph has no objections."

"Naturally." Neither one of them had reason to name a child after their fathers. Joseph was a good candidate and a good man. "And what if she's a girl? Josephine sounds nice."

"You're right. That does sound nice…" Cooper placed his finger on his chin, but Mary Anne elbowed him in the ribs.

"Joseph, be serious."

Cooper cleared his throat to kill off any giggles. Then, he glimmered with a hope I had long missed. "If we have a daughter, I'd like your permission to name her after you."

I shouldn't have been surprised. "Are you certain?" It was an honor, but there was so much history between us. If not for Mary Anne happily nodding, I would have been completely baffled. "Charlotte isn't even my real name."

"It's who we all know you to be." Mary Anne grabbed my shoulders and poured love into me, much more than I deserved, but it was what she had to give. "You're the most important woman in our lives. We both love you more than words can ever express, and it would be an honor to name our daughter after you."

"I appreciate that, but…" I truly didn't feel worthy of such honor, and her hands began to feel heavy. "…that's definitely a boy in your belly."

"Then, there's always next time!" She hugged me tight. I couldn't disappoint her. If Mary Anne wanted my name, she could gladly take it.

Cooper put on his socks, shoes, and jacket. Mary Anne was eager to be a good wife and helped with his buttons. Their eyes met a final time, and he grinned. "Be safe."

"You as well."

After Cooper picked up my bag, I placed my hand on his back and took us to my room at the boarding house. Then, he plopped my bag on the floor and dropped onto one of the beds, finally having a moment to take it all in. He was quiet and still like a gargoyle statue.

I eased onto the opposite bed. Everything was working out for the best, but Cooper wasn't wrong about the difficulties of his future life. Other buildings near Cooper's gym weren't harmed too badly by the riots. His place was targeted because he proved blacks could thrive in their world without permission or condescending sympathy. It would only get worse. "I'm sorry."

"No, don't apologize. You didn't do anything wrong."

Cooper tried to warn me when we first met that mulattos weren't accepted. Abby was killed trying to escape the Cohens' plantation, Dinah was treated like an object, and her brother didn't know how to stand up to the evils in this world. "Did I trap you into something you didn't want?"

"Mary Anne and I made a decision when we bedded each other. We're accountable for our own actions, and we're accountable to this child."

"But is it what you want?"

"Charlotte, everything has changed." Cooper raised his voice, just stern enough to silence my rattling brain. He was calm. Dare I say, the curve on his lips signaled content. "I loved you. Maybe a part of me will always love you. But I will never love another woman the way that I'll love the mother of my child. She's given me something irreplaceable, so that's what she'll always be to me."

"And it's that simple?"

"There's nothing simple about it. Love and family aren't simple matters that blink into existence, mature and sure of themselves. You make connections, and then you make commitments, because life isn't simple. This is going to work because we want it to, and we'll will it to be so."

I should have burst into triumphant cheer, or at least patted myself on the back. But when I tried to smile alongside Cooper, my heart shuddered. "Then come back home!" I hated that I was leaking so much, but my blasted eyes couldn't keep it together. What if he never got to hold that child? What if she had to raise their little one without him?

"I can't be a deserter. Other fathers and husbands are risking their lives. I can't ask them to do more than I'm willing to give."

Mary Anne had been through enough, and I couldn't stand the thought of watching her mourn him. "What if you die?"

"I won't. I have someone to live for." Cooper grinned. "Two someones."

"Three." Who was I kidding? It wasn't just about Mary Anne. No, we weren't in love anymore, but there would always be love between us. "I'll always need you."

"No, I don't think that's true, not anymore. You're in a new phase in your life, and that's alright. You've always been strong,

Charlotte, and now you're walking in it." There was such a bittersweet ring to his voice. My heart was like a banjo, losing strings each time it was plucked. Our paths may have diverged, but I believed we were always supposed to come back together.

"Then I want you, Coop, as my dearest friend."

The man I adored smiled as if he had gotten away with stealing the sun. That brightness in him was one of the many reasons I reluctantly fell in love with him, and I wanted the world to know his warmth and beauty. "And I need you, Charlotte, because I want to rescue our friends."

I did my best to restrain my true intentions. "I thought you didn't want me to risk my life."

"I don't, but…" He shrugged. "I'm being selfish. I know it's dangerous, and I shouldn't even bring this up, but when Mary Anne talked about our wedding plans, I kept thinking about who wouldn't be there. I want them by my side, and I want them to find their own futures."

"It's alright. If anyone's earned the right to be selfish, it's you." I couldn't hold back anymore. A scandalous curve slithered between my lips. "Besides, I was going to do it anyway."

"I know." Cooper leaned forward and mirrored my expression. "I saw it in your eyes."

Cooper said our friends were likely being held in Lake City, but he didn't know more than that. We'd have to investigate on the ground in a few hours, after most of the residents had gone to sleep. I paid Miss Rogers for three more nights, just in case our plans were derailed.

Cooper and I spent the time catching up. I mostly did the talking, since I read his correspondence with Mary Anne. He wasn't surprised by Dinah's revelation. He always knew there was more to Steven. He was astonished by how quickly our community was growing and by the powers in our arsenal. I also confided in him about how some of our newest recruits still wanted to be connected to their human families.

"Do you believe my child will have powers like Mary Anne?"

"I think so. It would be a shame if a power like hers wasn't shared. John believes Mary Anne's powers are potentially limitless. Perhaps they'll develop in more diverse ways, but that child is going to be a force."

Cooper was unnervingly quiet, and his brow wrinkled.

"Don't fret, Coop. We can teach your child how to use their powers, just like we taught Mary Anne."

"I'll love and care for my children, whether they have powers or not. I'm concerned about the Overseers. We can't let their hatred continue for another generation. We have to expose them."

"And risk going through human courts and human justice? John would rather kill them all."

"There's a high cost to operating outside of 'human justice.' John's 'Ghost' character is seen as a mass murderer to the world. Are you comfortable with your husband being seen as a villain while the true monsters are painted as innocent bystanders?"

No. I didn't like it one bit, but we both knew lawmen and politicians were corrupt. The zealots were well-connected, even in the North. "We collect evidence. If John ever came to trust human officials to handle matters properly, we'd have plenty. In the meantime, Mary Anne and the baby would be safe with us."

"Mary Anne doesn't want to abandon the hotel and the people there."

"And what do you want to do?"

Cooper hesitated as if he were ashamed to admit it. "I want to know that my wife and child are protected while I'm off at war. When I talked to Mary Anne about my concerns, she told me, 'Any place my feet tread is safe.' Then that killer gleam appeared in her eye."

"She's as arrogant as ever." It's not as though Mary Anne didn't possess a reason to be. But if Cooper was willing to entertain moving with us, I'd have to keep working on her. "We're going to snuff out all of the zealots. In the meantime, let's focus on taking out these Rebels and saving our friends."

It wouldn't be so strange for Runaway to rescue black soldiers from captivity in the South, but if anyone found Cooper with me, it wouldn't be difficult for someone to discover my identity. I blinked to the armory and quietly grabbed a couple of things before I was noticed. I didn't want to bother explaining what was going on. If anyone asked, they'd want to help. I couldn't put my people in that position. It was my fight to handle.

I came back with a long men's coat, larger than John's. Underneath, Cooper wore civilian clothing from his bag. I covered his face with a scarf and a mask. For weapons, I brought two pistols, a rifle, and additional ammo. Based on how he twirled the guns before placing them in holsters, I assumed he'd use them properly if need be.

As for me, it was a relief to wear my original colors again. I wondered what sort of legendary tales the rescued Union soldiers would tell after my heroics, and it thrilled me to imagine the future fury of the Confederates. It was an honorable pleasure to enrage unjust men with righteous deeds. I wanted that blue coat to be a symbol of liberation and defiance.

It wasn't difficult to get to Florida. We once chased down one of Steven's leads and found Alfie being pulled away by zealots. His parents' lifeless bodies were lying in a pile of snow. John was enraged and quickly manifested the boy's powers, plunging ice spears straight through their chests. The blood of vengeance baptized the boy, and he gazed at his savior with an otherworldly awe. When John reached for the boy's hand, he leapt into his chest as if he were already home.

Steven took care of Alfie and his parents' bodies. Then, John asked me if I wanted to see the ocean. The timing was a bit strange, but I agreed. He swooped me up in his arms and followed the scent of the wind. John gently set me down on the coastline, east of Jacksonville, and wove his fingers between mine. It was a warm September night, and the light of the full moon shimmered against the rocking waves. The skylight rested on his face, softening his chiseled features. I had almost forgotten that he still had the blood of zealots on his chest, sleeves, and face from when he hugged the boy. I recall thinking about how quickly I had become accustomed to death wielded in his hands.

"One day, we'll have to cross the ocean, Charlotte. There are plenty of our people in this land, enough to defeat the humans. But if we want to maintain our rule without wiping out all of them, we'll need more of our kin."

"And what makes you think they'll follow you to a new and strange land?"

John's eyes flashed to gold, and I knew within myself that he was capable of making his case. We all knew that our kind weren't safe under human authority and that John would do whatever was necessary to keep us safe. *"They'll come, and together, we'll live free like you wanted."*

It was different standing there with my hand clasped onto Cooper's. The moon wasn't full; it was little more than half, and it was almost chilly. I also didn't come to ponder the possibilities beyond our shores. My husband wasn't there to reap the lives of my enemies, so I feared that terrible duty would fall on me. I didn't like being left behind in battle, so John demanded a nonnegotiable stipulation. I promised John that I would value my safety over the lives of our enemies. If I were going to risk my life to save my friends, I couldn't be afraid to cross that line.

"Is this the closest you can get us to Lake City?" Cooper asked.

"No, but I needed to take in the view." I inhaled the salty air into my nostrils to help ground my memories. Beyond the dunes was an untamed forest, and the barren coastline was empty besides a few birds looking for a late meal. For miles, all I saw was black waters shimmering as the roaring waves tossed and turned. For the men not strong enough to survive, it would be the perfect watery tomb. "Hold on."

We weren't too far from Jacksonville. Union troops were dominant there, but it was still too far from Lake City. There was another spot closer, a plantation near the Santa Fe River. Plantations along the river had docking stations and ferries, making them distinctive landmarks to remember.

I had to keep moving to avoid being seen. Runaway was famous in those parts for freeing several families, and I did not doubt that I'd be shot on sight. Every time I landed, I glanced around for a good place to jump toward. Cooper was humorous as I tugged him along. It was the most ungraceful I had ever seen him, practically stumbling into every shrub and tree. He was out of sync with my intentions, so I'd have to pull him down when I ducked or yank him up when it was time to rise. He was frustrated, for certain. I would be in his shoes, but he didn't say a peep.

Once I found a railroad, I risked following along that clearer path to cut down on my jumps. I had become much stronger since I retired from the Underground Railroad, but I'd be pushing myself by night's end. I also didn't have John or Dinah in case something went wrong. There were Confederate troops peppered along the tracks—a few tents and a guard or two keeping watch. I'd either run parallel or blink past them.

I retreated into the pinewoods that surrounded the town. I sank into the sandy soil and caught my breath against a tree. Cooper was breathing heavily and holding his chest as if he had really been through something. "I'm the one doing all the work, Coop. What are you out of breath for?"

"Chasing you around is always tiring work." John may have laughed in agreement with Cooper, but it was just as likely that he would have taken offense.

"I need you to stay here while I search the town."

"I don't want you to go alone. Let me watch your back."

"You'd only slow me down while I canvas the area. Don't worry about me. I do this all of the time." I didn't grant Cooper the opportunity to argue with me. I had rescued enough men for him not to worry, but I hadn't done it alone in a while. Tillie and Dinah were often advanced crews, and John could blink around himself or send a swarm of beasts to clear out an area. I didn't have their help when I snuck across the South traveling to plantations, though. I was getting back to my roots.

A larger row of tents guarded the rails going into town. They must have been fewer than five miles away. I had a sinking suspicion that more troops would be guarding the rails westward, toward Tallahassee. Sure enough, more tents were present.

Lake City sat around the Florida, Atlantic, & Gulf Central Railroad. There was a depot along the tracks, guarded by a few men. They were wooden sheds, sure to house supplies for the Confederates.

The town was named for its proximity to bodies of water, such as Lake DeSoto in the center. The town was blanketed in darkness, with no streetlamps and hardly any candles or lanterns in windows. It made for a good cover as I snuck down the gridded dirt streets, hiding behind houses and storefronts. It was intensely quiet. In the background, the constant melody of chirping crickets accompanied the soft marching of Rebels patrolling the streets.

Five soldiers were wandering around town, and four were spotted near the rails. Ten were curiously stationed around a cotton warehouse. The windows were blocked, but I wagered that my friends were being held inside. It was large enough to accommodate captives and conveniently close to transportation. I could handle something like that, but the issue was the tents just outside of town. They could have arrived within thirty-five to ninety minutes in a hurry, unless I delayed them. There also could have been more soldiers in town, sleeping in homes or the church.

I needed Cooper to be a lookout, but there weren't many good options for vantage points. The best was a general store. I peeked through the window. I didn't see anyone inside, but it was dark. I blinked up to the second window to check for signs of life. The room was full of barrels and crates, and there were windows all around. If Cooper were a decent enough shot, he'd be close enough to pluck off Confederates like turkeys.

When I returned to my friend, Cooper's nostrils flared like he was about to blast fire. But then he swallowed his feelings and breathed in relief. "I'm glad you're alright, but don't blink away before we talk things through."

I resisted the profound urge to argue. "Fine, Coop. We're in this together, but you've got to trust me if this is going to work."

"I trust you with my life, but you've got to trust that a human can handle himself. I am the one who trained you. Remember?"

In my head, I understood that Cooper was a capable soldier and a fine fighter, one of the best I had ever seen. I used to think he was invincible, but I also thought the same about Dave. Unexpected deaths left irreversible scars in your heart, a constant reminder that the worst was always possible. But that was my defect to fight through. "There's a warehouse being guarded by about ten guards. I believe that's where they're hiding our friends. There was also a wooden shed and a small brick building by the tracks. I spotted four men there."

"That's likely a supply depot. It may have guns, powder, food, and uniforms." I liked the mischief that twinkled in his eyes. "If we take that out, we can do some real damage."

"I will blink us to the second story of a general store, so you can have a vantage point. I want you to watch the warehouse and pick off any threats I miss."

"Are there soldiers patrolling the town?"

"I saw about five men. I can pick them off, one by one. My greatest concern is the tents lined up just outside of town, east and west."

"How many tents?"

"Around two dozen on each side. Maybe a little more."

Cooper's eyes slightly enlarged. "There could easily be a hundred men, maybe two hundred on each side of us, Charlotte."

That was a lot more than I anticipated. If Kachina were there, she could swallow them up in an earthquake. Tony could have moved all the prisoners into his shadows, or he could have used them to dispose of the soldiers. Mary Anne could have easily killed the soldiers with a few powerful and precise explosions. My powers weren't meant for fights, and my fists could only take me so far. "We'll have to get our friends and leave."

"They won't want to leave all the others behind."

"I'm not asking their permission. I'm going to take them, and that'll be that!"

"Even if you only blink them to safety, we have to give the others their best chance to escape." Cooper took a moment to ponder. Within a few seconds, his plump lips mischievously curved. "A general store should have plenty of supplies to cause a distraction."

He was correct. We collected glass bottles and ceramic jugs, and divided kerosene and turpentine among them. There was also plenty of whiskey. I took inspiration from the rioters who tried to set New York City ablaze. We tore garments and soaked them in the flammable liquids for our wicks. We did our best to move quickly and quietly. We made two dozen and positioned them near Cooper's post before I moved onto the next phase of our plan. I also poured a few jugs of turpentine and four baskets of flour.

Then, I found some beef jerky, dried fruit, and rock sugar to grant a boost of energy. Cooper watched me as I washed it down with a glass of sassafras tea. "Will food make that much of a difference in your strength?"

"It's difficult for you to fight if you're hungry. It's no different for me, but food isn't enough. I'll need plenty of rest after all of this." I wished I had taken a nap before the mission, but at least that reddish tea provided a spicy bite to keep me up. "Keep working. I'll be back in a flash."

Cooper continued, and I made my way back onto the streets. I couldn't be certain how many soldiers were nestled in their beds and where, but the few strolling around town could be dealt with. My first victim was a man dutifully marching around the two-story courthouse in the center of town. My plantation raids taught me to be light on my feet while creeping along the sides of buildings. The poor fool didn't know I was behind him until I blinked and latched onto his back. He never got to see my face. The next thing he saw were black waves, shimmering like light against obsidian. A powerful burst of terror belted from him but was quickly cut off as I blinked away. I landed back on my feet.

Alone.

I did wonder how long he screamed before reaching the water. He was about four miles from the shore and lower than the height of Trinity Church. The impact could have broken his body like a fallen teacup. There was a chance he could survive, and a chance was all I was willing to give him. It would be a difficult swim to shore, and even if his body were intact, the Union ships were likely to find him first.

I told myself it was for my friends. If I had killed that man, I couldn't allow his death to be in vain. If my hands had to be soaked in blood, then they were going to be useful and successful.

Another guard must have heard me drop in and rounded the corner. I blinked on the roof to avoid him, then behind him while he gazed in a stupor. He tried to shout my name to warn the others, but it erupted into a screech as he dropped.

Returning from the skies of the beach made it difficult to be light on my feet. I drew some attention to myself, but the guards around town weren't quick enough to draw their weapons or warn their friends. They couldn't stop me from appearing above or behind them. One little tap was enough to carry them away. When the last one had fallen, my feet landed back on the wooden floorboards of the general store.

"Are you alright?"

"I'm fine." My strategy was to push. I wouldn't take time to sympathize with the enemy or to feel any limitations. My heart was excited to work, so that's what I did. "I'm going for the depot guards next."

"If you're overwhelmed, retreat. Don't waste your energy fighting them, Charlotte. Keep moving them. If you need me, come get me." His commands made me nostalgic for our days at the gym. I did have a habit of wanting to prove myself, but it wasn't in my best interest to tussle with the Rebels.

One was marching, two were standing together at the door, and another man was guarding the brick building. I went after the two guarding the door first. I couldn't blink behind him, so I arrived with a throat punch that sent him gagging and stumbling into the door. The eyes of the other man widened in fright, and he reached for his gun. I grabbed a hold of it as well and used that as the anchor to carry us both to the Atlantic. He fell, clutching onto his weapon, and I reappeared above the throat-punched man, who was furiously clutching his neck for dear life. He was stomping around in search of me as my feet landed on his shoulders. The unexpected weight pushed him into the ground, but we fell through the sky before kissing dirt.

I landed on my hands and knees before the man who was marching. He was skittish like a terrified street kitten, clutching his weapon as if it were a doll. "You're the Runaway!"

"Oh? So, you've heard of me?" I stood to my feet and smiled. "I'm flattered."

He pointed and yelled incredulously. "You're not a man!"

"Shh!" I began to raise a finger to my lips, and by the time it reached them, I was only a few inches from his face. "Don't tell anyone."

He jumped back, screaming so much that I had to latch my hand around his mouth. "Be quiet, or you'll wake the whole town." Terror poured from his eye sockets as the gravity of his situation pulled him down like demons at his heels. Then I pulled my hand away and allowed him to fully release his cries.

The last man had his rifle out, shaking and circling the area for me. He should have heard me landing on the roof shingles. Perhaps he was too focused on nervously spinning. He was a bit too unstable to come in behind or in front of him, but if he wasn't looking up, he certainly wasn't looking below. I sat on my bottom, then blinked to the ground. As he looked down and saw my widening smile, I latched onto his leg.

It was over for him then. My buttocks smacked on the wooden floor hard, and the jars rattled. "You alright?"

I gritted my teeth, hoping my tailbone wasn't bruised. "Yes, sir."

"If the depot is cleared out, take me there. We'll take some weapons for our friends." Cooper grabbed a canvas blanket, a carpet bag, and a crowbar. I touched his shoulder, and the scent of turpentine and liquor was replaced with sawdust and oil. Cooper's eyes danced around the room, then his feet moved with eerie precision as if he had been there before. I suppose it wasn't difficult for him to find what he needed when crates were stenciled in white. With a firm shove of the crowbar and lift, the lid popped open.

The first pistol was frightfully cold for something that could harness the power of an explosion. I tucked a few inside the carpet bag, and Cooper followed by stuffing a few brass tins inside as well. Cooper immediately moved on to a crate of rifles next, observing each weapon for a ramrod before rolling four of them in a blanket. I clumsily extended my hand, but Cooper resumed his search like a dog on a hunt. He gathered a few final items: a nipple wrench, a rag, and a tiny tin of oil, all of which slid into his pocket. "We're done here."

I pressed my foot on top of the rolled canvas and placed my hand upon Cooper's shoulder. A few seconds later, we were on the wooden floorboards, surrounded by jars of flammable oil. I set the carpet bag down near a clear corner of the room. Cooper followed with the blanket and unwrapped the guns like an eager child on Christmas day. He pulled a long grease strip from a rifle in one quick and loud rip. "Must you be so loud?"

"I'm trying to be efficient. Someone is bound to realize there are no patrollers soon, and we don't need all of the troops flooding the streets to investigate." Cooper kept his voice low and calm, though he worked fast. He had the steady and proficient hands of a soldier, making certain the guns were in working condition and empty before dropping the ramrod down the barrel.

I was familiar enough with rifles, so I reached inside the carpet bag for a cartridge box. Cooper promptly snatched it from my hands.

"I'll finish with the rifles. It'll be faster this way."

I pouted, but I kept quiet. He was quick, much quicker than I would have been. A sharp metallic scent filled the air as Cooper tore the cartridge open with his teeth. Then he poured the black powder down the barrel, like grains of fine sand sliding through a bottle. Then he dropped a Minie ball, and my stomach dropped in sync with the dull thud. As he tucked the bullet in tightly with the ramrod, the devastation that was soon to follow dawned on me. Someone's life was in his hands, and Cooper was steady as a rock. I wondered how many lives he had taken. Cooper had been in battle. I knew that much from his letters, but he hadn't written about killing men.

Cooper reached inside the carpet bag and pulled out a brass tin filled with percussion caps. To me, they were like thimbles for the rifle's nipple. Once he finished, Cooper set the rifle down and quickly moved on to the next gun. He was trained to load and reload. All four rifles were prepared in less than ninety seconds. I suppose I could have worked on the pistols, but I was so mesmerized by his hands. It was second nature to him, as if I were in a kitchen baking a pie. It was also a reminder that we had different talents, and Cooper could more than pull his weight.

"We'll leave these here." Cooper set the last pistol down on the canvas blanket and made certain the cartridges and percussion caps were also on it. "If the opportunity should arise, you can blink back here and grab the weapons."

I wasn't eager to see a firefight with my friends and the Rebels. What were the odds that everyone made it out alive? "Hopefully, it won't come to that."

"I don't see another way. Even if we could draw some of the warehouse guards away, some will remain. Eventually, more soldiers will come, and you can't blink us all. It's too great a strain. Some of us will have to stay behind to fight."

I didn't like that scenario either, but my limitations had forced me into such predicaments before. If only John or even Dinah were there. I could certainly move everyone with their added strength. "We'll worry about that later. Let's move on to the next phase."

We moved on to our combustible jars next. Cooper proceeded to light the rags on fire, and I blinked them to the next location.

The men of the Confederate camps were mostly asleep. They had become accustomed to soft, cold dirt. The flaps of the patched tent stayed open to circulate a breeze and air out the scent of sweaty men, packed together like street rats. Some were light sleepers, propping up at the sudden crack of glass. Some heard the gentle murmur of roasted canvas, but were unaware until wisps of smoke filled the air, and flames crackled and popped. No doubt, they confused the sound of my fires for the contained campfire in the center.

A few sentries were awake and looking for trouble. Two soldiers were talking by a roaring fire. I swear, they didn't look up at the raining jars of fire until I had dropped about six or eight of them. I blinked back to Cooper as he lit the rags, and I grabbed two jars at a time. There was an uproar in the camp as the men tried to save their things and put out the fires, but quite a few ran for their guns stacked outside their tents.

I couldn't throw from any higher, or else I would risk the fall blowing out the flames. I gambled with the wrath of their pistols. They were so busy looking up at the sky, they didn't catch me before I slung a basket of flour over the campfire. The specks incinerated midair and blasted like a dragon's breath. The men cried out in panic and rushed away. The flour burned up quickly, but it was enough time to throw more turpentine at the aggressive flames. One soldier was certain he had me in his sights. Perhaps he would have if he hadn't taken the time to watch me watching him, then smirk. I was gone before he pulled the trigger, and his friend behind me took the bullet. My last target was two wagons of supplies. One was definitely food. Based on the roaring explosion, the second had ammunition and gunpowder.

By then, the camp was too rowdy. It was time to move on to the west camp. I used the same strategy, but these men were far more alert than the east camp. I had to switch up my patterns more frequently, so they couldn't anticipate my movements. Some of them were, undoubtedly, shooting randomly in hopes of being successful. While throwing another jar midair, I felt a hot sting across my left side. A young man was the culprit, pumping his rifle into the air excitedly before reloading it.

I landed back on the wooden floorboards. As Cooper handed me two lit jars, he noticed a tear in my coat and blood. "You're hurt."

"I'm fine." I was angry, angrier than I should have allowed myself to be, but I didn't have time to rest or calm down. I blinked back to the camp and behind the man who wounded me. It was an instinctive response—breaking the jar of fire against his back. As he lit up like a match and screamed, it was the most intense flames I had felt yet. My stomach sank. I had dropped a dozen men, and more were due for their final appointment with their maker. Was this end any crueler than the others I had given? I certainly didn't want to be burned away, screaming next to John for the pain to end.

I smashed the other jar near the feet of a close soldier, who was also preparing to shoot me. Then I kicked the Rebel in his gut. As he doubled over on impact, that's when I carried his flaming body to the skies of the Atlantic Ocean. I didn't know if that fall would be more or less terrifying for him, but it would be a quicker death. That was all the kindness I could afford to give to my enemies.

When I returned to the store, Cooper hadn't lit any jars. He latched onto me to look at my wound. "I can blink away with you touching me. I'm much more precise than I used to be."

"You were only grazed, but we should get that cleaned up. We don't want you to have an infection."

"We'll worry about that later. It's too late to turn back now. We have to proceed, and we're on a tight schedule." It stung terribly, but I had lived through worse and fought through more painful wounds. I was most worried about when fatigue would finally catch up to me, so I had to stay ahead of it. "Come on, Cooper. Light them up."

The concern in his eyes was more vibrant than that burning Rebel, but Cooper sighed and lit another match. I carried Cooper with me, along with jugs of turpentine. Stacked crates were stenciled with white lettering that told us their contents: food, clothing, shoes, muskets, sabers, bayonets, and so on. We doused much of it with turpentine. Then we went to the brick storehouse where kegs of powder were on top of pallets. Cooper made a trail of turpentine from the pallets toward the door until we ran out. Two of the kegs, I blinked to the courthouse.

It didn't make me feel good to destroy so much of their property, and I certainly didn't want any civilians to be harmed. I figured the people would act fast to try to put the fires out. There was a lake in the center of town. They'd scramble to pass buckets and keep the fires from wiping out wooden homes filled with women and children. I imagine most of the men were off to war, and the preservation of the two would be left in the hands of the soldiers. I prayed they'd be successful as Coop threw lit matches into the trails of turpentine.

We blinked to the courthouse before the flames took hold of the depot. Before we could light our last jugs, an orange burst rose from the horizon. It burned and left an afterimage in my eyes, like staring at the sun too long. I looked away, and then a deep rumble rolled throughout the town, rattling walls, windows, and shelves. Dogs and horses pitched a fit, and a concert of screams was so perfectly in tune, I almost questioned if it were rehearsed. Towering puffs of thick black smoke rose like the hand of God about to reap vengeance on the land. It was a sight to behold, but we couldn't allow the crackles and roars to distract us.

We lit the last two jars and tossed them at the two kegs. We retreated to the store. Another burst of orange light filled the room, and the floorboards and walls shook like a tuning fork. Cooper threw himself on top of me for protection, but his fingers pressed close to my wound. I shuddered and whimpered in his grasp. He probably thought the quake was getting to me. We were mostly safe. The crashes and thuds mostly came from below us.

After the world stopped shaking, we watched the windows. Families rushed out of their houses and screamed at the rising smoke. Many yelled accusations about the Union launching an attack. By the looks of things, there weren't a lot of men in town. They were likely called to battle. Any man who wasn't a child or too riddled with age ran toward the courthouse. As far as the warehouse guards, the herd immediately halved.

"Go on, Charlotte. I'll cover you."

I nodded. The chaos in the streets was the perfect distraction. The guard in the back didn't know I was beside him until I touched his shoulder, and the same was true for the guards on both sides of the warehouse. The front was trickier because they were more alert, and there were two. I grabbed hold of one, but the other leaned away and prepped his gun to fire. I clenched my jaw and blinked one guard to the Atlantic Ocean. My heart was pumping fiercely as we fell. I was a bit rattled and couldn't imagine the scene behind the gunman, so my instincts brought me back to the general store, where a cloud of smoke surrounded Cooper.

"I said I'd cover you."

There was a sharp scream from a woman, and I peered out of the window. The soldier's body was on the ground, lying still as his gray uniform reddened in the chest. Cooper pulled my arm, so I wouldn't give away our location. As we stood for a few seconds up against the wall, staring into each other's eyes as horrified hollers filled the skies, it became all too obvious that this was not Cooper's first kill. I always thought Cooper shared similarities to John—their flirtatious nature, confidence, and stern leadership—but Cooper never possessed the cold resolve of a killer before.

"What is it?" he asked. "What's wrong?"

"Nothing." Cooper was so hesitant to kill Mary Anne's father, even when he was goading him into it, and he was a man who had hunted down slaves and handed his own daughter over to the zealots. If Cooper couldn't kill such a man, I assumed it wasn't in his nature, which was just fine. Not everyone could and should be like John…or Mary Anne. His innocence was yet another luxury taken by this cruel world. "I didn't know you were such a good shot."

"Well, I am a corporal." He offered the tiniest smile. Perhaps he was pushing it all down like I had decided to do. Every life was inherently valuable, but that didn't erase the fact that humans subjectively valued certain lives over others. We both needed to make it home to our families, and we had to live with the cost of our mission.

Cooper quickly reloaded his rifle and added it to the pile retrieved from the depot. Then he tensed his fingers, prepping to grab the holstered pistols on his body. I wouldn't know what we were running into, so it was the greatest risk yet.

"Are you ready, corporal?"

Cooper took a deep breath, then nodded. "Lead the way, Runaway."

A small crowd had scattered from the soldier's body, once it was known there was nothing that could be done for him. The source of the shot was also still disputed. A trained soldier would deduce the general store was the likeliest location, but it was mostly frightened women and children taking cover. That gave us enough of an opening to blink to the front door and barrel through. As a lantern's light peeked through the cracked door, the nozzle of the pistol came into my vision. I flinched and blinked to the next place my eyes could carry me, the staircase in the corner.

Screams followed as the crowd ran from the gunshot fired off into the street. I didn't have time to search the room. I had to disarm the soldier and protect Cooper. As he began to turn with his pistol-wielding arm straight out, I prepped my legs for a mad dash and blinked forward. My arms and chest collided with him as he turned, firing another bullet with reckless abandon. The stench of sulfur entered my lungs as I was enveloped in white smoke. I dropped that demon above the black waters, with enough time to scream to the Heavens for mercy.

I landed awkwardly on my hands and feet in the midst of chaos. The captured men were all chained on the lower level, and their cheers were an eruption. There were more than a hundred men, yelling excitedly for me and Cooper, who was exchanging blows with a burly guard. One guard lay on the floor, gurgling as blood seeped from his neck. Cooper's pistol was on the floor. The burly guard must have knocked it from Cooper's hand and received a blow for his trouble. His beard was stained with blood.

Cooper didn't have much time for a fist fight. One guard was barreling down the staircase, and another was shoving a ramrod down his gun barrel from a guard post on the second level. I reached and blinked toward Cooper's pistol, then appeared behind the guard on the top floor. He shook like a leaf once he heard the click of the hammer. He raised his hands and slowly turned to face me. He was just a boy, barely old enough to be drafted. He was as white as a ghost, with eyes shining with dread and tears. The commotion from the prisoners blotted out all other noise, but I swear he mouthed, "Please."

Both my hands gripped the pistol tightly. There was no way I was going to miss his heart at that range. I had likely killed several men that night. I didn't understand why I hesitated. My hands began to shake, and a bout of courage stirred within him. That fool began to reach for the gun, and he startled me enough for my finger to pull the trigger. My heart hammered harder than the recoil as my ears rang. Burning sulfur entered my nostrils as smoke drifted from me and to my target. The boy stumbled against a wooden railing behind him, and his rifle fell from his hand. His eyes were open wide as if he were so surprised to die, and as he dropped to the ground, the fatigue from my day hit me like a train.

I nearly dropped to my knees, gasping for air. If not for the roar of another bullet, I would have collapsed. Instead, I blinked to the ground level and watched as another guard fell. Cooper must have gotten the better of the big man he was fighting, and the tower guard who came to his rescue didn't know that Cooper had another pistol on him. Cooper shot him in the gut, just as the big fellah stumbled backward. The big man grunted and lunged at Cooper, who was quick with cocking the hammer back, and fired two shots into his opponent.

When he dropped to the ground, wheezing his final breaths as his lungs and mouth filled with blood, I couldn't help but wonder if that's what Dave looked like when he died, and if Coop had to relive it all over again. They didn't look the slightest bit alike. Dave was dark and clean-shaven. He wasn't a soldier. He died defending his friends in their place of business. He shouldn't have crossed my mind, but I couldn't help but think of those bullet holes in his gut and chest. He died because men didn't want to fight that godforsaken war.

"Runaway!" Cooper shook my mind loose with a good shake to my shoulders. He must have called me a few times, based on the desperation in his eyes and voice. "Are you alright?"

No. I had just killed someone. Definitively. And I was watching the light of life leave a man's eyes. "I'm fine…" I couldn't even lie properly; my voice was so hoarse. I tried again with a nod and wiped my tears away.

"Hang on. We're almost there. Stay strong."

I nodded again. So much was riding on my physical and mental strength. The soldiers were either sitting or lying on the ground, bound together and bolted to wooden beams with short chains. Many of their wrists and ankles were scraped and bruised, and some of them were poorly bandaged. Their trousers and shirts were tattered, and none of them were wearing shoes. It would be a difficult journey if they had to run for their lives. Their skin was dry, and their eyes were sunken. They were probably thirstier than an empty well. But most of them did have a spark of defiance in their eyes. They weren't ready to give up and die there, and I wasn't ready to let them either.

Amongst the sea of faces, one head rose higher than the others, and his eyes beamed brighter than any lantern in the room. His mouth moved as he began to speak my name, but then he slapped his mouth shut to protect my identity. Beside him was another familiar face, a little older and bigger. I inched toward them without considering that it would be strange if we knew one another. I stopped once I noticed Danny's right pant leg split open. His right thigh was bandaged. With all that had happened, is it ridiculous that my first thought was we probably wouldn't be able to dance together again?

Then my eyes furiously searched the room for Steve's older brother, Sam, but he was nowhere to be found. It would have been too suspicious if I had asked such a personal question. I had to wait, even though my heart was shriveling inside my chest. I knew the terrible truth without having to hear it.

"We have to find a key to these chains."

"I have a better idea." Danny and Steve were situated in the center of the soldiers. I wanted to run to them, but it would have compromised my identity. Instead, I rushed to the closest two soldiers and felt their chains. They were heavy, solid, and unrefined. I felt the rough grooves through my leather gloves. Once I tugged and felt them dangle, I knew them well enough to distinguish them from the soldiers. They were all clamoring for help, like desperate children waiting to be fed. It was a bit distracting, but I understood the chains enough to evade them. Once I was ready, I grabbed the forearms of two of the men and blinked about ten feet closer to the door.

The men looked at their freed hands and feet, amazed by my abilities. The men quickly stood, wincing and grunting from stiff and numb joints, then grabbed me in excitement. They yelled thanks, but Cooper was concerned by how they shook me and rushed to my side. He pulled me away with worry in his eyes.

"We don't need to strain you this much."

"I'm fine." Blinking people to where I could see was far less tiring than carrying them across the country. But it was a waste of a jump. I'd rather transport all that I could and then free whoever had to stay behind and fight. "I'll be right back." I went back to the general store to retrieve the loaded weapons. They were untouched, but I heard rustling from underneath me and the voices of men. If they discovered our hideout, they would try to breach the warehouse next.

I pressed my hands on the blanket and reappeared on the warehouse floor. "They'll be coming in soon."

Cooper looked to the group of over one hundred men. We didn't come here for all of them, but they were his brethren in arms. "Then we need to reinforce the doors and protect this place until everyone is free."

I freed a few more men, and Cooper directed them to reinforce the doors. He didn't raise his voice often, but he commanded and coached men in his gym with an unrelenting fierceness. The soldiers fell in line, rolling barrels of cotton to act as a barricade. They were several hundred pounds and dense enough to stop a few bullets. They took the weapons we brought, and the ones their captors had, then positioned themselves high on the upper levels to watch the streets. Cooper also had men positioned in case anyone got through the barricaded doors.

After Cooper had a brigade of about twenty men, I decided to move on to my true task. "I'm going to start moving some of you to safety. Please, be patient. I need to concentrate. I'll start with the injured and go on from there." I hoped I wasn't too obvious. There were other cripples among their group, but my eyes were on Danny, and I walked right to him. He was holding his breath, nearly turning blue. He couldn't have been in that much awe of my persona. When I knelt beside Danny and looked into his eyes, there was more than wonder and immense gratitude. There was a pride that nearly filled them with tears. I hoped the rest of the soldiers didn't take offense when I took hold of Steve, who was right beside Danny. "I trust you can take care of him, sir."

Steve's eyes glanced around the room, as if he were asking for permission. Cooper was right. The boys were too noble to leave the others behind, but I meant what I said about not giving them an option. I took a deep breath, then inhaled the salty air. I figured all was forgiven when they pressed me together like a good sandwich, hollering joyfully as we sank into the cool sand.

Danny held my face and kissed my cheeks, and I was reminded of how he held me close as we waltzed together in Five Points. "Charlotte, you've been the Runaway this whole time?"

I used to trade blows with Steve and Danny in Cooper's gym, fighting with all of my strength to win a sparring match. I could never knock them out, but they often gave up before showcasing their true strength as men. If only they had known how much I was holding back. "I'm sorry I never told you boys about my powers."

"You came for us. That's all that matters."

I smiled, remembering how handsome Steve was in his brown trousers and green shirt. He had a drink in hand to boost his courage, then he asked me to dance. His brother was sober, taking in our final night together with a clear mind. They were all so happy when Mick and I defeated the Irish in a dance battle.

But even through the cheers and laughter, the sadness in Sam's eyes was apparent. "Where is Sam?"

A great hush overcame us, only leaving the ocean hugging the shoreline. Steve faintly whimpered as I clutched his shoulder. He was like a dam struggling to keep the rush of a river at bay. I feared Steve was going to lose it, but he took a breath and beat it back. "He didn't make it."

His voice faded as if he had been washed away and held in the ocean's depths. Sam, Dave, and Cooper were close. They could have held the world together with the strength in their backs, yet Cooper was alone. Steve was alone, and I had lost another dear friend.

"Charlotte, he wouldn't want his death to distract you." Steve pleaded as I tried to sink into myself and sob. He grabbed my arms and shook some sense into me. "You've got to go back and save the others."

Their expectations were like anchors tied to my fragile heart, and I struggled to breathe. John was going to be furious that I risked my safety at all. Perhaps a few weeks of travel would cool him down, but I wasn't looking forward to his scolding. Even Cooper wouldn't like me pushing myself to the brink. But how could I allow myself to fall so far in their eyes? "My powers are limited. I came to rescue you boys. I can free them from their chains, but I can't bring them here…"

"Charlotte…" Steve tilted his head and smirked, bemused as if he knew a secret that I didn't. "I've read about all of your miracles. If anyone can do this, it's you. You just have to believe in your own power."

Even if I explained my limitations in great detail, I doubted they would accept it. They had known the legend of the Runaway longer than they knew Charlotte, but I hadn't been her since the Draft Riots. I needed help or time to rest and regain my strength. "I'm afraid I'm near my limit."

Sweet Danny dared to laugh at me. "Since when have you accepted limits, Charlotte?"

"I've never seen it," Steve replied. "This is the same Charlotte who ran from her captors and swam through the Ohio River."

"And then she became the first woman to train under Cooper and started a whole revolution."

"This is the same Charlotte who defeated the Irish in a jig. Who does that?"

"Think of all the adventures we had together, going to theaters and places people thought we shouldn't belong. That didn't stop her."

"No, nothing could!"

"Alright! You both made your point." Even if I never donned Runaway's mask and coat again, I would always be the person underneath. I was still Charlotte when I was tied to that stake, about to be burned alive. I pushed past my limitations then, when fire was nipping at my feet. I could do it once more. "I am strong."

I returned to the warehouse, and the men reached for me as soon as my feet touched the ground. I decided to be true to my word. "The injured will go first. I'll pick an injured man, and then a couple of you should put your hand on me or someone touching me. We have to make a connection. We'll try five men at a time."

The injuries weren't too bad. Some had slings for their arms, some had head injuries, and two other men were injured in the leg like Danny, but crippled slaves wouldn't have been too appealing. I wondered if the other injured succumbed to their wounds or if they were executed due to their lack of usefulness. Most of the men were exhausted from the hot climate and lack of water, but they would be good field slaves if they could be broken. After seven trips, I was out of injured men. But I still had about twenty-three more jumps to go, unless I raised my threshold.

Blinking had become second nature to me. It was easier for me to move from one location to the next than it was to run. There was a space that I traveled to between my destinations, where the rules of the world didn't apply to me. That secret world invited me into its bosom as if I belonged there. But when I carried others with me, I could feel the strings that bound them pulling and resisting the space of infinite possibilities. It turned each journey into a sprint, and every added person was a heavy load on every muscle I had. My lungs began to burn, and each time I reached for a soldier, my arms quivered. I kept pushing, though. Even though air scraped against my dry mouth and hunger carved my belly, I kept pressing forward. "I am strong. I am strong."

"Charlotte!" Cooper rushed to my side as I collapsed on my hands and knees. I probably looked like a mess to him, based on the concern in his eyes. Thankfully, he found a canteen up on the guard post, nearly filled with water. "Drink this and rest."

I was too distracted to know what had been going on outside, but there certainly was a lot of hollering and gunshots. Men were quickly pushing equipment and beams to the doors for reinforcement. I figured we didn't have much time to escape, and no one was getting out of that warehouse alive without my help. I had to keep pushing.

Cooper helped me guzzle the water. It was such a relief to feel moisture on my tongue again. It made a remarkable difference. I took a few breaths while Cooper signaled men to come toward me. One of the soldiers must have found the keys and began setting the soldiers free to spare me the energy of walking toward them. That little bit helped me greatly. Five men touched my back and shoulders just as I finished gorging myself. "Are you ready?"

I managed to barely nod.

"No, I want to hear you say it!" That was his tone reserved for his friends when he stood in their corner. He wouldn't tolerate defeat, because Cooper was the one who nurtured their gifts. He knew better than anyone that they would win.

"I am strong." I pushed on, even though their hands were like cords pulling me toward the ground. I think they began to feel it, too. Each drop-off resulted in sluggishness instead of celebratory running and jumping. The last ten jumps were excruciating. The air was hot in the warehouse; it smelled of smoke, and the booming of gunfire was more rampant.

Eight men remained, including Cooper, when I collapsed on my hands and knees. I would have screamed if I had enough air, and I would have cried if I could spare the water. I did feel heavy moisture on my face, and when it fell into my mouth, it was too thick to be tears or even snot, and it had a metallic taste.

"Runaway…" Cooper was much gentler this time, as if he were speaking to a child, and then he caressed my face. "I know this is torture, but you have to move the rest of us at once. We're out of time."

Every bit of me was shaking, and I thought I would unravel. I never felt heavier than I did at that moment. It was as if the earth had opened up and swallowed my arms and legs. "There's nothing left in me, Coop." I wasn't even certain that I had enough air to make that shameful confession audible for him.

"Charlotte…" Despite the worried wrinkle on his brow, Cooper had the same bemused smile as Steve. "What can't you do?"

My quick and shallow breaths surrendered to a memory of my hand reaching for his own. "Fail." It had been so long since we danced together in Five Points. He held me tight and told me that I could be a conductor. I was too afraid at the time, but Cooper's selflessness and strength inspired me to risk my life and my freedom in the service of others. I wanted the slaves in the South to know what it was like to be Joseph Cooper: free, fearless, and strong.

With what little strength I had left, I gripped onto the sleeves of his coat.

"Everyone, come now! This is the last jump."

I closed my eyes and buried my head into his chest. One more jump. That's all Cooper needed from me. It didn't matter how many cords attached and pulled me down. I hoarsely screamed and focused on the shore where my husband brought me and promised we'd make a better world. I didn't have the strength to say the words he made me state over and over again as a child, but in my mind, it rang truer than anything I had ever spoken. *"I am strong."*

Chapter Eleven

I remember light and crisp white sheets. The air was real cool on my skin, but under the tucked sheets was warmth and a body pressing up against mine. "Charlotte..." His breath heated my cheeks, and so did the brush of his thumb. "Charlotte, it's time to wake up."

"But I'm so tired, John." I snuggled deeper into our bed and nuzzled his chest. "I don't want to wake up."

"Come on." His tone had a playful flutter before his tender lips tickled my forehead, but then it became quite stern. "Charlotte, we need you to get up."

"We?"

As I raised my head, a dark figure enveloped me. I pressed deeper into a cotton mattress until his rough hands became familiar, and his pretty smile focused. "Cooper?"

"Welcome back, sleepyhead. Are you sticking around this time?"

It was a struggle to keep my eyes open, but I was too curious not to let my eyes wander. Soft light filtered in through closed shutters. I easily counted four crosses mounted on the walls. The space was enclosed with a door, so I wasn't in a hospital ward. There was a cabinet with bandages, rags, a washing bin, and other things. A bookcase with a few Bibles stood in the corner, and a fancy wooden desk was pushed up against the wall. Most of the light came from an oil lamp sitting on the table. "Is this a church?"

"A clergy's office, to be precise. The Union converted this church into a hospital. You collapsed from exhaustion, so we took you to Jacksonville, where you could be protected and cared for. You've been here for a week, in and out of consciousness."

"A week?" John should have been traveling with Moses, so he likely wouldn't have known that I was hurt or expected to hear from me. Mary Anne must have been worried sick. "You haven't fed me in a week? No wonder I'm so hungry."

Cooper chuckled with a heart full of relief. "I fed you broth and porridge, but you wouldn't take much else." I felt a tremendous load of guilt. He must have been terribly worried about me.

"Well, I want a ham sandwich."

He laughed again, quietly yet heartily. His pretty smile was enough to inject some life back into my lips. "I'll see what I can find." Before getting up, Cooper touched my shoulder and froze for a few seconds as if he had to be certain the moment was real. He would have never forgiven himself if I had died, but he wouldn't have lived long.

John would have killed him.

Once Cooper left me alone for a little while, I worked on wiggling and flexing my muscles. I wasn't sleepy anymore, but my body was still tired. I managed to push myself up and leaned against the wall. I was a bit curious what I might find on the cleric's bookcase, but my legs were going to be jelly until I got some food in me. I spotted my clothes folded neatly on the desk and my coat hanging on a rack. My mask was on the bed, next to the pillow. It smelled of fresh lemons.

Cooper came back into the room with a tray of food just as I set it down. I reached like a nursing child thirsting for their mother's bosom. Cooper set the tray on the chair where he had once sat. There was a blanket draped over the back of it, so I reckoned he slept in it, too. "Here you go."

I glared at it, and then at him. It was a plate of grits, a biscuit, a piece of fried salted ham, an orange, a glass of water, and black coffee. "This isn't what I asked for."

"It's close enough. Remember, it's breakfast time."

"How am I supposed to know the time? And heroes should get ham sandwiches whenever they please!" I was glad he got a chuckle out of my misfortune. I made do with my ingredients and tucked the meat inside the biscuit. There was a little bit of honey and butter in the center, so it helped mask the saltiness. The grits were decent, very buttery. The coffee was disgusting. Cooper got another good chuckle when I stuck my tongue out. I diluted it with water and squeezed a little bit of orange juice to make it tolerable. The orange was probably the best part of the meal.

"You certainly are incredible," Cooper spoke softly, as if in a daze.

I hid my eyes in the rest of my sandwich. "How you reckon?"

"In the pursuit of saving others, you pushed beyond your limitations once again. I never would have forgiven myself if you didn't pull through, but I never accepted the possibility that you would die. After all the loss we've experienced—Harvey, Dave, Sam—I should expect the worst. But I knew you'd wake up and become stronger than ever."

I ran out of sandwich, so I finally raised my head. Cooper's admiration was daunting, but it wasn't necessarily romantic. I suppose it wasn't impossible for him to open that door again, but I sensed it was, at the very least, firmly shut. "No matter what you decide to do with John and your people—whether I agree with it or not—I have no doubt you'll succeed. All I ask is that you don't cause unnecessary bloodshed of the innocent. At least keep John in check for that."

I certainly didn't feel like an all-powerful being, especially while covered in ham grease. I splashed some water on a napkin to wash the sticky citrus off my fingers, then dabbed my face. "Does everyone know who I am?"

"The military is extremely grateful to you. They're trying to keep things hush for your sake. Civilians don't know you're staying here, and no one has seen you without a mask, besides a few doctors and me. But it's big news, Charlotte. It made the papers."

"Then John might know already." I covered my face and moaned. "He'll be so angry!"

"The military is keeping my part in all this confidential, but my superiors needed to know. Otherwise, I would have been accused of desertion. As far as your identity goes, why would the government have any idea who you are? I think you're safe, for the most part. My only concern is that you came to visit me, so it's not impossible to link us all together."

I moaned louder, but I didn't have any regrets. We were alive, and Cooper was soon to marry our dearest friend. John was going to be unpleasant, but I could handle his rage. I had to believe it would all work out for the best.

"And the Rebels…" I peeled my fingers away so I could look Cooper in the eye. "How many survived the fall?"

Cooper swallowed as if he wanted to keep the truth down in the pit of his stomach. "Three."

A flash of faces overwhelmed my mind, and I tumbled into the pillow. I tried to tell myself that they were fighting an evil war and deserved their fate for trying to sell my friends into slavery, but those thoughts were quickly blotted out by their young and fearful faces. Despite their evils, they were made in the image of God. They may have done monstrous things—perhaps they were even monsters—yet God saw fit to love them.

I was embarrassed to sob and shake in front of Cooper. He had to kill soldiers, and I doubted he broke down. I didn't want him to think I thought any less of him for doing what was necessary in just warfare.

"I'm sorry."

I swallowed and did my best to catch my breath. "For what?"

"For saying you had changed." He smiled, full of sadness and relief. "You're definitely different, but you're still the same woman I fell in love with."

His words gave me much comfort. The night of the Draft Riots, I decided to harden my heart to become the woman John and my people needed, but I never wanted my heart of flesh to become stone. I had only hardened my resolve. My value of humanity hadn't changed. Cooper meant a great deal to me, so I was glad that he acknowledged my true feelings.

"Everything might change after today. Maybe everything already has." I reached for his hand, and Cooper was kind enough to oblige. I kissed his rough knuckles, healed from years of constant battles to prove himself. "I just want you to know that I appreciate everything you've ever done for me. I don't even have the words to express my gratitude."

"Well, that's awfully suspicious, Charlotte. You're normally so good with words." We had a good laugh together. It made it so obvious how much we had lost through our temporary separation. "You don't ever have to thank me, Charlotte." He kissed my hand in return, then grinned.

"I'm ready to go home now. We have a wedding to prepare for."

It blessed my heart to see the brightness in Cooper's eyes as he thought of his bride-to-be. "Your clothes have been cleaned. I'm going to let you wash. Do you need a nurse to assist you?"

"No. I'll be fine." Cooper caressed my cheek, smudging a trail of tears into my skin. It was a final gesture to make certain I was alright, and I offered a soft smile as confirmation.

I was able to get up just fine. My body was a little stiff, but a couple of stretches relieved most of that. The tiredness faded the more I kept moving. My arm was sore. Curiosity demanded I remove my bandage. There was a long, shallow stripe across my arm. It had scabbed into dark reds and browns. The edges were reddish pink, and the skin around it had bruised. John was going to be mad about that ugly thing. Hopefully, Zhang could still fix it before it became a scar. I was fortunate not to have any other wounds. My breasts were real tender, but I figured my monthlies were due at any moment. All the more reason to hurry and go home. Those pains could only be relieved in a scalding hot bath.

Washing supplies were on a cabinet. I changed into my clothes, combed my hair, then donned the infamous mask and gloves.

"Runaway?" Cooper knocked just as I was sizing myself up in the mirror. My jacket sleeve was stitched, but the seamstress did a poor job.

"Come in."

Cooper marched fast and formally, dressed neatly in a soldier's uniform and hat. A stiff hand came to his face, a proper salute that I had seen many times. Once he did, I noticed an extra stripe on his chevron. "You have a visitor."

A man stepped through the door, also dressed in a dark blue frock coat with brass buttons. A single star was stitched on his shoulder straps, and his boots were finely polished. His hat was respectfully tucked under his arm, and a letter was in his other hand. "This is Brigadier General Truman Seymour."

He was thin, with sharp yet calm eyes. "At ease, Sergeant."

"Sergeant?" A prideful smile burst on my face. Cooper tried to contain it, but I caught a smirk as he closed the door. "Congratulations are in order."

"It's well-deserved," Seymour said. "I've been briefed about the mission and your capabilities, but that was hardly a mystery. Your reputation precedes you, Runaway. Because of you, 151 brave men can return to their families or the battlefield."

I felt the heaviness of his presence and the importance of his rank, but it was difficult to be intimidated by humans when I slept with the most powerful man alive. "Thank you for your kind words. I wish I could have saved more."

"You may very well receive such an opportunity in the future." He presented a cream envelope to me and began to explain before I could read through it. "President Lincoln has decided to throw a party highlighting exemplary Negros, such as Sergeant Cooper, and notable abolitionists. The purpose of this gathering will not be common knowledge in advance, but the president hopes you will be his guest of honor. He and General Grant would both like to meet you."

It was a handwritten note, not written by the president but transcribed through a telegraph. I trusted that the Brigadier General's words were true. I had already done so much since rising from the slave shack, but going to the White House as a guest was never even in my wildest dreams. "I would love to accept their invitation…"

As its conqueror? That was far more likely, considering my husband. "But I have people I'm accountable to. Surely, you understand the chain of command."

Cooper was bulging his eyes from behind the Brigadier General. I probably embarrassed him. The Brigadier General's brows rose just a hair, but the rest of him was rather stoic. "I'm an experienced military man, and I've fought through many battles. Whatever obligations you have, it's crucial to recognize opportunities like this. If you're concerned about your safety, no one is going to execute you amongst such a crowd. Your safety is a priority to the president. He is an admirer of your work."

"He doesn't find my gifts to be alarming?"

His lips slightly curled. "President Lincoln has always been fascinated with the strange and unusual." He wasn't wrong. Mrs. Lincoln was an odd woman. She even had a séance at the White House. People assumed she was a bit mad with grief after losing her son, William. Lincoln himself enjoyed oddities such as Tom Thumb. I was the greatest spectacle yet.

I wanted John to make peace with Lincoln, deep in my heart. I was prepared for that not ever being a possibility. But even if we were fated to be enemies, it was a good opportunity to listen and learn. "I will consider this deeply. Thank you."

The Brigadier General offered an understanding nod. "I was distressed to hear about your injuries. Do you feel well enough to travel?"

"I do, sir. I've rested enough."

"Well, then, Miss Runaway, it was my pleasure." He bowed, and I became a bit bashful. Cooper straightened like a board and saluted his superior until he was acknowledged once again. "You're dismissed, Sergeant." His superior's presence lingered in the room for a few seconds, even after Cooper shut the door behind him and took a breath.

"That's all he had to say?"

"That's all he might have been authorized to tell you. I assume Lincoln doesn't want to scare you off." Cooper retrieved a big leather bag and a rifle that was tucked away in the corner.

"Can I say goodbye to the boys?"

"It's best if you don't. They'll see you in a few days at my wedding."

"A few days?"

"Well, heroes get to go on leave. Besides, I'd rather bring my wife to the White House instead of a pregnant mistress."

"I can certainly understand that." I latched onto Cooper's arm, amazed at what the two of us accomplished. There were a few things that needed to be done before I could return him to his lovely bride-to-be. I thought of the initials carved in my Odysseus tree. In a flash, Cooper let go of my arms and stepped back to observe the unfamiliar territory. "We're in my bedroom."

"Why?" He sneered as if revolted.

"Because I need to change. I can't risk being the Runaway while I retrieve my things from Beaufort. Mary Anne will come next."

Cooper softened as he circled the room. It was decorated with soft and muted colors to complement the white oak bed frame, which was the showstopper. "What's with the tree?"

"*The Odyssey* inspired John. I know it's supposed to be made out of an olive tree in the book, but those aren't readily available here." I gritted my teeth, contemplating whether I should reveal what was on the tip of my tongue. "We once got into a fight about this. John thought you were my Calypso."

He looked down at me, puzzled. "I don't follow."

My eyes could have flown right out of my skull. "You've never read it?"

"Woman, you know if I read books, they're about making money."

I gently shook my head and chuckled along with him. John was well-studied. There were certainly economic books among our collection, but most of what filled our shelves were things I wanted to read with my husband. John even had to build another bookcase into the wall around our headboard, so we didn't have to travel far. "It's not important. Forget I mentioned it."

Some of John's shirts were on the bed from when I packed his bag. Cooper's curious fingers began to inch toward one, and I snatched his hand. "I need to change. You should wait in the hallway. John will be able to smell you, and I don't want to explain why you were in his things."

He sneered once again. "Well, that's disgusting."

Cooper wandered out and shut the door behind him. I quickly changed into a brown long-sleeve dress to hide my bandage and into a comfortable pair of boots. Cooper was a good boy and didn't wander around the rest of the house. I took his hand, and we blinked to that tree stump off the path in Beaufort. Nobody was close, and there were plenty of trees blocking a far line of sight. From there, we walked back to the boarding house, and Cooper waited outside for me.

Miss Rogers was at the front desk. She clutched her chest as if she had seen a ghost. "Charlotte! Where did you go? I was so worried about you."

"I had to go on a special adventure for Coop's bride-to-be. Everything worked out for the best, but circumstances delayed our return. I hope you still have my things."

"Of course. I packed them in your bag and put them in my office. I'll be right back." She went into the room behind her, and the paper on the mahogany desk caught my eye. *Masked Runaway saves 151 Negro Soldiers.* There was a new sketch of Runaway, a silhouette cloaked in shadow. Though there were no discernible features, it had a slender and curvy form. The pronouns in the articles from witnesses made it clear that I was, indeed, a woman.

I didn't want to pick it up and draw more attention to myself, but Miss Rogers caught me peeking when she came out of the office. "Isn't it exciting?"

"This made front page news in Beaufort?"

"Charlotte, it's front-page news everywhere! From the South to the North, Runaway is the talk of the town."

"I suppose I was too busy with wedding plans to notice." I was concerned that other illustrations might be more detailed. Perhaps I should have worn a hood like John. "I never expected Runaway was a woman."

"It's inspiring." Miss Rogers picked up the paper and poured a reverence from her eyes that should have been reserved for God's holy scriptures. Then she whispered her words like a faint prayer. "She's just like us…"

I didn't understand how someone with such great power could be relatable without knowing anything else, but I was glad to make her smile. "I'd like to pay you for watching my things."

"No, it was no trouble. I'm relieved you're alright and that Cooper is marrying the mother of his child. It all worked out for the best."

"It did, thanks to you." I owed her a great deal. She had no idea how her small act of kindness rippled into that rescue. I wanted her to know, and I felt like I could trust her with my secret, but it wasn't fair to John to divulge that information. "You take good care of yourself, Miss Rogers."

I took my things, reunited with Cooper, and thought of Mary Anne's bedroom. It was cleaner than it was before. Much of her fabric had been neatly tucked away. There were piles of new baby items, and my booties were waiting by the door.

"Where might she be?" Cooper asked.

"Anywhere, but likely her office downstairs." We walked down together. It was quiet, too quiet, and there was an odd tension I couldn't shake. I just felt sick in the pit of my stomach, all of a sudden. At the bottom of the stairs, Bess spotted us.

"Mr. Cooper!" She ran excitedly toward us, but once she realized that I was beside him, she slowed, and dread filled her bright brown eyes. Instead of running into Cooper's chest for a good hug, she clutched onto my arms in terror.

"Where's Mary Anne?" Cooper let Bess's fear infect him, and she was the most obvious one to be concerned about.

"She went out shopping with Loretta. They should be back at any moment." The poor girl's voice trembled.

"Girl, what's got you so frightened?"

When her eyes locked with mine, I got a taste of her terror. "It's your husband."

The sickness in my stomach dropped down to my ankles, and I would have tumbled over if she weren't holding me so tight. "Is he alright?"

"He arrived about an hour ago, looking for you, and he was not happy."

My heart sped up. Better than the alternative, but my mind was dashing like a mad horse. There was no way he could have gotten Moses to Mick that quickly. Mick would have barely been in Cincinnati. "Where is he now?"

"The green parlor." John's mood must have been particularly foul. Poor Bess was near tears. "Are we getting evicted?"

"No. He's not angry about the hotel."

"Should I come with you?" Cooper was stoic, but there was just enough tension in his voice to let me know he was itching for a foolish fight he couldn't win.

"Absolutely not," I seethed. "Give me my privacy." I marched boldly through the hotel and stopped at the wooden door. I tugged on my dress and combed my hair a bit. I wished I had dressed prettier. Perhaps that would have calmed him down.

"Come in, Charlotte."

I bit my lip and whimpered. Of course, he could sense or smell me. There was no point in delaying the inevitable. I eased inside, and John was hunched forward in a chair like he was ready to pounce. The boy was nowhere in sight, and I still had my powers. "Where is Moses?"

"He's with Mick, disappearing as we agreed."

"How? You said it would take a month—"

"I was made by the Confederates." His volume was low, but his tone was like a dog prowling toward his prey. "From there, I let the boy know we were in a life-or-death situation, and if he wanted to survive, he had to let me save him. Fear is a powerful motivator, even for a child that small."

"Then he can control his powers?"

"Charlotte!" John hopped to his feet with the paper in hand. I didn't mean to jump back, but he was beginning to burst like a boiling tomato. "We are not about to get distracted when you know precisely what I want to talk about!" He flailed it around like a war flag.

"John, I know you're angry—"

"Angry?" His burst of laughter after shouting was certainly unnerving. "No, when you dropped a piano on my head, I was angry. I don't know what to call this."

I hesitated. I didn't want to start speaking if he was going to yell over me. "John, I had to—"

"We made a promise! After what happened to Asha, we weren't supposed to put ourselves in harm's way for these humans ever again."

"I didn't involve anyone else. It was my choice to make for myself."

"*Our* people are not to get involved in human affairs—"

"They're my people, too!" I tried to remain calm, but my heart was stirred. "These were my friends who kept me safe and taught me how to fight. They know what it's like to struggle in this world with a black face, and the Rebels were going to bind them with chains. I couldn't let that happen."

"Oh, yes, you could have, and you should have. You had no right to make this decision on your own." It wasn't John's rage or the fact that he was hollering in my face that infuriated me. It was that he cared so little for the lives of the people who defined me.

"Why? Because I belong to you?"

"Of course you belong to me! You're my wife. And I belong to you. We're one flesh!" I was ready to go feral on him, but his eyes were glittering with infinite possibilities of failed missions. "If I had done something so reckless and risked my life without your blessing—without your knowledge—you would be livid."

"It wasn't reckless…"

"Charlotte!"

I pouted and hung my head low like a scolded child. "You're right. I would have been furious." John sometimes made decisions that I didn't agree with, but I deferred to him as my husband. He mostly tried to come to a compromise, but even if I were upset, I knew what his plans were. But those were matters involving our people. "I should have waited to talk to you, but I didn't have the time. I had to make a decision. Was I supposed to let my friends be sold off into slavery?"

John growled, his voice rising in frustration that I hadn't learned a definitive lesson after all these years. "You know that your life is more important than these humans. It always has been, and it always will be."

"Hey!" Mary Anne pushed through the door that I had left slightly open. Cooper, the fool, was right behind her. I thought I would have to worry about him, but she was the one who barged in with her hands on her hips. "Do I need to separate you two?"

John blinked hard, and his head propped up. "Mary Anne, you're different."

"Yes. Of course." She laughingly rubbed her belly. "I'm seven months pregnant." Cooper placed his hand on her shoulder, hoping to establish the new dynamic between us all.

"No, it's not that." John's eyes fell to me, full of hope. "Your scent has changed."

I touched my stomach and looked down at my tiny belly. Undoubtedly, John's child was growing in my womb. It seemed obvious at that moment. The future we had been dreaming about was already with us. And when I looked back up with a smile full of wonder toward my husband, the hope in his eyes began to fill with golden terror.

"John, no!" I plunged into his chest and took him home to our bedroom. He shut his eyes tight, grunting and hollering in a type of pain I hadn't heard him express since he used Mary Anne's powers to blow up the looters at the Colored Orphan Asylum. Veins popped through his skin and around his head, like snakes wrapping around his mind. And though he shielded me from his golden haze, I felt it through his skin and panicked breaths.

I had never seen John's sway grip him so fiercely.

"You have to fight it, John. Please." I felt the terror in his heart from watching his mother be burned alive and the disdain for humans that he carried as a result. It was nurtured on the Cohens' plantation as he watched the oppression of the slaves. The shame he carried for whipping me was like great stones tied to his neck. And his fury was born after Lady Cohen was helplessly murdered.

I screamed with what little air I had in my lungs. If I only felt a portion of his anguish, I couldn't fathom how he faced each day. His rage and bloodlust were so plausible at that moment. The humans would never stop. They killed Lady Cohen. They killed Asha. We couldn't let them take our children, even if they all had to die.

"No!" We both fell to our knees, trembling like leaves battered in a storm. "John, just because you feel or think something, doesn't make it right. It doesn't make it true!"

"I can't…" He was so red, and his skin was hot. I was afraid he'd activate Mary Anne's power and burn our home down. "I can't let them hurt you!"

"I know you're afraid. I'm afraid, too! I am. But we can find another way." I kissed his cheek, smothering tears on my beloved. His grief was like a burst of smoke in my lungs. I had to fight to see, think, and breathe through it all. "All parents have fears, but we can't protect children from the whole world. I know you wanted the world to be different from what it is now, but we can't destroy it for their sake. Our job is to prepare them and teach them how to build a better one. I know we can do it together. We have to."

I held him tight and struggled to get my breathing under control. I wanted his breathing to sync with mine. If he could calm down, I could reason with John—*my* John.

"Charlotte..." He began to pull away, still shaking and breathing heavily. The veins on his head had begun to recede, and his skin resembled a pig more than a tomato. I braced myself as his eyelids raised, releasing two fresh tears and a golden haze as beautiful as a morning horizon. "We can do it together."

As his pinkish color faded and his skin smoothed, John appeared to me more beautiful than he ever had before. I held his face, feeling his strong jaw and cheekbones. He was a model of perfection, more handsome than any master sculptor could build. Only the Creator could mold such a being for me. "We are strong."

"Stronger together."

I collided into John, pouring my whole heart out to him. I allowed him to taste my hopes and my fears as I tasted his lips. I was grateful for wearing that ugly dress, because his fingers were impatient with the buttons, and he tore it open. I swear my heart wanted to leap right through my chest as he trailed my neck and bosoms with soft kisses. I breathlessly pleaded with him not to destroy another one of my corsets. John fiddled with his own clothes while I kicked off my boots and peeled off layers of fabric. From there, my husband carried me over to our bed, crafted by his own hands.

I had made love with my husband more times than I could count. Not because it wouldn't bring me joy to recount them all, but because it seemed innumerable. We had acted with reckless abandon, wild passion, and caressed each other in the most tender of ways. He made me feel lovely and admired as well as dangerous and fiercely desired. I had been thoroughly pleased and well-fed as a wife, yet he still managed to surprise me.

We had never been that vulnerable with one another, emptying ourselves into each other and mixing into something new. As we tumbled under our sheets and tasted each other's tears, it was clear that we had broken away from John's vision of a new world.

We were in uncharted territory, one that we had the liberty of exploring together.

Chapter Twelve

The sun was high and blaring through the window. It was harsh on one side of my face, but I couldn't bear to close the curtains. John rested on my stomach and hadn't moved in a long while. I was hungry too, but I didn't want to spoil the moment. I spiraled his locks, hoping our child's hair would be easier to deal with than mine.

"I can hear her."

"John, you don't know if it's a girl, and you certainly can't hear her. She's too little."

"I know what I hear." He pouted and sounded like a stubborn child. There was no sense in talking him out of it. It was a lovely sentiment.

"You don't want your first heir to be a son?"

"You know I don't care about that."

A deep grin spread across my face. "I know. I just wanted to hear you say it." I felt fortunate to have such a man. He had his flaws—certainly—but his benefits were immaculate.

"Have I been a good husband to you?"

"I have no complaints so far." My mind was numb to any current failings. I only possessed wonderful tingling and hopeful desires.

"I want you to know that I'm going to be a good father." John raised his head and rested his chin on my stomach. It was a more uncomfortable position, but he looked like a child—a *normal* child—full of hope and void of a lifetime of heartache.

"I have no doubt, John."

He smiled and sat up, almost bashfully. "There is something I want to give to you and now feels like the right time."

It was obvious that John's surprise would be a ring. We were married in such a hurry that he didn't have time for anything other than a simple gold band. I didn't care much, but John promised to get me another one, and I didn't press him. There were matters more important than jewelry. I did wonder at times about the delay. It's not as though he couldn't afford something grand.

I wasn't surprised John left the bedroom to retrieve his gift. Any obvious hiding place, I would have discovered. Sure enough, he returned within a minute with three boxes in his hand. Two were black, the other was red. "You're overdoing it, aren't you?"

"I know it's uncommon, but I figured we should both have one. If you belong to me, I belong to you."

I about melted when he placed that black ring box in my hand. Inside was a gold signet ring with our initials together, protected by a thin wreath of olive leaves. The sides were engraved with olive branches. John's ring was similar, but masculine. It was bigger, the lettering was different, and there was no wreath. The center was more oval, and the olive branches on the side were larger and more detailed. They were both beautiful, but not the refined work of an experienced artist. "Did Kachina make this for you?"

"No, I made it myself."

I laughed shortly in disbelief. "Since when can you make something this intricate? I've never seen you manipulate gold either."

"As long as raw materials from the earth haven't been industrialized, Kachina's power can manipulate them. It wasn't easy for me, and I had a few failures. It took months to get this result."

"You've been secretly at this the whole time?" I raised my hand, so John could remove the plain band and replace it with his crafted piece. And after I placed John's ring on his finger, I nearly released a sudden wave of tears. The ring certainly wasn't anything I imagined. The olive branches weren't symmetrical, the face wasn't perfectly round, and the texture of the band was uneven, but I absolutely adored it. "And what's the red box for?"

His jaw tightened. "It's a backup in case you didn't like it." He flipped the lid open, revealing a glittering mine-cut diamond on a thin gold band. I would have picked something like that in the store, but it didn't glow as beautifully as the ring already on my finger. "You can have both if you like."

I wrapped my arms around John and kissed his cheek and lips. "How did I ever become so fortunate?" We could have reengaged with intimacy—he certainly deserved it—but my belly rumbled between the smack of our lips.

John laughed and crawled out of the bed. "We have to feed you, my dear. You're eating for two now."

He closed the curtain, finally granting relief to my face. "There's not much to eat here."

"Then I shall have to take you out."

"Not without a bath. I haven't had one in over a week." I had to eat to hold me over. Luckily, I had crackers and apple butter. A handful of walnuts and raisins also tamed my hunger long enough for John to fill our bath.

The house was chilly, so the warm water was too tempting not to dwell in. I leaned on my husband's chest, determined to rest there until it became ice cold. He was also relaxed, stroking my arm as he stared at the ceiling. "Everyone is going to be thrilled about our baby."

We'd have to warn Emma to remain calm before telling her the good news. I didn't want her to squeeze the baby out of me. The children would be excited to have a new friend. Kachina and the others would be glad for John's sake, perhaps even outright happy for the both of us. The new people didn't know us, but who didn't like babies? There was only one concern. "Dinah might not be happy…"

"She'll get over it."

"I don't know, John." I struggled with whether I should tell him about Dinah's behavior. I didn't want him to retaliate too harshly against her. There was also a tiny possibility that she wasn't lying. "Dinah told me the story about how you two met. She said after you played poker in her room, you…" I watched his eyes. He didn't seem nervous or guilty. I felt sick even saying it out loud. "…slept together."

His eyes widened before he threw his head back and laughed. He could have been overacting to cover up his role, but I knew my husband well. It seemed genuine, especially when the laughter tapered off, and annoyance crept into his voice. "And you believed her?"

"No, but she said it to upset me, and she was a bit successful."

John pursed his lips into a devilish smirk. "You were suspicious of me on our wedding night."

"No! I said you seemed rather experienced."

"And I said you were the only woman I've ever been with."

"And I believed you. It just didn't seem like your first time. It was a compliment."

He chuckled and continued to stroke my arm. I couldn't put my finger on it, but it always seemed like John knew something that I didn't. "If I had slept with Dinah, would you be angry?"

I think my heart stopped pumping blood and blasted rage straight through me instead. I sat up and tried not to shout. "After all of your heartfelt confessions, pretending like I was the only woman in your life? Why wouldn't I be upset if you never mentioned her?"

"Fair enough." He raised his hand in surrender, then sank back into the bath. "But she propositioned me at a difficult period of my life. My mother had just been killed, and you left me alone to bury her." If he had a pistol aimed at my heart, it would have been loaded with bitterness. The hit was direct, and my lungs were filling up with grief.

"John, I'm so sorry—"

"When I chased you down, I found out that you were in love and living with another man. You were my whole world, yet you replaced me in a few months."

I wanted the roof to cave in and take me out. I felt so awful. How could I explain my relationship with Cooper? I did love him by that time, but I wasn't *in* love with him then. It wasn't going to bring him comfort that I fought off my feelings for Cooper when he never had the capacity to love another woman at all. But even when I was finally ready to surrender, after John's hands had been stained with too much blood, I still couldn't let him go. "You were never replaced. You were as irreplaceable as you can get."

"But it was the darkest time of my life." John was remarkably composed, but the hurt in his voice was deep. Whatever came out of his mouth next, I prepared to be understanding, even if it broke my heart.

***

"I want to please you."

"No." I had just ducked away from Dinah's lips and grabbed her hands. I saw her as a strong-willed woman with tremendous potential, and I despised her father for forcing her into a life of impropriety. "You don't need to do this for your father."

"For the first time in my life, I'm doing something for myself."

"Even so, I can't accept." I repositioned to grab her hand, meaning to kiss her goodnight like a gentleman. I also wanted to tell her my heart belonged to someone else. But when my lips touched her hand, a flood of memories poured in. It wasn't only her memories of manipulation and abuse, but the memories she had also taken on, including those of Uncle Landon. I was brought to my knees from the sheer weight of her burden, and I had to release her power before it completely overwhelmed me.

"John, are you alright?"

My head was pounding. If not for my enhanced healing ability, I suspected my mind would have shattered. "What a terrible power…"

"I'm sorry." She helped me onto the bed and poured a glass of water. She didn't say much until I had ceased wincing and grunting from the pain. "How come my powers don't hurt me?"

"Your mind is built for it. I can copy other people's powers, but I can't match the original."

"Unless they die."

"That appears to be the case." At the time, I only had my mother's abilities to verify. I didn't want to hold onto Dinah's ability. If I wanted one like it, I'd get it from Steven. He could take on someone's memories and their form, but Dinah didn't appear to have a talent for that.

What I did see in Dinah's memories was that she had been waiting for a man strong enough to defy her father's rule. She knew I was that man the moment she laid eyes on me. "Well, if you feel up to it, mischief awaits you."

I was successful in kissing Dinah's hand goodnight on the second attempt. From there, I blinked through the window and out past the edge of the plantation. Dinah's father was assembling a team of zealots to come and find me, due to the vile words of jealousy from my uncles and the nature of their untimely deaths. I wanted to slaughter them by my own hand, but that would put me under more suspicion and make it impossible to purchase land in the future.

I saw a mockingbird perched in a tree and was able to call it to me. I had seen my mother control animals. I wasn't able to do it in the past, but I was certainly more powerful than before. I sent it to gather others, and a few more returned. They left, and a flock of all kinds of birds came back. I tried my luck with other animals, anything in the area with teeth. It started small, but bigger predators made their way.

When I sensed the approach of a carriage, I hid up in the trees and waited. They came in fast, cloaked in shadow. Only one lantern guided their way, and it wasn't enough to stop the barrage of white-tailed deer that flung themselves in front of the carriage. Their sheer force and speed of the bucks knocked the carriage on its side and dragged the horses down with them. The driver was thrown to the ground and trampled by the spooked animals he once tamed. The men inside the carriage were shaken, but mostly unharmed. They quickly climbed out and helped one another. There were four of them, the last was an older man cloaked in white. I recognized him from Steven's memories. He was present the day Steven's mother was burned.

He splashed oil in her face and chanted before another man lit up the pyre.

My rage flared, and the animals instinctively knew to attack. Five black bears emerged from the trees, baring their teeth. One man tried to aim their pistol, but they were shoved to the ground before they could shoot. The others tried to run, but the bucks blocked their path. The old man never made it out of the road. He saw me, watching from above with golden eyes. With a weary hand, he pointed at me. If a bear hadn't ripped his larynx out, he would have warned the others before bleeding out.

Another horse headed our way at a brisk pace. I recognized the approaching scent as Steven's father, and blood was in the air. I assumed he heard the screams, and I rushed to him before he had the opportunity to turn around. I leapt from the trees in front of his steed, taking charge of the animal's mind. He pulled the reins, but the horse continued toward the carnage and wouldn't stop until his master met the swipe of a mother bear.

I reveled in every scream, squish, and tear. He truly was a pitiful man who was cruel to everyone who knew him. Everyone he knew was a tool, including his poor wife. But that was just the way of humans. I could have ignored those crimes and minded my business if not for his involvement in my mother's demise. I would have liberated Steven and Dinah—one way or another—but the day he sided with the zealots was the catalyst for me standing above him on that dark night. "Tell me, Master Ward," my golden eyes shone brightly, "do you still believe my uncles weren't killed by a bear?"

After one final blood-curdling scream, his spirit was released to the depths of hell where it belonged. I expected to find Steven relieved and grateful that he and his sister could live a full life free from Ward's oppression. Instead, he was cradling her body, which was naked and wrapped in a white bed sheet. She had stab wounds and a busted nose. Steven told me that their father found out they were aligned with me, and then he attacked Dinah. Steven tried to stop him, but failed.

In hindsight, I reckon once their father discovered I had gone, he likely tried to attack Dinah. Steven finally stood up to his father and was punched and stabbed. Ward left his son to die, not knowing the extent of his capabilities. He must have convinced Dinah to take his place, while he took hers. He was only wearing pants at the time. I imagine his shirt had stab wounds and too much blood to explain.

We buried who I thought was Dinah together. And as he stared at her grave, I noticed a fire in his eyes that hadn't been there before. "Whatever your cause is against the humans, I pledge myself to you." Steven had already pledged his father's land to me, but I didn't expect that he'd be able to kill for me. Now, I knew he'd be willing to do anything. He was completely devoted.

"Then let's prepare for a new world."

***

It was sad to think about. I never had a blood sibling, but losing Mary Anne would have shaken me down to my foundation. I wondered if Dinah forgave Steven, in the end, for being such a coward. "Dinah said it was safer to be a man. Do you believe that's why she took her brother's identity?"

"Steven must have talked her through how to switch places with his dying breath. He always felt guilty for not doing more to help his sister or his mother. In his mind, passing off his identity was him trying to make up for his failures. It made Dinah the heir to their father's property and allowed her to start again. I wouldn't have held Dinah's past against her, but others certainly would have."

As I watched John from the opposite end of the bath, I pictured him hovering over Dinah's father. I doubted he smiled as the bears consumed his flesh. He was probably as cold as a stone statue. "You were quite the fearsome foe."

"Isn't that why you decided to become my ally?"

"I was willing to face you!" My beloved got a good chuckle out of my arrogance. I quickly calmed and eased back into the water. "But it was difficult. It was like cutting my own heart out." For John's sake, I hoped he believed me.

"Well…" John threw his head back, laughing once more. "…I didn't enjoy fighting a woman mad enough to drop a piano on me."

"Well, you shouldn't have underestimated me."

His eyes swooped down like a hawk and took hold of my thighs. "Oh, I have never underestimated you." I squealed as he pulled me close to smother me with kisses. They were all so ticklish. I begged him to stop, and he did not relent. I blinked out of the tub and quickly tried to wrap myself in a towel, but as soon as it was on me, John scooped me up in his arms. "When have I ever let you escape me, woman?"

I began to doubt my resolve when it came to birthing his ten children. It was easy to get swept up in his beauty, strength, and charm. For the happiness he bestowed upon me, I genuinely wanted to please him. John gave me a final kiss and sat me down on the bedroom floor. I did scold him for treading water throughout the house, but he was a sweetheart and cleaned up while I got dressed.

I went to the closet to retrieve a coat and remembered the envelope given to me by Brigadier General Truman Seymour. My stomach rattled with nerves when I thought about broaching the subject. I glanced back at John, lacing up his boots. I told myself that if I wanted to please him, he must have possessed the same desire for me. "I need to show you something before we leave."

John had a curious curl on his lips when he took the letter. His eyes dashed across the paper, and his face straightened out. "You can't go."

"It's a good opportunity."

"You're the most wanted woman in the nation. The bounty on you is greater than the one on me."

"Well, at least I finally beat you in something!"

"Charlotte…" John stood up and gently took my hands. "It'll be far too dangerous. Risking your life is one thing, but you have our child to consider."

"Oh, I hate when you make perfect sense!" I glanced at the letter on the bed. What if famous abolitionists whom I admired were there? And not everyone had the opportunity to meet the president. "You should at least go."

"As a land baron? Certainly. But it'll be strange if I don't have my wife by my side."

The only answer was obvious. I waited a few seconds for John to propose it, but he kept his mouth shut. "What if we convince Dinah to pose as Runaway?"

"I thought you said she was angry with you. Women don't just get rid of anger."

"We can ask! We don't have to push her. It's an opportune moment for her to gather information from the most powerful men in the country. She wouldn't want to pass up on that, and you shouldn't either. If Lincoln requests a private audience, we can switch places."

"Having you appear in public with Runaway would protect your identity from anyone suspicious." John sighed as he weighed the options. "Spoiling Runaway with praise after such an extraordinary rescue is a worthy enough reason to request an audience, but I doubt there isn't more to it."

"Then we should hear him out." I wrapped my arms around his waist and gave him a firm squeeze. "Come on, John, aren't you curious?"

John grinned widely and had to turn his head, but that wasn't enough to resist my charms. "I'll grant him a possible audience with you, but that's all I'm willing to agree to right now."

I squealed and blinked us inside the tavern on our land. It was supper time, so it was crowded enough to bump into Christopher.

"Charlotte! John!" He took the liberty to hug me tight, and I didn't mind. He had a drink in his hand, so I assumed his inhibitions loosened. "Where have you been?"

"We know where she's been." Caroline was sitting with her brother at a table. There was an unmistakable tension in the room. Questions and bodies suddenly surrounded us; a couple of faces John was unfamiliar with.

"Don't crowd my hungry wife. Let us eat and gather our bearings. Round up Kachina, Tillie, Nathaniel, Adam, Zhang, and Dinah. Have them meet us in the back room." The tavern was the communal place to get a good meal, so it was often crowded throughout the day. The maximum capacity for the front might have been fifty, but there was a back room reserved for special meetings that fit about ten people comfortably.

The food in the tavern was suited to my Southern sensibilities since the cooks were mostly liberated slaves. It was how they earned their keep. One of our own always managed them. Zhang liked to come by and share cuisine from his homeland, but Mr. Clark mostly managed things. He was a plump man and wasn't much for fighting, but he had perfect senses. His enhanced flavor profile was probably the reason he was around three hundred pounds. For the record, he thought my sweet potato pies were perfect.

Mr. Clark had one of his servers bring out a tray of cheese, crackers, and fruit until he could send for more. James and some other men shot turkeys earlier, so I was ready for a good meal. A few minutes later, they brought a basket of bread and turkey legs with boiled potatoes. I didn't know what my baby could feel, but I liked to imagine they were dancing.

Henry ran and gathered everyone John requested. Adam came first, then Nathaniel with Zhang. Dinah came in next and sat in the furthest possible seat, avoiding my eyes. Kachina and Tillie came in last, and Tillie certainly gave Dinah a mean glare when she walked by. "It's good to see you alive, John. Does she have to be here?"

"You all didn't make up while I was gone?"

"Some things aren't so easily forgiven." Kachina settled in on John's left side, taking the place Steven usually occupied. Tillie sat beside her. Adam, Nathan, and Zhang sat on my side of the table.

"You don't have to forgive Dinah, but as long as we all have the same goals, we should work toward them."

Kachina's jaw was tight as she stared at her master. "I hate to bring it up, but—"

"What about what Charlotte did?" Tillie asked. "Tony brought us some papers. She's everywhere."

I was prepared to speak for myself, but John's hand softly rested upon my own before I could even mumble. "The humans were going to sell off some of her friends, and given Charlotte's history, she felt compelled to save them. I understand not everyone will agree with what she did, but not all humans are worthless, and she owed them a great debt."

Kachina was stoic. Tillie was not, but she kept her bird mouth shut. Adam cleared his throat, as if to test the waters. John remained calm, so he eased into his question. "Does this put us at risk?"

"Her actions have given us an opportunity. President Lincoln has invited Runaway to the White House for an important event." All of their heads propped up in amazement. Even Dinah's eyes had finally found us. "If Dinah poses as Runaway, she'll be able to gather important intelligence about the war, their future intentions, and whether Lincoln himself has any ties to the zealots."

If Tillie still had talons, I swear, she would have used them to tear out Dinah's eyes. "You trust her with such an important mission?" They were all stunned at the request, no one more so than Dinah herself.

"I'll also be attending with Charlotte on my arm. Mr. Cooper and Mary Anne will be newlyweds by then and also in attendance. Should the opportunity arise for Runaway and Lincoln to speak privately, Charlotte and Dinah will switch places."

"That is," I chimed in, "if Dinah agrees to it."

She blinked hard, then batted her eyelashes until some sense came back into her. "Of course. I'm honored that you trust me…" She was still baffled, and that was fine enough. At least she wasn't angry anymore.

Adam nervously tapped his leg and sat with his arms folded. "And what happens if Lincoln is a zealot sympathizer?"

A hush fell on the room. It wasn't a belief John held, but it wasn't one he had ruled out. The zealots had Union sympathizers, and there was no question about it. "Then we'll have to gather appropriate evidence and consider the possibility of ending his life."

"And what if he's as good as the humans say?" Kachina almost sounded disappointed. If she were itching for a war with the humans, others must have felt the same.

"Then we'll consider adjustments with that in mind."

I did my best to contain the silent gasp within me. John had never considered cooperating with the Union since we were wed.

"It sounds like a good plan." Nathanial nodded a few times. "We trust you." The rest of the room continued their praise of John in unison.

"Zhang," John spoke softly, "a bullet grazed Charlotte's arm during the rescue. If it isn't too late, heal her wound."

Zhang humbly bowed his head and grabbed my arm, right under the wound. It was still sore, but the pain immediately alleviated as soon as his light spread across my body. A simple wound like that was nothing for him, but a hint of dread entered my mind as he raised his head with widening eyes. "I feel two energies."

"Two?" Nathaniel asked, remarkably puzzled. "Two separate energies…as in from two different humans?"

"Yes…" I wanted to be annoyed with Zhang for spoiling the reveal, but it was impossible to be angry with him. So, I bashfully wrapped my arm around John and leaned into him. "We have wonderful news to share."

John had a straight face for the duration of his conversation, but he finally beamed like a bright sun. Judging by how that sun bounced off everyone else's face, they caught onto the news. They still waited with bated breath until John kissed my forehead and said, "Charlotte is with child."

Our friends cheered and greeted us with hugs and hearty handshakes. Though Kachina and Tillie both vied for John's affection, they held me tight and praised me for making him happy. Dinah abandoned her exile across the room and offered her hand as a man would. John accepted it, but I chose to embrace her. She gave me an awkward pat in return. "I am happy for you, Charlotte."

"Thank you, Dinah." I felt the tiniest bit of guilt, knowing that Dinah would never be able to carry a child in her own womb.

"Have you considered what you'll name the child?"

"If I'm blessed with a boy, I'll name him after his father."

"Of course," John nodded.

"And if it's a girl?" Dinah asked with a big smile.

"I'd have to think on it…" Even if I wanted to pass my name down to our baby, I had already promised it to Cooper and Mary

Anne. "I like 'Hope' or 'Liberty.' Those are fine names. Perhaps something meaningful."

John lightly pulled me close for a squeeze, but he didn't speak. It was one of those moments when someone is so quiet, you can feel it. He was smiling, almost like he was suffering through it.

"What about you, John?" Dinah's tone was a little less curious and a bit more leading. "You must have thought about it."

John pressed an uncomfortable grin to his face and shrugged his shoulders. I had never seen my husband bashful or hesitant to say anything.

"It's an awful name, isn't it?" His birth mother hated her name, but he might have been inclined to suggest it. Or maybe he had concocted some sort of nonsense name that would give me a good laugh. "You can tell us."

"Come on, John," Nathaniel insisted.

"Yeah," Tillie joined in. "I'm sure it's a fine name."

He looked just like a little boy, hopeful and afraid that I'd reject him. "I've always liked the name Lillian..."

I swear, the blood in my veins turned ice cold for a few painfully slow seconds. Then, the temperature shot right back up to a boil. I don't know how I managed to keep a smile on my face and speak in a normal tone. "Well, it is a beautiful name. We'll have to figure all this out in private."

John kissed my hand, and I worried that I concealed my emotions a little too well. "In the morning, I'll want to meet all of our new residents. Charlotte will be off to help her friend prepare for her wedding."

"Just in the morning," I assured. "I'll come back at night."

"We should build a baby nursery," Kachina said matter-of-factly. "I know you have your home in New York, but you should surely have one here. John's heir should be around his people."

The house John built made me reminisce about a less complicated time, when our dreams were simple and innocent. Raising my child in a palace was certainly more than I had ever anticipated, but constantly separating from our people was probably decreasing morale. "Yes, of course. That would be a wonderful project, and I'd love your help."

That little commitment was enough to brighten the room. Over time, other women would marry and help expand our empire. Our children would have friends to laugh and play with, in a land where they could be free to express themselves and their power. They would grow, have children of their own, and we'd truly be a nation.

There was only one uncertain obstacle to deal with. "Would you all mind clearing the room so we can talk to Dinah in private?"

Dinah's eyes widened a bit, and Tillie responded with a smirk full of villainy. "Absolutely." Tillie had the most obvious attitude, but they were all slow-footed, as if they had been waiting for John to return and give her a good tongue lashing.

Once the door closed behind them, Dinah had to grab her arms to stop herself from trembling. "I do apologize for deceiving you all this time."

John glared as he breathed righteous anger through his nostrils. I prepped myself for his fury. I think I even desired it, but he released his frustration with a sigh. "I understand why you did it. I don't understand keeping it from me this entire time. I thought we had more trust than that."

Dinah's lips quivered, and her eyes glistened. "The truth got away from me…" She held her throat as it rasped up, then whimpered. "When you live a lie for so long, you become terrified that the truth won't bring you freedom. Besides, I thought it might be better to be treated as a man."

Ironically, I don't think John would have been as soft-spoken if he thought she was a man. "I know you had different opinions about the boy, but he's in safe hands."

Dinah was fighting for dear life to keep those tears at bay. Eventually, she quickly brushed her finger across her face. She was so upset; her words were barely a whisper. "I trust you." Those words released an uncontrollable amount of shame, and she sobbed in her hands. I thought she might need comfort, but John nudged me back. I obeyed and gave her some time to compose herself. She took a few deep breaths and forced herself to stop shaking. Once she was composed, John nudged me forward.

"Now, are you going to apologize to my wife?"

She reluctantly transferred her gaze to my eyes. "It was a ridiculous thing to lie about. I was hurt and drunk. I was even afraid that we might lose John after losing two of my friends." Her heart was pulling on me like a child tugging on your leg. I wanted to trust her. I very much needed to, but I wasn't certain that she had learned her lesson.

And when I failed to respond, she turned to John. "I don't plan to disappoint you again. I'll keep my eyes on the mission for as long as you'll have me. Nothing has changed regarding my resolve. I'm still the same person who fought by your side."

Dinah held her breath as John, stoically, took a few steps forward. She jumped a bit when he placed his hand on her dainty shoulder. "You're an important part of our vision. What we've built here, we've done together. The others will come around in time. You'll have to give them reason to trust you again."

If I could trust anything about Dinah, it would have been that blooming smile. "Thank you, John." I offered a grin to affirm my husband's decision and let that be the end of it. Dinah gently bowed her head as the two of us walked beyond her.

John took my hand, and we rejoined the crowd as they finished their meals. We were congratulated by happy faces and hugs as soon as we stepped through the door. Adam spoiled our news, so word quickly spread in the community. John indulged the men in a celebratory drink, while I made small talk with the women. Evelyn was especially happy for me, and she expressed her desire to have a family. The way Adam kept looking over, I suspected we'd have another wedding to plan for in a few months. My child would be the beginning of a new generation, living free and boldly as their true self among people unafraid to do the same.

If she were a girl, Liberty would be a suitable name. I hoped to convince John of it. After all, he wasn't the one who would have to carry and birth her. But that was a discussion I planned to have later, when he was less emotional about it.

However, when we decided to retire for the night, John requested that I take him back to New York. I didn't question him. I began my nightly routine, and once I climbed into bed, expecting him to proposition me once more, he sat up against the headboard and spoke sternly, as if he had been stewing the whole night. "What's wrong with Lillian?"

"Do we have to argue about that now? We had the most wonderful day together."

"What's the difference in arguing now about it or later?"

I threw my head back and moaned. "You know I don't like your mother. You know what she did to us, and there's no need to rehash it. With that being said, make your case." I folded my arms and waited for his failure.

John's face tightened, and the intensity in his eyes increased. "She rescued me as a child from the zealots and took me in as her own. She didn't want to marry Mr. Cohen, but she wanted me to be safe and taken care of. I know she didn't always treat you as well as you wanted—"

"As well as I wanted—?"

"But she did look after you for twelve years!"

Anger stirred in me so fast. I had a dozen things to say, but I would have yelled them out. I had to calm myself if I wanted to seem reasonable in my rebuttal.

"She died rescuing me. She wasn't my blood, but she's the one I think of as my mother. It's too difficult to think about my birth mother. Every time I try to dwell on our good memories, it always turns into the night I watched her burn. And maybe that's wrong of me, as a son, but I was only a boy then. To be honest, I didn't have much of a world until you came into it."

The anger in me completely melted. I wished I could go back in time and hug him, but he was such an odd little boy. I wished I had understood his pain back then.

"When I met Lillian and took on her power, we were like kin. I don't expect you to understand it, but I think of her as my real family."

Oh, I understood it better than he thought. I didn't remember my mother or much of anything before Lady Cohen brought me to John. She gave me a name and responsibilities. She wasn't kind to Abby and her mother, but she wasn't cruel to the rest of us. I understood that I had special privileges around the plantation, and it made me feel like I was possibly close to being seen as a person. Perhaps that's why it hurt so much when she made it known that I was potential prey and set me up to be beaten. Her actions led Abby to run away and be mauled to death. He didn't see her chewed up and wheezing to death. John only experienced the warm nuzzle of a mother's embrace. I experienced her fangs. "When I think of Lady Cohen, I think of her covered in blood after butchering your uncles. She made me believe that I could be next if I stepped out of line. I think of being whipped."

"But I'm the one who did it!" John sank into his hands after bursting with frustration. I was stunned and gave him a moment to breathe, so he could ask the question that had been plaguing his mind since the two of us joined in holy matrimony. "Do you hate my mother, so you don't have to hate me?"

"Of course not, John!" I held my beloved's face and felt the shame he harbored every time he gazed at the scars on my back. I recalled the way his voice quivered when he told me to close my eyes. He desperately needed me to be strong, while each lash stripped something from him. "You didn't want to do it."

"I could have chosen differently, despite the consequences."

"No, John. It was my decision." Allowing Master Cohen to murder all of the slaves was unconscionable, and if John had murdered his father and uncles, we would have been hunted by the authorities and the zealots. It was better that only our masked versions were hunted by our enemies. "The past is the past. I don't hold it against you, so stop torturing yourself."

"If that's how you feel, then I want you to forgive my mother. If you can't do it for yourself or for her sake, I'd like for you to do it for me. She was important to me."

I was entitled to my rage. Lady Cohen rightfully earned it. But my husband looked so pathetic; his eyes were big and dopey like a pup begging for a bone. I knew within my soul that I deserved to hate her, but I also knew that John's soul needed my forgiveness.

And I didn't think he would accept that I had unless we named our daughter after that wretched woman. "I will consider it."

He stared for a few seconds, as if I were going to change my mind instantly. I stared harder, perhaps with too much aggression, and he kissed me on my cheek and mumbled, "Thank you."

Neither of us was interested in having intimacy then. I lay in my bed, wide awake and pondering about the past. He went off to war, and I was left to work in the field with Abby. I was never comfortable when Landon was nearby. If his eyes were any indication of the vile fantasies concocted in his mind, then I was violated at least a dozen times. After Master Cohen died, Lady Cohen brought me back inside the house. The Cohen men were not pleased, and I didn't feel safe. To make things worse, Abby was distraught after witnessing her father put a bullet in her mother's skull. She asked me to deliver a message of hate at his tombstone, but I couldn't bring myself to do it. When I returned home and found her body, she was relieved I didn't say anything. She said hate was tiring.

I rolled over and met John's eyes. I was going to scold him for staring, but he didn't need to hear me nag again. I decided to wrap my arm around him and lean on his chest. He stroked my hair like you would a cat. It could be a hassle, but at least it was soft. "Am I a good wife?"

"There's always room for improvement. Would you like a list?" I pinched his skin and twisted until he hissed. "Ow! Sheesh, woman! I was only teasing."

"Well, I'm being serious."

John gently pressed his forehead to mine and chuckled with the whimsical heart of a child. There was a magic sense of wonder to him as he caressed my cheek and his lips curled. "Charlotte, you are divine."

I don't know why I bashfully retreated into his chest, but I was satisfied with his answer. I wasn't angry at John—not for anything that happened on the plantation or afterward. His power and resolve could frighten me, but their possibilities also thrilled me. He was a terrifying force, but he was also gentle and thoughtful. He would do anything for me, so I decided never to allow another sun to go down upon my wrath.

Chapter Thirteen

Bright and early, I brought John to our territory and then went to the hotel. I blinked outside of Mary Anne's door and knocked. I was relieved when Cooper heard my voice and came out of the room next door. "I'm glad to see you and Mary Anne aren't living in sin."

"And I'm glad to see you're alive. Last I saw you, John was losing his mind."

"Charlotte!" Mary Anne opened her door and attacked me with her arms and gigantic belly. "We were so worried about you!"

"I'm fine. John is fine. The baby is fine."

She gasped wide enough to swallow an elephant. "My bosom sister is having a baby?" She held me tight and shook me real good. "Oh, Charlotte! What if we're having a boy and a girl, and our children fall in love and get married? Then we'd all be one family!"

"That's…a lot." Cooper peeled me away from his bride-to-be's grasp, and I was grateful to breathe again. "That is wonderful, Charlotte. I'm happy for you."

"Not happy enough for your son to marry my daughter."

“John seems like a very intense father-in-law, so that will be entirely up to Little Joseph…or Little Charlotte. We don’t know what they’ll be yet.”

“Have you decided on names?” Mary Anne squealed.

“Not exactly, but I’m not here to talk about my baby. I’m here to help plan your wedding, and we don’t have much time.” I visited Bess in the kitchen and acquired some coffee, bread, fruit, and bacon. Cooper and Mary Anne sat next to each other in her office, snuggling up like they had been together for ages. I sat across from them, taking important notes. The most crucial thing was Mary Anne’s dress. She had already designed something simple and comfortable for her belly. With my help, we were going to have it on her body within a week. Cooper was more than capable of finding himself a suit.

The ceremony was going to be short, ten to fifteen minutes. I was to be the maid of honor, and Cooper was going to have his brother, Elijah, be his best man. Cooper traveled to Chicago for his wedding, so it was only right for Elijah to do the same. His other brother, Isaiah, was a Union physician and couldn’t attend. Cooper hadn’t broken the news to his parents yet. He planned to do that in person with his bride. Cooper would find someone to officiate the wedding.

“How many guests should we expect?”

“Not very many,” Cooper said, perfectly serious. “Thirty would be the max.”

“Thirty? Are you mad? You’re one of the most respected men in town. Loads of people would want to celebrate your wedding, especially if we had free food and liquor afterward. We always throw the best parties.”

“Things have changed,” Mary Anne said, rather solemnly. “The Draft Riots frightened so many people. Folks Joseph used to know, and those who supported him largely left. Even for the men who stayed behind, I don’t think they’d want to risk the trouble of coming…”

She didn’t have to finish. Their faces made it all too clear that they had pondered and discussed the dangers of having a mixed marriage. I understood Cooper’s feelings, so I moved on.

The location was obvious. It was too cold to have it in the garden, so the ballroom would do perfectly. "We must have a reception, so I can dance with my husband."

"In your condition?" Cooper teased with a naughty curl of his luscious lips. His arm rested behind her on the rim of the chair, and he stroked her soft and creamy arm with every given opportunity.

"I'm pregnant, not dead, my love. You will dance with me."

"Well, if you insist…"

"Excuse me!" I snapped my fingers before the two of them nuzzled like animals. "We need to focus!" It became a pattern with the two of them. They were always close, touching one another, giggling, and whispering flirtatious remarks. They didn't argue once during the planning. They decided on a live band, food, floral arrangements, and everything, without even the slightest pushback, with one exception.

"John and I would like to pay for the wedding as our gift to you."

"No." Cooper was firm, and I wasn't surprised. "I don't need John's money. I can pay for everything."

Mary Anne dug her elbow into her beloved's ribcage. "It would be rude not to accept." I didn't pry into their personal finances, but Cooper wasn't pulling in money like he used to, and Mary Anne paid herself a modest salary as the landlord. John didn't care what they did with the hotel, as long as the bills were paid.

"Come on, Coop! What's the point of being friends with a bank robber's wife if you don't allow me to spoil you once in a while?" I didn't want Cooper and Mary Anne to hold back on anything due to expenses. I wanted their wedding to be a magical day they could look back on, when they were both old and gray, with no regrets. Besides, John and I didn't have a proper ceremony, and I was looking for a good occasion to dance. "You can still buy your own suit, if you want. And this way, that can be your focus."

Cooper's vanity practically had him salivating. "Fine then. I'll accept your generous gift." I swear, all he cared about was that suit. I also assigned him the tasks of hiring a band and inviting the guests. Mary Anne had no interest in reaching out to her family in the South. As far as she knew, a cousin had taken over her father's property, and she was just fine with that. Bess and Loretta were going to handle the food. It wasn't a banquet, but there would be plenty of cold meats, fruit, vegetables, bread, and my famous pies. They would also handle the decorations.

I charted out what needed to be done and what days the tasks needed to be completed. "When will Steve and Danny be home?"

"Danny has been honorably discharged due to his injury, and Steve was granted leave for a little while. They should be boarding a train tomorrow."

"Shouldn't we have a memorial for Sam? We'll all be together…" I nearly choked on those unbelievable words. I hated to sour their delightful mood or intrude on Mary Anne's big moment.

"Of course, we should." Mary Anne rubbed Cooper's hand for comfort. "I know what Sam meant to you all."

"We were torn up about it, but caring for Charlotte took priority. Grieving together is a good idea, but that's entirely up to Steve. He might not be ready to do anything without Sam's body." It was likely that Sam was buried by the Confederates and placed in a mass grave. If there were a memorial, it would have to take place the day after the wedding. Finding him any time soon simply wasn't possible.

I decided to focus on what I did know and what I could do. Mary Anne and I searched for a bridesmaid dress and outfits for the White House event. For the wedding, I found a burgundy gown that complemented my figure (while I still had one) and flowed at the hips. I planned to add some white lace on the trim and a bow on the waist. I also found a pair of white gloves that went just past my wrists. Since John was going to accompany me, I purchased a matching burgundy vest.

For the White House, I found a green velvet gown that hugged and flowed in all the right places. It was modest and hid the scars on my back and the base of my neck. A wonderful gold and emerald brooch brought the whole thing together. Mary Anne had a difficult time finding something grand and comfortable to wear. Much of what she liked was too snug for her waist, and she still had some growing to do. After her tenth dress at our third store, she had a completely mad idea while we rode together in a carriage. "We should make a dress ourselves."

"Absolutely, not. We don't have time. We have to make your wedding dress."

"We can dye my wedding dress after the reception!"

"I thought your mind would be ready for something else after the reception."

"Alright, *you* can wash and dye my dress. I certainly won't need it." Mary Anne was older than I, yet I often thought of her as my younger sibling. Despite the product of fornication growing in her womb, I had yet to get used to her giggling like a Greek nymph.

"Isn't it the custom to wear your dress for breakfast with your in-laws after the honeymoon?"

"Joseph won't be interested in that. Besides, he's got to get back to fighting." Mary Anne's tone turned rather melancholy. I didn't envy her predicament with Joseph's parents. The only time he went to visit them was when he paid back his loan and became the sole owner of the gym. He couldn't wait to sever that tie. I didn't anticipate Mr. Cooper making Mary Anne feel welcome, but I hoped for the best.

"Well, if it'll make you feel better, I will dye your dress." It was a bother, but I enjoyed watching her face brighten like the sun. She and Cooper were quite a handsome couple. I hoped the world would be ready for their grand debut.

It was my duty to make certain the blushing bride was as beautiful and regal as possible, given the time constraints. Luckily for Mary Anne and me, we were trained seamstresses. I didn't require patterns, and the silhouette was going to be simple enough. Mary Anne was a talented sketch artist. The fitted bodice would end at the waist and be cinched in by a delicate bow. From there, the cotton satin would flow to the floor. I measured, draped, and got to cutting. Generous seam allowances were considered for her condition.

After we cut our pieces, it was time for me to return home to my husband. He asked about my day, but I kept my recollection short for his sake. I was much more interested in his day of bonding with our new citizens. We had a doctor, among the newly liberated, so John interrogated him to see if he was fit to preside over my labor. I was most excited once he told me Adam was completely smitten with Evelyn. I suspected another wedding would be upon us soon.

Margaret and a few others also inquired about their families. John told them he would look into it, but he wasn't keen on accepting too many humans into our community. I asked John how he felt about inviting Cooper to live with us. He was not amused, to say the least. But if that was the only way to entice Mary Anne and her child, he agreed. With John's reluctant blessing, it was left up to me to persuade my friend.

The next few days were a blur. I hardly had any time to spend with the boys once they arrived, but Cooper entertained them. While I constructed the skirt, Mary Anne was busy with her in-laws. She cried a bit once she returned. They didn't say anything cruel to her, but she could tell the Coopers were disappointed in their son. I reminded her that Mr. Cooper always took issue with his youngest son and not to take it too personally, but that didn't make her feel any better. It took seeing the lace flowers brilliantly laid on her skirt to smile.

It brought me joy working with Mary Anne again. She was a talker and shared her adventures of being a landlord. The tenants and the city gave her grief from time to time, but she and Mick were resourceful. She asked questions about my life. I had plenty of adventures to share, and Mary Anne vowed to hate Dinah on my behalf. I mostly told her stories to see her expressive face and to hear her childlike giggle. I hadn't realized how much I had missed my dearest friend.

As for the dress, it wasn't too difficult to put together, but we certainly didn't want it to look like it had been pieced together in a few days. The seams and hems needed to be flawless. Every bow and button needed to be perfectly placed. The lace collar was the most difficult to get right, and it was pivotal. Mary Anne made her veil with wax orange blossoms, while I created a hairpiece. The morning of the wedding, John fetched fresh orange blossoms from the florist, and I bound them with ribbon for our bouquets.

Mary Anne's cheeks were pink, and her lips were blood red, as usual. It was such a lovely contrast with her raven locks and skin, creamy like a fresh glass of milk. Her long curls were pinned neatly, barely long enough to cover her scar. The lace detailing from her neck to her chest added a steamy allure while also displaying modesty. Cooper wasn't exaggerating when he said Mary Anne was one of the most beautiful women he had ever seen. As I accompanied her to the double doors of the ballroom, I kept thinking about how she looked like a princess stepping out of a fairytale. Mary Anne was the perfect angel, dressed in white cotton.

Steve and Danny stood at the doors, waiting for their musical cue. I was so relieved to see them on Cooper's big day. I had to fight off tears. I did a good job until Mary Anne took a deep breath and whimpered. "Don't tell me you're afraid."

"No. I'm just overwhelmingly happy." Mary Anne smiled and grabbed hold of my hand as if she would never let go. "Thank you."

"For what?"

"For not leaving me alone with John." Mary Anne's voice trembled. "I don't know what I'd be today if you had."

"Thank you for not walking out of Cooper's door to go find him. I don't know who I'd be without my sister."

We held our heads high and fanned our eyes. If I focused on how much I loved Mary Anne and how empty my life would have been without her, I would have broken down on that floor. That day wasn't about me. There was a wonderful man inside, and this was the beginning of their happily ever after.

The music inside slowed, and after a few notes, I recognized the tune. It was the same song that Cooper and I danced to in Five Points when I slipped and confessed that I loved him. I was still so very much in love with John; I didn't know what it meant to open up to another man. I was stunned by my words, even embarrassed that he noticed. But before I could even acknowledge what was spoken, Mary Anne stepped into our world, and it was never the same.

The doors opened wide, and a warm glow filled the hall. Willie and the crew made certain every chandelier, glass object, and wooden surface was polished and shone for days. The light was softened by draped fabric and brought to life with greenery dispersed throughout the room. The decorative flowers and vases were all very beautiful, but paled in comparison to the sea of black faces that met us as we walked down the aisle.

I recognized the barbers who did the boys' hair, and the shoemaker who made the boots I danced in with Cooper. I saw bricklayers and masons who helped build my room in his gym, and cooks who fed us when I was too busy or had a taste for something different. There were writers and local abolitionists who passed on valuable information to Cooper, so I could do my work as Runaway. There were service workers who came to the gym to learn how to defend themselves and entrepreneurs who invested in Cooper's vision. The faces that laughed and danced with us at Harvey's were wholesome echoes of the past. There certainly weren't enough chairs for all of the onlookers, or enough food. There were well over a hundred people.

Mary Anne squeezed me tighter, and my eyes were bound to the love of her life. I always loved Cooper's smile, and it was no less than stellar as he gazed upon his blushing bride. Mary Anne could hardly stand it and whispered, "He's so handsome!" Cooper wore an expertly tailored black wool frock coat and vest that complemented his physique. He looked so fancy with his silk cravat and golden pocket watch. I was surprised he resisted the temptation of a top hat.

Cooper reached for Mary Anne, and she stood in awe for a few seconds, as if she couldn't believe this handsome prince truly belonged to her. I had to kiss her hand and nudge her off. But even as I let go, she tugged on me once more and looked my way with big eyes. I didn't know whether she was seeking my blessing or needed a final push of encouragement, so I gave her a heartfelt smile and nodded. Then she let me go and took Cooper's hand.

"There are so many people here," she whispered.

"They wanted to pay their respects." If you had asked Cooper before the wedding, he likely would have said he didn't care if his parents were present, but his momma seemed so sweet, dabbing tears with a handkerchief. His other brother, Isaiah, managed to attend after all and sat with them in the front row. He and Elijah had such pride in their eyes. Mr. Cooper, on the other hand, was like a stone.

As the chaplain spoke about the holy covenant of marriage, Cooper and Mary Anne fell deeper into each other's gaze. While most of the audience watched them, John's eyes were on me. I was grateful to be longed for, but I never could have been truly happy if my friends couldn't experience something similar. "Joseph and Mary Anne, you may now declare your vows before God and the witnesses."

Mary Anne began to tremble. "I'm so nervous. I'm not as good with words as Charlotte."

I considered coaching her, but Cooper spoke so tenderly. "They're your words, Mary Anne. No one else can speak for you."

She bashfully smiled, then took a deep breath to calm her racing heart. "Joseph, you cared for me when I was only a stranger. You nurtured my potential before I was even a friend. That's what you do. That's why all of these people are here for you. You're a good man, Joseph Cooper, and I needed your goodness. You and Charlotte changed my life!" Mary Anne stunned me by turning around and grabbing my hand again. "Words could never be sufficient to express my gratitude, but I'll live my life pouring my whole heart into my duties as a wife, a mother, and a friend."

Cooper was a lot more solemn than expected. He wasn't even smiling, and the atmosphere shifted into something intense. "Mary Anne, you were there for me when no one else was. You stayed by my side when you didn't have to. If I've ever come across as unappreciative of your sacrifice, I apologize." He recovered Mary Anne's missing hand and pulled her close until their eyes kissed. "I want you to know that I've always seen you—the real you."

I think she meant to smile, but she burst into tears and fell on his shoulder, quietly sobbing. That didn't stop him from speaking in her ear, loud enough for me and the rest of the wedding party to hear. "I noticed how hard you try to make people feel safe and loved. You did your best to make Charlotte smile when her heart was closed off. You gave me your ear when I needed counsel about her, despite your own feelings toward me. I noticed your tenacity and willingness to push yourself beyond your comforts. You wanted to prove that you weren't wasting our kindness and mentorship, and your strength has become incalculable. You've broken from a cycle of hate from your family, and you seek to make a better world for our child and our country."

He lifted Mary Anne's head and signaled his brother. Elijah pulled a hinged leather box from his pocket. The interior was lined with crimson velvet. It held a sacred treasure, a golden band nesting a blood-red ruby even richer than her quivering lips. "I do love you, Mary Anne, but more importantly, I trust you."

The ring was not small. It dulled and darkened in Cooper's steady hands, but once he placed it on her trembling finger, the light set it ablaze. "I, Joseph Aaron Cooper, for as long as I live, vow to make you and our child my priority. I swear this as a man before God."

I was fairly certain the chaplain was supposed to say something next, but Mary Anne's feelings got the better of her, and she kissed him long enough for the young chaplain to clear his throat and skip to the end. "With the power vested in me, I now pronounce you husband and wife."

The crowd applauded and wooed once Cooper dipped Mary Anne. Mr. Cooper was still stone cold, but his boys and Cooper's friends hollered in excitement. I waited patiently for all of the guests to congratulate the newlyweds. The uninvited guests understood that we weren't prepared for them and didn't expect to stay for the extra festivities. They came to shake money into Cooper's hand or slyly stuffed his pockets. They talked about Mary Anne's beauty and reminisced about the glory days. Many thanked Cooper for his service and bravery. Many asked about Mary Anne's pregnancy and wished for a healthy baby.

After Isaiah made his way through the receiving line, he curiously looked me over, and I returned the gesture. "You are exactly how Joseph described."

"Funny, he didn't say much about you."

"Oh?" His lips curled. "My baby brother didn't talk about his brilliant, handsome brothers who graduated from a prestigious medical school and—?"

"Oh, you are related!" He wasn't quite as handsome as Cooper, but he had an inch or two on him. When I hugged Isaiah, he certainly didn't feel as solid as his brother, but he was fit. "I thought you couldn't pull away from your duties."

"The army insisted. My little brother has made quite the impression."

Cooper's parents came to greet the couple next. Mrs. Cooper was buttoned up, with a golden cross being the flashiest detail. Her face retained a youthful glow. If I didn't know any better, I would have thought she was an older sister. "You look so beautiful," she said to Mary Anne. "And your dress is stunning."

Cooper raised his head, elated by his mother's approval. "Mary Anne is an impressive seamstress. She made it with Charlotte."

"Yes, I remember hearing much about Charlotte..."

I grinned hard, though I wanted to disappear.

"You did the right thing," Solomon said to his son as he patted his shoulder. "The honorable thing by Mary Anne."

"And she's a great woman," Elijah interjected, trying to ease the tension on his brother's face. "We're blessed to have her as a new addition to the family."

It was painful, waiting for more words to be said between Cooper and his father. All the boys favored him, and they were blessed with height, broad shoulders, and healthy bodies. No one was as large as Joseph, but his father had an intimidating demeanor. But I wasn't afraid of him.

"Charlotte, may I borrow you?" John was so quick to grab the back of my arm. I didn't even see him move from the corner of the room. I very well couldn't refuse my husband, so I reluctantly joined him, away from their ears. "You are prying in matters that don't concern you."

"Coop is my friend."

"Relationships between fathers and sons are complicated. You worry about what you can handle, like this reception." I didn't want to leave it at that, but John was right about my obligations. It was time to herd the uninvited guests out. Cooper's parents left with the big crowd and went back to Brooklyn. John helped to arrange the tables and chairs, so we'd have plenty of space to dance. Willie, Bess, and Loretta began serving food. Mary Anne rested her feet, and I personally brought over a plate. Cooper remarked that having my sweet potato pie made the occasion extra special. John was annoyed that there wasn't an apple, as if I had time for that.

As soon as the band struck up a lively song, I grabbed John's hand and dragged him to the dance floor. He didn't put up a fight like Cooper used to. "Do I need to teach you, Mr. Cohen?"

"You underestimate me, woman." He took a firm hold of my waist, and I swooned. He had excellent rhythm, and he seemed familiar with the communal dances. John never stepped on my feet, every twirl and lift was perfect, and he was particularly graceful during the waltz.

"You've never danced with me before. Where did you learn this?"

"My mother." I wasn't surprised. Lady Cohen knew all there was to know about being a lady, so it only made sense that she conditioned her son for ballroom.

"You taught me piano, but you didn't teach me how to dance?"

"Oh, you never *learned* how to play piano. I *tried* to teach you."

"I am not that bad!" I slapped his chest, and he laughed. I certainly couldn't play well enough for a party like that. Even the expert fiddlers would have been thrown off by my clumsy timing. I was a much better dancer than musician, anyhow.

When the music slowed down, Mary Anne stopped stuffing her face and danced with her beloved. As John and I glided across the floor, I kept my eyes on her dreamy face. She had the look of a woman who had gotten everything she ever wanted, and Cooper was glad to know he gave it to her.

"Perhaps we got married too hastily. I should have given you a grand wedding."

After I promised to marry John, I blinked to Ripley, Ohio. I knew there was a fine dress shop there, and I found a plain white cotton one in my size. The shopkeepers remembered me and were thrilled to serve my needs. Then I traveled South to our magnolia tree. It was broken from our fight, but flowers continued to bloom. I created a bouquet and placed a few in my hair. I still felt like I hadn't done enough, but John was in awe.

John found us a little chapel to exchange our vows in. A minister wedded us, and a shopkeeper and her son served as our witnesses. As a thank you, we often shopped in her store. That's where John always purchased my tea.

"No, everything was perfect, John." I could have jumped over a broom and been satisfied. I never dreamed of my wedding day. I dreamed of my marriage. "Our life is perfect."

After Mary Anne's first dance, other men wanted a chance to dance with the bride. Isaiah, Elijah, and Steve all had a turn. Even Big Willie got a little one-on-one time. Cooper was fine talking with his guests while she bounced around the dance floor. Danny talked with him for a while, but his eyes wandered to the dance floor often. Cooper encouraged him, and he eventually hobbled over to me.

"May I cut in?"

John gave him the most disrespectful eyes I had ever seen. "You may not."

"John!" I seethed. "This is my friend who was in the Battle of Olustee."

"So, you endangered my pregnant wife?"

"No," Danny nervously laughed, "that would be Coop. I just benefited from her bravery."

John sneered and looked so mean. I hoped Danny thought it was out of jealousy and didn't pick up on how prejudiced John was against humans. "Let me dance with my friends for a little while. We have a lifetime to dance together." I eased toward Danny before John could shoot him down.

The tempo was a little fast for him, so I slowed my pace. I also did my best to let Danny lead. It was awkward with his cane, and he winced here and there, but at least he didn't step on my feet. "I'm sorry. I'm not as good as I used to be."

"You're here. That's all that matters."

John remained on the dance floor with his arms folded. It was comical how little he wanted to socialize. He very well knew how to speak to humans and blend in. He just didn't want to. As soon as the song was over, he meant to take me back, but Cooper had been watching from afar and rushed to tap my shoulder. "Would you appease the groom with a dance?"

Oh, I felt John's glare before I had the courage to look. Cooper thought it was hilarious. "Come on, my love. One dance with a friend."

"Come on, John." Mary Anne came to our rescue and pulled on his arm. "We haven't danced in a long time."

John wasn't ungentlemanly enough to refuse a pregnant bride. And since Mary Anne wasn't human, he didn't have to be disgusted the whole time. He was annoyed with the arrangement at first, but they began to converse with one another. She even said something that made him laugh.

"Should we be worried?" Cooper asked. "They were once betrothed."

"We'll have to keep a close eye on them." Mary Anne was slowing down. She only had maybe one more dance in her. Besides, I had to get her out of that dress, remove the lace, then wash and dye the fabric.

"It'll be interesting traveling together to Washington. This party is supposed to be a catalyst for change."

"I know. It's not every day you get to meet the president."

"There's more to it than that." Cooper was serious; he spoke as if he wanted me to feel the gravitational pull of each syllable. "Lincoln is under a lot of pressure right now, due to the war and his reelection. He needs to win his second term, and after that, he wants Congress to abolish slavery before the war ends."

I nearly gasped. I had wished for such a thing to happen, but I knew better than most how resistant the country was to such change. "What happens if he can't make Congress act before then?"

"Many Americans, even in the North, are not ready for abolition. They accept it as a means to cripple the South and win the war, but many are prejudiced and don't want to compete with free blacks. They also fear things like this."

"You mean mixed marriages?" Cooper nodded, and it made me so angry. It's not as though whites and blacks hadn't been making children for ages. When it was a little bastard slave child who could be used like Abby or Dinah, they didn't pay any mind to them. It was only a threat when they were born out of love and mutual respect. Cooper must have been worried about his child, who was soon to be born into our intolerant world.

"If abolition doesn't happen before the war ends, it might not happen at all. Lincoln is going to make some moves, and this party is a ploy to soften the hearts of power players in Washington. He wants to display our courage and conviction. Hopefully, it will inspire our politicians to find a bit of both to finish the fight."

"I believe they have plenty of courage and conviction to do the wrong thing. They don't need courage. They need shame."

"Well, I pray your moral clarity is contagious."

I didn't have much time to enjoy the dance. We didn't even get halfway through the song before Mary Anne wobbled over while rubbing her belly. "Mind if we trade? I think I'm near the end of my night, and I'd like to be with my husband again."

"Of course not." I rejoined my husband, prompting a big smile. He held me close and took in my scent. He truly was greedy for me, and I didn't mind. "Mary Anne gave you a good laugh. What did she say?"

"I inquired about her joining us, and she complimented me for not fearing that her superior power would emasculate me in the eyes of our people."

"Oh, dear." I tried to hold in my laughter, but even John thought it was amusing. Mary Anne looked so sweet, leaning on her husband's chest as they rocked back and forth.

"She's really become something else. I blame you."

Maybe it was a little bit my fault, but Mary Anne certainly wasn't an angel when she tried to seduce him in the past. But her arrogance steadily grew over time. "When you have that sort of power, it's likely to go to your head. You know that better than anyone else."

Cooper looked over our way, and our eyes locked. I truly was proud of him for keeping good on his word when it came to Mary Anne. I had never seen her so happy. More importantly, she was right about needing Cooper's goodness.

"I'm glad Cooper kept his conversation with you professional." There was almost a threat in John's voice.

"I want us all to be friends. You can get to know him better on the train."

"I know plenty about him."

"Knowing of a person isn't the same as actually knowing him. Please, promise me you'll behave."

He pouted, as if he contemplated the opposite. "I promise."

"Good." I pecked his lips, though I felt a bit guilty. I didn't plan on being particularly well-behaved. He was going to hate my plan, so I had to keep him in the dark for the meantime.

I took John to the mansion and told him I would pick him up in the morning. He needed to brief Dinah on our plans, and I would be working well into the night on Mary Anne's dress. Cooper moved his party to the parlor so he could play cards with the boys. He said he would give us a few hours and then expected to spend time alone with his wife.

"I'm sorry for all this trouble," Mary Anne said as we began to remove the lace. It wouldn't dye well, so we had to handle it separately.

"Oh, don't worry. You'll make it up to me tonight."

"How so?"

I blinked home and retrieved a bag from the closet. When I returned, I removed the velvet gown and laid it across the bed like a mad scientist. "We're going to change my dress."

Chapter Fourteen

We didn't have access to or knowledge of what happened to Sam's body, but Steve wanted to say goodbye to his brother with a few of his friends. In the morning, Cooper, Mary Anne, Steve, and Danny rode in a carriage to the site of Cooper's gym. John and I followed behind in a separate carriage. We had a small ceremony. Steve had a photograph of us all together at the gym before they left for war and before Mary Anne showed up. We lit a few candles and traded stories about Sam and Dave.

It was difficult to be back there with Cooper, knowing the world we built together was burned to the ground. All of us, except for John, wandered around in horror at what had been destroyed and awe at what remained. But at the same time, it was nice to see Cooper standing in the middle of the rubble while holding Mary Anne's hand. He was happier than when I found him in Beaufort, and despite us being there to honor the dead, Mary Anne was glowing from the new life inside of her.

John stood beside me the whole time and didn't say a peep until after we said a final prayer together. "Daniel…"

Danny gulped as John stretched his hand with an intensity in his blue eyes. A white light came into John's palm, and he squealed like a frightened kitten. He took a few steps back and bumped into Steve. Danny was flabbergasted, touching himself and shaking until he was certain. Once he knew there was no pain, he hollered. "My leg!"

They all stared in disbelief at John, while he gazed at them blank-faced. "If I ever grant you the opportunity to dance with my wife again, I hope you'll be a better partner."

Danny nodded with the pace of a sloth, completely unsure if the moment was real. John didn't speak again. He walked out of what was left of the front door, expecting me to follow. Cooper had to elbow Danny to pull him back to reality. "Thank you, John!"

I was a bit in awe myself. John was so nonchalant about the whole ordeal. If I hadn't brought it up in the carriage, I don't think we ever would have talked about it. "That was a real kind thing you did for Danny. You just changed his whole life."

"Well, he's important to you…"

I cuddled up next to my husband, experiencing a mix of immense gratitude and guilt. I knew he would try to understand the scheme I cooked up with Mary Anne, but it would be difficult. He was even going to be furious. I needed a little bit of time, but I would let him know the truth before I pulled the trigger. I prayed that when the time finally came, he would understand.

Mary Anne's dress dried overnight. We spent the day sewing the lace detailing back in. The ivory flowers contrasted beautifully against the Prussian blue, and the dress matched Cooper's uniform closely. She was going to look like a real princess, and more importantly, she was married to her child's father and wouldn't appear to be a scandal.

When the evening came, we set sail on the ferry to New Jersey and caught our train to DC. It was going to take about twelve hours to arrive. It was the first time John and I traveled so far like ordinary humans. We thought it was important to create a paper trail and plausible transportation paths. John, like Lady Cohen, desired privacy and purchased a car.

The oil lamps were lit low, the benches were abandoned, and the room was filled with the hum of the locomotive. About an hour after departure, the staff brought us supper. About an hour afterward, they returned to help convert our benches for sleeping. John and Cooper weren't tired, but Mary Anne and I barely had any sleep after sewing our dresses for the past week. I was still determined to do a little bit of reading before bed, but John swiped my book and told me to take better care of his baby. I gave him a good glare for committing such an egregious sin, but I agreed to be obedient on one condition. "You be nice to Cooper while I sleep."

"I don't plan to be a bother to anyone."

"I don't want you to ignore him. I want you to be nice."

With a blank face, John tossed his side of the blanket over my head. By the time I pulled it down, he had already pulled the privacy curtain to block my vision of him. I did need to sleep and mind my baby's health, so there was no need to chase after him.

I was the first to sleep and the last to wake up in the morning. I got dressed just before the porter came with our morning meal. Bread was wrapped in soft linen, tea and coffee were served in fine china, and we had our choice of pork or smoked fish. John and Cooper took both options. I sat with Mary Anne during breakfast, and the boys retreated to empty benches. Perhaps they had words while I slept, but other than that, they were quiet like the dead.

There was no escaping each other's presence once we got off the train and shared a carriage. Mary Anne was the first one in, and John helped me next. I decided to spice things up and took my seat next to Mary Anne. The boys both had similar flashes of annoyance on their faces once they realized their predicament. They folded their arms and tried not to look at each other.

It was a mercifully short journey, less than twenty minutes to Pennsylvania Avenue. I had been across the nation and seen men in uniform armed with bayonets, but it felt more significant to be in the nation's capital. We were in the heart of the Union stronghold, and the home of the Commander was like a beacon of strength and hope.

We stayed at the Willard, which was only a five to ten-minute walk to the White House. It was bustling with men in fine suits and soldiers in uniforms. I shuffled around in the cushy carpet while observing the dark polished wood and high ceilings. There was a smoky glow in the room as the guests enjoyed their morning cigars and gossiped. John and Cooper took note of every face, pistol, and exit.

"What is she doing here?" Cooper's eyes darted to Dinah, disguised as Steven, drinking coffee with a group of men in the lobby. Dinah glanced at us, then ignored our presence.

"She's busy working," John said quietly. Senators, congressmen, aides, and foreign dignitaries stayed at the Willard. One little touch, and all their secrets belonged to her. Dinah was always good at engaging with a crowd. I wondered how many times, while she worked the room in her father's harem, did she envy her brother's place. I was surprised to see his face again, but it was the skin she was likely most comfortable in.

Before going upstairs, John scheduled a time for a fine meal to be brought to our rooms. The bellhop wanted to carry our bags, but John and Cooper insisted they do it themselves. Mary Anne's room was a few doors down from mine. John and I had a suite to ourselves. I wasn't sleepy, but the first thing I did was lie out on one of the two beds. It was far more forgiving than the train. It was a shame I wasn't tired. "You should sleep. You didn't get much on the train, and I need the father of my baby to be alert."

"That's not a bad idea." John must have been tired since he didn't argue. He took off his clothes and neatly placed them in a drawer. "Don't wander around the hotel. Wake me in four hours to eat. We should keep our energy up for tonight. Will you have my suit steamed?"

"Of course." As he climbed in, I got out. It was my job as his wife to make certain our clothes were in pristine condition. I tailored John's suit myself, so he was going to look perfect. When it came to me, I was a bit conflicted. If I wore the green velvet dress, I didn't need to steam it. I could wait until the very last minute and not afford my husband the proper time to oppose it. I also brought a backup dress: a sweet, pleated silk pink dress with ruffles. That would need to be steamed.

John had already dozed off by the time I decided on what I was going to do. I sent our clothes off to the Willard staff, and Mary Anne did the same. In the meantime, I sectioned my hair into pieces, softened it with pomade, and wrapped it in rag curls.

Then, I relaxed in a robe and read until I was hungry. I woke my husband just before noon. A few minutes later, Dinah came to our door still wearing the appearance of her deceased brother. Shortly after she arrived, a bellhop rolled in a cart with linen and silverware for our small dining table. By the time he was done setting it, another bellhop rolled in with a cart of food. They also did the same for Mary Anne and Cooper. Eating in the room gave my curls more time to set, and it offered us privacy.

Our first course was a bowl of turtle soup. I wasn't too keen on trying it, but Dinah insisted it was delicious. John liked it too, so I succumbed to their pressure. It was odd, but a good mix between chicken and pork with a briny taste as well. Next, we had poached salmon followed by roasted duck. Once John saw that I was reaching for a fruit tart before finishing my plate, he fussed. "You better feed my baby those peas."

I glared. "If our baby wanted peas, I would crave them, and I don't want any peas."

"It's good for the baby, so eat all the peas and turnips."

Dinah got a good chuckle out of us. "Is it going to be this way for poor Charlotte the entire pregnancy?"

"Can you believe he wants me to do this ten times?"

"John, that's preposterous. How is a busy man like you going to raise ten children?"

Dinah posed a perfectly rational question, and John grew frustrated the longer we waited for a reasonable answer. "I like peas and turnips, so my child will like peas and turnips, and they're good for you. This child needs to be healthy and strong."

I shook my head but succumbed to my beloved's pressure. I wished I still had some potatoes to mask their flavor, but I powered through it. "Have you enjoyed your spy time, Dinah?"

"I have. The frustrations with Lincoln are palpable. Humans have weak hearts and stomachs. They need an end to the war or at least a decisive victory to lift their spirits."

Cooper's words about the party weighed heavily on me. Dinah clearly didn't care much for humans, but as a fellow former slave, I wondered if she cared about abolition. "What are the odds Congress votes to amend the Constitution to end slavery?"

"Immediately? Very low. They aren't hungry for it, and Lincoln doesn't possess that sort of political capital to push it through."

I didn't respond, and I tried not to look too disappointed. In my mind, I was more resolved in what I had to do.

"Did you gather enough information on the White House layout?" John asked.

"Yes, I know it well. I can blink right inside."

"Good. You'll hang back for the first hour. We'll keep our eyes peeled for danger and act if necessary. You'll arrive, shake some influential hands, and see if Lincoln offers to meet with you later in private. And if there's any trouble, I want you to blink back here. I'll neutralize the threat and meet you after the party."

"Understood." Dinah had taken my face many times, but she had never pretended to be me. I was nervous about her performance as Runaway, but it was something I needed her to do. Charlotte Cohen had quite the task of her own to pull off.

John decided to canvass the area. Dinah knew the area well enough, so she stayed close for our safety and wandered around the hotel. I had the staff remove our dishes and bring a portable hip bath. I brought my concoctions from home to make myself fragrant. Once I was done, I polished my skin with almond oil, rubbing it generously on my knees and elbows. Mary Anne was kind enough to come over and rub cocoa butter on my back, taking her time to massage life into every welt and crease.

"Have you told John what you're doing yet?"

"No," I confessed through a pillow.

"That's a bad call." I moaned as the pressure of her palms increased. It had been a long time since I had one of her masterful massages, and she had a talent for getting all the knots out. "If John still has my powers, he's going to blow something up."

"I'm going to talk to him." A bellhop brought our clothes after I finished with the bath. I laid them out on John's bed, so the dress's frills were staring right at me. "I could always wear the pink one."

"I'm surprised you own something so sweet. Doesn't seem like you at all."

"I can be a sweet lady."

"You're a warrior, Charlotte, in every possible way." Mary Anne's fingers trailed down my back one final time, and I recognized every scar she grazed. Each lash was such a terrible experience, but it paled in comparison to watching John be whipped on my behalf and Maddison's murder. Even though I was a slave, I thought I had a sense of freedom by being favored by John and Lady Cohen. Those lashes were a reminder that no matter how comfortable you are in captivity, someone can always rattle your cage. Only true liberation was acceptable.

I sat up and covered myself with a robe, feeling relief in my back and shoulders. "I certainly miss your magic touch."

"Well, you can blink to the hotel and get a massage whenever you like."

"Or you could come stay with me." I wrapped my arm around Mary Anne and clutched onto her shoulder. "We can raise our children together, and Coop can have a nice plot of land to make his own. I've already talked to John about letting him stay. He could be among the human representatives in our community. It can be like old times, us against the world."

"I would love that…" Mary Anne had a smile on her face, but it carried a terrible burden. "But I can't do that, Charlotte."

"Why?" I wasn't angry that my friend rejected me, but I assumed she allowed her arrogance to blot out any good sense. "You know if zealots ever find out what you can do, they'll do their best to kill you."

"Their best isn't good enough."

"Mary Anne, this isn't a game!" Peter and Hotah weren't as strong as Mary Anne, but they were strong, and John could have also died in our last battle. "We just lost two of our people to the Overseers. What if a new group of zealots rises with more ways to get rid of our powers?"

"The zealots aren't the only danger in this world." She rubbed her belly and longed to hold her growing child. "My husband is a Union soldier, and he's fighting in the bloodiest war our nation has ever seen. He could die. It's likely he will, and if he does, he will die as an American. Our child is an American, and that's what I choose to be. I don't begrudge you for wanting to start a new nation, but if this is the country my husband dies fighting for, then I want to die in it, too."

It was a hard truth that I didn't care to be reminded of. If it were up to me, I'd swoop them both up and put them under my protection. But Mary Anne had such a strong resolve in her blue eyes. "You're normally so cheery. I didn't expect such a grim explanation."

"I read the papers. Joseph is optimistic and determined to come home to us, but I'm not a fool. I'm prepared for a long life with the man I love, but I'm also prepared for the worst." Mary Anne took my hand and clasped it like she was about to recite a prayer. "Do you believe war with humans is the only possible outcome? War is such a terrible thing."

"I can't say for certain." I hated that I couldn't smile through an optimistic prediction of the future, but I had seen and experienced too much of the world to live naively. "John always believed that the United States wouldn't be able to help itself. Just like the Egyptians enslaved and sought to kill the children of the Israelites when they had grown too numerous and powerful in their land, the same would happen to us. I hope that he's wrong, but human nature doesn't change. Gaining power and being prepared to strike back only makes sense. I don't know if that war will happen in my lifetime, but I'd rather not burden my children with that future. I'd rather find a way to have peace."

"And what about John? What does he want?"

"What he wants is irrelevant." I pulled from Mary Anne's grasp and rubbed my belly, while imagining a beautiful child who looked like her father. "He'll do whatever it takes to keep his family safe. Whether that's through war, peace, or a massacre is entirely up to the people of this great land."

Mary Anne had an uneasy look on her face, but she gently nodded as the consequences of my words rested in her mind. "Cooper thinks Lincoln is a good man."

"Well, he needs to be more than a good man to impress John because he doesn't believe such a thing exists."

"Not even Joseph qualifies?"

"I fear our former relationship skews John's opinion." It was frustrating, but John wasn't interested in friendship, and

Cooper didn't seem too keen on it either. "Perhaps tonight will give them a chance to bond and appreciate one another."

"I hope so." Mary Anne slid off the bed and stood on her feet. "Well, I've got to prepare for tonight. Thank you for helping with my dress."

"Thank you for helping with mine." It did seem wrong not to wear the green dress after Mary Anne delayed her wedding night to help me. I was proud of it, but I became more terrified of John's reaction the closer I got to the party. I tried to calm my nerves with a good book, but I was too nervous to remember what was on the page. I might have lasted ten minutes before I gave up and lay in the bed, paralyzed by John's future rage. That silly pink dress would offer a night of peace, but that's not what I wanted.

I waited a little while longer, then continued preparing for the party. I laid out my powders and pastes on the desk and made up my face. I applied everything lightly: rice powder to reduce the shine, burnt cork on my lash lines, rouge for my cheeks, and beeswax mixed with berry for my lips.

Next, I tackled my hair. It was very curly once I removed the rags. I pinned most of it up but sectioned the back of it off so it draped down, no further than my collarbone. The gold and emerald necklace I brought was large enough to cover the scar on the base of my neck, but you could never be too careful. I finished the look by sewing the flowers I used for the wedding into my hair.

There was nothing left to do except embrace the mischief I had sewn. I wore a hoop skirt and a petticoat to give some volume. For the top layer, I couldn't wear anything underneath. The bodice was modified with boning to add structure, and it was padded and lined to be comfortable. As I looked into the full mirror, I was pleased. My chest was well defined, yet modest. My shoulders were bare, yet tasteful. The sleeves extended just past my elbows and were decorated with intricate gold embroidery: acanthus leaves, looping vines, and floral rosettes. All in all, it was a beautiful dress that I could be proud of.

The door handle began to jiggle, and I hopped back in a panic. I held my stomach and my breath, bracing for what was to come.

The door slowly opened, and my husband came in with a basket and a bright smile. "I brought you some pastries..." John stood stupefied, barely capable of shutting the door behind him. His eyes twinkled, and he forgot how to utter human speech. He muttered and giggled like a child understanding music for the first time. John set the basket down on the dining table and nearly rushed me. "You look divine—"

"Stop!"

John's feet froze in place. His hands were prepped as if he were going to grab me. Surely, he wasn't going to rip the dress off an hour before Lincoln's party! "Do you not like it?" He noticed the pink dress on the bed. "This one fits your personality much better, Charlotte. You're stunning."

His flattery was unsettling my stomach. I could barely look at him. "Please, do not be angry with me. Try to understand."

A little bit of worry settled in his voice. "Understand what?"

I held my head high, anticipating his grief. It pierced my chest, and I clutched onto it, hoping to regain my breath. I wanted to be confident and persuasive, but as I turned around and revealed my bare back, I trembled.

Silence thickened like molasses until I could hardly breathe. I expected rage so all-consuming that it would scorch the oxygen between us, but all I felt was the chilled air on my open back. The only sound for a good while was my quiet, panicked huffs of air, until an unexpected thud shook the floor.

I jumped and turned to face my husband. He had collapsed on his knees, wide-eyed and pale like a ghost. The horror and grief on his face were distinct, like we had been pulled back to the moment when he cradled my bloody body in his arms. "Charlotte, you mustn't wear this! It's indecent!"

"Indecent?" I recalled the crisp ripping sound as his hands tore my dress and exposed me to his monstrous family. They witnessed my shame and reveled in my torture. "No, what they allow to happen to slaves is what's indecent. That look of shame on your face? That's what I need them to experience!"

John couldn't muster any fight in him. His mind traveled back to that awful day when he split my back open, ten excruciating times, and held my shaking body in his arms. The pain was so severe that I could only see the ache in John's eyes. "Are you punishing me?"

The fury within me shattered, and I quivered from his torment. "Sweetheart, no." I held John's face and pulled him toward me, so he'd have no choice but to rise on his feet again. "I love you, and I would never do that to you."

"Then why do you want to show them what I did to you?" The poor boy looked so miserable; I didn't know what else to do but wrap my arms around him. He wouldn't return the gesture.

"John, I meant what I said about forgiving you. I don't want to cause you any pain, but this is bigger than us." I eased my grip so John could see my eyes as I pleaded. "Cooper told me this party could influence Congress to abolish slavery. That's Lincoln's aim. If my scars can make them see—if putting a face to the pain can make blacks human in their eyes—then I have to do this. If I have the power to make a change, then I'm obligated to bring it to pass."

"Charlotte…" Dear Lord, he was shaking. "I don't know if I…" Shame took his breath, but I knew what he was too proud to ask. Perhaps if I were a kinder woman, I would have relented and put on the pink gown. But we would have never forgiven ourselves, and the added shame would have been intolerable for him.

"You're not the only man who was ever forced to do something that split your soul apart. This evil thing that we've allowed to fester in this nation has created victims and monsters, sometimes both. It's hardened the hearts of so many and taken the lives of women and little children." My voice faltered at the memory of Abby's wheezing and how close she was to freedom when the dogs tore her down. Steven found his courage just in time to die. How dare I even consider not living as boldly and loudly as I could?

"I can't guarantee that making these powerful people face their evil will soften their hearts, but even if I can't change their hearts, they deserve to see it and live with the consequences."

As John lowered his head and gently pressed it against mine, the weight of his pain was like a locomotive on my mind. I felt guilty for exposing such a terrible wound. But I couldn't remove his burden. I could only lighten the load. "We can't change past mistakes. We can only atone for them while we still have time. I need you to trust me and stand by my side in defiance of these unjust laws and the cowards who uphold them."

John's body had calmed, but his eyes seemed distant, as if he were still trapped in the past.

"No one has to know what you did. I promise, John, I won't tell another soul."

He took a quiet, yet deep and uneasy breath. Then, another. Slowly, the pressure began to fall away. "The pink one…" John's voice wavered. "…is much too sweet for you anyhow."

I fought back tears and jabbed John in his chest. He chuckled. "Hurry and get dressed."

John didn't take much time preparing himself. I ate a few pastries while he quickly washed, then I helped him with his clothes. The charcoal frock and trousers truly brought out his pretty blue eyes. The frock was single-breasted with narrow lapels, tailored close through the waist. His vest was a dark olive, and his cravat was a shade darker, matching my gown. I made certain his high collar was perfectly placed. A gold pocket watch and his signet ring were the proper finishing touches. "You look handsome."

"Handsome?" John's arms wrapped around my waist as he smiled. "But I called you divine."

"Well, you'll have to work on catching up to me." I nearly collapsed when his lips tickled my neck. "Come on, John. We can't be late." I gently pushed him off of me, but his gaze was certainly a temptation. I hoped we would both be in the mood for pleasure after a successful evening. In the meantime, I covered myself in a mink capelet and bonnet. John didn't want to bother with his coat, but I insisted and grabbed a top hat as well.

Mary Anne grinned from ear to ear once she saw me in the hallway. She was just as lovely as on her wedding day, wrapped in white rabbit fur. Cooper gave a measured nod of approval. He couldn't be his flashy self since he was dressed in his uniform, but carrying Mary Anne on his arm would grant him more than enough attention.

Though the White House was within walking distance, Cooper hailed us a carriage for the benefit of his pregnant wife. Cooper helped me get in after Mary Anne, then John followed. I touched my husband's thigh to reaffirm that I would always be by his side. He gently grinned and brushed my wedding ring with his thumb. "No diamonds tonight, Mrs. Cohen?"

"No, Mr. Cohen. You and I will be spectacle enough."

Chapter Fifteen

We approached the White House, and the duality of the president's mansion became more prevalent. Yes, it was a grand place to raise his children, but the armed soldiers patrolling and standing guard along the building made his role as the head of the executive branch clear. We were about to meet not only a man of great political power but the commander-in-chief. He could come to be our greatest ally or a foe that needed to be eliminated.

A servant helped us out of the carriage, and I gazed at the columns in awe. The burden they carried was astronomical, and some of its weight rested on my chest. The power to wage war and grant freedom was decided in such a place.

"Are you ready for this?" John asked.

I gripped his arm tighter. "Of course."

Cooper walked slightly ahead of us with Mary Anne on his arm. There was a line in front of us and more coming up from behind. Cooper and John handed our invitations to a servant and told them our name. Another man checked a list and marked our arrival. We weren't patted down for weapons before entering, so the same must have been true for other guests. John looked displeased, but we entered anyway. A flood of light enveloped our bodies, and servants came forward to ask for our coats and hats. The men quickly obeyed. My bonnet came off easily enough, but once my fingers grazed the latch of the capelet's brooch, I froze.

The entrance hall quickly filled with noise, but Mary Anne's soft voice was clear to me. "Come on, sister, this is your big moment." She winked while Cooper stood beside her with a proud smile. John was smiling too, but I knew he was masking fear.

That was alright. I would put on a brave face as well. I released the brooch, and my husband was kind enough to remove the mink. I didn't wait to watch the reactions from the servants or the guests behind me. The buzzing in the room quieted and turned into whispers, and those whispers and subtle gasps granted me power.

To be fair to the gawkers, the dress was cut below my rib cage. Even without the scars, it would have caused a scene. Any shame I could have possibly felt paled in comparison to when I was exposed on the plantation. If I could endure the brunt of each lash, they could certainly bear the brunt of their existence.

As the servants wrangled us into the East Room, black faces gave subtle nods and raised brows. It was under the twinkling chandeliers that the horrified gasps of white women became apparent. Some of them raised fans for privacy to gossip with their friends, without bothering to avert their eyes. It wasn't too long after that white men began to gander. Even the aristocratic gaze of George Washington seemed to be in on the scandal.

"There are Union Democrats here." John's keen eye swept the room and rested near the back corner on the right. "That's Andrew Johnson. There are all sorts of interesting political rumors surrounding him. Dinah will have to shake his hand."

"I see a few abolitionists." Cooper had respect for many esteemed visionaries, but it was rare to hear such excitement in his voice. "There's Charles Lenox Remond and Captain Robert Smalls."

"Robert Smalls?" I spoke loud enough for him to hear from across the room. We all turned our heads and pretended like we weren't the culprits. I had never been so embarrassed in my life!

John's expression remained muted. "Who is that exactly?"

"I learned about his daring feats in *Harper's Weekly*. Surely, you must have heard something about a slave commandeering a Confederate ship and sailing to freedom with his family."

"Oh, yes, that account sounds familiar." It was unbelievable how unimpressed John seemed as he stared at such a prolific man. His stature was smaller than John's. Smalls was neatly groomed and seriously composed, but that was the case for just about every other dark face in the room. He performed such a Herculean task yet appeared so remarkably ordinary in his naval uniform.

"He pilots the USS Planter," Cooper said. "He came to our base to inspire us. He's a native of Beaufort."

Mary Anne tugged on my arm and pointed toward the Entrance Hall. "Isn't that man with the big hair the one you're always raving about?"

My heart leapt out of my chest, and I squeezed onto John's arm. I immediately knew who Mary Anne meant before I laid eyes on that thick mane. He was known for his rich, dark brown hair, but it had salted from his wisdom and life experience. He was 46 then and one of the most influential voices in the world.

"I think you've read everything Frederick Douglass has written," John remarked. "Do you want to meet him?"

"Me? No! I mean, I do, but not right now. I'm fine. Don't mind me." I was so flustered. I would probably sound like a fool. Besides, there were already admirers ready to pounce as soon as his coat was removed. I wanted to be a bit more refined.

"Why are you so nervous?" John seemed a little annoyed, as if he were offended on my behalf. "You're the most famous person in this room, and you've rescued more lives than any abolitionist. Ever."

"I can make it happen," Cooper said with a confident smile. "We can go together."

If I had Mary Anne's complexion, I certainly would have been bright red by then. "I'm fine. Truly."

"Excuse me," an olive-skinned servant with short curly white hair approached us from behind. "You are Sergeant Joseph Aaron Cooper, are you not?"

"I am."

"The president has requested an audience with you."

Cooper remained remarkably calm, but Mary Anne and I pawed at him like excited pups. "May I bring my wife and my friends?"

He glanced us over, "Your wife may accompany you. The others will have to stay here."

I withdrew from Cooper and returned to my husband, who raised a brow with the tiniest hint of intrigue. Cooper took the hand of his wife, who was already smiling brightly. I did notice a trail of gawkers in their wake. Perhaps the observers were merely curious why a trusted servant of Lincoln was leading them somewhere private, but the sneers from a few white faces seemed more emotional than that.

"You look a little flushed." John touched my cheek. I felt a little warm, but not sickly. "Can I get you anything to drink?"

"Something cold."

"I'll be right back, my dear." He gave me a quick kiss on the cheek and proceeded to the next room. There was food and drink for the attendees, but it wasn't as grand as I had imagined. Their spread wasn't much different than Mary Anne and Cooper's wedding reception. I was too nervous to eat.

I lost sight of Douglass, and Robert Smalls moved on to a different room. I didn't want to chase after them and disappear from John's sight. I waited and watched the room, noticing more eyes on me. I turned and locked eyes with a white woman in a dark blue frock coat, whose eyes were widened in shock, then embarrassment. Then she composed herself and marched toward me with a purpose. I prepared myself mentally to defend my choice of dress, but when she came within five feet of me, she smiled. "Good evening. My name is Josephine Griffing."

"Good evening," I responded more defensively than I should have. "I'm Mrs. Charlotte Cohen."

"Mrs. Cohen, I apologize if this is too forward, but you look as though you have a story to tell, and I'm connected with many abolitionist networks that would be interested in hearing your perspective." She reached into a small purse and handed me a brochure that made her intentions clear. It contained an illustration of a dark-skinned slave pleading with clasped hands, bearing scars on his back. "Three days from now, there is going to be a meeting at Hope Harvest Church here in Washington. We want to inspire women to be more engaged in the fight to abolish slavery, and I believe your boldness will do just that."

"You want to put my scars on display?" I didn't plan to cut any more dresses, but it wasn't out of the question.

"If that's what you want, but I was hoping you could speak to our group."

I was stunned. I thought a few politicians might be challenged, or I might end up in a well-circulated photo. I wasn't much of a speaker. "Well, I…"

"She would love to!" John said from behind. I looked up at him with bulging eyes, urging him to retract his statement, but he focused on Josephine. "Charlotte loves to read and has a gift for words. We would love to attend, and as her husband, I'll be by her side."

I forced a full smile across my face. What else could I do? I couldn't admit that I was nervous. I didn't even understand why I was.

"Wonderful. I'll be sure to add Mrs. Cohen to the schedule."

"That's fine, Mrs. Griffing." I began to tug on John's arm. "Now, if you don't mind, I need to have a word with my husband."

"Of course."

There wasn't much room for privacy, but I didn't want Josephine to hear. We walked deeper toward the back corner, and she retreated to her friends. "Your sudden interest in advocacy is puzzling."

"Speechwriting is a skill any writer should have. It's your dream. Why wouldn't I jump at the opportunity for you to perform, speaking on a topic you're passionate about?" He handed me a glass of water, and drinking gave me the opportunity to calm down. "Your humility may be charming for some, but I know the truth of who you are. The time is fast approaching when the world will know as well."

John's supremacy aside, he was correct about how I should present myself. If I wanted to make the most out of that opportunity, I couldn't be falling all over the abolitionists in the room. I was the wife of a wealthy land baron, and it was time I played the part. I pretended the last swallow of water was courage and gulped it down. "Lead the way."

Lady Cohen taught her adopted son well. John masked his revulsion with a charming smile and inserted himself into conversations with politicians. I watched their reactions once he introduced me as his wife. Representative Thaddeus Stevens looked like a stiff prune, but he cracked a smile. John commended his efforts as a Radical Republican and pledged to send generous donations to members of his party. Once politicians were aware of our wealth, John was a magnet.

The Union Democrats were much more pained, but they recovered quickly from the news of our nuptials. They wanted to win the war and unite the Union and Confederacy into one nation. Their greatest struggle with abolition—or at least the concern they voiced—was Southern resistance to reuniting if their way of life was completely rejected. John told them that he was a Southerner, and while none of them liked being told what to do, plenty of Southerners were either apathetic or even personally against slavery. "I released my father's slaves as soon as I inherited his land. Plantation owners are holding onto slavery out of pride, not good business sense. Even if we set moral questions aside, feeding, sheltering, and guarding slaves is a financial burden. Shifting that burden on freed workers while paying competitive wages is the future.

"Humans are stubborn and can't all be convinced with logic and reason. Some people, you must defeat and bring them under submission. They may resent it for a little while, but they'll come to be grateful for the forced change after the benefits become apparent. We are now approaching a crucial time in this nation's history: embrace liberty or die."

Even if they wanted to disagree with John, he was an intimidating and charismatic figure because of his natural presence and his mother's power. They would usually respond with something like, "Here's to peace," and raise a glass. If they properly fawned over his insight, he promised to donate.

We made our way through the Green and Blue Room. After many conversations, I spotted Douglass in the Red Room, having a chat with Mrs. Griffing. She could be the perfect opening for a proper introduction. "John, I'm ready to meet Douglass now."

"Are you John Cohen?" A man asked with a raspy voice. He had a mustache that curled and short hair that pressed onto his face in organized waves. "I have long-awaited to meet the owner of the Crimson Hotel."

"If you've come seeking to purchase the property, it's not for sale, Mr. …?"

"Stemple, and I'm not interested in purchasing the property." Mr. Stemple's piercing blue eyes cut me in all kinds of ways. "Is this your wife?"

John placed his hand on my shoulder. "Yes, this is Charlotte Cohen."

"How do you do, sir?" I offered a polite bow of acknowledgement, but his eyes swiftly returned to John.

"She cleans up rather nicely for a nigger."

John's chest immediately pressed against my back, and I held out my arm to stop him from causing a ruckus. He was blowing fumes through his nostrils. If not for the crowd of people, John wouldn't have let me stop him.

Stemple's smile faded, and he took a few steps back. "I don't mean to offend," his voice quivered. "Her kind aren't usually tolerable, but you've managed to find an exception, Mr. Cohen."

If we were anywhere else besides that room, John would have torn Mr. Stemple's head clean off his shoulders. John stopped fighting me. He was unnervingly still after clenching his fist and tightening his jaw, making his words all the more menacing. "Why is someone like you at an event like this?"

"I heard the infamous Runaway would make an appearance. It's a pleasant surprise to find you both here. Eyewitnesses said Runaway saved orphan niggers that now reside in your building." I gathered he might have been the man poking around the Crimson Hotel, or he was connected to him.

"If you don't like people like me, what business do you have with Runaway?"

That snake of a man wouldn't bother to look into my eyes, only John's. "I want to see her up close. The last thing the world needs is magical niggers."

"Oh, I can think of something else the world doesn't need…" John stepped closer to Mr. Stemple, and he trembled. I sensed the bloodlust in my husband, and the eyes in the Blue Room began to take notice.

"Come on, John. Let's get some fresh air." I took his hand, and he didn't move on the first tug. I had to pinch him, then he obeyed. I would much rather never have the chance to speak with Frederick Douglass than to have John embarrass me in front of all those people, even if it were on my behalf.

We didn't wait for our coats. We stood on the lawn, far enough from the ears of guests and soldiers. When I shivered, John took off his coat and covered me. "You can't kill him."

"Don't tell me what I can't do."

"That man thinks I'm Runaway."

"Dinah will prove him wrong."

"He may have spoken to others. If he goes missing, it might raise suspicions." I pressed on John's chest, hoping to calm him down. "He's obviously a person of influence to be here. Dinah can find out who he is."

"Then I will kill him."

"You can't kill someone for insulting me. Even terrible men are made in the image of God."

"And he petitioned me to send him to his Creator once he disrespected my wife."

I chuckled, thinking back to when Mary Anne defended my honor against two racist women at the Barnum Museum. "You are very sweet in your own way." They could both be so terrifying, but I had no doubt they loved me fiercely. "If he's dangerous, we may not have a choice. But if he's a simple prejudiced man, we can practice the teachings of Christ and turn the other cheek."

John grumbled like a stubborn child.

"What are you two doing out here?" Mary Anne called from the steps, wearing her husband's coat. Cooper was kind enough to help her down.

"John needed a minute. How was your audience with President Lincoln?"

Cooper tried to hold a dignified face, but he couldn't contain that beautiful smile, especially when Mary Anne burst with glowing pride. "He honored Joseph with a private commendation letter and this watch."

She pulled a slim leather box from Cooper's coat and opened it for us. It was a shiny silver watch with an eagle embossed on the cover. When Mary Anne's gentle hands flipped it open, an engraved message was revealed: "For a man of legacy."

"Oh, Coop…" It was recognition and respect well-deserved, but beyond that, I saw a glimmer in his eye that signaled that respect was needed. "I'm so happy for you." I wrapped my arms around his neck, and he gave me a good spin. As my feet dangled in the air, I felt a new sense of hope for the future.

A good throat-clearing from John abruptly ended that, and Cooper sat me down. "The President and General Grant have gathered to meet their guests."

Cooper began to lead the way, but John placed his hand on his shoulder. "Cooper, keep an eye on Dinah when she arrives. I can keep her safe if there's trouble, but I'd rather not draw too much attention to myself. A soldier acting courageously shouldn't stir suspicion."

"I'll stay alert. Don't worry."

"I won't."

I wasn't worried either. I gleefully took Mary Anne's arm, and we gushed over Cooper's new treasure. It was signed A. Lincoln. I could hardly wait to show Danny and Steve, and it would make a lovely heirloom to pass on to his child. I bet even Mr. Cooper would crack a smile and admit to harboring pride in his son.

The party had reorganized into a greeting line from the East Room to the Green Room, where his wife was waiting. Then, she welcomed guests into the Blue Room. There, we would finally meet Lincoln and General Grant. We were at the very back of the line. Mary Anne and I passed the time by admiring the gowns and suits, and Cooper chimed in a few times. He even teased about financing a seamstress business, which John did not find amusing.

The servants did their best to move everyone along promptly. It wasn't long before we saw Mary Todd Lincoln's fluffy gown, decorated with frills and beads. She had bright and tremendous smiles for her husband's guests that only wavered at one moment. Mary Anne pointed out a fine pair of golden boots, and I turned to admire them. When I faced Mary's direction again, she raised her fan and averted her eyes. But for a brief second, she was stricken with pain. Mary composed herself well, and she avoided my eyes until we were right in front of her. "Mr. Cooper, thank you for coming into our home."

"Madam President. You've met my wife, Mary Anne. These are our friends, John and Charlotte Cohen."

"Thank you for hosting us, Mrs. Lincoln." I was content with John speaking for both of us, but she directly stared at me, and her smile evolved beyond a simple hostess desiring to please her guests. It deepened into something far more bittersweet.

"You're the one who's been causing all of this ruckus?"

My eyes widened a bit, and I swallowed all the air necessary for a proper response.

My husband rubbed my hand as a quiet comfort. "Hopefully, Charlotte is causing a good ruckus."

"A necessary one, I'm afraid." I sensed within her a yearning for liberty, and it made me hopeful about her husband.

"Well, if I can't fight on the battlefield, Mrs. Lincoln, my contribution had to be far more creative."

Mary propped her head higher, and her eyes brightened. "You have certainly succeeded in your aim." She took a small step to the side and welcomed us into the Blue Room. Her husband immediately stood out, since he towered over the other men in the room. The difference between Lincoln and the bearded man in uniform was more than half a foot. He was even taller than John and Cooper.

John had a curious gleam in his eye as he stared straight on at Lincoln. There were three people ahead of us. Based on the brief interaction Grant had with the man in front of us, I assumed the flow of people was partly his fault. Lincoln was polite and social, and Grant was brief. Since no one was talking to him, I pulled on John's arm and eased over toward the general.

Cooper and Mary Anne followed our lead. Grant offered a slight nod, and Cooper did the same. "Sir."

"Sergeant Cooper." His voice was low but soft and crystal-clear, like a river.

"You already met my wife. These are our friends, John and Charlotte Cohen. John is a land developer and owns the hotel we manage."

"It's a pleasure to meet the man who will put an end to this war." John reached out his hand to Grant, and the two engaged in a firm grasp. "Your terms of 'unconditional surrender' certainly inspired the nation. I'm not surprised by your promotion."

"The press repeated that line from a dispatch."

John paused, expecting clarification, but I thought Grant's words were final. My husband hesitantly continued. "The press loves to sensationalize, but I'm sure you'll live up to our expectations."

A brief moment of silence spread between us again. Men had been flattering John all night, but Grant seemed content to let the conversation end.

"Do you enjoy parties like this, General?" I asked.

He slowly exhaled. "It's necessary."

"Certainly, and I do love a good party, but I enjoy being home with a good book more."

His eyes brightened a bit.

"Uh, oh. Do we share the same weakness, General?"

"That depends on your library."

One author immediately came to mind, and it made me bashful. Unfortunately, it was the only name I could think of. "Jane Austen is perhaps an uninspiring answer."

"She loves adventure stories," John quickly chimed in. "We've read Homer's works and Dumas together, though she was devious and read Walter Scott without me."

"Only *Ivanhoe*. We were going to begin *The Lady of the Lake* together."

"Frederick Douglass took his surname from the book." Grant spoke so softly and plainly. My excited gasp seemed unwarranted, but I couldn't help it.

"You're right! Douglass wanted to hide from his master, so his friend renamed him. He wrote about it in his autobiography." Though Grant was still a bit stiff, I felt the most relaxed I had been the entire night. "Did you enjoy *Ivanhoe*? I loved it!"

"Charlotte—" Cooper meant to urge me to stop, but Grant gently raised his hand, prompting him to hush up.

"I did, Mrs. Cohen. What did you enjoy about it?"

I took a moment to think of something that would resonate with a man of his position, with the weight of the nation on his shoulders. "I loved that living honorably was important, even in dishonorable societies and dishonorable circumstances."

"It's a good lesson."

"It's necessary."

Grant released the tiniest huff of air, and I think it was meant to be a chuckle.

"My wish is to share some of that resolve. That's why I'm here with my husband instead of home with a new book."

Grant finally cracked a smile and darted his eyes toward John. "Men with this kind of resolve are hard to come by."

Cooper was tense for most of our conversation, but he had finally begun to breathe. "If we had a hundred men like Charlotte on the battlefield, the war would already be won."

"You wouldn't need a hundred," John said with a dubious grin.

"You gentlemen need to think a little bit bigger." I raised my head higher. "After all, warfare isn't won by men alone."

"What's this talk of sending women to the battlefield?" A high and nasally voice asked. I hadn't noticed that Lincoln's guests had moved on, and we were holding him up. Cooper's body straightened, but the president placed his hand on his shoulder. "At ease, Sergeant."

Cooper kept his arms down, but he didn't relax. "Charlotte has a lot of vigor, sir."

"She must. This is the most I've seen Grant speak tonight."

"We bibliophiles speak our own language." I smiled at General Grant. "I feel as though we are kindred spirits." Grant's eyes were, thankfully, on me as John reached his hand toward the president. I only managed to catch a glimpse of gold out of the corner of my eye.

"It's a pleasure to meet you, President Lincoln. I'm John Cohen." As Lincoln's hand connected with John, I sensed the earth shift beneath us, in a monumental metaphorical sense. Cooper noticed as well, and his eyes briefly flooded with panic.

He must have been terribly conflicted, watching John clasp Lincoln with both hands as if he were subtly bragging about their new dynamic. If Cooper called out to warn the president, he would expose us and endanger his wife and unborn child. But if he stayed silent, Cooper and the United States of America were at the mercy of an inhuman killer.

"It's a pleasure to meet you, Mr. Cohen."

Chapter Sixteen

John and President Abraham Lincoln engaged in normal chatter that sounded like garbled and faded noises. The only distinct detail was the beating of my heart, which I felt pulse through my ears. I was trying my best not to display panic, but Cooper's face had yet to relax.

I reminded myself that John could not control Lincoln. Animals? Yes. Anything more complex was a challenge, though not impossible. Master Cohen was unwell from Lady Cohen's poison when he forced John to beat me. It was the cruelest and most insane I had ever seen him. After their blowup, I never expected Master Cohen to pass his land onto his stepson while his brothers were in his ear. John later confessed that Lady Cohen used more than her womanly wiles to manipulate Master Cohen while his mind was fragile.

Lincoln was a different story. He was educated, strong, and had enough will to wage war for the soul of the nation. Control was out of the question, and even using it to help persuade him was too great a risk. What if Grant had noticed John trying to hex the president? What if Lincoln noticed? John's sway can be felt, yet they kept on talking like old friends.

"Isn't that right, my dear?" John's hand fell on my shoulder, and it startled me.

“I’m sorry. I’m a little flustered.” I touched my stomach, hoping for a convincing excuse as to why I wasn’t paying attention. “I think it’s my pregnancy. I’m getting used to the early changes.”

A heartfelt smile deepened on the president’s face. “How wonderful for you both. Is this your first?” The solemn joy he possessed was infectious.

“Yes, sir. We’ve only known for about a week.”

John wrapped his arm around me, not grasping that I was putting on an act. “I need a quiet place to sit my wife down while she catches her bearings.”

Lincoln looked at his light-skinned servant, who had helped to manage the crowds. “Mr. Slade, please accompany Mrs. Cohen to the State Dining Room.”

“You mustn’t bring her there!” Mary left her perch in the doorway and joined us. “It’s a mess.”

“I’m sure Charlotte will enjoy the work-in-progress. I trust her not to touch anything.”

I was humored to see other couples bicker. She didn’t press it further, but I recognized the reserved hellfire in her eyes. She was hardly over five feet, but every inch of her was going to give him trouble later.

Mary Anne quietly excused herself and followed behind us. We were escorted out to the vestibule and walked to the State Dining Room. There were no other visitors going in and out of the space, and that mostly had to do with the giant unfinished portrait leaning up against the wall. The table was filled with sketches, maps, newspapers, books, and photographs. Oilcloths were laid across the floor, chairs were stacked in the corner, and the room smelled of turpentine.

“I’ll have some water and food brought to you ladies.”

“Wait!” Mary Anne called out to Mr. Slade before he closed the door. “What’s being painted?” The painting was mostly dark colors. Eight figures were sitting around a table. None of their faces had been attempted yet, but I could make out Lincoln’s figure by his hair and beard.

“It’s the first reading of the Emancipation Proclamation.”

I took a breath of air and felt the weight of every molecule. I recalled celebrating at Harvey’s the day the document was signed. The crowd was drinking and dancing all night, yet Cooper was very reserved. He was happy for the Confederate slaves, but voiced concern about slaves living in border states. I remembered the words he spoke into whiskey, close enough to fog up the glass. *"It's brilliant for warfare, but it's cruel toward our cause."*

As soon as Mr. Slade shut the door, I clutched onto John. "What are you doing? Using your sway here is reckless!"

"I'm sorry, my dear." He had such a big smile as he caressed my arms and softly kissed my cheek. "You know I can't always help it when it comes to our kind."

"Our kind?" The curious glimmer in his eye made perfect sense, and that lustful smirk on his face was further confirmation. "You mean—?"

"He's one of us." John kissed me again, then walked to the corner to get us chairs. His low laughter made it feel as though the floorboards beneath me were shaking. He was unaware that I pretended to be ill, but my knees did start to wobble. John held the heart-shaped crest as I eased into the rosewood chair, contemplating whether I was slipping into hell or paradise.

"Mary Anne, will you take care of her?" John asked. She nodded, and he scurried off to his alleged new subordinate.

I looked back at the massive painting and Lincoln's unfinished face. I had yet to learn who he was as a man rather than an ideal. I always hoped that Lincoln would prove himself to be a trustworthy and honorable man, capable of softening John's heart and quelling his bloodlust. Now, I know the truth. He was always more than just an ordinary man.

Mary Anne reached for my hand and wove her fingers between mine. "Is this a good turn of events?"

"I have no idea." Even if Lincoln was more persuadable, he still had his own will. And even as president, he had limitations on his own power. Grant was also an influential force, and I doubted Cooper would stay silent as John took over the country.

"I wonder if Lincoln even knows he's different."

"That depends on what he can do." Perhaps there was a reason why he was fascinated with Barnum's oddities. He could have been trying to find an explanation for himself.

I tried not to dwell on it. John would tell me as soon as he knew. I didn't want to worry about anything and risk making myself or the baby sick. Slade did send a servant girl with food and water, and we cleared off some of the table to eat. Mary Anne and I mostly sat for a few minutes, nibbling on cheese and meat slices, while we hoped for the best.

We stayed until hollers erupted around the White House. I hopped out of my chair and pulled Mary Anne along. When we came into the vestibule, the esteemed professionals were huddled around a figure in a blue coat like a mob swarming Jesus. Dinah glanced toward the East Room, then reappeared there. The crowd was surprised at first, then elated. Her little trick solidified her identity in their minds.

"Runaway!" The white women were especially loud as they reached for her.

"I didn't know you were this famous," Mary Anne said.

"Neither did I…" I wished we had warned Dinah. She had to blink inside the Green Room, which ended up working out. It was a smaller and more private room. The White House staff quickly blocked off the entrances and pushed the people back. Mr. Stemple hung back in a corner and watched the chaos in horror. It was probably his worst nightmare. He did see me and even did a double-take.

"Mary Anne, is he the man who came to the Crimson Hotel asking questions? His name is Mr. Stemple."

She followed my eyes to him. "I wouldn't know. Mick was the one who dealt with him, and he never gave his name."

Once Mr. Slade spotted us, he helped sneak us back into the Blue Room. John happily slipped his arm across my waist. He was overjoyed. Cooper, Grant, and President Lincoln and his wife were in the Green Room with Dinah. I doubted they were discussing anything sensitive with a mob waiting to meet her, but she absolutely shook their hands.

Waiting in the Blue Room were some prominent politicians, like Andrew Johnson. Mr. Slade also escorted Robert Smalls and Frederick Douglass. I felt John's eyes on me, but I wouldn't look at him. They were patiently waiting to meet the famous Runaway, and it seemed intrusive to interrupt that moment.

They weren't about to fall all over themselves like the white women, but there were stars in their eyes.

"Why is Cooper inside?" Mary Anne asked John.

"I suggested he stay beside Runaway for protection, and Lincoln agreed."

John's boisterous smile slipped once Mr. Slade directed the first group into the Green Room to meet Runaway. It was Andrew Johnson and four other Democrats. They were inside for about two minutes. It wasn't much time for a chat, but Dinah likely discovered all there was to know.

Thaddeus Stevens and a group of Republicans went in next, and then Douglass, Smalls, and other abolitionists. About ten of them went in together for a short time. When they exited the room, an undeniable cheer was spread across their faces. I might not have spoken to Douglass myself, but pride rested in my belly like a warm bowl of soup.

"Come on," John spoke in my ear once Mr. Slade motioned for us. "It's our turn."

It wasn't odd standing across from someone wearing my face, but it was unnatural pretending to be surprised and even honored. The President was even the one to introduce us. "Mr. and Mrs. Cohen, Mrs. Cooper, I'd like you to meet the legendary Runaway."

"It's a pleasure." John offered his hand. Dinah wasn't wearing my signature gloves. They were leather, but they were fingerless and without any brass on the knuckles. I offered a slight bow and a big smile. Mary Anne kept her hands balled and at her side, but she did offer an unconvincing smile.

"Thank you for being here." That, I sincerely meant.

"Thank you for having me," she spoke in a lower pitch to distinguish the two of us. I wasn't terribly worried. Clothes, hair, and powders transformed many women. With much of Dinah's face covered and her hair pulled back in a bun, I didn't think anyone would think we were identical. In truth, my jaw and cheekbones had sharpened a bit since Dinah had first taken my form.

"My wife and friends were in New York during the riots," Cooper said. "You saved many lives that night."

"We won't forget your bravery," Mary Anne added, though it came off rather flat.

Thankfully, Mr. Slade was ready to swap us out with the next group. Mary Anne and I headed for the door, but John propped himself up against the wall next to Cooper. "I'd like to stay and protect our brave heroine."

"Yes," Lincoln nodded. "That'll be fine."

Grant squinted, just a little, and I feared John was laying it on a little too thick. He probably could have talked Lincoln into allowing all of us to stay, but I didn't want to. I trusted Dinah would be successful in her tasks.

Since I was, inexplicably, the belle of the ball, I wasn't nervous anymore. I spotted Douglass as he drifted back into the East Room and gazed up at the portrait of George Washington. Mary Anne nudged me forward, and I quietly stood beside him and admired our first president.

Douglass's posture was perfect: raised chest, arms behind his back, and his broad shoulders enveloped the room. His eyes were brown but bright, lit from the passion of his own convictions. "If not for the enslaved, the fires lit by the British would have consumed this portrait." His voice was just as rich as I imagined, a powerful baritone.

"Is that so?"

"First Lady Dolley Madison is credited with the honor, but without staff and slaves, it would have been an impossible task."

It was a very large painting, even taller than Lincoln. It was hard to imagine that while Mrs. Madison's life was on the line, she'd be so desperate to save a portrait of a dead man.

I had read a speech from Douglass, written years ago, "What to the Slave is the Fourth of July?" He had such intolerance for the evils of slavery, yet held our forefathers and Constitution in such high regard.

"Is it true that Washington rotated his slaves between Mount Vernon and Philadelphia to avoid Pennsylvania's emancipation laws?"

Douglass's arms relaxed and fell to his side. "Yes, that's true, and Washington also went on to emancipate his slaves in his will."

I didn't even care for the portrait's style or the pose. George's hand was extended as if he were about to deliver a speech, yet his lips were clamped together. I felt as though he had swallowed costly words that needed to be spoken. "Courage is wasted on the dead."

His shoulders shook from a faint chuckle. "Washington may have been many things in life, but he had no lack of courage."

I searched for whatever Douglass's thoughtful gaze had discovered, but Washington's melancholy expression gave me nothing. I understood that if the Founding Fathers had demanded no slavery when the colonies came together, there would have been no nation. Politics was complicated, but public compromises first began in hardened hearts. "Then why didn't he do more?"

"'Sin lieth at the door.' Evil embeds itself in the hearts of even the greatest of men. It makes their feats no less great, but 'no one is good—except God alone.'"

"No one, huh?" It was difficult to argue with a master orator, especially when he quoted my Lord and Savior. "My name is—"

"Charlotte Cohen." He humbly bowed his head. "Mrs. Griffing informed me of you. She's looking forward to your stirring words."

I thought all my nerves were gone, but my heart fluttered. "Do you have any advice for a novice like me?"

He offered a kind smile, like I imagined a father would. "Be true to God. Speak for Him, and He'll be your advocate."

I felt as though I had years' worth of questions to ask him, but he had already said all that needed to be said. I looked back up at the painting and wondered what Washington would think of the mess the country was in. Would it have been worth rebelling against King George III if he had known it would be torn apart in less than a hundred years? And would he have fought such a bloody war to stitch it back together?

A loud thud distracted my heavy thoughts, and then a horrifying shriek. I believed it was Mrs. Lincoln's voice. I began to rush toward the Green Room, along with Douglass, Smalls, and other guests. There was some hollering from a man I didn't recognize, some more shuffling, and another thud. If the hollering man meant to fight, he had no chance with John and Cooper in the room. The staff and military pushed us back toward the entrance hall. Within a minute, they insisted we gather our coats and leave.

"Our husbands are in there!" Mary Anne told an insistent soldier.

"Ma'am, please, we need to secure the premises."

As he tried to shuffle us toward the entrance, I saw John exit the Green Room and wave. "John!"

The soldier continued to push us, but then a wave of dread loomed over him. When his back hit John's chest, he looked up and lost about ten years on his face. John didn't need to speak. He just scurried off like a child expecting discipline. John had a slight sneer that screamed his annoyance, but he forgot the soldier as soon as the boy moved on.

He pulled us away from the crowd and spoke quietly. "There was an attempt on Runaway's life."

My chest ached with a rush of guilt, and I clutched my belly. If I hadn't listened to John, our child could have been harmed. "Is she alright?"

"Yes. I sensed bloodlust from one of the guests and warned Cooper. He brought him down easily enough, but the man came with a bloodied knife." Based on John's steely eyes, he came to the same conclusion I did.

"Where is Cooper now?" Mary Anne's voice was shaky from her elevated heart.

"He's keeping the zealot restrained. He asked me to get you ladies to safety, and I obliged. Runaway disappeared with the weapon, but not before touching the would-be assassin." John couldn't have been happy about the zealot being alive, but Dinah would have invaluable information. If the zealots still had a stockpile of Moses's blood, then we needed to destroy it.

The staff worked quickly to retrieve coats and hats for the swarm of guests. The military was uncomfortable with so many people inside, so we were asked to wait on the porch and lawn. John searched for a carriage while Mary Anne and I huddled together for warmth. I would have suggested walking to the hotel, but Mary Anne had stretched and touched her back on more than one occasion. She needed to be off her poor feet.

Once we had our things, John helped Mary Anne in the carriage. As he guided me up, his attention was snatched like a dog sniffing an intruder. "John, what's wrong?"

He didn't answer. John immediately proceeded down the curbed road, two carriages in front of us. He was already in front of Mr. Stemple by the time my feet hit the ground. Stemple didn't have time to retreat or block. He could only grit his teeth and wait.

"John, no!" I wasn't fast enough to stop John's mighty blow to Stemple's face. He spun on one leg, then bounced when he hit the ground.

"Did you think I would let you get away with disrespecting my wife?" As he yelled over his defeated foe, I couldn't help but think of Cooper standing over a knockout.

Mr. Stemple was bleeding, but he covered his face too much to know the extent of the damage. He had enough strength to holler, so John showed a great deal of restraint. I was a little embarrassed by the gasps and gawkers. I hoped Mrs. Griffing or Frederick Douglass weren't around to see. Just my luck that Cooper's timing was excellent, and he angrily looked on from the portico steps.

"Come on, John!"

John winced, then stumbled as I pulled him back to the carriage. It couldn't have been from the pain of the punch. Even if he didn't have Emma's power, the strength he carried from his mother was plenty to punch a human without any discomfort. But he definitely wasn't super strong. Then, while getting inside the carriage, he nearly fell backward as he grunted and gritted his teeth. If not for Cooper pushing him from behind, John might have collapsed on the ground instead of on my chest.

"What's wrong with him?" Mary Anne asked.

I had never seen him in pain quite like that, but I recognized the cause. It was only going to get worse, and I didn't want to cause a scene when we left the carriage. I wasn't even certain if he'd even be able to walk to his room. "I'll be right back." It was a risk, but I blinked to his hotel bed. I would much rather have John squirm in a feathered pillow.

"What happened to him?" Dinah was sitting in a chair by the desk. She had removed my coat and wasn't wearing my face anymore. A Bowie knife was sitting on the desk; its blade was stained red.

"I think he took on your power to gather information on a suspicious character. We feared he might know Runaway's true identity and possibly be an Overseer."

"I wish he hadn't done that." Dinah rushed from her seat and stood beside me. Mr. Stemple must have been around thirty years old. Everything he ever learned, said, experienced, and thought was running through John's head because of her ability. Dinah was practically squirming alongside him. "He could have asked me to do it."

"I don't think Stemple would have let you touch him. Besides, John wanted to punch him." He wanted to do more than that. John managed to show restraint and gather necessary intelligence. Despite his temper, he was a good leader. "Take care of him. I'll be back soon."

I blinked back to Mary Anne and Cooper before Dinah could distract me with questions. The carriage hadn't moved yet, and Mary Anne was silently praying that no one came seeking John for retribution. I think everyone was too busy trying to get home. Normally, people leave parties in waves. The congestion slowed our journey to a crawl.

I huddled in closely, so the driver wouldn't hear our conversation. "Dinah is watching over John. He copied her power to see Stemple's memories, but his mind isn't naturally suited for such a task."

Cooper's brow curiously rose. "I didn't know John had any weaknesses."

My eyes narrowed, and my jaw tightened. "I wouldn't call them weaknesses. They're more like deficiencies."

A low and unimpressed chuckle escaped him. "And what's the difference?"

I pondered how best to convey John's abilities. "Think of the maximum amount of weight you can carry. What would happen if I tried to carry the same amount?"

"You would die."

I slapped his chest, which got another good chuckle out of him. "I am not a weak woman."

"I don't mean to offend, but I'm a lot stronger than you. It remains a fact." Something about the tone of Cooper's voice—perhaps a slight drop when his lips flattened—made me concerned that I overshared. "So, how does John carry your abilities?"

I looked at Mary Anne, hoping she would agree that Cooper's questions were too personal, but her eyes glittered with intrigue. I suppose I would have been curious in their shoes as well. "I haven't noticed any drawbacks that harm him, but John can only blink to what he can see."

"What about other drawbacks? What if he copied…fire, for example?"

"After copying Nathaniel's fire powers, John awakened a natural fire resistance. I think it's inherited from his real father—not that it's any of your concern…" I leaned away, not intending to say anything else. Cooper leaned back, but the look on his face mirrored that portrait of Washington. I figured I didn't have long before whatever was on his mind came out.

There were too many people for a conversation when we stepped out of the carriage. Many guests from the party stayed at the Willard, so the lobby was buzzing and the halls were lively. There was no privacy afforded until I reached my room, and even then, Mary Anne and Cooper were right behind me and waiting to be asked in.

I quietly sighed and opened the door. John was asleep. Dinah was kind enough to remove his coat, frock, and shoes. She was sitting on my bed and watching him intently. He usually looked like a cherub when he entered deep sleep, but his face was still tense. "John is sleeping through his headache."

"Speaking of John..." Cooper unclasped each button on his coat with the utmost determination. Then he tossed it on a chair, reminding us of the blue uniform on his body. "What did he do to Lincoln?"

A flutter of laughter escaped Dinah's mouth. "Oh, you mean John's sway?" That petty woman smiled deliciously as if she had devoured Lincoln herself. "That was a wonderful surprise, indeed."

"What does it do?" Cooper's eyes were directly on me. "What did Lincoln feel?" I couldn't blame him for being concerned. I was willing to physically fight John to keep him from using it on Mary Anne.

"It's difficult to explain, and my experience isn't like everybody else."

"Oh…?" Dinah stood on her feet. "Why don't you tell them the truth, Charlotte? Explain what it's like."

I didn't appreciate all of their eyes interrogating me, especially when I didn't know how to articulate it. "Unless John's power has dramatically changed, Lincoln is still a free moral agent."

"That's not what my husband asked." Mary Anne found a chair to rest her feet. Her brows were furrowed as she rubbed her belly. "What would the sway have done to me?"

"That was a different circumstance," I spoke a bit more forcefully. I hoped, for her sake, that Mary Anne didn't press it further.

Dinah eventually scoffed and rolled her eyes. "If you won't tell him, I will." She practically floated over to Cooper, and I recalled the last time they got into a tussle. Dinah could have killed him, yet Cooper didn't move an inch when she stood half a foot from his face and grinned like the devil. "John's sway…" Her voice itself was intoxicating, as if she expected her revelation to be seductive. "…it shows us that he makes sense."

Cooper's head tilted, and his eyes narrowed. "What does that mean? Sense about what?"

"His power. His resolve. His conclusions. His protection. To join him. To fight by his side." Each statement was a stake, rooting her further into the truth of this world. "I have a choice in the matter, of course. I always did. But why would I choose anything or anyone else? He makes perfect sense!"

Dinah had paused like a rousing preacher, expecting to receive vocal support from the audience. But Cooper maintained a stoic face until it slipped into something pitiable. "I always thought of you all as a small and persecuted group being targeted by zealots. The truth is you're two cults warring with each other."

Dinah rolled her head in my direction and glared through lowered brows. "How could you have fallen in love with a man with a mind this small?"

"Dinah, stop!" I grabbed her arm, hoping to derail further escalation.

"No!" She wasn't stronger than me in that form, but she managed to shake me off. "I know this man. Alright? Better than you!"

It was difficult to say that was true, since she copied Cooper from before his gym was destroyed. But she did have a good grasp on his thoughts and witnessed parts of his life that I never could. Admitting this makes me ill, but I wanted to know what made her lip curl in disgust. "He's asking these questions to interrogate the past—your decisions about joining John and choosing to love him instead of being Mrs. Joseph Cooper." Her tone fluctuated between outrage and mockery. "That's when John first used his sway on you, right before Cooper's proposal."

His eyes widened. There was hurt in them, but not from losing a life with me. He seemed content with his marriage to Mary Anne. But I feared he believed I had been deprived of a life with him.

"That's not why you refused Cooper," Mary Anne asked softly, "is it?" She was so happy to hear Cooper was going to propose, and even sadder than I was after the night ended in a fight.

"She never rejected it," Cooper corrected sadly. "I withdrew because I knew she would never let John go." His sympathetic look deepened as my eyes filled with tears, but I mourned nothing. I loathed his pity, every single drop of it. I wanted to rebuke him, but if I had opened my mouth at that moment, I would have disturbed the entire hotel with screams.

"Do you all have to be so loud?" John sat up, moaning and still wincing. He took a moment to inhale, then released a gust of wind and Dinah's power. He shifted his head, side to side, cracking his neck as his worn mind healed. Once he was finished, his eyes opened and focused on his prey.

"Mr. Cooper, if you're so curious about the effects of my sway, I could always use it on you." He stood and walked so calmly and quietly, but the quickness startled Dinah and Mary Anne. I also cleared a path. "But it wouldn't be very effective because of *my* perception. You would see me as a threat—not your leader—because that's what I am to your kind."

To Cooper's credit, he didn't move an inch. He kept his face firm, though his eyes weren't as steady.

"You could cower and obey me, and many humans would. But that isn't your way."

"You got that right."

The left side of John's lips curled. "To Dinah, I'm the man who will lead my people into the Promised Land by slaying giants, rather than wandering and whining for forty years."

"And Charlotte?" Cooper dared to ask, offended on my behalf.

"It doesn't matter how Charlotte saw me. What matters is how I see her." John stepped a little closer, and even though Cooper had about an inch on him, he seemed to rise higher. "She's always had a choice because this was always all for her."

Every golden gaze never held me captive. Each one held me in high regard. I could be his queen. I could be a god. He would shape the world for his muse.

"He needed me." I had to catch my breath. My heart was stirring, and I couldn't stop the tears from falling. "After the slaves sold me to the zealots for their freedom, the world didn't make any sense to me. Maybe it never did…"

Cooper's shoulders relaxed, and his eyes softened. Mary Anne held her chest, aching for me. They knew I was hurting back then, but I kept the depth of that wound to myself. At the time, John was my enemy, yet without his help, I would have been burned alive.

"The only thing I have ever been sure of, even if you ground me to dust and left nothing but a speck of my soul, is that even that speck would know I was always meant to be with John."

Dinah was uncomfortably quiet and clutched her arms like she didn't know what to do with herself.

"Dinah is wrong," I told my dearest friends. "The first time John ever used his power on me was the day I chose to stay with you two. John's sway never took my choice away. He has only ever shown me how strong I am." My chest felt hollow. I gasped for air and felt as though I'd never get an adequate amount. But I needed them to know, once and for all. "You may not respect the choices I made, but they were mine to make."

Cooper's heart broke for me, and he began to rush toward me. "Charlotte—"

"Don't touch her." John's hand was powerful enough to knock Cooper off his heels and into the dresser against the wall. He caught himself before hitting the floor. It was not within Cooper's nature to tolerate such disrespect, but any anger locked within him faded once he looked up at John's indignant sneer. "You made her cry."

He looked beyond John and quieted as he watched me pitifully sob. "I didn't mean to make her sad."

"I'm not sad!" I yelled, far louder than I intended to. "I'm angry, and I'm furious that you think I'm that weak." I turned away to hide my face, contemplating blinking away to gather myself. Then I felt Mary Anne's belly press into me, and I very well couldn't fight off a pregnant woman.

"Come on, sister. You're alright." I was angry with her, too, but Mary Anne only ever had concern for me, and she never hated John. I bore no true ill-will toward her. "Of course, we respect you, Charlotte. We're just trying to understand what happens next."

John looked down on Cooper one final time before peeling me away from Mary Anne. He let her rub my back as I leaned on his chest. John smelled of lavender and rosemary, and his tender kisses to my forehead were gentle. I could have slept safely in his grasp for a thousand years, if not for the pleasure of waking up beside him. "What happens to the nation entirely depends on Lincoln's choices."

"And Runaway." Dinah's eyes waltzed around the room, gauging our resolve after such a fine mess. "He wants to see her at midnight."

Chapter Seventeen

A deep hush rested in the Entrance Hall of the White House. There was no chatter or eager footsteps. Faint traces of perfume lingered, but all other evidence of a party had been polished and swept away. It was dark in most areas, but the stars and moon shone through the windows, and warm gaslights flickered from the Red Room.

I blinked through the other rooms quickly, searching for servants, guards, or assassins. I didn't spot another soul. I returned to the Entrance Hall and took a breath. He was in there. I recognized the quiet rustling of paper. He must have looked up from his chair once my footsteps were close enough to hear. As I entered the room, President Lincoln rose from his chair and bowed his head. "I expected you would still come."

I had already forgotten how tall he was. As I stepped through the doorway, I was swallowed by his presence. "Of course, Mr. President."

***

"Lincoln is clairvoyant."

Mary Anne and I stared at Dinah, stunned. The revelation weighed heaviest on Cooper, as he slowly lifted his head. "To what degree?"

"He can see the future. Sometimes it comes as feelings or metaphorical visions. Most occur in his sleep. A few come clear as day."

Mary Anne clung tighter to me. "Then what does he know about all of this? The war? The nation?"

"And our identities?" I asked. "Does he already know I'm Runaway?"

***

Lincoln motioned to an upholstered chair. He wouldn't sit down until I took my place beside him. "I apologize for the attack that happened today. The staff was selective about the guest list and familiar with the attendees. The lapse in security was unexpected. The responsibility rests on me."

"Does that mean you knew the man who attacked me?"

"Not well, I'm afraid. Mr. West was in the employ of Congressman Wood. He wasn't one for the spotlight. He's a trusted and persistent fellow." Lincoln removed his low-perched spectacles and set them on his pile of newspapers. At a glance, they were about the war. At least one was about me. There was also a leather-bound Holy Bible resting on the table.

"I didn't notice any watchmen tonight. Do you not care for your own safety?"

"There are soldiers nearby, but after what happened, I wanted you to feel at ease."

"That is rather thoughtful of you." I had no gift for reading minds, but my instincts told me he was sincere. "Still, you are the president. You should consider your own safety more carefully. You've been in danger before. What if an assassin came for you?"

I'm not certain whether it was the small oil lamp casting a shadow on half of his face or the faint scent of coal burning in the fireplace that made me feel out of sorts, but his halfhearted smile gave me no comfort. "Death is like an old friend. They may reappear during inconvenient times. When they do, one cannot refuse them."

***

"Lincoln has a Reaper's sight," Dinah spoke low, her voice rough with fatigue. "His visions are of death alone."

"Death alone?" Mary Anne cradled her belly as she sat on my bed. She took a deep breath and leaned back to ease the strain. "That must be awful."

"How often do they manifest?" Cooper asked.

"It began before the death of his young child, Eddie. It started as feelings, but by the time he lost Willie, the power had strengthened. Friends. Loved ones. Even enemies. He's seen their passing. The war has made them constant."

***

I had seen a portrait of Lincoln when he first became president. His face was weathered, but steely with determination. The man before me was far more worn, with new wrinkles and sunken eyes. I could not imagine his exhaustion. I glanced up at the portraits on the wall. Some depicted beautiful landscapes of the nation. Others memorialized great men, dead and gone. "You should still take better care of yourself. No need in worrying your poor wife."

"Hmm…" He nodded a few times. The shadow cast from his powers darkened as I gazed into his hollow eyes.

***

Mary Anne looked at her husband. Her eyes were heavy, pleading with anyone who would answer. "Why doesn't he try to stop it?"

"How do you stop death while waging a war?" John's words cut deep, not cleanly. Mary Anne lost her breath.

"He's never been able to stop death, not without consequences." Dinah lifted a brow, and it stirred intrigue and dread in me.

"What sort of consequences?"

Her lips almost smirked. "When the Lord sends a destroyer to smite, the target cannot escape."

***

It was odd sitting next to the president, knowing how great a burden he bore. I always thought my gift was liberating, despite persecution. His burden was evident, pulling at his shoulders. "Why did you ask me here, sir?"

"I wished to thank you personally again for your service to the Union." A small yet bashful smile brought color to his hollowed cheeks. "And if I may be honest, my curiosity got the better of me."

I mirrored his expression. I didn't know why I was surprised to see he was an admirer. I assumed I was more exciting than Tom Thumb. "What are you curious about?"

"At first, you were a rumor, then a hopeful tale spun by the enslaved. But after dozens of corroborating stories, your presence was undeniable. Bounties printed in papers, wanted posters at every train station and general store. You had become a legend, solidified by your appearance in the Draft Riots." His tired voice sharpened, as though he were addressing a crowd. "But that was your last sighting until you and Sergeant Cooper rescued 151 soldiers."

"You want to know where I've been for the past eight months or so?"

"If you would, please."

I couldn't tell him that I had joined a federal bank robber in holy matrimony, not yet. I loathed the idea of disappointing him. It wasn't easy to explain John and me. Ghost and Runaway was a far more complicated tale. "The man who tried to kill me was not acting alone. He's part of an organization called God's Overseers, and they've been an enemy since my gift awakened."

His bushy brows sank deeper into his wrinkled face. "And what is their aim?"

"To rid the world of abominations." I sighed deeply and braced for whatever reaction would follow. "I hate to disappoint you, Mr. President, but the truth is I retired from the

Underground Railroad before the Draft Riots. The Overseers became too great a threat to travel alone. I only rescued those men as a favor to Sergeant Cooper."

His head tilted, and his eyes pressed in. "And who is Sergeant Cooper to you?"

I reminded myself to continue answering in a lower tone. "He's a pillar in the negro community in New York. Our paths inevitably crossed. He wanted me to rescue his friend's family from slavery, but I never could find them. That same friend was among the 151. I figured I owed him." There was no harm in using the truth to hide the truth. The weight of such a failure created a reasonable obligation.

"Hmm..." He nodded again and kept his eyes on me. That inquisitive hum was a little maddening. I kept reminding myself to stay calm, or else I would expose myself. "And would you, Miss Runaway, be open to more operations of this sort?"

***

"Unless there is lamb's blood on the door," I said to Dinah. "The Israelites were also under God's judgment, but they escaped a plague of death meant for the firstborn in Egypt. The blood of the lamb was God's mercy."

Mary Anne's face brightened with a revelation, then she uttered her desires as if in prayer. "What if God gave us these powers for a reason?" It had been a long while since she had such soft and humble eyes toward John. "You have my power, Lady Cohen's, and Charlotte's. You could end the war yourself if you wanted to."

It was harrowing how cold my husband's gaze was. "'If' is the operative word."

Mary Anne winced, and her jaw tightened. "My husband could die."

"An admirable decision he—no doubt—grappled with. I would hate to affect Mr. Cooper's choices. You know how he detests that."

Cooper leaned against the wall and quietly sighed, bearing the responsibility of John's subtle rage. "We don't need anything from him, Mary Anne."

"This isn't about us!" Her voice and heart elevated, as if she had been waiting to express her true fears for seven months. "It's about the nation. It's about hundreds of thousands of lives. Wives losing husbands. Mothers losing children!"

"John…" I pleaded softly. I didn't want him to hurt my friend, though I recognized that my friends had greatly offended him. But I also contained memories of Mary Anne's reddened face and the explosive destruction in her wake, and her pink cheeks had already reddened.

Perhaps that was my ingrained fear, and Mary Anne posed no particular threat—even as a pregnant, angry woman, because John had absolutely no sense of danger when he leaned closer to her and spoke plainly. "The war has served as a fitting distraction while we've built our ranks—without you, might I add—Mary Anne."

"But the war will end." Dinah, thankfully, sucked all of the oxygen out of the room and put out that fire. Her tone was far more assured than hope, even prophetic. "Grant is a butcher. He'll do whatever is necessary to achieve victory. He has enough resolve to stomach the losses."

Mary Anne and I shifted our glances between Cooper and each other. I never wanted him to join the army, and I had such a terrible sense of dread. Was Cooper already a calculated sacrifice for Lincoln and Grant? Was his destiny to be like the fallen heroes of Fort Wagner, and was I wrong to stand in the way of such honor? And the quiet in the room was killing me, hearing so clearly Cooper's breath, in what could be our final night together. "How much longer do you think it'll last?"

Dinah pursed her lips and shrugged nonchalantly. "Perhaps a year or two at most. Neither side could stomach a third."

I fell back into my husband's chest; my head pressed in and hidden. I had already lost Sam to the war, Dave, Harvey, and Asha to the riots. Steve was going to return to battle, and I expected Danny might as well. What were the odds that I wouldn't have to prepare for another funeral with not even a body to bury? "I know you wanted to grow silently in the chaos, but that won't last long."

John's hands held my arms, and he kissed my forehead. I hoped his heart would soften toward my position.

Dinah must have feared that to be the case. "The Union will prevail, the South will pick up the pieces, and the nation will focus on expansion." She spoke as if it were a threat. "And if niggers are suddenly equal, who do you think the humans will turn their hatred toward?"

***

I had looked away—in shame, I suppose—but forced myself to meet his eyes again. "To be honest, sir, I presently would not."

He became very quiet. Lincoln's face didn't change, but his shoulders slowly sank. I feared I had disappointed him.

"I trust that you have nothing to do with the Overseers, but they have their hooks deep in this nation. Federal and local governments have turned a blind eye to it, and I don't understand why. My life, and the lives of others like me, will continue to be in peril long after the war unless they are stopped."

Lincoln leaned back in his chair and crossed his long legs, considering my words. They were difficult to digest. "What evidence do you have against these Overseers?"

"I have documentation detailing connections, bank accounts, crimes, locations, and more."

"You've gathered this evidence yourself?" The subtle, heightened pitch in his voice assured me again of his admiration.

"No, sir," I said, suppressing a smile. "But I can vouch for it."

I began raising my hand, intending to pull back my collar and show him where the zealots branded me. I'll never forget the scent of my burning flesh or the way my skin sizzled. "They've burned people like me. I was almost burned alive myself…" My hand faltered and returned to my lap. If I were to show him my scar, it would be easier to identify Charlotte as Runaway. I wasn't ready to surrender that part of myself yet. "If I am to help the Union in any further operations, I must know we share the same enemy and possess the same sense of justice."

***

"We're a long way from equality," Cooper reminded us. "The Senate is going to vote on a constitutional amendment to abolish slavery. There is no doubt it will pass, but it's likely to die in the House."

That would have been a grueling disappointment, if not for Dinah's low and hysterical giggles. Cooper and I gazed as if she were mad. "I pity you humans. You lack the power necessary to forge your own futures. How blessed I am to have evolved beyond your limitations," she sneered.

That arrogant woman raised her head higher. "Mary Anne had a point about your power, John. With me, Kachina, and the others by your side, we could defeat their demoralized armies. Even united, they wouldn't be enough."

"We don't have the numbers to survive any sort of a victory," I said dismissively.

"There are more of us out there. They'll join us. Besides…" Her mouth twitched into a small smirk before her face became like a stone tablet etched in judgment. "…we don't have to worry about our small numbers if we shave theirs down. Significantly."

The horror on Mary Anne's face made me embarrassed to be associated with Dinah. But I knew John had those feelings immediately after learning of my pregnancy. It wasn't a plausible option. Perhaps if we wanted to win a battle or a war, but not to build a nation for our children.

Cooper didn't bother taking the time to be horrified. "You're a demon." His judgment was simple, and it wasn't done in rage.

Dinah shifted her entire body away from Cooper's direction and spoke to John. "Why is this human even in here?"

"You know, that superiority complex coming from you is rich: a black woman, impersonating a black man, impersonating a white one."

Dinah rolled her head back toward Cooper's direction. The expression on her face was difficult to explain, but it reminded me of my clumsy piano playing. Everything can be fine until your fingers press on two notes that don't belong together, and the sound scratches your brain. "Can we please put this human out in the street where he belongs?" she asked John, more firmly.

"The street?" Cooper fully showcased his stunning smile as he chuckled and threw his hands in the air. "I know you moved up in the world since becoming a mass murderer, but perhaps you could remind the room what your last profession was?"

Oh, Dinah was rattled! Rattled enough to holler, but her voice didn't quite sound like her own. The pitch and tone rose, becoming clear and pure like a bell, as her pigmentation and hair lightened. She began reaching and running toward Cooper with shortening limbs, until she was swallowed in my clothes. John had stoically watched their altercation, but my husband's eyes instantly widened in a way that frightened me. He disappeared from my side and reappeared beside Cooper, so that his fingers latched a hold of Dinah before Emma's fingers could smash my friend's head through the wall.

They disappeared again, then reappeared behind us all. John had just enough strength to toss Dinah on his bed, but if she persisted, he couldn't defeat her with strength alone. "Sit."

John did himself no favors if he was trying to convince the world that he didn't control Dinah or, at least, had her trained as a pet. She was eager to jump and attack Cooper again, but she dropped onto the mattress, huffing, grunting, and gritting her teeth. John's voice was particularly menacing; it sent a shiver down my spine. His eyes also fiercely shone with authority until Dinah's breathing calmed, and she was a pouting child.

John stepped away from her, having confidence that she would not defy him. Mary Anne was awfully quiet as she stared at the child across from her, one eye slightly narrowed. She hadn't moved to protect Cooper or even screamed.

"Just so we're clear," Dinah seethed, "your husband was three seconds from having his head knocked off."

Mary Anne circled her stomach like a crystal ball before smirking. "And just so we're clear, you were two seconds from having your brains splattered across this wallpaper."

Dinah screamed within a closed mouth, but John's voice swept over and snatched up her whole soul. "Hush."

I watched Cooper play cards a few times. He had a wonderful poker face. It was nearly impossible to tell when he had a bad hand. Dinah wouldn't have killed him in front of us, but she had a history of hurting Cooper. Still, he didn't allow fear to show on his face. He didn't even flinch. Then again, I would have had all the confidence in the world if Mary Anne were in my back pocket.

"You have to excuse Dinah," I told him. "She has so many voices in her head that she says all of the insane ideas out loud." I briefly gave a good glare in her direction. "We aren't going on a killing spree. That's not the world I want to build for my child."

I had no talent for games. Cooper could always tell what I was thinking, and I hoped he saw the sincerity in my eyes. What we shared was far more important than being past lovers or friends. We were parents of children who deserved endless possibilities.

"Then work with us."

A minimal brow raised on my husband's face. I was a little surprised myself.

Cooper had to take a hard swallow of his pride. It's not as though he hadn't come to the revelation that we were too powerful to defeat, but I didn't expect him to plead to John. "Humans have more in their hearts than hatred. Try preying on their gratitude."

"Helping to end the war would make families extremely grateful." Mary Anne tried to sell her story with a cheerful smile. "The government would feel like it owed you something."

John predictably scowled. "The government doesn't owe you anything and never gives without taking something of value away."

***

My husband's words still lingered in my thoughts. He knew more about politics, but I knew a great deal about determined men. For all his power, the president was still a man. "I take the attempt on your life seriously, Miss Runaway, and I'll continue to pursue the men responsible. If you possess evidence, I will pursue every lead until we achieve equal rights and protection for all citizens of these United States." The existence of the Overseers was a stain upon the nation he governed, and Lincoln was embarrassed and offended by his failure to stop them.

"If you grant me three days, I can provide all the evidence necessary to bring these zealots to justice."

His lips tightened, unsatisfied with the delay. "And then, Miss Runaway, what are your intentions?"

***

"Runaway is such a big success. Tonight is proof of that." I was glad that Mary Anne witnessed a room of esteemed professionals losing their minds over me. She always cared about recognition, and she loved us so deeply. "You'd be heroes if you ended the war."

"Not with men like Mr. Stemple." John's disgust was controlled to a sneer, but he spoke so matter-of-factly. "He's not even an Overseer. He's just a rich American influencer, concerned about someone who looks different having power." The last thing John needed was to see the ugliness of this world like Dinah. Stemple probably affirmed all of his fears.

"Then how about someone who looks the same?" Mary Anne's smile fell, and her voice was no longer that of a pleading wife, terrified of becoming a widow. She was calm, and she waddled over to us as if she owned the room. "I'm calling in your debt, Mr. Cohen. If Runaway can't be the face that ends the war, then it has to be yours."

***

My eyes fell to the playful thumbs in my lap, then quickly reverted to Lincoln's gaze. He had leaned in, eager to hear my answer. I had to be mindful of every word and not advance our plans too quickly. "There is much I have not explained, and much I would love to trust you with. Forgive me. I am honored to be here, but I ask that you grant me patience and trust."

I wished I could read his thoughts as he carefully picked me apart with those gray eyes. "The nation owes you a great debt of gratitude. The least I can offer, for now, is my trust."

My stomach was in knots. I was tempted to tell him more—even a little desperate—but it wasn't the proper time. "And if all is well once we meet again, I would like to introduce you to someone."

"Someone like you?" He did well, masking his curiosity.

"Someone much more powerful."

His face firmed, and he nodded a few times. "Someone like Ghost?"

My heart slid down to my stomach. I shouldn't have been surprised that the president invoked his name. It would have been odd if he had never mentioned a killer with such extraordinary power. "No, I hope not. A man like Ghost would never cooperate with you." I masked my nerves with a solemn smile. "This man is different. This man is better."

***

Years ago, Mary Anne had no idea how to control her power. She didn't even know what it was. Lady Cohen told her that John was in trouble, and she had the power to save him. She acted out of reckless love for a conman, and her combustion saved him. More importantly, Mary Anne kept me alive in Five Points during the Draft Riots. John openly declared that he was indebted to Mary Anne. Was preserving an entire nation a fair cost for preserving one life? Perhaps not normally, but John's guiding belief was that my life outweighed everyone else's.

John's hardened brow softened. I had a duty to my dear sister to nudge him along. "You don't have to order the others to be involved, John. You can keep your vow."

John raised his eyes to the ceiling, then closed them as he breathed. "Can we trust Lincoln?"

Dinah sat with her legs folded, slumped forward. "Lincoln won't be president forever."

"The obvious successor would be Grant, if he wants it." Cooper smiled hesitantly, small but optimistic. "You could do a lot of good for your people under another twelve years of Republican presidencies."

John took a few seconds more to ponder this monumental shift. It was not the path he expected to walk. When John exhaled and lowered his head, the ground beneath us finally stabilized. "If I am to help the humans, I would require more than gratitude. Much more."

***

As the roaring fire and Lincoln's breath faded into the background, the White House felt a little too quiet. I felt as though I was intruding, and I certainly didn't want to keep Mary awake with worry. I had someone waiting for me, as well. "I really should be headed back, Mr. President."

"Before you go…" Lincoln said as he rose, taking hold of the Bible. When he placed it in my hands, it felt heavier than it should have. "Take this token of appreciation."

The leather was stretched and worn. I flipped through the pages. A folded letter from him rested inside. I planned to read it privately. The pages were boldly printed, which explained the weight and thickness. Passages had been circled, underlined, with notes scribbled in the margins. In the very back was a short, handwritten message: *"All moral courage shares the same source. May you continue to seek refuge here. A. Lincoln."*

I nearly panicked when a teardrop hit the page and wrinkled it. I closed it and wiped my face before more damage could be done. "Thank you, sir."

"You're most welcome." He gave a small, humble nod. "I shall await your return here, same hour, three days from now."

I pressed the Bible to my chest and gave a final nod before returning to John to shape the nation's future.

Chapter Eighteen

Before I met Lincoln, John insisted on destroying the knife with Moses's blood and confiscating the zealot's supply. Mr. West was trusted enough to infiltrate the halls of Congress, but he didn't know where all of the blood vials were kept. Steven at least knew where Mr. West kept his portion of the supply, so John went with him. They removed the blood from Mr. West's residence and burned it somewhere secluded. It was best to keep such things out of the hands of human authorities.

After I returned, I briefed my friends on the conversation with the president. Dinah appeared a bit bored, but I suppose it was easy enough for her to predict our conversation. Mary Anne and Cooper were impressed with Lincoln's gift and short letter. Lincoln expressed concise words of gratitude on behalf of the Union. My friends were also curious about my husband's plans.

John was quiet as I explained. A grin broke through when I mentioned Lincoln knew of the Ghost persona. There was a gleam of pride as he held my mementos, but he offered no commentary. When the questions came, John said he needed to sleep. Even after they left, John and I barely spoke. He didn't even try to entice me.

My mind was too excited to rest. The events of the day repeated in my head, from John on his knees to standing by my side, proudly proclaiming me as his wife, to men who wanted to keep me in chains. We came a long way from dreaming about a simple porch swing, and there were more dreams to be had. I was able to ease my mind about an hour after John dozed off and drifted to sleep myself.

"Charlotte…" A faint mumble nudged me from my peaceful slumber. It wasn't the first time he called out for me, but I didn't want to leave our porch swing. John's arm was wrapped around me as I held our baby girl. I didn't let it go until about the third time he called my name.

"What is it, John?" I reluctantly opened my eyes. He was indistinguishable, shrouded in darkness. "John?"

My husband moaned as if he were in pain.

"John?" I got closer to him. He was tossing and turning. He was normally a light sleeper and quiet like the dead. "John…" I touched his chest, and his hand clasped onto my arm. I winced, but John immediately loosened his grip once he recognized me. "John, what's wrong?"

"Nothing." His voice was trembling, and so were his hands. His heart was dancing for dear life.

"John, be honest with me…" He had his mother's powers, my powers, and Mary Anne's. He had Dinah's but released it. That meant he had one more, and it certainly wasn't Emma's. "You saw something, didn't you?"

"No. I didn't see anything." I hadn't heard that much pain in his voice since I left him after his mother was killed.

"Is it me? Or is it the baby—?"

"No." John pressed his hands upon my back as if he would never let me go, but I didn't find much comfort. "I didn't see any death, but you felt so far away from me…"

"Well, I'm not going anywhere." I tried to be unshakeable for him, but my voice wavered. Even though we had been in dangerous situations, I hadn't taken much time to ponder my death. I was certainly willing to die for my loved ones, but there was a child within me who needed my heart to beat. "We'll never be apart, John. We're going to die together, old and gray."

His heavy breaths weren't the reassurance I wanted. He held me tighter.

"Promise me, John. I'll die in my sleep beside you after we've watched our grandchildren grow up. We'll have the perfect life together."

"I promise…" He mumbled. He didn't sound confident, but John wouldn't lie to me.

I nudged John, and he scooted over for me. I listened to his heart until it slowed to a steady pace. His breathing deepened, and his body calmed down. John couldn't live without me, and I depended on that fact. Even if I were to die prematurely, he would rescue my soul before an angel could escort me elsewhere. We would be fine. I had to believe that with all my heart.

I awakened to soft lips pressed upon my own. I grinned and sank deeper into the sheets. John was dressed for the day. "I overslept?"

"Your friends are about to leave for the train station. Cooper and Mary Anne are at the door."

I hopped right up and got dressed as quickly as possible. We were supposed to ride the train together back to New York, but that was before I met Mrs. Griffing. We had to stay in town long enough to deliver my speech. John and I would keep our room booked for the next few days, but we would go home once I was dressed.

I opened the door, and Cooper's eyes were immediately drawn to John, who was glaring from behind. Cooper suffered through a few seconds of silence, but John did not relent. "John, may I speak to your wife in private?"

"No."

"John…" My voice was firm, but my hands were gentle when I reached for his hand and kissed it. "Would you be a dear and fetch me some tea? And some fruit, please? For the baby?"

John's eyes didn't wander from Cooper, but he did head for the door. "I have to fetch you some morning flowers, anyhow."

Mary Anne and Cooper stepped out of his way, but John made it a point to glare harder as he passed by his rival. It successfully made them both uncomfortable, and I was a little embarrassed. "He brings me flowers every morning."

"That's romantic." Mary Anne practically swooned. "You two truly are wonderful together. I'm happy for you both." Her voice was sweet and sincere. I happily welcomed her inside, and her husband.

Cooper slightly bowed his head. "I wanted to apologize for what I said about John last night. I hope you can at least understand why I was concerned."

"Of course. If the accusation were true, it would be a horrible thing." I crossed my arms. "But it wasn't true, so you can understand why I found the accusation to be so horrible." Much had happened since our argument. I didn't have time to dwell on my anger, and I didn't intend to keep it. "John isn't a bad man. At times, he's even extraordinary."

Cooper's lips tightened, and he nodded a few times. "I hope so, Charlotte. You know I think the world of you."

"We both do." Mary Anne's smile was warm and bright. I prayed that I could keep her happy, but that highly depended on Lincoln.

"Take care of little Charlotte." I took the liberty of holding her stomach. I couldn't believe Mary Anne wasn't already due.

"Well, you take care of little Mary Anne." She giggled, but I knew her well enough to know she was a little serious.

"I wish." It would have been wonderful to return the honor she bestowed upon me. "John wants me to name our daughter Lillian Cohen."

"It is a beautiful name." I must have glared at her, because she laughed. "Just because you take on someone's name doesn't mean you become them. After all, you're the new Lady Cohen."

That was the first time I heard the title and hadn't flinched. "Lillian never dreamed of anything this grand before." I felt Mary Anne's belly flutter. I didn't have John's talent, but I had a sense the next generation would be powerful. Mary Anne's family was going to be a part of that, so our husbands needed to be allies. "If you find my husband before you go, please apologize to him."

"I will," Cooper assured, and he was a man of his word. I hugged them both, and they went on their way. John told me later that Cooper saw him in the lobby and apologized. John wanted to give him a hard time, but he accepted Cooper's hand for my sake. I had hoped our trip would make them friendly, but I settled for their alliance.

After breakfast, I held my bouquet of geraniums to my chest and took John's hand. The time for snow had passed, but it was still cold in the Dakota Territories. Nathaniel's fires kept the mansion warm. John gathered our closest allies in a parlor and shared key details from my meeting with Lincoln. The most surprising piece of information was certainly his power.

"Does this mean we've already won?" Tillie asked, her voice brightened with hope. All of them had similar wide-eyed expressions, except Dinah. She was quiet and still seemed rather bored.

"We shouldn't get ahead of ourselves. He has a lot to consider for the nation, and his power isn't absolute. In the meantime, Lincoln's abilities shall remain a secret between us. If the zealots discover them, he'll become an irresistible target."

"John…" Nathaniel's voice was soft and soothing. "If you do fight in the war, you don't have to do it alone."

"Nate is right," Adam said. "We can defeat the Confederates in no time."

"No." John was stern. "I made a promise that I wouldn't risk the lives of my people for human affairs. I meant that. No casualty is acceptable to me. As your leader, I will bear this responsibility."

Adam sighed heavily, shook his head, then smiled at the man he admired. "You are a man of legend, a true warrior king."

I watched their faces to see how my fellow Americans would react to such a title. Adam was used to a monarch, but we were somewhat removed.

No one even flinched.

"I can handle the Union and the Confederates. Your tasks will be centered around growing and protecting our community."

The most important task went to Dinah, who was charged with finding wherever the zealots were hiding more vials of blood. John assigned Tony and Hoshi to assist. Hoshi could offer extra hands if needed, and Tony's mastery of shadows made it easy to sneak around. They'd be good for a heist mission. John wanted to keep the killing to a minimum until he had met with Lincoln himself.

Tillie was upset that she couldn't act in her normal role, but her knowledge of the zealots made her invaluable. She had to sort through our evidence for Lincoln. James and Adam were assigned to help, and when Evelyn learned of it, she volunteered.

As for Kachina, Nathaniel, and Zhang, they were tasked with continuing to build up our community. We had to fortify our security, continue building homes, and places for children to play. Javier was a carpenter in his old life, and he worked well with the former slaves as they put their trade skills to good use. Our abilities assisted them well. Arthur could fly supplies or tools to any location. Henry could also build fast. He didn't begin as a good craftsman, but his speed let him practice quickly. Emma enjoyed carrying bundles of material to work sites, and Goldie's sparks were good for welding.

John kept himself busy as he oversaw all tasks, but he prioritized training men. We had many skilled Indian warriors who could help train the depowered people. They respected John's power and had accepted him as their chief. I had faith they were willing to die to protect their home.

I would have loved to watch John, shirtless, dominate every man bold enough to try his luck, but I was given a different task. He wanted me to prepare for my big speech and take care of our baby. I didn't have the heart to argue, since I honestly needed the time. I didn't want to show my scars again. They would be too great a distraction from my words.

I sketched a fitted frock coat with puffy sleeves. It would be Union blue and decorated with golden buttons. I was tempted to sketch a pair of pants, but I decided that it would be too masculine. A flowy blue skirt was more appropriate. Under the frock coat would be a lacy white high-collar and long-sleeved shirt. It was too big a task for me, so I asked two former slaves, Martha and Agnes, to help with construction.

There was much I wanted to say. I could have rebuked the nation for allowing slavery to take root and being slow to abolish it. I could have cheered for utter destruction in the South, but how many people were like Sheryl and Richard? They risked a great deal to help me and other slaves escape. They were much better than the mob in New York that nearly killed me and burned Harvey alive. I wanted to speak to the strength and promise of America, but I didn't know how much I believed in it. There was also the audience to consider. I imagined it would mostly be women, and there was only so much that women were allowed to do.

I paced along the marble floor as I pondered. I gazed out the giant windows and tried to soak in the beauty of early Spring sunshine, but quickly grew tired of the light. I unlatched the plush red curtains, and the bedroom filled with darkness. I lay across the unfamiliar bed and stared at the crown molding. Kachina had such fine details and creativity, but I was an uninspired mess. Eventually, I told myself that if I sat at the mahogany desk, the words would flow onto the page. I must have written a dozen versions of the same speech, and all of them ended up as kindling.

The night before my big debut, John came through the door and witnessed me burning the thirteenth attempt. "Woman, what is wrong with you? I'm certain that one was fine."

"How would you know? You haven't read it."

"I would if you let me." He was so desperate to help me, and that frustrated me even more. I sat on the floor and watched my words crisp and break into embers. "Charlotte, whatever you write, I know it'll be perfect."

"You don't know that…" His praise added pressure to my chest. If it weren't for him, I wouldn't have been in such a fine mess. "I don't know what to say."

"Of course, you do." He spoke with a chuckle. "You're amazing with words."

"What if we only think I am?" I hid my face in my hands and shook with shameful fright. I had dreamed of writing for so long, yet I couldn't put two lines together without it sounding awful. "What if no one else likes my writing? What if the one thing I always wanted to do is something I'm not good at?"

I hated myself for having doubts and shattering John's illusion of a fearless woman. Waiting to hear his response was torture. "Art is subjective."

"Nothing is completely subjective!" I uncovered my face. John's expression was more baffled than disappointed. "You can hone your skills, but you either have a gift or you don't."

"Charlotte," John smiled and reached for my hand, "take us home."

When I looked at the white columns and deep red curtains with gold trim, it made me feel like a character in a Roman epic. But I did miss the quiet space John crafted for me. I took his hand, and as I rose to my feet, I carried us both to familiar wooden floorboards. It was cold and dark, but John guided me to my desk effortlessly and set me down. Then he kissed my forehead and took a step back. "No one else matters."

I directed my frustration into a heavy sigh. "That's what you always say, John!"

"And it's true." My beloved grabbed an extra blanket from a chest and draped it over my shoulders. There were matches on the mantle and blocks of wood stacked by the fireplace. He had a roaring fire in less than a minute. He wasn't one to complain about the cold, but he stretched his palms toward the flames. "These words will be perfect because you'll say what needs to be said in your own voice. Charlotte Cohen only answers to herself, her husband, and her Creator."

I latched on tighter to the blanket. "It's not that simple—"

"You were right about that green dress. I'm right about this." He lit a candle for me and set it on the desk. Then he took some paper from a drawer and set a pen beside it. I imagined him to be a stern teacher, overlooking a shy and talented student. "Whatever you say to those humans will be an honor bestowed upon them. If they don't receive it, it's their loss."

I don't know why I found his snobbery to be so amusing. "I'm sorry."

"For what?"

I shrugged. "For being afraid."

I braced myself for a lecture or more supremacist views as he knelt beside me. Instead, he smiled. "It's good to remind me that you're not perfect. It keeps me grounded. I'll have to add it to my list."

I glared and pinched his hand.

"Ouch." I couldn't have hurt him too badly. He was hauling lumber with Emma earlier, so he was strong enough for whatever I threw at him.

"Am I…" I was so embarrassed to ask; I was blushing. "…still divine?"

"Always." He only pecked my lips. I hid my disappointment in the blank pages. I would have gladly allowed him to distract me for another hour or so, but focus was required. John got ready for bed. When he was under the sheets, he casually placed another burden on my shoulders. "Have you thought of a proper name for our land?"

"I've given it some thought…" Only one answer seemed appropriate to me, but I didn't know if John would like it.

"Well, it will need to be decided by the time we speak to Lincoln. I'm certain he'll want to know the name of our budding nation."

I placed that monumental responsibility in the back of my mind. The speech came first.

John's words reminded me of Douglass's advice. I pulled John's Bible from the bookshelf and went through my annotations. I still didn't have many sentences to string together, but certain verses spoke to me. I jotted them down, reflected, and prayed until I was at peace. If the Holy Spirit could imbue Stephen with the proper words to say to defeat his critics, I would trust in God's power as well.

In the morning, I decided to cook breakfast in the tavern. One of the cooks was a lovely, dark woman with calluses on her hands from harsh days in the field. Now, she worked tirelessly in the kitchen, always with a smile and a lovely hum. I added salt to her grits, and she swooned after a tasting. "Thank you, Lady Charlotte."

"My pleasure, Bethany."

When I brought out a plate for my husband, he was conversing with Adam. Evelyn was predictably at his side. My surprise was that Nathaniel and Goldie were in the corner, enjoying a meal with Emma. "Mind your business," my husband warned with a smile.

"I am…" I eased toward the kitchen, but my eyes wandered back to them. They had been working together rather closely, but I hoped Spring would be blooming more than flowers.

After breakfast, I polished my notes and said a few prayers before my beautification process. Martha and Agnes helped me get dressed. They did their final tucks and stitching, so the fit was perfect. The frock's buttons weren't functional. They were decorative beads, and I had a pair of earrings to match. The ends of the frock were pulled together by a leather belt, and only at my waist. I wanted the lovely lace flowers and the skirt to be visible.

I looked in the mirror as Martha brushed my hair. I thought of how John would pet it and remark on its softness. It did look lovely, cascading down my shoulders. "I think I want to wear it down."

"Down?" Martha asked, surprised.

"Yes. I'm certain." My hair stretched down the center of my back and could become a beast if not properly tamed. It wasn't comfortable when Martha braided along the crown of my head and pinned it down, but it did make the loose hair manageable. She gently brushed my curls, so a bouncy wave remained. Agnes added pomade to give it a nice shine.

There was a knock at the door just as they finished. I assumed it was John and positioned myself for his immediate line of sight. "Come in."

I lived for the smile that spread across his lips. His feet were drawn to me. John's hand settled at my nape, feeling my tightest and thickest curls. "You're wearing your hair down?"

"I felt like embracing my femininity today."

"You did a marvelous job, ladies, though you had a marvelous canvas to play with."

Martha and Agnes bashfully bowed and left us to ourselves.

John's hands moved to my shoulders and down my sleeves. His eyes lingered on my chest. I was covered, but the top was sheer.

"I was mindful of you, John. No need to tear the buttons off."

"How thoughtful of you." He kissed the top of my neck, and I resisted the urge to completely wilt in his arms.

"You have something to look forward to, if you behave."

He pulled away but gazed a little while longer before taking my hand. "Let's be off."

We blinked to the Willard, found a carriage, and then traveled to Hope Harvest Church. We were fifteen minutes early, and a crowd was still coming in. It was mostly white women with their friends, a few with their husbands. The room was ten percent black and twenty percent men.

"If you were Emma, you'd be breaking my hand."

"Sorry…" I eased my grip, but my heart wouldn't let up. I didn't expect over a hundred people to be in attendance. It was standing room only, and the aisles were crowded.

A woman excitedly waved us down and motioned us to the front pew. There was a spot reserved for the two of us. "We're pleased to have you, Mrs. Cohen."

"The pleasure is all mine." My voice trembled.

Mrs. Griffing was sitting on the other end and got up to greet us. "Charlotte, I am absolutely elated to have you here. Are you excited?"

"You could say that."

"You'll be wonderful. I can tell. You have one of those faces. And you look wonderful, full of life!"

"Thank you."

Mrs. Griffing touched my arms and smiled deeply. "You'll close out our program, so take time to breathe. You'll be wonderful."

I nodded and took deep breaths. John and I sat and quietly observed. Pastor Baldwin opened the program with a greeting and a fiery prayer, but it was his wife who introduced the speakers. Two black men told their stories of life on the plantation. A black woman who had lost her husband in Fort Wagner also gave a tearful speech. It reminded me of the secret dread Mary Anne kept hidden behind her supportive smile.

Every so often, I pulled my folded notes out of my pocket. John stroked my hand as a reminder to stay calm.

Mrs. Griffing came up next. She made an immediate demand for the abolition of slavery, calling on the House to pass the Thirteenth Amendment. She said any other action was cowardly and an affront to God. She referred to the physical suffering of the former slaves and the anguish of the widow. I shouldn't have been surprised when her hand pointed in my direction. "God bless Mrs. Cohen, who was brave enough to bear her lashes to the cowards of Washington. I pray the conviction of the Almighty grips their hardened hearts, if not his just and vengeful wrath."

My face remained still, but I caught myself squeezing John's hand again. He didn't make much of an expression, but his jaw tightened. I did wear the dress for attention, so I shouldn't have been uncomfortable.

But I felt so much pressure.

A few hymns were sung next. The psalmist was talented, and the congregation sang along. The songs soothed me, but Pastor Baldwin followed. He gave a wonderful, condensed sermon, noting that men-stealers are supposed to be put to death, abused slaves are supposed to be set free, and the runaways are meant to be cared for. He rebuked the slaveowners who removed holy scriptures from the Bible and pastors who twisted God's words to appease devils. It was the most excited the room had been. The black voices were especially loud.

Once he began to wind down, the woman who seated us pointed to the stage and mouthed, "You're next."

I reached for my notes again, but John's hand rested on mine. "You'll do wonderfully, my dear. Just remember who matters."

Thunderous applause followed the end of Pastor Baldwin's speech, and my heart dropped. He spoke a few more words. I didn't realize he was introducing me until my name was spoken and his hand reached toward me. Still, the moment didn't seem real until John nudged me.

As I stood, I felt so tiny, like that little girl Lady Cohen brought home to the plantation. I was accustomed to keeping my head down. I never looked in the eyes of white people, but Lady Cohen wanted to see me. Then there was John. He wouldn't be satisfied until I had grown out of my shyness. He wouldn't allow me to be like everyone else.

The steps to the pulpit seemed abnormally large, but that might have been my nerves. Pastor Baldwin took my hand and helped me rise to the top. The feeling of being small in such a big moment didn't go away, but as I approached the podium, I remembered who was truly most important. As I looked out at the audience, I didn't see the faces of attentive men and women, clamoring for inspiring words. I saw the blue eyes of a little boy.

"Don't you know that you're strong?"

I took a deep breath and prayed that God would speak through His willing vessel.

"Good evening, ladies and gentlemen who long for liberty. I would like to thank Mrs. Josephine Griffing for inviting me to this blessed gathering. I would also like to thank the ladies of Washington who labor tirelessly in the cause of abolition, and Hope Harvest Church for providing this fine venue. Your courage and conviction are not only admirable; they are necessary.

"My name is Charlotte Cohen. If I may be so bold as to presume that if any of you know me, you—no doubt—recognize me as the woman in the green dress who donned her plantation scars at the White House. I did not come before you today to bear my flesh. I came to bear something much more intimate.

"This dreadful war has taken fathers, sons, lovers, and dear friends. As women, we don't stand in the front lines to face an army of guns and bayonets. We're at the bedside of our children as they say their nightly prayers. We sit in pews with our heads bowed and hands clasped, appealing to an Almighty God for peace and mercy. And we stand in the doorways of our home, waiting for letters from chaplains and commanding officers with the most dreadful news. These tasks may appear small in the moment, but they are monumental in the eyes of God. We teach our children to hope. We demonstrate our faithfulness to our Creator, and we accept His divine will, even if it is beyond our comprehension. Our children not only watch us when we thrive, but also when we suffer.

"When the Apostle Paul spoke of Timothy's sincere faith, he spoke of its origin: his grandmother, Lois, and his mother, Eunice. Our children and grandchildren are our first disciples. We tend to our home. We teach our sons to love God by honoring His commandments. We are called to love our neighbor, yet we do not treat them with any modicum of dignity that should be afforded to another soul loved by an eternal and unchanging God. Are the enslaved not also made in His image? Is the flesh split open by the slave master's whip not the same flesh that God so wonderfully knitted in the womb?

"It is our responsibility, as women, to marry respectable men, bear innocent children, and guide them with kindness. But kindness must never become weakness. They must be kind enough to push past their fears and delicate sensibilities. They must be kind enough to offend and even hate evil. They must be brave enough to stand against a storm of adversity, even if they find themselves standing alone.

"Women make homes. Men make war. Men have the strength to win battles, and women must preserve the world they fight for. But before a single shot is fired, they pack up your teachings and take them on the battlefield and in the halls of Congress. So, I ask you today, what kind of men have you raised, and what kind of men will you choose to raise today?

"It is not only the place of men to defeat unjust laws and unrighteous enemies. When Pharaoh ordered Hebrew midwives to slay Hebrew boys, they disobeyed his command because they feared God. Jochebed sailed her child in a basket up the Nile River, and through God's abundant grace and divine mercy, that child became a leader who unleashed God's judgment until the enslaved were free.

"We mustn't fear God's plans for our children, nor should we reject the necessary travailing it takes to will them into this world. If Hannah had not persevered through her grief and dedicated her son to a higher purpose, Samuel would not have been born to anoint David as King. And if Ruth had not continued to show loyalty to her mother-in-law and her God, after they lost their husbands and Naomi lost a son, the House of David would have never come to be. God's Providence is often demonstrated through the diligent hands of a woman. Those hands may hold a tambourine in worship, or they may drive a tent peg into the heads of the enemy. However God chooses to anoint your hands, let them be used to initiate necessary change.

"Women were brave enough to stand at the cross when their Savior was slain before the world, and they wept at his tomb and witnessed His Glory. We may lack the physical strength of men, but our power is demonstrated in our perseverance through longsuffering. We find a semblance of joy in our broken world and inspire men to rebuild civilization—with and for us. Adam had the whole world to himself, yet God gave him a woman because it was not good for him to be alone.

"I didn't come here today to bear my scars. I came to bear my soul. I have gazed into the rabid eyes of slave masters, foaming at the mouth like the beasts they used to chase me down. I have seen men who claimed to be pious resort to the cruelest of measures to preserve their order, not God's design. I have seen humans used, broken, and disposed of like tools. I have seen evil sitting in the seats of power, and I have seen evil in the hearts of the weak and oppressed.

"Evil is a choice. Any human can decide to indulge in its bitter fruit, and any human can refuse to stand against it.

"Are you too afraid to speak of the suffering slave to your friends? To your sisters? To your brothers? To your husbands? To your children? Surely, you are like Queen Esther and have been called for such a time as this.

"We may be the weaker sex, but we are not helpless. We have their ears. We hold their hearts. They need your courage, conviction, and even your words of rebuke. They need your compassion and your fire to spur them into action. Revolutions don't begin on the battlefield or in the halls of Congress. They begin at kitchen tables, at the cracker barrels in general stores, and in pews like these. Whispers of hope have always preceded cannon thunder.

"I stand before you as a woman and a wife. A few short years ago, I was a slave who could only dream of the life I have today. Now, I am called to make the dreams of others come true. I am made in the image of a loving and just God, and He entrusted me with the burden of bearing a child made in His image. You may be asking, 'What manner of child shall I raise?'

"One who shall act justly.

"One who shall love mercy.

"One who shall fear God rather than man.

"And one who shall be free."

The room erupted in applause. The crowd had been interjecting cheers of excitement throughout my speech. By the time I finished, everyone was on their feet. I had become bold enough to walk down the stairs and down the center aisle. Men whistled and hollered, while women waved their handkerchiefs. Some were openly weeping. I was grateful for their affirmations, but the louder they became, the more inaudible they were. The people reached for me. Some wanted handshakes, others just wanted the opportunity to pat my back or at least graze my garments. Mrs. Griffing greeted me with a hug and tears, but her words were lost in the noise.

Only one voice stood out: John's whistle at the end of the front pew. I rushed into his arms, and he squeezed me tight. "They haven't realized," he spoke in my ear, "they've been watching the rise of a queen this entire time."

I imagine Mrs. Baldwin was supposed to return to the stage, thank me for my riveting speech, and close out the night in prayer. Instead, the crowd broke out into every verse of "Amazing Grace." The psalmist led us through them, and hymn sheets helped the congregation after the first two. Many women were crying too much to even sing. Instead, they waved their hands in prayer.

I couldn't sing much myself. I was overwhelmed by the moment and would have certainly cried. I leaned on my devoted husband's arm, knowing that my place in this world was forever changed.

Chapter Nineteen

The halls of the White House were quiet and dimly lit, much like my last visit. No guards. No other visitors. Warm light seeped from the Red Room. I eased to the door and saw Lincoln sitting alone and reading a newspaper. I blinked out of the White House and returned a moment later, reappearing before him with two leather satchels filled with documents. I placed them at the president's feet just as he rose to greet me.

"Miss Runaway."

"Good evening, Mr. President." I made certain to lower my voice. "I hope you're in high spirits."

"Higher now that you've arrived." He motioned toward a chair. "If you please…"

I considered whether I should fetch John before making myself comfortable. Lincoln's tone was a bit firm. "Thank you."

Lincoln sat after I did. He didn't reach for the satchels. He kept his dark eyes focused on me. "There's been a grave development with Mr. West."

I felt as though the shadows cast over the President intended to swallow me as well. "What do you mean?"

"He was murdered in his cell." There was an inquisitive glimmer in his eyes. I prayed it was merely light bouncing off his spectacles. “A man impersonating a guard stabbed and left him for dead.”

I remembered to control my breathing, so he wouldn’t be suspicious. “I had nothing to do with that.”

“How am I to be certain?”

My body stiffened. I didn’t enjoy having my integrity questioned, but the pool of suspects was small. Any reasonable person would at least question me. “If I wanted to kill Mr. West, he would have never been left behind at the party. He was likely disposed of by an Overseer.”

I returned his gaze. I had done nothing wrong, and I didn’t ease up until Lincoln sighed and reached for the first satchel. “Their reach is troubling.”

“We share the same enemy. I do hope we can successfully work together.”

He took a stack of papers and quickly glanced through one before moving on to the next. I stayed silent to give him time to digest. Eventually, Lincoln removed his spectacles and raised his head in terrible awe. “Ghost gathered this evidence.”

Lincoln happened to take a stack of documents containing Emmett Willis’s picture and a copy of his decoded logs. Out of all the Overseers killed by John, Willis certainly had one of the flashiest departures. The stories in the papers were gruesome. But that confrontation led to invaluable leads and rescues.

“He did.”

Lincoln set the papers on the table and hunched forward. His bushy brows wrinkled, and his fingertips pressed together. “How acquainted are you with this man?” The judgment in his voice was unmistakable.

“He saved my life and others like us. We have been at odds, due to his methods, but I have learned that most of his killing has been retribution.”

His knee nervously bounced as he pondered. “Where is your friend?”

He knew. There was no getting around it. I was hoping to break it to Lincoln gently after we had more rapport. He was already tense.

"I need your word before I bring him. What is spoken in this room shall remain between the three of us. We need the freedom to walk away if we cannot come to terms with each other."

President Lincoln took a breath and sat upright. He even towered over me while in his chair. "I shall extend my trust in you, Miss Runaway."

I exhaled a breath of relief and nodded. Lincoln watched quietly as I shut every door. I did trust him, but the White House was a home. I didn't need his family or his workers to be prematurely exposed to our identities. As I shut the final door, I questioned if I was making the right decision. By that time, it seemed entirely out of my hands. I couldn't let Runaway and Ghost be the end of the story.

I appeared before my husband. He was sitting on our porch swing, sipping a glass of lemonade while he watched the stars. It was a lovely night, as if God had flicked speckles of white against a dark blue canvas. I was tempted to sit beside him and enjoy what was left of our private life. "It's time, John."

I picked up his suit jacket that was folded over the seat. Before standing, John raised his glass to the sky before devouring the rest of it. After an audible gulp, he smirked. "For New Seneca."

"For New Seneca." I helped my husband with his jacket, then straightened his tie and collar. The world might have thought John to be a monster, but I had come to believe there was a little monster in all men. I once told John that we could learn from the humans' mistakes and build a better world. As I wove my fingers between my husband's and cherished his blue eyes, our future was clearer than the night sky.

Lincoln sprang to his feet as soon as he recognized my husband. "Mr. Cohen."

"Lincoln."

The president's eyes widened, but he remained remarkably calm as his gaze fell upon me. "That would make you Mrs. Cohen?"

I was so used to wearing my mask; I had to remind myself to pull it from my face. "I am," I said in my normal voice.

Lincoln clenched his hands to restrain their tremble. "How did you bamboozle us all?"

"There are several abilities in our arsenal," John spoke plainly. "I assure you, Charlotte is the real Runaway. Given her condition, I couldn't allow any possible danger to come to her."

I touched my belly, and Lincoln took notice. "I take it your child is the reason why you refused more rescue operations."

"Mostly." Even if I weren't pregnant, John would have fought against taking such extraordinary risks. "My husband is a far more powerful ally than I."

Lincoln winced, understanding the truth of my words. "Are you the man known as Ghost?"

John's head perked up, and his chest poked out. "That's what the papers call me."

The shadows on Lincoln's face spread and darkened as his anger grew. "You've taken dozens of lives."

"You're mistaken," John said. "I haven't 'taken' any lives. I have only reaped what was forfeited after committing atrocities against my people."

Internally, I was screaming at John to be more restrained. Outwardly, my face was a steel beam when Lincoln's gray eyes tried to pump me full of judgment. "It wasn't your place to seek vengeance."

"I wouldn't have needed to seek vengeance if the United States had sought justice." John's eyes narrowed, and his tone finally sharpened. "While President Polk was busy expanding into Mexican territories, my mother and I were tied to a stake. They made me watch her burn."

John couldn't speak of his mother's death without pain breaking through his voice. "They had already shot my father. They were simple people. Performers. You would have liked them…"

Lincoln's face softened for half a second before a quiet, righteous indignation overcame him. "And would they be proud of the man they raised?"

John winced, barely enough for me to notice. "They didn't raise me. A woman named Lillian did." His voice slowly rose. "Perhaps if Andrew Jackson cared more about that little girl and her family, instead of putting down slave rebellions and forcing Indians off their land, the zealots wouldn't have made her a bitter orphan."

"The deeds of men dead and gone do not excuse your actions, sir."

"My actions don't need to be excused." The timber of his voice rattled my spine. "I was content with living a secluded life with Charlotte. But while you were busy with your war, the zealots came again. They killed Lillian and nearly burned Charlotte alive. It was necessary to take matters into my own hands."

John's hand slipped from my grasp as he took a step closer to the president. He lifted his gaze to meet Lincoln's, and his golden shine reflected in the president's eyes. "I've done you an immense favor. The Overseers would raze this house to the ground if they knew what you were. I'm purging a great evil from your nation."

"If you managed to purge all evil from this nation, would you be left standing, Mr. Cohen?" I did admire Lincoln for not cowering to John. He had a strong will and the choice to oppose John's sway. But he must have been feeling the inevitable truth that persuaded so many of our kind. "Why choose to expose your misdeeds to me now?"

"Because your feelings about my choices pale in comparison to what I can offer you." John eased away and motioned me to take a seat. I walked to the opposite end of Lincoln's couch. John sat upright in a chair, his hands resting on the arms like a regal king. Lincoln held his breath as he eased into his seat.

"My wife has always been kind and optimistic. While I sought vengeance and you waged war, she risked her life freeing slaves." John's voice brightened from his admiration. "You and I are both responsible for the end of many lives, but Charlotte never had a taste for blood. She's only killed to save my life, then to save your 151 soldiers. She doesn't talk about it, but I know those decisions weigh on her."

I had to turn away from my husband if I stood any chance of holding back tears. I didn't enjoy killing zealots, but I didn't lose sleep over them. Those Confederate boys were a different story. They were young and ignorant glory seekers with their whole lives ahead of them. Of course, John noticed my pain, even if he couldn't share it.

"Charlotte is truly a compassionate person. She seeks peace for our kind and for the Union. She convinced me to end the Draft Riots, even though she and her friends suffered from the mob's violence. Despite everything, she chose to love her enemies."

I struggled to suppress Dave's bloody and lifeless body in the Crimson Hotel. If John saw my shoulders shaking and heard me whimpering, it might have flared his past rage. I couldn't be a distraction.

"I took Charlotte's hand immediately after, and I've also taken her counsel. I am here today because of her."

I wiped my face and turned. John kept his eyes on Lincoln, but he glanced to make certain I was alright. I gave a small smile, and he reciprocated.

"Mr. President, I am here to offer you Atlanta."

The room fell deathly quiet. Only the kindling cracked in the fire. Lincoln's sharp eyes were frozen for several uncomfortable seconds. Then it thawed into a raised brow. "Atlanta?"

"Yes."

Lincoln looked to me as if he expected me to say otherwise. His nasally voice heightened when he asked, "And that is something you can procure?"

"He certainly can," I spoke before Lincoln could insult my husband further. "And he can do it without losing tens of thousands of men."

I thought my words would bring relief, yet they pressed on Lincoln's chest as he sank deeper into the cushion. There was little light in his eyes, and his breaths were shallow, as if the war itself were pressing the air from his lungs. John also took a shallow breath. "I'm well aware of your sight, Mr. Lincoln."

The president's face was unchanged, and he continued his short and quiet breaths.

"I know the burden it places on your mind and heart. As the president, you must feel responsible for each life lost during this terrible war."

Two hundred thousand Union dead weighed on his shoulders, and just as many Confederates dragged at his heels.

It was a miracle he could even stand at all. “What are you asking in exchange?”

“I have procured land in the Dakota Territories. We call it New Seneca. It’s home to liberated slaves, Indians, and others like us with extraordinary gifts. It is my priority to protect them. Therefore, if New Seneca is to stand beside the Union, I require five items.”

Lincoln offered a quiet nod.

“The first is to declare the Overseers as enemies of these United States. They will be known as hostile conspirators, justifying federal prosecution, military action, and covert missions.”

Lincoln’s stiffened and wrinkled face was unchanged.

“The second is amnesty for past crimes dealing with these hostile actors and the robberies. These two items are for your benefit. There will be no need for the Union to seek retribution against my people if we’ve committed no crimes. This inspires cooperation rather than future hostility.”

“Every coin your band stole must be returned to the Union.” Lincoln’s voice was incredibly stern.

“Of course.”

“And I must consider your evidence…” His eyes were drawn back to the stack of papers. “But I am inclined to agree if you can do as you claim.” Willis wasn’t the only man of influence connected to the zealots. Lincoln was obligated to pull that thread until it all unraveled. “What are your other items?”

“We are a small yet growing community. I have ten thousand acres of land, but I would like the United States to reserve and gift more to us.”

Lincoln’s head curiously tilted. “Ten thousand acres is already a considerable amount. Who governs this community?”

“I do, and my wife. We’ll continue to grow, and I’d rather avoid conflict in the future over land. As the head of the executive branch, you hold this power.” John had the funds to purchase more land, and he certainly had the power to seize it. In John’s mind, it was a benevolent demand.

“What is your next item?”

"New Seneca seeks to be a haven for our kind, and that invitation extends beyond the borders of the Union. I require immigration rights for foreigners who wish to assimilate."

Lincoln paused, rightfully sensing where the conversation was headed. "And what is your final item, Mr. Cohen?"

John managed to restrain a budding smirk. "Sovereignty."

"That is something I cannot permit," Lincoln said, quickly and emphatically. "It would undermine our war efforts. If we won't acknowledge the Confederacy as a nation—"

"They had the right to secede. The Tenth Amendment—"

"John…" I seethed and bulged my eyes.

Lincoln smiled, though, arrogantly like Cooper before stepping into the ring. "The Union supersedes the Constitution and is perpetual. The Southern States are engaged in active and hostile rebellion. We do not recognize the Confederacy, and we certainly will not recognize a new nation within our territories."

I silently prayed that as John's lips tightened, he would bring his political grievances under submission. The last thing I needed was for the night to end in a spirited debate about the legitimacy of income taxes.

"Your acknowledgement has no bearing on how we operate and grow. Again, I am offering cooperation rather than future conflict."

"You speak of rebellion."

"I speak of liberation and self-determination."

"Let's not derail the conversation!" I was assertive. I had to be to get a word in. "Mr. President, I understand the delicate position you are in. Of course, you can't acknowledge a new nation while dealing with open rebellion.

"However, we are a people consisting of Indians who have been betrayed and denigrated by this government, former slaves who aren't even considered persons—let alone citizens—and gifted who have been hunted and abused. You cannot expect loyalty from people who have never received it from their government."

Lincoln was doing a fine job taming his facial expressions, but I had a sense he sympathized with victims of injustice. He understood the price of the Union's moral failings more than anyone. "The loyalty of New Seneca is to John. They'd die for him. That won't change."

Lincoln's gaze intensified, and he spoke softly yet firmly. "The Union can take Atlanta."

"At what cost?" Surely, Lincoln had spoken to enough widows and soldiers who would never be whole again. "Sergeant Cooper is my dear friend. I want to save the Union soldiers. John can do that, but displaying such power comes with great risk." My heart raced. I'm not certain if it was due to my desperation to make him see or the anticipation of future dangers. "We'll attract enemies, even create them. Separation and legitimacy will grant us some protection. We can't depend on the United States, but we can protect ourselves."

"The government has made treaties with the Natives," John said.

"Tribes were willing to secede land for peace and compensation." A cynical smile graced Lincoln's lips. "You're asking the United States to do the opposite for no compensation—after stealing from our purse, mind you."

"My alliance is priceless."

Lincoln laughed, and it was too harsh to be a good sign. "And this 'alliance' is permission to conscript your 'gifted' for battle?"

"No." John raised his nose to the president. "This is a solemn oath you make with me and me alone. I will not trade their lives for humans."

Lincoln huffed through his nostrils and stewed in his frustrations. With folded arms, he pondered in silence. I looked at John, but he lightly shook his head. Now wasn't the time to interrupt Lincoln's internal struggle. He was a strong man, but the stress of the war weathered his face like the elements against a mountain.

"Before major battles, I tend to have recurring dreams." Lincoln's words were soft, as if he were lulling us into the dream with him. "I'm standing at the helm of a rushing ship, leading a fleet toward a final destination. Lately, the storm has been overwhelming. My ship continues, but thousands of ships are lost at sea." I felt as though I was tossing and turning on that boat with him. Perhaps his words carried that much weight, or perhaps his abilities allowed me to share a piece of the storm's pressure.

"For weeks, I've had the same dream every night..." Lincoln offered me a hopeful smile. "...until I met Runaway." His relief brightened his eyes, and I smiled as well. Unfortunately, Lincoln's burden returned as he turned toward my husband. "Or so I thought..."

When John took Lincoln's hand at the party, he must have felt what Dinah and so many of the others did. He may not have understood it then, but he knew trusting in John was logical. "What changed in your visions?" I asked.

"My ship hasn't slowed, but the storm has softened." I had a terrible feeling about the dream, like a chill resting on my very soul. "I do believe you can change the outcome of this war, Mr. Cohen. Your wife believes in your power, that's why she's chosen to stand beside you."

John's face tightened. He didn't appreciate Lincoln using me against him. "I cannot expose my power to the world for anything less than sovereignty."

The fire crackled as John and President Lincoln tested each other's conviction. Was Lincoln willing to let tens of thousands of men die to preserve the legitimacy of the Union? And would John let those men die, knowing how much it would weigh on my heart? Neither man wanted to walk away, but neither could afford to lose.

"Give me one week," Lincoln said. "If your evidence is sufficient, I will grant your first two items. The other two, I can grant after a demonstration of your power."

John narrowed his eyes. "If you aim to take advantage of me—"

"Presidents have immense power, but they answer to the electorate and serve with others." Lincoln did have a reelection to consider. It was certainly in our best interest that he was successful. "You have my word, Mr. Cohen. I will take executive action to reserve another ten thousand acres, and that promise will be good until the end of my second term. If you do not take advantage of these years, it will be no fault of mine."

John took a moment, then nodded.

"As far as your final item, the best I could offer is a compromise."

John's nostrils flared, but he did not interrupt.

"You would still be subjects of the federal government, but you would be free to govern yourselves. And you may not require our financial support, but infrastructure and technology will be useful to a growing community. Isolation is a death sentence for a landlocked country."

Being landlocked didn't matter to a people who could slip in shadows, travel through the air, and literally move the earth, but John had no intention of revealing the full depth of our power. He swallowed his tongue and sat on Lincoln's offer.

Lincoln then set his sights on me. "You have my word, Mrs. Cohen. Being an American means something of great value. We are not—nor have we ever been—a perfect Union. But people like you make it better. I will not allow you to shed ties with the Union. We'd be a lesser nation for it."

I tried to contain the swelling in my chest, but a smile broke through. Who could have imagined that a little girl purchased for $500 would be courted by the president? I shouldn't have needed his validation, yet I was overjoyed enough to shed a tear.

"You can trust in this great nation, and you can trust in my word."

John watched this man of immense power pull a handkerchief from his pocket. I dabbed the few teardrops and chuckled. I didn't expect to be so taken by him or his plea. When John rose to his feet, I jumped up. For a moment, I feared I had ruined everything.

"President Lincoln…"

Lincoln stood and towered over me once more. "Mr. Cohen."

John didn't crack a smile, but he extended his hand. "You had best value your word as much as I value mine."

Lincoln grinned and took a firm grip of my husband's hand. "I swear on my life."

The fire popped behind us, and Lincoln's cheap tobacco lingered in the air, yet the moment felt unreal. I had bottled so much fear about the consequences of their meeting, yet they were uniting as allies. I was genuinely thrilled, but as I rubbed my belly and tried to imagine the possibilities of our shared goals, I couldn't help but feel a terrible ache. Perhaps it was paranoia or the cynic in me looking for another way to disrupt my peace.

The last time I felt that uneasy was the day the zealots introduced the boy.

Chapter Twenty

We celebrated in our private home. Between tender kisses, John often referred to me as his queen. I wasn't enticed by the power entrusted to me, but his joy was thrilling. I lived for the smile on my husband's face as he kissed my belly. I played with his hair, wondering how his strands would mix with mine. I wasn't sold on ten children, but only having two seemed impossible. He was a fitting distraction from my anxieties, and peaceful sleep followed our lovemaking.

In the morning, I blinked to New Seneca and told Nathaniel to have Dinah bring him, Tillie, Kachina, Zhang, and Adam to our home in New York. I returned and sent John into town to fetch a few things. We cooked a late breakfast for our friends, who arrived just in time to help set the table. Kachina was kind enough to make my morning daffodils the centerpiece. We had Johnny Cakes, pork, potatoes, fruit, and eggs.

"Well, well, well…" Adam smiled as he scooped his portion of eggs onto his plate. They were less solid than usual. "It looks like you've come to see my way of doing things."

"I'm trying something a little different," I said in his ear, perhaps a bit too aggressively. "Don't get used to it."

That was the first time we invited them for a meal, and I didn't cook for them often. All plates were cleared. The boys even asked for seconds. Once they were full, John explained our meeting with Lincoln. They all tried to keep their expressions limited until John opened the floor for questions and commentary. Their eyes wandered across the room, wondering who would be the first to break the silence.

Nathaniel led things off with a smile. "This is a good deal. Many of the Indians and former slaves are pregnant or have infants. We should focus on laying roots, not burning bridges."

Adam nodded. "I agree with Nate."

Tillie rolled her eyes. "It's no surprise that the two of you would rather make love than wage war. Perhaps you boys are thinking with a different brain." She pursed her filthy lips and glared.

"Having children is a priority," John said. "We're already outnumbered by humans, and they're multiplying. If any of you can get married and start a family, you have my full blessing."

Dinah's eyes dropped to the restless hands in her lap. "Additional land will become necessary faster than we can imagine. We'll eventually need more than twenty thousand acres."

"That's what I'm worried about," Kachina said. Her voice trembled, but certainly not from fear. "Humans have betrayed the Natives and violated their treaties. How can we be certain they'll live up to their word?"

"We can't be completely certain." John looked into Kachina's intense brown eyes and spoke calmly, and even soothingly. "But I trust in Lincoln, and I trust he wants to use my power. My offer for peace was too enticing, and making me an enemy would be devastating."

Kachina leaned back into her chair and contemplated in silence. Their eyes wandered the room again. I wouldn't be surprised if they all shared her concern. Even Dinah and Tillie locked gazes for a moment.

"Peace would be nice…" Zhang had a solemn smile. He was such a kindhearted person that it was easy to forget he ran from across the world. "New Seneca is our home, and we must keep it safe."

Tillie grimaced. "Is it too late to change the name?"

"It serves as a reminder that even though humans failed, we don't have to." I was glad John spoke up. He wasn't terribly fond of the name—due to the connection with Cooper—but he liked my reasoning. "New Seneca shall be an autonomous community, governed by Charlotte and me. You all will serve as my trusted advisors, keeping the peace and executing my will. If the federal government oversteps or betrays us, they'll face my wrath. It's that simple."

Tillie, Kachina, and Dinah wore worries on their faces. I wondered if their displeasure was about the deal or if intuition made them nervous about something else. If I dwelled on their anxiety too long, I would have wrinkled my forehead as well.

"We must remember what is most important." I took my husband's hand and kissed it. "We can trust in John. We all share the same vision of freedom, and he has the strength to protect it."

John kissed my hand in return. He had such passion in his eyes; I imagined him to be making a vow. Despite my concerns about the unknown, I had the utmost faith in my husband. Soon, those wrinkles smoothed on their lovely young skin.

"I do have another suggestion regarding New Seneca."

Tillie rolled her eyes and threw her head up to the ceiling.

"We need a symbol, some kind of banner. I wanted something beautiful and strong to represent us, so…" I sighed, seeing that Tillie prepared herself to resist my idea. "Wouldn't it be appropriate if it were designed after Tillie?"

All eyes landed on our formerly feathered friend as she brought her head down, and her eyes widened. I didn't expect she'd be too stunned to respond.

"That's a wonderful idea," Zhang said.

"She was John's first recruit," Kachina reminded. "I agree with Charlotte."

"I do as well," Dinah offered a small smile to her former friend. "It's appropriate."

Everyone else verbally agreed. Once John gave a nod of approval, Tillie collapsed into her hands and sobbed. I was tempted to wrap my arms around her, but John rubbed her back. She much preferred that. It was best to let her cry it out until her composure was restored. She was far too emotional to speak out loud, so she nodded in agreement, and we left it at that.

We spent a few hours together sharing ideas. Zhang had infrastructure requests we could make to Lincoln. We couldn't always rely on Arthur and Henry to spread information around. With all the children born and soon to come, schools were going to be a must. We had even outgrown our tavern. When everyone's powers were restored in a few months, John was going to be incredibly busy with training. Nathaniel also confessed that he was courting Goldie. Adam didn't need to confess, but he did as well. I was thrilled for weddings to come! New Seneca's future was bright, but there was much work that needed to be done.

We had another week before meeting with Lincoln again. John wasn't ready to completely give up his identity, but he couldn't be Ghost while fighting for the Union. I visited Mary Anne in New York. She was a marvelous designer, and her sketches were always lovely. She was too busy to construct it, but Martha and Agnes were also master seamstresses. The inspiration was the Union uniform, but the fabric would be a darker blue and tailored to his body. His face would be hidden by a mask made of fitted leather and a cloak. Kachina collaborated with tradesmen to craft a signature belt with a hawk emblem on the buckle. They also made buttons, holsters, and a scabbard for a saber. With everyone working together, we'd have a refined disguise by the meeting.

In the meantime, I also had other obligations. My speech in Washington, D.C. was such a hit that I was invited to two other events. John supported my speeches, as long as my travels were early in the pregnancy. The first was in Upstate New York, not too far from home. The second was at P.T. Barnum's Lecture Room, which seated 3,000 people. Mary Anne told everyone she knew about it. Danny and Steve were both still in New York, so they were recruited to pack out the theater. Mary Anne invited every adult at the hotel, Steve reached out to our old associates, and Danny passed out flyers in Barnum's Museum every day.

When I told John about all the fuss Mary Anne made, he had a gleam in his eye, as if he felt challenged. Then, he invited the former slaves, every other black resident of New Seneca, and our closest friends. Word kept spreading until about a hundred people wanted to go, but then John realized transportation would have been taxing for me. If no one wanted to travel with Tony (and no one ever did, besides his sister), we had to lower the maximum to sixty. I don't know if Dinah wanted to go, but John informed her that she was required to help carry the load.

Many of the residents didn't have clothes for the theater, so I thought it would be good for Caroline and Tony to accompany me to New York. She wandered around the shops, glancing at pieces with her arms folded. Every time I asked her opinion on a dress or a man's frock, she shrugged. Tony apprehensively gave his opinion but would always defer to me. "Whatever you like, Lady Charlotte." At least he was good at holding our purchased items. When no one was looking, he stored them in his shadow.

After our third store, Caroline stopped in the middle of the sidewalk. An extravagant green silk dress was in the window, decorated with peacock feathers. She had wonderful glimmers in her eyes, and it had been a long while since I had witnessed that in her. "You should get it."

She shook her head. "It will be too expensive and much too extravagant for the occasion."

"Too expensive for who?" I touched her shoulder and smiled. "I plan to give you the world. I can certainly afford a dress. You more than deserve it."

A bright smile spread across Caroline's face before she rushed inside.

Tony chuckled and shook his head. "She always had an eye for the finer things, things we couldn't afford growing up." His smile had a great deal of sadness and relief. Much of it was for his sister's sake, but I recognized the burden John had placed on his shoulders.

"You both have done a great deal for New Seneca. There's no point in fighting for a world we can't enjoy." I tilted my head forward so he would go inside. We picked a few dresses, but mostly separate pieces that the former slaves could put together. Once Caroline had her own dress, she was much livelier and opinionated. I was grateful. I needed their help to gather shoes.

Most former slaves had only one or two pairs for work and were worn.

It was a great spectacle when we returned home and Tony unloaded our haul. I had Arthur fetch John to help dress the people. Though he didn't mind deferring to me, he had a natural sense and learned plenty from his mother. Caroline was also happy to help. Men and women cradled shiny shoes as if they were newborn babes. They bowed and kissed my hands in gratitude.

I caught John watching and blushed from embarrassment. He tilted his head and began to walk toward me. I giggled but managed to compose myself by the time he held my waist. "We should find more occasions for such things."

My brows rose in surprise. "Yes, they do look nice." As the women twirled in their fashions, I imagined a bustling town full of pleasures to enjoy. "We should have dances and plays." I bit my lip and giggled again. "We can always put your circus blood to good use."

John chuckled and held me tighter. "Perhaps, my dear. Perhaps…" I could tell by the brightness in my husband's voice that he knew his wife was correct.

The day of my speech at Barnum's, Mary Anne made certain the ballroom at the Crimson was clear for our arrival. John, Dinah, and I brought everyone in groups of twenty. Mary Anne also made arrangements for omnibuses and carriages to stop at the hotel and transport our people. The freedmen might have dressed like city folk, but they gawked as if we had landed on Mars. Despite being able to fly, Arthur hadn't traveled much. He was amazed, like everyone else.

I didn't expect 3,000 people to show up at the theater, but it was nearly at capacity thirty minutes before the curtain rose. Once I arrived backstage, the crowd made perfect sense. The legendary Frederick Douglass was conversing with Mrs. Griffing. I thought I had gotten over my nerves, but no one informed me that he'd be in attendance.

"Remember who you are," John gently squeezed my hand. His confident eyes steadied my heart. "Go and be great." He kissed my hand and nudged me forward. His pride was a reminder to keep my accomplishments in perspective. I didn't want to overstate my importance, but I had no reason to be afraid or to shrink myself in their presence.

And, even if I had any doubts, Douglass's smile was a proper affirmation. "Well, if it isn't the Great Charlotte Cohen. I've heard such wonderful things about you."

"Well, a master orator gave me wonderful advice at the White House." I hoped he hadn't heard too much. My speech was mostly unchanged. I'd have to write more as the opportunity came.

We talked for a little while. My husband watched from the background until I motioned for him. John let the room know how proud he was to have such an intelligent and driven wife. He was a proper manager. He built me up and kept me calm. When Mrs. Griffing and Douglass offered more opportunities to speak, he readily agreed. "If anything can break the bonds of hatred, it's the piercing words of my dear Charlotte."

We met other abolitionists on the program. One white man saw us at the White House and was desperate to shake John's hand. "How lucky you must be to have such a beautiful and brave woman."

"I like to think of Charlotte as my personal blessing from the Lord."

Everyone was truly kind and encouraging. They were also talented, and I enjoyed their words. Before Mrs. Griffing was to take the stage, she told John, "I made certain to schedule myself before Charlotte. She's a tough act to follow."

I was flattered, but John raised his brow. "And who follows Charlotte?"

"Only Mr. Douglass."

"Hmm…" John nodded a few times and pressed a hard grin to his face. "Fascinating."

"Good luck," I told her. John and I stood in the wings while she captivated the audience for the next few minutes. I searched for friendly faces. John made certain our people had good seats. Many of the freedmen were in the first couple of rows. His trusted leaders were seated in a private box. I couldn't find Mary Anne, but I knew she was watching with my friends. I never imagined when I saw plays with Danny and Steve that they would, one day, watch me take center stage.

Mrs. Griffing took her bow during a roar of applause, and then we waited for my name to be called. I slipped through John's fingers but held his gaze for a little while. He knew, with every bit of his soul, that I would be wonderful. The audience did as well. I still didn't see Mary Anne and the boys, but I recognized their voices from all the years of hyping up fighters ringside.

I took a deep breath and prayed for the Spirit of God to speak through me. In the bright limelight, I made my case before the abolitionists I admired, friends who uplifted me, former slaves who shared my burdens, and subjects who needed to be convinced of my influence and worthiness. I didn't allow their numbers or faces to distract me. I looked past them and straight on to the future. They didn't come into focus until deafening applause filled the auditorium. I finally found Mary Anne, Steve, and Danny whistling and clapping from the tenth row. I waved to them and took my exit.

John congratulated me with a hug and a kiss. Douglass immediately followed, so he only had time to shake my hand and say, "Well done."

John stayed in the wings to watch his performance. I took notice of his choice of words and when he changed the pitch or speed to emphasize a point. The stage didn't swallow him; he filled it with his performance. The auditorium was captivated. I would have been, too, if not for John's curious eyes. "He's a seasoned speaker, yet you're already on his level as a novice."

Believe it or not, that was high praise for Douglass. The crowd was mad for him, though. They were mesmerized for fifteen minutes. Then, they erupted.

After the event came to a close, Mary Anne and her giant belly attacked me in the lobby. "Charlotte, I am so proud of you! You were sensational!"

"We're so proud," Danny patted my shoulder, since Mary Anne hadn't released me from her death grip. Steve was laughing at how uncomfortable my face was.

Slow and hard claps came from behind me. "That wasn't so bad," Tillie smirked. I returned the gesture with a playful glare.

"Not bad?" Caroline said. "Lady Charlotte was incredible!" Caroline had wrapped her hair the night before, but it didn't hold curls well. However, she was stunning in that peacock dress.

Dinah didn't say anything, but she had the tiniest smile on her face. I didn't expect her to praise me, but others from New Seneca certainly did. Arthur was so excited, I was concerned he was going to float off the ground. "You really are going to change the world, Lady Charlotte. I can see it." I appreciated every compliment, but the fire in his eyes was the greatest honor. That same passion was in the eyes of the rest of the freedmen. I always believed Cooper's role in the world was crucial because he represented what life could be outside of slavery. I was proud to finally be that representation for someone else.

John stood close and didn't say much, besides the occasional boast. He had a curious look in his eye, as if he were up to something. I didn't question him. Instead, I lingered in the triumph with our people.

The next morning felt different. I woke up with a smile on my face, and it wasn't just from my husband's lovemaking. The air was a little lighter beneath my feet, and I wasn't the only one experiencing it. When John and I went to the tavern, Bethany's bright smile was a brilliant contrast against her dark skin. I meant to compliment her, but she spoke first. "You were inspirational, Lady Charlotte."

"Thank you, Bethany. That's kind of you to say." I noticed John had a peculiar smile as he watched us, and it was quite distracting. "You look so lovely today."

"Oh, you're too kind, Lady Charlotte. Too kind." She bashfully sank into her shoulders. "I'll bring you a plate—sausage and grits—real fast."

"Thank you." Once she scurried off, I noticed other freedmen were staring at me. John was, by far, the oddest. He leaned on his hand, with his elbow on the table. "Why are you looking at me like that?"

"Like what?"

I shrugged. "I don't know. Like you're smitten."

"Oh, I'm certainly smitten." John's smile deepened.

I eyed him suspiciously but didn't press him further than that. He relaxed by the time the food came, but Bethany and many of the others remained enamored with me. I wasn't certain how I felt about it, but I assumed that's why John was so happy.

After breakfast, John had a final fitting before we met with Lincoln. He put on every piece carefully, as if he felt the weight of every hand that crafted them. Every cut and stitch told a story. Every button and patch was thoughtfully placed. Everything fit perfectly, from his frock to the mask. John smiled at the eagle engraving on his buckle as I spread his cape across his shoulders. With part of his face covered, John's strong jaw was pronounced. Once I raised his hood, his blue eyes sparkled like diamonds in a mine.

"The cape might be too long." Martha bent down to get a closer look at the hem. It nearly swept the floor. "We don't need Master John to trip and fall."

"He can fly," Agnes said flatly. "Besides, he'll be taller with his boots on."

John put on his new boots to make him a little taller. He walked across the floor with a domineering expression but could barely hold it once the girls and I giggled. He was very handsome, though. "Do you have an opinion?" I asked John.

"Even if I did, you'd do whatever you want, woman." He gazed into a mirror and watched Martha as she contemplated the hem. "You ladies looked so lovely yesterday. I am inclined to trust your marvelous instincts when it comes to fashion."

Martha bowed her head and blushed profusely. "Thank you, Master John."

He turned around and stared at Agnes and Martha with narrow eyes. The girls fidgeted nervously until he raised his brow. "What did you think of Charlotte's speech?"

"It was wonderful!" Agnes's smile came into full bloom, and her eyes were bright. "She's an inspiration to us all."

"And are you grateful to live in New Seneca with us?"

"Of course. Lady Charlotte has been very kind. You have, too, Master John." Her voice quivered from nervousness, but she seemed sincere.

He took a long and quiet breath. "If it's all right with my wife, I would like for you both to act as Charlotte's ladies." I managed to mask my shock with a smile when his hand touched my shoulder. “Tend to her needs and help care for children. I promise, you’ll be well taken care of.”

Martha clutched her chest as if she feared her heart was about to leap out of it. “That is a high honor!”

John smirked and turned to the mirror again to admire his cape. As he stretched it wide, he regally raised his head. “Perhaps we should test it out. You may wait for us outside. We’ll be there shortly.”

They both bowed their heads, then left with radiant smiles. Even if I wanted to reject them, I didn’t have it in me to disappoint them. They were capable when it came to service. However, they’d be of little use in a battle. “I’m surprised you trust the care of our children to mere humans.”

John reached for my hand, then pulled me into his grasp. He kept his eyes on my reflection as he rubbed my belly. “They’re loyal subjects of New Seneca, and they adore you.” I would never grow too old to enjoy the way his lips pressed upon my skin like soft pillows. “Devotion to a common cause is powerful, and so is devotion to a worthy figurehead. They love you, so they’ll love our children.”

I grew concerned that John truly wanted me to give birth to ten children. “You’re thinking about a dynasty.”

“Aren’t you?”

In all my years of imagining our lives with children, I hadn’t thought of them beyond being little, running in the field, kissing their father’s cheek, or sleeping peacefully in their beds. I never fathomed that royalty rested in my womb. “Lincoln won’t care much for that, or any president who follows.”

“They’ll always have their feelings, but they’ll lack the power to do anything about it.” John’s eyes shimmered with gold, and he kissed my neck once more. “Humans fear power, yet they’re drawn to it. One day, we’ll be so beloved and innovative that humans will flock to serve underneath us. Nations thrive on resources, and we’ll capitalize on our abilities. Who wouldn’t want to live in a nation where we can control the weather, have mastered our crops, and heal sickness? The Indians left their tribe to join us. I doubt they’ll be the last.”

It was remarkable how fearful I used to be of those golden eyes. They changed into a source of comfort as my husband plotted a peaceful path for our family. I only hoped Lincoln, and any leader who followed, chose to walk that chartered course. "So much has changed since you left for war. You've matured."

"And so have you, my dear." It was too early to know how my body would handle pregnancy, but his affection and excitement were persuasive. I believed we could raise good men and women who would change the world for the better. "After you, Mrs. Cohen."

We blinked outside to the front of the mansion. Martha and Agnes had wrapped themselves in shawls and were huddled together. It was a sunny day, but the breeze was strong and cool. I immediately felt a drop in temperature once I slipped from John's grasp, and he took to the sky.

He truly looked marvelous, like an angel. The sun shone off the golden eagle as he rose higher. Truly, John would be a vision of hope for the Union and an agent of judgment for the Confederates. If Runaway could become famous for rescuing slaves, how would humans respond to a man who could save the nation? The citizens of New Seneca, who had watched John take to the skies many times, still stopped and stared in awe.

John picked up speed and rolled through the air. Alfie and other children ran to keep up with him, pointing and cheering. I imagined a few of our future little ones jumping and calling out to him. And even one day, if they shared his same ability, they would join their father in the sun.

What an unstoppable force they'd be.

Chapter Twenty-One

Once again, we met at midnight while the White House was dark. When our feet touched the floor of the Entrance Hall, a figure stood in front of the Red Room, illuminated by the warm gaslight. "Who are you?"

John immediately clenched his fingers, preparing to strike the man down.

He was a hard-looking man with a mustache and a diagonal scar from the right side of his cheek to his chin. He was well-dressed, perhaps in his early fifties. He stood perfectly still until the president came out of the Red Room to greet us. "Apologies for the alarm. This is Mr. Pike, and he'll be acting as a liaison."

John glared. He didn't like surprises. Fortunately, he was disguised in his new getup. "A liaison for what?"

"Mr. Pike is a man of…" Lincoln pressed a hard grin to his face. "…many talents. He's tasked with coordinating with agents of New Seneca to bring destruction and justice to the Overseers."

My chest began to rise as if a sun had grown inside of it. "We're moving forward?"

Lincoln nodded. "Yes, Miss." I tried to dull my excitement, but Lincoln's grin only brightened my mood.

"From what we can confirm, your evidence against the Overseers is legitimate." Mr. Pike was a soothing baritone. "Careful details will begin to come out in the newspapers. President Lincoln will sign an executive order in the morning designating them as enemies of these United States."

I looked at John. He refused to smile and glared at Lincoln. "You were given our trust, yet you brought in Mr. Pike. What if our faces weren't concealed?"

"Mr. Pike has been investigating Runaway and Ghost for quite some time." Lincoln paused, and that brief breath felt like an eternal rush of anxiety. "He already had his suspicions about Mrs. Cohen."

John's expression didn't change, but my eyes certainly widened.

Mr. Pike smiled. "And since a colored girl told me Ghost kissed Runaway in the lobby of the Crimson Hotel during the Draft Riots, I had my suspicions about Mr. Cohen as well." Perhaps I should have been stoic at that moment, but I glared at John while his brows furrowed. "Of course, your clever alibis gave me pause, but it was too great a coincidence that Charlotte visited Mr. Cooper in Beaufort, and he next appeared in Lake City with Runaway."

I gasped as Mick's warning became evident. "You were the one lurking around the Crimson Hotel asking questions!"

Mr. Pike bowed his head. "I couldn't pinpoint your location for the longest time. I had no leads until the riots. It struck me as odd that Runaway would have been in New York in time to save Superintendent Kennedy from the mob. It made the most sense that she lived or worked near the city."

My shoulders dropped. I could only be upset with myself. John warned me that getting involved with the riots would expose us. "Does anyone else know?"

"No, but my hope is you'll come to feel comfortable enough to share with a few more key figures." Lincoln's eyes searched John's getup, from his boots to his hood. "In the meantime, what am I to make of you, Mr. Cohen? Certainly, you're not considering fighting for the Union as Ghost."

John folded his arms. "My wife named me Archangel for your war. That is how the world will know me until the rest of our agreements are fulfilled."

Lincoln's eyes narrowed as he pondered. It was one thing to fight for a cause. It was an entirely different matter when it came to becoming a symbol. Lincoln believed Runaway was worthy of such a burden, but trusting John was a gamble. Eventually, he nodded and stroked his beard. "That is acceptable."

Life began to move at a blistering pace after that meeting. John ordered Tony to return the gold bars kept hidden in his shadow to the federal government. Once Mr. Pike saw Tony's talent, he wanted to use him to assist with raids against the Overseers. John was adamant about none of our people being involved in the war, but capturing and killing zealots was different. Tony wasn't as prejudiced, hot-blooded, or bloodthirsty as Dinah. He made for a better partnership with Mr. Pike. Dinah—disguised as Steven—used her ability to point them to other conspirators. Soon, other political aides, promising future politicians, and other men of influence were arrested and taken in for questioning.

Lincoln was true to his word. He pardoned us and deemed the Overseers enemies of the nation. Headlines flooded the newspapers:

Secret Society Under Federal Investigation
Burnings in the South Confirmed by Federal Sources
Heretics Wreak Havoc on 'Gifted' Citizens
Witness Testimony Links Influential Men to Attack on Runaway

Journalists had written about an attempt on Runaway's life after the White House party, but they didn't speak to Mr. West's motivation at the time. Details about their dogma and cruelty were slowly introduced to the public. Since the Overseers were largely stationed in the South, their influence in the North was painted as an invasion of heresy.

The story of their cruelty could not be told without speaking of their victims. They were given accounts of "Gifted" burned alive, unaffiliated with New Seneca. Their abilities were a mystery, so the country was buzzing with curiosity.

Lincoln arranged for John to meet with General Grant, who was not fond of their agreement. He didn't believe John's powers were necessary for victory, and he didn't appreciate that John leveraged his power instead of choosing to fight out of obligation to the Union. Lincoln's cabinet also had concerns.

The President made it clear that using Archangel's power wasn't up for debate. John was kind enough to arrange a little presentation. They were impressed enough when John took to the sky. He decided to tease Lincoln's men by making the ground beneath them tremble. The Secretary of State, William Seward, did his best to appear unimpressed. John descended from the heavens, unamused by his stoicism, and held out his hand. "May I have your hat, sir?"

Seward's eyes slightly narrowed, but he looked to the president for guidance. Lincoln nodded, and Seward reluctantly surrendered his hat.

John observed the feel of the cloth, its shape, and size before smiling. It was well-crafted. "You have my thanks." John flung his arm into the air, prompting a horrified gasp from Seward and a few others. A few seconds later, the hat exploded into a radiant burst of fire. Seward couldn't stop his eyes from bulging from their sockets.

Lincoln placed his hand on Seward's shoulder and grinned. "It's better we utilize this sort of power than the Confederates."

"Certainly…" Seward and the rest of the cabinet marveled as John took to the skies once more, pulling about a hundred pebbles with him. Seward wasn't completely convinced of John's necessity until he directed the rocks higher into the sky and focused with his eyes closed. Then, a rumbling rippled across the sky with scatters of light. I was told it was an impressive display, like fireworks. I was also told that Seward uttered another harrowing thought. "Let's pray the Confederates don't also recruit such terrible power."

As for me, I continued delivering speeches across the Union. Travel became bothersome. Pregnancy symptoms were the worst on the train. Whatever I tried to feed my child, they quickly rejected it. My ladies were with me, holding my hair and rubbing my back as I vomited. I didn't need them to make such a fuss, but they liked feeling needed. "I'll bring some water to your seat, Lady Cohen."

"Thank you, Agnes." Martha gave me a towel to wipe my face, then accompanied me to my seat on the train. Since John was busy with government business, Dinah took his form and traveled with me. She kept her eyes on the paper as I took a seat.

"They say you teleport."

"Excuse me?" I was still queasy and a bit dizzy. "You mean telegraph?"

"No. It's in the paper. They've coined a term for what you do." She pointed to a front-page article. I hadn't done anything as of late to merit such a prized spot, but my name apparently sold lots of papers. "Since you carried all those soldiers such a far distance, they combined the Greek word 'tele' with the Latin word 'portare' to make the word."

"Teleport?" I was well enough to understand the explanation, but it still seemed so strange. "And it means to carry far?"

"Essentially."

I frowned. "I invented it. Shouldn't I have the right to name it?"

Dinah shook her head and chuckled. "You can call it 'blinking' if you like, but the journalists are the ones who make the people decide. You can't defy them all."

I could tell Dinah preferred the paper's term. It seemed like a losing battle, so I sighed and picked up *Ivanhoe* for another read.

"That one again?" Dinah asked, rather bored.

I shrugged. "I was considering *Frankenstein*, but John doesn't want me to read it without him. Besides, I don't want to start something new while I feel so terrible."

"And I suppose you relate to the lovely Lady Rowena."

I was taken aback. Rowena was a fine character, and Ivanhoe pined for her, but she was too passive to be me. "You've read it?"

"No, but I've touched people who have." She turned in her seat and gazed harder at me. It made me uncomfortable, which made her smile more. "You think you're Rebecca, don't you?"

I don't know why her mockery was so embarrassing, but I could match her. "Do you think you're Rebecca?"

"Who says I'm not Ivanhoe?" She raised her brow. "Or Locksley?"

Even though she wore my husband's face and spoke in his voice, I couldn't unsee Dinah. I knew John too well, and I certainly knew her well enough. "Never mind." I didn't want to argue about who had a claim over a fictional character, certainly one she had never taken the time to personally discover. Agnes came with a glass of water and crackers, and my baby graciously accepted. The dizziness subsided, so I dove into the book once again.

We traveled to Pennsylvania, Ohio, and made our way to Michigan. When we stopped at hotels, Martha and Agnes stayed in one room, and I was booked with my imposter husband. I let Dinah have the room, then normally blinked to the mansion when it was time for bed. During our downtime, the girls liked to travel around town and shop for brooches or decorative pins. It was their way of remembering our journey together.

Dinah would follow us from a reasonable distance. Besides acting as John's alibi, she was there for protection. While the girls haggled over prices, I eased out of the shop and joined Dinah in an alley. "You don't have to isolate yourself. The girls would love to pick out a brooch for you."

"I have no use for something like that."

I must have made a face, displeased with her tone.

"Apologies. That wasn't very John-like." Dinah pushed off against the wall she had been leaning on and hovered over me. "Well, at least not the new John…"

I followed her eyes to Agnes and Martha as they walked out of the shop. They were giggling and holding their new prized possessions. They couldn't have enjoyed such freedoms while enslaved. I didn't understand how Dinah could be unaffected by their happiness. "John has always cared about the well-being of his people."

"He's always kept their kind at a distance, though. Now, he's entertaining the idea that a common cause and ideals bind people together, rather than shared heritage."

"Heritage isn't irrelevant, but new people can always become your people. Ideals are everything." I hoped my smile would lighten her mood, but Dinah was unmoved.

"The major question is how humans will react once John displays his godlike power."

"There's only one God," I corrected. "He was overgenerous with John's creation, but we're all still ashes and dust."

"And the Breath of God," Dinah said with a faint smile. "You mustn't forget that." I hadn't heard her talk much of God, yet she raised John's head a little higher. "Perhaps there's a little more in us than there is in them. This power must come from somewhere and for a purpose."

"This is our purpose." I meant to give her a rousing lecture, but that was the moment my stomach decided to rumble, and it was not quiet. I held it, embarrassed, and Dinah chuckled.

"Come on, Charlotte. John will be crossed if you don't feed his little heir."

"Of course…" I was grateful my baby was finally ready to eat. During our meal, Agnes and Martha wanted to listen to my stories about New York. Dinah didn't say much, besides interjecting certain details I had forgotten. Once we returned safely to our hotel, Dinah changed and took on her brother's form. She liked to drink, smoke, and gamble. I didn't scold her for her filthy habits, as long as she was sober when we went to my meetings.

Martha and Agnes were always excited by my delivery, but I worried about boring Dinah. My speeches had recurring themes, but I introduced new topics from the newspapers. I urged the House to pass the Thirteenth Amendment and equal wages for colored soldiers. If soldiers were paid differently based on the color of their skin, then that meant the nation thought less of their sacrifice—great men, like Sam. If we were a nation worth preserving, then we had an obligation to preserve the inherent dignity of our soldiers. Apparently, that sort of thinking earned me the reputation of being a radical. Fortunately, I found a welcoming place among other radicals who loved liberty and longed for equality.

Dinah liked to watch for the room's reaction while I spoke. She clapped and whistled as John would have, but she couldn't mimic the pride in his eyes. At least she was easy with returning a smile when admirers made conversation.

"Your wife is a wonder, Mr. Cohen! You must be so proud."

"Yes, Charlotte is rather impressive." She seemed sincere, though I never got used to her hand on my shoulder. "I have no doubt she'll change the world."

I had one more speech to make before my tour came to an end. I went back home and slept next to the comfort of my husband after exchanging stories about our day. Even though John intended to take Atlanta himself, Grant believed it was too great a risk to put it all in the hands of one man. Therefore, Major General William T. Sherman planned and prepared for the invasion. He was going to spend a lot of time in Tennessee before the battle. John stroked my arm while looking up at the chandelier. "The humans are fools. They don't believe I have the power to break the Confederates."

I snuggled closer to his chest. "Does their lack of faith offend you?"

"No." His eyes fell back down to me, and he spoke matter-of-factly. "I find their ignorance pitiable."

I pressed a smile on my face and shook my head. "You are quite a man, Mr. Cohen. They'll see that soon enough." I was almost terrified for them. It was dangerous to step inside the ring with a contender who completely outclassed you. I had seen Cooper knock opponents out cold with one punch. John didn't even need to raise his hands.

In the morning, I expected Dinah to be dressed by the time I blinked to the hotel room. Instead, I saw a long figure in the bed. A pair of white feet poked out from the end, and a wrinkled hand rested on the covers. I was alarmed at first, until I realized he was tall and too big for his nightshirt. His back was to me, but as I stepped closer, his hair and beard became clear. "Dinah?"

I inched toward her, then nudged her back. "Dinah, are you alright?"

She whimpered in pain, just like John had.

"Dinah!" I shook her hard until she sprang up, eyes wide open and heaving for air. It took her a few seconds to realize I had awakened her. Her eyes danced around the room and squinted at the daylight peering through the curtains. Then her breathing calmed, but she collapsed into her hands. I assumed Dinah was embarrassed, so I stepped away. Her skin darkened, limbs shrank, and it softened into a feminine form. She still wouldn't speak.

I eased onto the edge of the bed. I waited a few more seconds, then decided to ask the obvious question, "How long have you been doing this?"

Dinah's answer was muffled by her fingers. "Since we met him."

I sighed, remembering how distraught John was after his vision. She must have been torturing herself. "Are you that afraid of the future?"

Dinah's eyes intensely glared through her fingers before she removed her hands and stiffened her posture. "I'm not afraid of anything. I'm concerned about what I know of human nature."

It was difficult to argue about what she had seen. I genuinely worried about how the horrors of the zealots' memories, or countless other humans' memories, affected her sense of self, yet I was also impressed that she could walk, talk, or even think. Her mind was a wonder. "What did you see?"

The loose nightshirt slipped off Dinah's shoulder as she shrugged. "Rushing ships. More of the same. I have to get used to it."

"No, you need to sleep. Normally." I adjusted her sleeve. Her hair was disheveled, and her eyes were heavy. "You don't want to age this beautiful face rapidly."

"Hardly anyone ever sees it anyway," she mumbled.

"That won't always be the case. Besides, John is getting older. You won't be able to impersonate him for much longer. It won't even be feasible to keep pretending to be Steven."

"I guess you're right…" Her lips trembled, and her blue eyes glittered with pain. Dinah tried to hold in a rush of emotions, but once she heard herself whimper, it burst forth. She pulled her knees to her chest and sobbed. I don't know why I found it so shocking. I had seen her cry before. She had even bitterly wept, but not with that face. She was light enough for her forehead and cheeks to turn red.

I rubbed Dinah's back until she allowed me to pull her to my chest. We had seen so much death, had taken lives ourselves, but you never truly get used to it. Even if you come to accept its power and inevitability, it always feels burdensome, even if it offers some liberty. She apologized for her outburst, and I told her there was no need. I gave her some space while she quickly dressed.

Our next stop was about an hour away by carriage. We were all going to ride together, but I had another sent for us, for Dinah's sake. She would be more comfortable if Agnes and Martha weren't gossiping in her ear. She sat with her arms folded, in John's form, staring through the window. Her eyes were still heavy, but I don't think she intended to rest.

"Do you truly dislike humans?"

She raised her brow.

"All of them?" I was always baffled by her demeanor. She had seen terrible things, sure. But if I had wonderful experiences with humans, she must have possessed thousands.

Dinah kept her eyes on me as she contemplated her answer. She swallowed, then took a breath.

"I liked Dave."

Tears rushed to my eyes, and I had to turn away. The grief came upon me so strongly that it felt like a hole was torn open in my chest.

"He was a bit filthy, but in an amusing way—not threatening. He was handsome, liked to laugh, and was fiercely loyal to his friends. He was willing to die for them, and he did." From the corner of my eye, I witnessed her stature shrink. Her skin darkened, and her voice lightened. "Maybe in another life, I could have escaped my father's plantation and met you all in New York. I could have been the woman he always dreamed of settling down with."

I turned to judge her sincerity. She was a masterful liar, so I could never be certain. But she was the type of beauty he would have raved about. He would have loved her spiraled curls, made some joke about her looking like his morning coffee. They could have smoked cigars together with Harvey. He wouldn't have judged her past. He would have protected Dinah and tried to make her smile.

"But of course, the humans killed him," Dinah spoke bitterly, as if we shared the same pain. "Good people aren't meant to last in this world."

I thought of Cooper loading his guns into the Confederates. Sometimes, I smelled the smoke from the nozzle. Sometimes, when I closed my eyes, I saw the breath of life leave their bodies as their eyes dimmed. War was such a horrible thing. But I liked to tell myself, when I was haunted by the faces of screaming young men falling to their watery graves, that it was an unfortunate consequence to keep my loved ones safe. When John rained hellfire down in Atlanta, it wouldn't be good—but it would be necessary for our children.

"That's why we're making a new one."

Dinah tilted her head and slowly curled her lips into a smirk. "Amen to that." She leaned her head against the carriage wall as her body filled out the clothes. "Would you read to me?" She asked in my husband's voice. "It helps John sleep."

I did as she asked, starting where I had last left off in *Ivanhoe*. The story's hero was cared for by the wise and skilled Rebecca. It wasn't long before she drifted off to sleep.

I didn't know if anything in this life could heal Dinah of her wounds, but I was determined not to make more children like her. That was the vow I carried with me into my final speech. The ugliness of war was necessary to create beautiful futures. Evil needed to be purged with total victory, or else it would cull all goodness in this world.

Chapter Twenty-Two

It was dawn on the fourth of May when I stepped onto the balcony of my New York home to say goodbye to my husband. We hosted a grand party the day before, then spent a quiet night together, wrapped in each other's arms. I lifted my chemise so he could kiss my stomach. My belly was still small, but I liked to imagine our child could feel their father's ticklish lips. I wondered how magical their laughter would be.

"Take good care of our baby—and Mary Anne."

I ran my fingers through his hair. John looked so handsome when hope softened his features. "You take care of yourself." I raised his hood, and John stood on his feet. Darkness shrouded his face. He would be terrifying to the Confederates once the earth began to tremble.

"What's wrong?"

I placed my hands on his chest. "I want to tell you to be merciful and only do what is necessary to achieve victory. The truth is, I don't want anyone to die—Union or Confederate."

"But…?"

I bit my lip, swallowing my pride. "But I need to tell you what you've told me." I looked up into his blue eyes as they caught the breaking light of day. "If you're going into this war, you must value your life above theirs. I want you to make good decisions, John, but the most important decision is to make it back home to us."

He smiled and rubbed my shoulders. "Don't worry, my dear. Only God Himself could delay such a reunion."

"Only delay?" I asked hesitantly, hoping he wasn't committing blasphemy.

He chuckled and inched toward my lips. "Why would God stand in the way of something so good?"

I couldn't disagree with him. Every time I ever kissed John, it certainly felt like it was meant to be. Despite our trials and tribulations, we were an inevitable conclusion—predetermined before the foundation of the world.

"There's no need to worry, Mrs. Cohen." John bent down and picked up the heavily packed bag. He had everything I could think of, including some pie. "I've seen your future, and you are glorious in it."

"If you say so, John…" I took his hand and kissed it as he rose off his feet. He didn't stop his ascent, but he bent just enough to kiss my hand before rising into the sky. I watched him until he vanished into the golden haze of morning, beyond my reach.

It was best not to worry about John. He could handle himself, and the fighting wouldn't begin for a few days. I had a very different task ahead of me, so I returned to the mansion and began packing a bag. Tillie came to bother me, leaning against the doorframe with her arms folded. "You know, Mary Anne could have her baby here. This is where she belongs."

"I don't disagree, but I can't make her. She's too stubborn—and too powerful."

"She defies your orders, and you're going to wait on her hand and foot? How is that fair?"

I stopped folding and stared at her in awe, so much so that Tillie straightened up.

"What? What is it?"

I had to pick my jaw up off the floor. "I think you're jealous of my best friend."

Tillie scoffed dramatically. I laughed. She walked over and plopped onto the bed—glaring—but it broke into a smile. Then she sighed and handed me a silver rattle from the bed. I cradled it, and she rolled her eyes. "This is serious. The zealots are on their heels, and they'll be more desperate."

"I can take care of myself, and Mary Anne can certainly take care of both of us."

"Charlotte…" Tillie said with sharpening eyes. "The world is more dangerous—not less." She mumbled. "And you're sort of our queen…"

"I'm sorry, what was that?" I leaned closer.

"Forget it!" She pushed me away and stomped off, more embarrassed than angry.

"If you need me, send for me!" I called after her. She was close enough to hear, and Kachina and Nathaniel knew that as well. They weren't thrilled I'd be gone for a while, but they could manage. I placed the rattle in my bag, then imagined myself in Mary Anne's office.

It was early, so I went into the kitchen and helped Bess, Loretta, and Big Willie prepare breakfast. My speeches had become a bit famous, so they had lots of questions about my adventures and the abolitionists I'd met. I didn't know Big Willie was such a fan of Frederick Douglass. He spent the next half hour quoting portions of his speeches.

I carried a breakfast tray up to Mary Anne. Before I could knock, the door opened. "Morning, Charlotte." She was radiant in a white cotton gown—though clearly uncomfortable. I didn't think her belly could grow any larger; it hung low.

"How did you know it was me?"

"Pregnancy is a fascinating thing." She stepped aside and motioned me to come in. I was intrigued but walked hesitantly. I set the tray down on a table, and Mary Anne wobbled to a chair. I held it steady as she eased into it. Even that small movement left her out of breath. "He's a big one."

I began to pour some tea for her. "Oh, so you believe he's a boy?"

"I know he's a boy." She rubbed her stomach, and it began to dance. "I can feel him." She certainly could. He stretched her skin so much that he looked as though he might stand up or break free. "Charlotte…"

I followed her eyes down to the tea, which was nearly about to spill over. "I'm sorry!" I knew babies moved, but I didn't know they could press so fiercely against the body. "What do you mean by 'feel' him?"

"I can feel…" Her eyes drifted around the room before she shrugged. "…everything."

"Everything?" The word felt heavy on my tongue. I couldn't fathom it. "Everything like what?"

"My baby, the rising steam, the air between us. It's like you have a special rhythm and heat. It all feels different. People. Objects. I know I have a son because of his shape." It was difficult to believe, but Mary Anne seemed so certain, almost unbothered by her heightened awareness.

"Can you sense outside of this room? Can you sense John or Cooper?"

"No. It doesn't go that far. Just a little beyond this room." She sat up and readjusted just as her belly calmed. "I suppose I could always feel everything before, but I had to concentrate."

"John said your ability was to move the smallest parts of something fast enough to make it explode."

"Well…that makes sense." I tried to imagine what Mary Anne might be seeing as she looked at me, but all I could see were crumbles of biscuit that fell onto her stomach as she ate.

"Are you in pain?"

"No…but it is strange." Her eyes wandered in the distance while she tried to put it into words. "I feel—"

"Overstimulated?"

Mary Anne laughed so hard she snorted. "I was going to say more powerful than ever, but sure. It's a lot, but I'll get used to it."

John was the only person who could hope to understand her, but I couldn't call him away from battle. Dinah might have been of some use, but I never wanted her to touch Mary Anne at all. "Will you consider having this baby upstate? I think you should be away from people, in case you lose control during labor."

"And you'll teleport my doctor there?"

I bit my lips to hide the initial displeasure. That silly word truly caught on. "Yes. I can blink a doctor there, but I think it will be better if we use one from New Seneca who will understand your power."

Mary Anne smiled as if I were a naïve child. "I understand your concern, Charlotte. I do, but my powers aren't out of control, and I have a high pain tolerance. I'd rather stay here in the city, close to everything I could ever need. And…" Her soft voice quieted. "…if you're concerned about the doctor's knowledge, Cooper told Elijah about my abilities."

My whole body tensed. Telling her own secret was one thing, but our stories were indistinguishable. "And did Cooper tell him about me?"

Her smile expanded, flashing her pearly whites.

"Mary Anne!"

"Elijah won't tell another soul! He hasn't even told Isaiah."

I was not pleased, but I also didn't want to upset the pregnant woman, who was more powerful than ever. Besides, I was curious about the depths of her abilities. "If you can feel a boy inside of you, can you…?" I don't know why I was so bashful all of a sudden.

Mary Anne grinned very sweetly. "Come here." I stood up, and she reached for my hand. She stayed seated and pulled me toward her. Then, Mary Anne closed her eyes and took a deep breath. I tried to keep still, but my heart began to race.

"No."

My heart raced so fast that it shattered against a wall. "No?"

She opened her eyes and leaned back. "The shape isn't distinguished enough. But I feel the rhythm." A lovely curve spread across her lips. "It has a strong heartbeat."

I held my belly, absolutely stunned and near tears. "How can something that small have a heartbeat?"

"Miracle of life, I suppose."

It was, indeed, a miracle. I was grateful God trusted me to nurture such an incredible little being.

I wished all there was to growing a child was smiles and happy tears, but the breakfast I shared with Mary Anne came back up. We both ended up lying in her bed next to one another, waiting for Elijah to arrive. I wasn't too dizzy by the time he knocked. I opened the door myself.

"Charlotte Cohen." He said my name as though it were a song. "As I live and breathe…" He definitely knew my secret. He was curious about me at the wedding (along with the rest of his family). Now, the gleam in his eye was of pure admiration.

I guided him in and closed the door. "Do you have any bags, Dr. Cooper?"

"Willie took them to my room. Thank you." He handed me a tin of crackers wrapped in parchment paper. "Eat small portions throughout the day instead of large meals. Bland foods will be better for you."

I sighed with the fire of hell in my lungs. "I don't cook bland food."

"You can manage for a few weeks. I've been told you can do anything." He laughed at my expression and turned to Mary Anne. His eyes widened when he saw her stomach. "You were right to send for me. I don't think you'll make it to forty weeks. How have you felt?"

"I've felt some pressure, but I'm alright." She smiled, but there was discomfort in her voice.

"Well, it won't be much longer until I get to meet my nephew." Elijah made himself comfortable in Mary Anne's rocking chair. "In the meantime, I'd love to hear your stories."

I figured I could trust Cooper's brother. I kept many details about John to myself, but I didn't mind telling him about my adventures as Runaway. There was plenty to keep him satisfied. He was curious about New Seneca. Cooper had mentioned the possibility of moving to a settlement of others like Mary Anne, and that was all he knew. I didn't divulge much information, beyond it being a safe place for humans and Gifted alike. It wasn't appropriate to tell an outsider all of our abilities.

His questions were a much-needed distraction. It kept my mind off John. He could have flown down to Georgia himself, but he thought traveling with the soldiers was good for morale. He teased, "Perhaps they'll pledge their loyalty to me by the end of the battle." I didn't think that would be the case, but building rapport with Lincoln's generals was a good strategy. And after the battle was over, and facts turned into myths and legends, the soldiers would remember that John was more than a sheer force of nature. They could attest that he was also a man.

I also had my own questions for Elijah. Cooper was a good man and worth being proud of, yet Solomon had such a sour look during the wedding. But even Elijah seemed baffled by it. "My father always admired education. When he was enslaved, he was beaten for wanting to learn to read. He decided he would be free and put his sons through school. JoJo chose to brawl instead."

"JoJo?" I laughed.

"Don't tell him I told you that." He spoke sternly, but there was a sly smile on his lips.

"It's adorable!" Mary Anne squealed and rubbed her belly. "I absolutely love it."

"Anyway, it's our fault Joseph was so good at fighting. Isaiah and I used to rough him up, but we were only horsing around. He started fighting other kids and finding ways to train. My father used to tell him, 'I'm raising healers, not bleeders.' Joseph responded with, 'You're not raising us, you're always working.'"

Our mouths dropped. "What happened?" I asked.

"Joseph found out our father had some fight in him, too, and ended up with a busted lip. Father said, 'Don't talk like a man unless you're willing to face the consequences like one.'"

Cooper always said his mind, even at the risk of being lynched or arrested. "I take it he didn't learn much."

"He learned to take a punch from people bigger than him, but he tried not to disrespect our father again. After that, he preferred not to speak to him."

"And Solomon carried his disapproval to the wedding?"

"He likes Mary Anne fine. We were just…surprised." He didn't need to go into further explanation. His big eyes and silly smile gave it away. "She's a wonderful woman—very beautiful—but my mother had hoped her boys would marry virgins. We're very religious people."

Mary Anne frowned and looked away. "I didn't mean for it to happen this way."

"What's done is done." Elijah's pretty smile looked so much like Cooper's. When he placed his hand on top of Mary Anne's, I knew it brought her much-needed comfort. "What's important is that you're a part of our family, and we'll have a new JoJo soon."

We wanted to keep Mary Anne off her feet, so I helped Willie and the others tend to the tenants. I cooked, read to the children, and played checkers with Elijah. Most of the time, I stayed with Mary Anne. We talked, knitted, and I helped her bathe and get dressed. I thought she handled her pregnancy beautifully, but I didn't realize how taxing it was until I saw her out of breath from simply crossing the room and how often she needed to relieve herself. It was something to look forward to, I suppose.

In the late afternoon of May 6, Elijah examined Mary Anne after expressing discomfort. She was in the early stages of labor. She could still walk and talk fine. When I handed her JoJo's silver rattle, she cradled the duck and swayed. "He'll love it. I'm sure he will!" I admired her joy, despite the pressure she must have felt in her spine.

Elijah kept a close eye on her and spoke softly. It lessened my worry, but I still decided not to leave her side in case the pain became overwhelming. Around midnight, I helped her to the water closet. Once we began making our way back to the bed, she gripped my arm tighter. "Something's shifting…"

"Shifting?"

She held her stomach just before a sudden rush of fluid spilled from her. We were both so naïve, screaming and flailing as though the baby might come at any moment. Elijah came and helped Mary Anne back to bed, but JoJo wasn't ready to come yet. She still had hours of increasing pain to endure.

I was too anxious to sleep. Besides, Mary Anne liked to squeeze my hand during contractions. Eventually, she didn't want to speak or even listen to me talk. She conserved her energy for control. By early morning, her hair was drenched in sweat. I continuously searched the room for fires or small explosions, but none came. Even the expected painful screams were just grunts.

About a quarter to seven, Elijah gave her one final examination. "Alright, Mary Anne. It's time to push." It was then that she turned bright red. I didn't know she was that strong until that moment. I squeezed back to alleviate some of the pressure, but she was inhuman! It was a price I agreed to pay, though. Cooper couldn't be there, and I sent Mick away to protect Moses. I was her chosen guardian. I could risk breaking for Mary Anne.

In twenty minutes, we heard the cries of a newborn baby. The new mother slowly breathed, as if her child's presence made the air sweeter. Mary Anne squeezed me tighter for every second Elijah dared to hold him before handing him over. She silently whimpered as the cord that tethered them was severed. Then she released my hand, reaching for her little child.

His uncle smiled so lovingly, resembling the boy's father, as he wiped the child with a damp cloth. "You were right. It's a boy."

Mary Anne reached further and began to cry harder. The child wasn't completely clean, but Elijah placed the naked boy in his mother's arms. The hope and wonder in Mary Anne's eyes were hard to describe as she caressed his brown skin. I had never seen her so incandescently happy. Her whole world was in his little face. "He looks just like his father." Her tears soaked his cheeks, and she whispered her great love for him.

Elijah came over and gently took my red-and-purple hand. I hissed, and his brows furrowed. "It's not broken, but there's going to be a nasty bruise."

Mary Anne would have apologized, but she was too busy kissing her boy, who was peacefully breathing in her arms. It was a lovely and quiet sound, but louder than any past heartbreak. "My little JoJo…"

"It was worth it," I told Elijah with tears beginning to break. "Everything."

Our beloved Joseph "JoJo" Aaron Cooper II was born on May 7, the day John invaded Georgia. As Elijah rubbed ointment into my skin and wrapped my hand in a bandage, John was granted permission by Major General Sherman to advance against enemy lines. While I watched Mary Anne nurse her child for the first time, John sent hawks to scout the rolling hills of Dalton. I changed Mary Anne's bedding while he blinked along the ridges to assess where it was best to attack.

The historical accounts from Confederates claim the attack began with rumblings. The earth opened up beneath artillery lines and swallowed dozens of men at a time. That wasn't nearly as terrifying as the mass explosions: weapon depots, carts of black powder, and even firearms in the hands of soldiers spontaneously combusted. High-powered shrapnel shredded soldiers, and many gasped and gagged on the battlefield and in the hospital, with no hope of recovery. To them, the onslaught was nonstop, but John strategically rested. Though he could rapidly heal, overusing Mary Anne's power could overwhelm his mind. With Kachina's power, he exercised tremendous control of the earth, and they happened to be in the foothills of the Appalachian Mountains.

General Sherman's correspondence to President Lincoln contained the name I gave him, so the North reported: *A Miraculous 'Archangel' Takes Victory in Georgia*. The soldiers John chose to spare reported a flying man, engulfed in black smoke and golden embers. The South quickly came to know him as the *Blue Devil in the Ridges of Dalton*.

I stayed up with JoJo while Mary Anne recovered. She woke up to feed him, and then I rocked him to sleep. I was awake when Elijah told me news of John's victory. The Union army was still marching to Dalton. Elijah wasn't fond of war and intended to remain a private doctor, but he watched it closely for his brothers' sakes. He was proud of them, but rightfully afraid.

Elijah stayed with us for a few days, in case Mary Anne and JoJo had any complications. JoJo was healthy—long and plump. I wasn't surprised Mary Anne wanted to lie around for a few days while I doted on her. It didn't completely distract me from worrying about John, but it helped. He didn't move ahead until the Union caught up in Dalton. It was plenty of time for him to rest before waging a new onslaught.

Once Elijah deemed mother and child healthy, he returned to his family in Illinois. I stayed with Mary Anne through the night and blinked home to New Seneca in the early afternoon. Tony relayed updates that he received through Mr. Pike. John moved ahead to Resaca. He destroyed the earthworks and artillery within a few hours and disrupted railroad lines that would have sustained them. The Union soldiers arrived a few days later and secured supply points.

The Confederates tried to regroup in Adairsville and Cassville, but Archangel annihilated their defenses. Wooden posts that fortified the trenches were scattered into splinter bombs, blinding and even paralyzing men. He even used his sway to spook many of the horses to stop their escape. His golden eyes became part of the "Blue Devil" myth. He moved on to Rome, then Dallas, then Kennesaw Mountain, and then Chattahoochee River. John rained exploding rocks on them like Hellfire, a horrifying pattern from ridge to ridge. Archangel defined himself as an unstoppable force, but the Confederates said no angel would litter the battlefield with soldiers praying for death. A survivor of Kennesaw Mountain wrote that a flock of crows surrounded John like an extension of his cape. The Blue Devil was a menace, unbeatable by conventional means. By the end of the month, John was on the outskirts of Atlanta, preparing for his operation.

John entered the city dressed in civilian clothes, bypassing military checkpoints by blinking in. If anyone inquired about him, he offered his father's name, Mr. Davis. He claimed to be an acrobat. His proof for patrolling Confederates was a series of flips. John became something of a phenomenon for the children, and they begged for a performance multiple times a day.

Because he was easy on the eyes, women were freer with their lips. They had a great hatred toward the Union for invading and unleashing the Blue Devil. Wealthy families began to flee in fear of the chaos. John even overheard women gossiping about the Overseers and cursing them for not killing the demon. Some even wished to conjure their own to fight back.

Late at night, John snuck around the city with my blinking power to spy on the Confederates positioning. He wrote down important information and commissioned a hawk to take it to General Sherman. While he was playing spy, the Union forces surrounded the city across miles, from the North, Southwest, and Northeast.

After a few days of rest and good Southern food to fill his belly, John snuck out of the city and began his offensive on their enemy lines. Confederates said he swooped in like a plague of death. A burst of sound and a rush of wind swept across the land, followed by tremors. Trenches collapsed instantly. Cannons flipped in the air soon after. Men screamed and clung to the sky, fearing the Blue Devil was swallowing them up and dragging them to hell. After decimating their outer lines, he pressed inward to their main lines. Redoubts were broken, one by one. Ammo ignited and triggered a sea of fire across the battlefield. Then he moved onto the city itself. Barricades were useless against him, and he did significant damage to the train tracks. The Confederates' defenses were meant to bleed armies for weeks, and John tore through it all in a day. The damage to their minds and spirits was devastating.

John did his best to keep explosions in the city to a minimum to avoid civilian casualties. He broke through their barricades with earth manipulation and even engaged in some hand-to-hand combat. While he blinked and broke men's bones, some tried to shoot him. That's when he activated his combustion. On a rare occasion that he was wounded, he instantly healed, which hollowed out the hope in his enemies' eyes. Fanatics tried to fight to the bitter end, and that's what they received. One man tried to stab John with a makeshift spear. Instead of exploding his weapon, John focused on his skull. Once his blood and brain were sprayed across the streets, many soldiers laid down their arms. Most fled. When the Union soldiers arrived, they expected a fight. Instead, they received silence and raised hands.

It was the second of June when I heard Atlanta had been conquered. I was with Mary Anne late into the night, rocking JoJo in the moonlight.

"You don't have to stay here." She sighed and sat up in bed. "I have to get used to being alone, at least for a little while."

I was surprised by JoJo's grip around my finger. I wouldn't be surprised if his father taught him how to fight before teaching him how to crawl. "Do you think Cooper might come home soon?"

"He might, but John could be home any moment. You should be there to greet him."

I loved the touch and scent of JoJo's skin. He was soft and perfect, like a spotless lamb. He was completely unaware of the terrible things my husband did for his sake and countless others like him, and I would love them both all the more for it.

I kissed his cheeks, handed my nephew to his mother, then blinked to New Seneca. I couldn't sleep. My mind was too restless to enjoy a good book. I paced the halls of the mansion, then decided the cool air of the night would do me some good. I walked to a play area for the children and sat on a stone statue of a turtle. One day, I hoped JoJo and my baby would climb and jump from it. I let thoughts of their future soothe my mind as the day began to break.

The glorious ring of bells filled the sky, and I searched for my victorious angel. I knew he would likely land closest to the manor, so I blinked to the side that faced our bedroom. From afar, his colors blended into an infinite canvas of warm blues. His approach slowed once he saw me, and the glow of the sun swallowed him whole. I winced but dared not look away. The edges of his cape were frayed. The fabric draped around his neck had been stained with blood—no doubt from the strain of Mary Anne's ability. His suit had been cleaned, but dark spots from his enemies remained. There were also stitches in his uniform, a few tears, and holes here and there. His gloves were also missing. A tired smile brimmed across his lips, but when he gazed upon me, his eyes were just as bright as the dawn.

It was selfish of me to blink us to our balcony in New York as soon as our hands met each other's arms, but I wanted a quiet moment with the hero of the Union. I squeezed him, just to make certain the moment was real. If his muscles didn't give it away, the smell of smoke would have. "You really could have done it for us, couldn't you?"

He raised his brows and leaned closer. "Done what?" His voice was low and rough.

I peeled back his hood, and John bowed his head so I might loosen the straps that bound his mask together. My heart fluttered once our eyes met again. I had nearly forgotten how handsome he was. "Destroyed the world."

A smirk flashed on his face, then fell as he cupped my cheek. "I think it's more difficult to save it." Every inch of my skin tingled in the best possible way. It had been too long since our last touch.

"I want to show you something." I unfastened my coat and let it fall to the ground. My husband pursed his lips with scandalous intrigue. I giggled and lifted my chemise, prompting him to drop to his knees in awe.

"She's growing!" His hands were filthy, but I dared not spoil that moment. He held and kissed my belly with such reverence that he could have been kissing the face of God. I didn't know if the war weighed heavily on him or if that moment was just that precious, but his eyes glistened. "Her heartbeat is strong."

"Of course. This is our baby."

"And you've been well? Are you keeping food down?"

"My sickness has passed." As I traced the edges of his jaw, I thought of asking about the toll he paid, but he would never confess if it were high. He would have told me it was pennies compared to the gold in my womb. So, I guided John to his feet, washed him clean, and rested beside him. The world might have been anxious to know what the Blue Devil of the South and the Archangel of the North would do next, but their world could wait.

We always made time for our own.

Chapter Twenty-Three

The myth of the Archangel swelled into a behemoth. Tall tales of Archangel levitating entire battlefields and creating rings of fire spread in less reputable papers. Soldiers who weren't stationed in Georgia lied about seeing him on the battlefield. Even reputable papers printed false sightings.

While John decimated Confederates in Georgia, General Grant launched a campaign in Virginia, resulting in heavy casualties. Many hoped that Archangel would appear and make victory decisive. President Lincoln had such a hope and relayed his request at their next meeting.

Agnes sent for me once John returned. When I walked into the parlor, the mood was sour. Dinah was in her brother's form, sipping a glass of bourbon in a chair. John was leaning over the fireplace mantle, watching the fire. He also had a glass in his hand. He couldn't get drunk, so he must have wanted to taste the burn.

"What's wrong? Did Lincoln not sign the executive order?"

John kept his eyes on the fire and took another sip. "It's on the desk."

Lo and behold, a piece of paper bearing the president's signature was on the mahogany desk. It was likely a duplicate, but I wiped my fingers before I dared to touch it. I read every line with care, so I could determine the source of their anger.

President Lincoln reserved ten thousand acres to be designated by the War Department, for the purpose of security and preserving the Union. A federal agent would be designated to oversee the land, including the settlement and protection of "persons deemed of strategic, humanitarian, or national importance." These persons of special interest could be presently in the United States and beyond. The inhabitants were permitted to determine their internal affairs, as long as they did not conflict with the Constitution and the laws of the United States. It was an impressive deal, but Lincoln was no king.

> "This authorization shall remain in effect for the duration of the present rebellion, or until such time as it may be amended, superseded, or revoked by executive authority."

I set the document down and took a deep breath. That was an issue of contention, but it wasn't a surprise. "Lincoln already told us about his limitations. He needs Congress to make New Seneca permanent, and he said it would be a legislative priority."

John kept his eyes on the flames. "He can't afford to push the issue until his reelection and the passage of the Thirteenth Amendment."

We couldn't disrupt the chances of that being passed. Other abolitionists and I had worked too hard, and John knew what it meant to me. "I trust that he'll get it done." I smiled, though wearily. "Do you doubt him?"

John took a final swig of his liquor, swirling it in his mouth before the last hard swallow. He sneered at the burn, then flung the glass into the fire. I jumped back as shards scattered against the stone wall and onto the floor. His eyes turned to gold as a few drops of alcohol fed the flames. He scowled like a beast.

I turned to Dinah for clarification. Her brow was low, and her rage was ingrained in every syllable. "They dropped Hamlin from the ticket."

Lincoln wanted as little attention to his executive order as possible, so the backdrop of the National Union Convention served as a distraction for the press. John couldn't attend, but Dinah did as Steven. We had heard rumors that Vice President Hannibal Hamlin would be replaced, but we hoped for the best.

"Why?"

"Because 'Radical Republicans' like you are a legislative distraction." It was unfortunate enough when Dinah saw the ugliness of the world through mankind's memories. The convention was a time for passionate men to debate out loud and whisper deals behind closed doors. Men who shared my convictions about abolition and equality were right—but politics was a game of compromise. Dinah heard them villainized and painted as power-hungry fanatics. "These politicians are more concerned about making nice with the South than they are about equality. Hamlin added nothing to the ticket, and Johnson is a Democrat from a Confederate state."

"Andrew Johnson?" I finally understood why there was shattered glass on my floor. Surely, John would have voiced his displeasure to the president. "After the victory in Atlanta, why would Lincoln require a compromise?"

"The president stays out of the convention process—at least, on paper." John finally turned from the fire. His eyes held more than rage. My husband was disappointed.

"Archangel assured Lincoln's skeptics that he can win the war," Dinah said, "but the Democrats are concerned about the depths of his power and how Lincoln will choose to wield it."

If the Democrats knew the truth, they would fear Lincoln's arrangement even more. "Did he ask you to help Grant?"

"Of course, he did." John was irritated but tried to suppress it.

I pressed my lips together tightly, trying to conceal my true feelings. Cooper was marching to Petersburg. "And you turned him down?"

I did not appreciate the way his eyes cut into me! I glared back, and John quickly fixed his face. "Lincoln can't give me what I want, and he's still in our debt until Congress formally recognizes New Seneca."

"And he wouldn't move on sovereignty? Not even after all the casualties from Grant's campaign?" I asked the question, but I knew the answer. Tens of thousands of men had already died.

That must have weighed heavily on the president's mind. Cooper could be next. He was fortunate not to have been part of the main assault at the Battle of Cold Harbor.

"Lincoln believes remaining in the Union is the best for New Seneca. It's difficult to argue with a man who believes he's right on both sides of the issue." I believe Lincoln's sincerity satiated most of John's rage. He was frustrated about Johnson, but I trusted that the president was taking what he believed to be the best path for everyone.

Was it wrong of me to ask John to take Virginia? He could have done it, but every time he stepped out onto the battlefield was a risk to his life. He couldn't take such a risk without guarantees. "What do we do now?"

John took a breath and met me across the room. He wanted to hold my arms and take in my scent to refocus. "We take Lincoln's advice and develop the land. They'll be less prone to interfere if we can make use of it—not that we'd allow them to take it from us."

"That would be an act of war," Dinah stated matter-of-factly, and it was a fact.

Though it didn't have to be inevitable.

"Then we focus on New Seneca." I took John's hand and placed it on my belly. "We grow our numbers, train our ranks, and become an economic force."

My husband nodded and kissed my forehead. We didn't like Johnson, but Vice Presidents might as well have been window dressing. Lincoln had already done a great deal, and I chose to believe he would do right by us as President of the United States.

Grant's campaign saw more losses than the Confederates, but he had more men to spare. His engagements were bloody but deemed a strategic success. Lincoln's likelihood of reelection increased while the South's contempt of the Union deepened. They bitterly continued fighting.

As far as the bloody hands of the Blue Devil, they were put to good use building a pavilion in Communion Circle. The end of Spring was fast approaching, and we needed places and activities for the people to enjoy. I told John it was finally time to put his circus blood to good use. He had until the end of the month to plan a performance. He would be the main attraction at a festival!

Adam and a group of freedmen had already begun to build a church. I had no doubt that he hoped to marry in it. A carpenter by the name of Paul bonded with Adam during the construction. He asked many questions. Paul was raised on an edited Bible meant to keep slaves obedient, but he secretly discouraged the teachings of their local pastor. He said it didn't sound like the Lord. Once he heard the missing passages, he felt called to live his life for the God who set the captives free. Adam planned to share his education so Paul could become a fine preacher.

Goldie and Nathaniel didn't wait for the church. We had a ceremony under the new pavilion and decorated it with ribbons and flowers. Emma wore a simple white muslin dress with a yellow sash. As she carried a basket of flowers as a symbol of their love, I wondered how lovely Asha would have looked standing beside her. Though Asha would have been too old for a flower girl. If she were alive, I'd be teasing her about boys and hoping to marry her off in a few years.

While we celebrated love and new life, the Confederates tried to preserve their rebellious nation. Cooper wrote to Mary Anne about killing a young boy. Since he was the father of a son he had yet to hold, it haunted his sleep. At the beginning of the year, the Confederates' conscription expanded to accept ages seventeen to fifty. They accepted younger volunteers. After Atlanta fell to Archangel, and so many men fell to Grant in Virginia, the Confederates began taking boys as young as fifteen to fight Lincoln and his "Butcher."

It was an awful price of war—one to consider while sewing puppets with Margaret, Scarlett, and a few other girls. Effie wasn't quite big enough to handle the needle, but she was a marvelous tester. It was in those moments that I reflected on Ecclesiastes. For everything, there was a season. There was a time to be born and a time to die. There was a time to plant and a time to uproot. There was a time to weep and a time to dance. There was a time for war and a time for peace. Our smiles wouldn't last forever, so we had to treasure them while we could.

John said he and the Indians were preparing a big show together, so I had to spoil him with apple pie. Dinah remarked that my sweet potato was better, and I decided to reward her. I blinked down South to my usual General Store of choice with Arthur and Henry. Their supplies were scarce due to the war, but I managed to scrape up two bushels for them to carry.

"Miss Charlotte?"

I froze with a potato in hand. I hadn't heard that voice in such a long time, and it surprised me when she didn't snatch my hair. But I no longer lived under her reign of terror, and I had changed. I placed the last potato in Henry's basket, then turned to face her with a big smile. "Actually, it's Lady Cohen now." I rubbed my belly, so she could see the shape of it through my dress.

Miss Ruth took a step back as her eyes enlarged. "You and Massa John married?"

I raised my hand that carried our initials. "We've been wed for nearly a year."

She stared at the signet ring in disbelief. It was an unusual wedding ring, but we were an unusual pair. "I'm really happy for you, Charlotte." A solemn smile crept on her wide face. "Lady Cohen would be happy, too—God rest her soul."

It didn't shock me that Miss Ruth still held such loyalty to Lady Cohen, but that loyalty did keep her from telling my secret. It was funny. John had invited other liberated slaves to live in New Seneca, but he never once suggested inviting any from the Cohens' plantation. "What about you?"

"I was working for Mrs. Mayflower, but she recently passed."

"Oh, I'm sorry to hear that." I once traveled with Miss Ruth and Lady Cohen to Mrs. Mayflower. She was much older but enjoyed Lady Cohen's company and Miss Ruth's cooking. She was a widow who lived with her son, but he died in the Mexican-American War.

"She had no family, so she left her property to me."

I held my chest and had a deep breath. "I'm glad you did well for yourself, Miss Ruth."

Miss Ruth's eyes looked beyond me to the man working the counter. He was distracted by the morning paper. The wanted poster of Runaway, tacked to the wall behind him, was hard to miss. "Be careful. The people here…" She signaled me to come in closer, and I obeyed. "They say such terrible things about…what you do."

Miss Ruth had been a force of nature all of her life, like a giant ball of fire. I don't know if I had ever seen fear in her dark, beady eyes. "They'll hurt you and Massa John, if they can."

I was so flattered by her concern, though I assumed it was mostly for Lady Cohen's sake. "Don't worry about us. We can give worse than we take."

Perhaps there was a bit too much resolve in my eyes. I believe she went from being afraid *for* me to being afraid *of* me. I must admit, it was exhilarating. "Are they like you?" Her eyes darted to the boys behind me.

I only offered a smirk as confirmation. She already knew too much, but there was no need to deny it. "Take care of yourself, Miss Ruth."

Arthur and Henry hadn't said a word, but their eyes were loud with intrigue. I paid for our things, then left. When we were far enough away from prying eyes, we blinked home to prepare for the festival.

On the last day of the month, John and I were awakened by a constant tapping on our window. I curled with my pillow in defiance, but John leaped out of bed and pulled back the curtain. "Tillie!" He opened the window, and a red hawk entered the room. I didn't love having a bird in our space, but John was excited like a child experiencing his first snowfall. "Come here, girl." He stretched his arm like a perch, and she came to him. I didn't know what to make of the way she nuzzled his neck, but I don't know what other way a bird could show affection.

"I'm happy for you, Tillie. This is wonderful news." Our eyes met. I didn't have John's talent, but I assumed most of the burdens of the past few months were alleviated. I never would have wished for what happened, but in a way, I was grateful that we had grown closer. "Take flight."

She nodded before spreading her wings and exploring the sky. I grinned at my husband, but he was contemplating something and grinned, almost mischievously.

"John!" I rushed to the window once he dove after her. He was riding the wind like a leaf in Autumn, graceful and free. It would have been a sentimental moment if he were wearing more than a nightshirt. "At least come back and put some trousers on!"

Thankfully, he didn't stay in the sky long. We had much to do. The area surrounding Communion Circle had been turned into a giant park. Wooden tables and chairs were set out. Another pavilion was built for shade while people ate. There were areas for people to sit down and enjoy games like checkers, chess, and Weiqi—a game Zhang taught us. Kachina crafted all the pieces and boards herself. She also crafted stone statues that resembled animals, and the freedman built rope walls and swings. It lacked the greenery of Central Park, but that beauty would come soon. As Evelyn walked with her arm wrapped around Adam, I noticed the tints of red in her hair turned a peculiar shade of pink. I assumed it was a sign her powers were beginning to bloom.

We had competitions all day. The Indians dominated archery. Benjamin was the best at shooting rifles, and that was without his powers returning. Emma wasn't allowed to compete in any tests of physical strength, but we did allow the winners to test their might against her. They failed. Henry also wasn't allowed to participate in tests of speed, but the winner could test their luck against him. He happened to lose. The poor boy tripped right at the start and hit his face. Zhang healed him, and Martha cleaned him up.

Throughout the day, there was meat, sweet bread, fruits, and desserts to eat. Everybody raved about my pies. I had Agnes ask everybody who had one to write down which was their favorite, so I could finally end the debate with John. Unfortunately, he stole the box with the ballots and burned it with Nathaniel's borrowed power. When I scolded him, John said, "I'm your husband. My vote is the only one that counts."

I rolled my eyes and went home to change. Everyone wore fancier attire to watch performances in Communion Circle. It was the first time it was filled. A puppet show told an exaggerated and humorous tale of Ghost and Runaway. Everyone had a bellyaching laugh when my puppet dropped a piano on Ghost's head. They even made fun of my battle at the bank against Hoshi and the Draft Riots.

"The city is on fire. People are dying. What should we do now?" Runaway Puppet asked in a soft and delicate voice.

"Hmm…" Ghost Puppet thought deeply, then flailed about. "I want to kiss you!"

John and I watched with reddened faces, half covered, as the puppets smashed together and audibly smooched. Everyone had a good laugh, so I suppose it was worth the embarrassment to see children pointing and falling over.

I thought to myself that I should write a book, so puppet shows and wanted posters weren't the only tales about me and my love.

Next, we had a few songs. The children performed a hymn, and Emma led the song. I didn't know she had the voice of an angel. If wrestling and carpentry didn't work out, she had something to fall back on. A small choir followed, comprised mostly of freedmen singing negro spirituals. A few white faces, like Adam and Christopher, swayed along with a peculiar rhythm.

John was amused as I bobbed my head and clapped. "I thought you didn't like songs from the slaves."

"It's different when you're already free." The songs were too sad when I was on the Cohens' plantation, and I truly didn't understand them. Once I was free and began rescuing others, I recognized them as a call to action and a means of survival. Now, they were stories of resilience and deliverance. How could I not love my history?

John kissed me when the song ended, then left to prepare for his performance. He would be next after a dance. One of our residents immigrated from Italy and trained in ballet. Agnes made her a skirt from tulle, and Javier built an elegant set. With John gone, there was an open spot next to me. Emma was sitting on the ground, close to the stage, with the other children. I tried to get her attention subtly, but she was enamored by Maria, who had the grace and beauty of a swan. I was about to call to her, but a figure, dressed in black, slinked down the stairs as the sun set. "Mind if I join you?"

It was Dinah, in a black frilly dress. I hadn't seen her all day, so I was curious. "Of course."

She didn't normally flaunt her real figure, but her open shoulders were quite steamy. Her corset hugged her tiny waist and propped up her bosoms. She even took the time to apply burnt cork around her eyes and blackberries to stain her lips. "Where did you get that dress?"

She raised her head and smiled. "If you can sew, I can sew."

It was well-made and stylish. But it was also familiar. I swore I had seen that lace choker with a heart pendant before. "It looks like something Mary Anne would make."

"Does it, now?" She fluffed out her frills while her words hung in the air. She enjoyed playing games with me, so I didn't want to overreact. To my knowledge, Dinah had yet to touch her.

But Dinah could go anywhere she pleased and do nearly anything she wanted.

I had gotten to know her well enough, and beyond her smoky eyes was a distressed mind. She never found peace, even as Maria floated around the stage to violins. "You don't seem well."

"I thought I cleaned up rather nicely." She meant to speak low and seductively, but there was a quiver in her voice.

"Dinah, what's wrong?" I didn't smell liquor, so she wasn't drunk. Something else had her pretty eyes shining.

She tried to hold her smile, especially as Maria took her bow, but it quickly inverted and trembled. I gave her a stern look to let her know I wouldn't let it go. The crowd applauded, and her fingers clutched the frills in her lap. I leaned over so Dinah could speak in my ear. Even then, she took a deep breath as if to give me time to change my mind. "I had another vision."

I wasn't pleased, but that sort of power must have been tempting. "Was it more rushing ships?"

She shook her head slowly, then clapped along with everyone else. She clearly wanted to wait to tell me the dream in private, and I tried to respect her wishes. I had been waiting forever for John to show me his roots, and he had such a big smile on his face as he graced the stage with nine Indians. Five of them had instruments and stood in the back. John was dressed in their fringed suede pants and war paint. They had headdresses, but John's was more elaborate. Kachina got a good chuckle out of it. He certainly stood out from the crowd.

"Ladies and gentlemen, it is my honor to address you all tonight as subjects of New Seneca." He pointed me out to the crowd. "I was informed by my lovely wife that I had an obligation to give you a show. So, without further ado, I bring you 'Flaming Arrow.'"

He stretched forth his hands and closed his fists, causing all the candles and torches to go out. The children screamed. Many were young enough to be afraid of the dark, and the moon was only a thin crescent. The next flicker of light came from matches, lit from both ends of the stage and used to set two arrows on fire. Two Indians quickly drew their bows, and a collective gasp swept the auditorium as they simultaneously shot John.

To no surprise, he caught them both, then burned the fire hotter until they turned to ash. However, the shape of the arrow remained in the flames. John smirked as the crowd cheered. He truly was the showman he was born to be. As the flames circled his body and the Indians danced around him with fire batons, I wondered what could have happened if John's parents had never been killed. We likely would have never met. Lillian would have had no need to adopt him and marry Mr. Cohen. He probably would have married a nice acrobat or a beautiful ballerina. I wondered if he would have performed on Barnum's stage. He had the charisma and talent to make something of himself.

I didn't know where I would be, though. Who else would have purchased me for $500?

Dinah released a fearful gasp. She trembled as the dance and music became more intense, even though John was in complete control. It ended with the Indians seeming to swallow their flames, while John unleashed a powerful breath like a dragon of legend. The crowd hopped to their feet. I clapped along and smiled so I wouldn't alarm my husband. I was the first person he looked for once the torches were lit again.

The men took their bows, and John leaped from the stage to engage with the children. They were his greatest admirers and loved the way he looked. A crowd also formed around the other performers. They humbly took their praise with bows and bashful smiles.

Dinah's desperate hand gripped my thigh. "It was a burning man…"

My entire body became cold. "A what?"

"The vision…" She whispered as John approached and forced a smile.

I didn't want to keep a secret from John, but he was radiant as he tried to hug me. I took a step back and raised my arms as a shield. "I do not want your paint all over my dress!" It was all white, and I managed to keep it clean. I even sat on a blanket during the performances.

John laughed. "Fair enough." He glanced at Dinah. I think he tried not to stare too hard, since her chest was quite pronounced. "You look unwell. Have you eaten?"

"No, I was busy finishing this dress."

"Well," he smiled like a demon in her face, "there's still plenty of apple pie."

Dinah glared. "I wonder why that is."

"Excuse me!" I pulled her away. "There's plenty of pie because I made plenty. Alright? There's some sweet potato, too. John is just being messy." I pushed Dinah, so she would go compose herself and get something to eat. Worrying on an empty stomach would only make her sick.

"You sure you don't want a hug?" He stretched out his arms and grinned wider.

"John, don't you dare!" He moved, so I blinked a good ten feet away from him. He tried to catch me, but I blinked further away. Unfortunately, when I tried to blink away a third time, John was able to sense where I'd be and caught me. I hated that he could do that. Of course, he sullied my dress. I wasn't happy about it, but I did always love what happened when he caught me.

"I want to kiss you!" Alfie shouted mockingly, and a burst of childish laughter followed. John certainly was kissing me, but he let me go to chase the little ones.

The night ended with dancing to fiddles and tambourines. The baby didn't slow me down much. I danced with everyone I could, men and women. Caroline's eyes glittered as we spun, and I believed she'd be soaring in the skies with Tillie soon enough. I pulled Tillie into our circle and made her dance. She only rolled her eyes once before laughing along with us.

Dinah was watching against a wooden beam, moping. I couldn't take it and blinked to her. "Come on."

"Charlotte, I'm not in the mood."

"You're never in the mood." I yanked on her arm, and she stumbled forward. "Sometimes, you have to make yourself enjoy life." Though she was dressed to mourn, I pulled her into our circle. Tillie's face fell, but once she noticed my commanding eyes, she fixed her face.

"Bygones."

Dinah's brow rose in surprise, and then she nodded. "Bygones."

I was relieved when Tillie took Dinah's hands and began to dance. I would have dragged Kachina over, but she was rather engaged with Benjamin all night. He was a handsome fellah. I hoped she remembered our rules about waiting until the depowered were back to normal. For many, it could have been any day from then.

After I danced my final dance with John, Martha and Agnes prepared us a bath, and then we got ready for bed. John hadn't stopped smiling the whole night. I didn't know how to talk to him about Dinah's dream. As we cuddled, I figured it was best to let Dinah explain it in the morning. I didn't know many details myself.

He was quiet for a while, but I could tell something was on John's mind as he brushed my hair. "What would you think if we changed our name?"

I sat up, completely surprised. "And I became Lady Davis?"

I had asked laughingly, but he offered a slow nod.

Perhaps this was the out I had been looking for. I had wanted to separate myself from Lillian Cohen and the terrible things his stepfather and step-uncles did. "Does that mean I can name our baby Adelaide?"

"Absolutely not."

I laughed again. That was the only time his smile fell. "I was only teasing." No, he loved that woman. No matter what she did, Lillian was a part of him. "I wouldn't mind being Mrs. Davis, but the federal agent assigned to New Seneca is John Cohen. All of your business associates and the politicians know you as Mr. Cohen. They know me as the radical Mrs. Cohen."

"I know…" I rubbed his cheek just as he smirked. Everything we ever were would have always been. There was no point in disregarding or running from it. For better or worse,

I was Lady Cohen, and he was my husband. "It just felt good to be John Davis again…"

John Davis was certainly a looker. If I had found a way to visit that traveling circus with his family, I certainly would have found a way to love him again. If God remade our souls a thousand times, I would find a way to love him a thousand and one. "Your father seems like he was a good man."

"He was." He caressed my back. Then I fell into his chest as he whispered, "I miss my momma, too." It wouldn't be much longer before John had his chance to hold his own child. Though he loved his father immensely, Mr. Davis couldn't protect John or Adelaide from the world. That's why John fought so hard for Lillian's vision of a haven, and we had built it.

Together.

Chapter Twenty-Four

Summer came and went quickly. I attributed that to everyone's powers reawakening. When John told Margaret that the zealots took her father's life, she was so emotional that it sent a wild thunderstorm to us. John was able to use a combination of his sway and his own control of the weather to calm the storm. Margaret was sad for a while, and it rained a whole lot. We did our best to raise her spirits. Children brought her food and dresses, and they tried to play games with her. She didn't break a smile until John took her hand and taught Margaret how to fly. Once he mastered her power over wind, he taught Adam to do the same.

Most others didn't give John that sort of trouble, and Dinah was a help. As the people became more accustomed to their powers, we found more ways to advance New Seneca. Thanks to Evelyn, we could grow nearly any crop we could ever think of rapidly. Margaret gave us excellent weather, and the land was plenteous. We had more food than we knew what to do with, so we became an exporter.

I visited Mary Anne when I could to keep her company. It was difficult for her to watch JoJo grow, knowing his father hadn't seen him. She sent him detailed sketches and plenty of letters. His correspondence became more intimate. He longed for her and dreamed of holding his son. Cooper nearly died at the Battle of the Crater outside Petersburg. It should have been a success led by colored troops, but a last-minute decision stripped them of command and put inexperienced white men at the helm of a massacre. Colored troops were disproportionately killed, and many who tried to surrender were murdered. Cooper said Mary Anne and JoJo were his anchors, and they gave him strength to continue.

His parents came to visit. Mrs. Cooper held JoJo the whole time, and Mr. Cooper presented a box full of hand-carved animals for his grandchild. His wife did most of the talking, but Mary Anne very much felt loved. She was thinking about visiting Elijah for Christmas, so JoJo could meet his cousins.

One day, while we were having tea in the garden, Mary Anne reached over and touched my belly. "John is right."

"About having a girl?" At that point, I wasn't surprised. He couldn't "feel" things as well as she could, but he had been consistent and adamant. "You couldn't tell him otherwise."

"Then all of the pretty bonnets I've made for her won't go to waste." Mary Anne sank into her chair as if she had fallen into a dream. "Our children are going to get married, aren't they? We'll be in-laws."

"Well," I lifted my teacup nonchalantly, "that's for JoJo and Lily Anne to decide…"

Mary Anne's eyes widened, and she practically levitated back up. "Lily Anne? Anne…as in…?"

I took my sweet time sipping the tea, but I couldn't hold back my smile. "John said he loved the name."

She attacked me with a ferocious hug. If JoJo possessed ferocious power like his mother, there was a chance John would want to betroth our babies like monarchs. I didn't know about all that. I preferred for them to have the liberty to love whomever they and God decided on, as I did. But no matter what they chose, Mary Anne, Cooper, and JoJo would always be my family.

She agreed to stay with me in New Seneca once I hit 38 weeks, but due to some bleeding, John forbade me from using my powers. My doctor committed me to bed rest, and my ladies waited on me hand and foot. John said Lily Anne's heart was still strong, and she was certainly a kicker.

I kept myself entertained by reading to the children. We had been reading *Beauty and the Beast*, and the girls marveled at the revelation that Beauty was the daughter of a good fairy. That explained much of her otherworldly attraction.

"Is Miss Evelyn a fairy?" Scarlett asked, and for good reason. Evelyn's hair had turned completely pink, her eyes were vividly blue, even glowed at times, and her skin was flushed with life and smelled of rosewater. She had such a beautiful wedding in the church, draped with flowers. It was no surprise that Adam was fruitful and multiplied. Evelyn was bigger than I was at 16 weeks, but John said he felt more than one heartbeat. She was as real as Gaia would ever be.

"Caroline looks like a fairy," Emma said. She was another one who barely stayed on the ground. It was comforting to see the warm glow of the sun on her skin again.

Effie gently pressed upon my stomach. "You look like a fairy, Lady Charlotte."

I didn't mean to laugh at such a kind sentiment, but I didn't feel very beautiful. I felt heavy, tired, and like I always had to relieve myself. "Thank you, Effie. That's sweet."

There was a knock at my door, followed by an immediate entry. My handsome husband entered with a weary smile. "School time in my room again?"

"We just finished." I playfully shooed the children off. Most of them headed through the front door, but Margaret headed for the window. "Can you use the door like a normal child?"

She huffed, annoyed. "But I'm not normal!" Margaret was obedient and followed the other children. She quickly hugged John as Dinah slid inside. Then, he shut the door.

"She's growing up a little too fast," I told him.

"It's better than her being miserable and docile. She is thirteen now." Margaret was practically malnourished when we brought her in, but she was a healthy, growing young woman. "They all feel like our children, don't they?" He sat next to me on the bed and touched my belly.

"Thank God they don't all kick this hard." I was excited when I first felt Lily Anne move, but I very much wanted her to stop attacking my ribs. My husband was trying to grin through it all, not wanting to add to my discomfort, but I knew the world outside of our walls was going to hell. "How was your meeting with Mr. Pike?"

"We don't have to talk about that right now—"

"John, please. I'm not a child. I'm having one."

His brows furrowed, and he kissed my hand. John consulted with Dinah, and she nudged him through the air. Then he sighed and kissed my hand once more. "The Confederates always saw this war as a states' rights issue, and Lincoln was a tyrant overstepping his bounds." John never wanted to protect slavery, but as a Southerner, he did share some of their sentiments.

"Go on."

"They didn't like the designation of the Overseers as terrorists, especially since so many of them are stationed in the South." He was avoiding my eyes, perhaps because they were so sad for my sake. "They're being protected."

"Protected?" I sat up higher against my headboard, trying to make sense of his words. Dinah walked closer with a sneer on her face and a quiet rage that began to burn inside of me. "They've burned people."

John's thumb rubbed against my skin, so softly, before he met my eyes. "They don't think we're people."

I held my chest, feeling ill. Perhaps my morning meal was about to come back up, but that could have been the baby pressing against my insides.

"Just as this war has become about liberating slaves for many in the North, it's become about fighting a tyrannical government that conjures demons to impose its will."

"Demons?" I bitterly laughed in disbelief, summoning furious tears.

Dinah gave a small nod to confirm his words. "Abolitionist preachers inspire equality. Supporters for the Overseers inspire purification." Dinah spoke quietly, but every syllable possessed disgust. "Since so many men have gone to fight and die, women have taken the stage to rally their cause."

I hated to cry. It was distressing news, but they were mostly tears of frustration. "But we're winning. The Union will win."

"The Union will prevail, certainly." John lightly hunched his shoulders. "But who's to say what it will take to bring down the fanatics?" His head tilted toward me, his voice barely a whisper. "How many boys will Cooper and Grant have to butcher?"

Truthfully, I felt more than rage. I was devastated that I got to sleep every night next to my husband while Mary Anne felt Cooper's absence, and I mourned the pieces of his soul that were stripped away with every loss and life taken. In the end, I wanted it all to be worth it for them. "What will happen once the Union is whole?"

"You mean after we absorb their bigoted Senators and Congressmen?" Dinah asked. "After their fanatics vote in the next presidential election?"

John paused. He was remarkably reserved, and it made me nervous that he was more concerned about my pregnancy than he led on. "Dinah doesn't believe reunification will end well for us."

"Will it?"

John reached for my stomach again, as if he were trying to calm Lily Anne down. "Lincoln will have more flexibility now that he's won reelection, but his goals for the war won't change. I believe he'll try to keep his word, but it would be more difficult if the South has a say." He released his hand once her assault ended. "I will do whatever it takes to keep us safe."

I didn't take it personally. Lily Anne was trying to make herself comfortable. I hoped she felt better than I did.

"Are you in pain?"

I hated that I wrinkled his perfect skin with worry. "I'm sorry. I feel so uncomfortable." There was so much pressure on my pelvis. I couldn't believe she wasn't already halfway out of me.

John frowned and kissed my forehead. "I'll fetch your doctor."

Dinah had her arms folded and lips tight as John walked past her and out the door. Her eyes were…deranged, as if she had to suppress every evil thought in her head.

Eventually, she took his place by my side. "Thank you…"

"For what?"

"Making me content with barrenness."

I harshly chuckled, and Lily Anne repaid me by kicking my spine. "Don't be glib. With all the miracles in this world, it's possible for you to conceive—if you want to."

"No." Her eyes might have fallen to my stomach, but her mind was elsewhere. "The few men I've cared for end up being killed. The only survivor is John."

"Well, he's durable." I patted her hand. "We'll have to find someone durable enough for you."

"Good luck…"

I drew a sharp breath as another bout of pain came upon me. I gritted my teeth and reached for Dinah's hand on instinct. Her eyes widened, but she didn't draw away as the pain pressed downward in a way I had yet to experience.

"Perhaps Emma would be more equipped for this…" She clenched her teeth as well, until the pain subsided for both of us. "That was different…" She pulled away and nursed her poor hand.

"It felt different." Martha and Agnes came in with a water basin, soap, cloths, and stiffer pillows to prop me up. The pain came again, but they kept time for me. Dinah watched me grunt and groan, almost mesmerized. "You don't have to stay. My ladies will be here until John and Dr. Bingle arrive."

The way she stared didn't make me feel any better. "Zhang should be here—in case something happens."

"Zhang is away fishing." I chuckled as her eyes bulged. "John copied his power. We'll be fine."

She sank further into her shoulders, resisting the urge to scold me. "I'll be in my room if you need me." Dinah lingered for a few seconds, mirroring my expressions. Eventually, she patted my hand and moved at a turtle's pace out the door.

John came with Dr. Bingle as the next rush of pain came. He was in his fifties and had plenty of experience delivering babies, especially as of late. He hadn't found many opportunities to use his powers, besides entertaining children. He could gather a form of blue energy in his hand and make it take shape. John liked to wield it as a sword.

Agnes took his coat and hat, then he rolled up his sleeves and washed his hands. "How far apart are the contractions?"

Agnes answered, because I could not. “Four to six minutes, I believe.”

“Hmm…” He felt my abdomen and assessed the contraction, my pulse, and observed my breathing. He was quiet—too quiet—and his jaw was tight. Then it came time to examine my pelvis. The doctor did well controlling his face, except for the twitch of his brow. “The good news, Lady Charlotte, is that you’re in active labor.”

I tossed my head back and sighed in relief. “Thank God.”

“But you’re already several hours in.”

John had his arms folded. He did a remarkable job remaining calm, but I knew his eyes well enough. “How much longer will she be in pain?”

“It’s difficult to say. Unfortunately, this is the process, and Charlotte still has quite a ways to go.” He patted John on the shoulder and offered a grin. “Delivering children is the easy part. Discipling them is a far more trying adventure.”

My husband returned a weary smile.

“Keep her propped up and in bed. She shouldn’t leave without my orders.”

The pain came upon me again, this time bending me over. I clenched my hands until I felt my husband’s fingers fighting to intertwine with mine. I loosened, just enough to weave us together. As it eased and I caught my breath again, John held my hand to his chest. “There’s no need to fear, Charlotte. I’ve seen your future.”

I hoped my smile wasn’t too cynical. I assumed that was just something John liked to say and never pressed him on it. I wasn’t worried about the delivery, though. I didn’t expect it to be easy, but I could certainly handle it if Mary Anne could push that big baby out of her.

John wouldn’t leave my side, other than to relieve himself. If he needed water or food, my ladies fetched it. John kept busy by reading. He started in 1 Samuel, which was one of my favorite books of the Bible. It was difficult to focus due to the pressure. After a while, time blurred together, and only a few sounds were distinct as I suffered. I asked John to stop so I wouldn’t look like I was being exorcised.

"Breathe," the doctor reminded. "Don't fight it. Don't hold it in. You were made for this."

Damp hair held to the front of my face while it puffed on the back of my head. Martha tried to keep me hydrated while Agnes removed blankets and dabbed beads of sweat. John's hand was always there, ready to take a good squeeze. He could have at least winced, but I suppose I gave him enough distress.

In two hours, a gush of fluid came. I wished I felt relief, but the pain steadily increased and came more frequently. Doctor Bingle often gave an encouraging smile, mostly covered by his thick mustache, but once he examined me again, his face fell.

"Doctor, what's wrong?" John asked, rubbing my hand. "Is Lily Anne alright?"

"Her head is well positioned…" He paused, then donned a veil of stoicism. "Her hand is resting on her head. It's not ideal."

"Not ideal?" John's voice was slightly elevated. "What does that mean?"

"Her posture is slowing the labor. She will come out, but Charlotte could tear, or her arm could be injured—"

"No!" I shook my head profusely, and two tears came loose. "I don't want to hurt her…"

The doctor firmly pressed his lips, then bobbed his head. "Then I'll attempt to move it…" The doctor's voice was stern, so we both understood. "And this will hurt."

John continued to hold my hand, kissed my forehead, and braced my shoulder with his other hand. I felt guilt for making the strongest man in the world feel powerless. But he didn't know how much it meant to have him by my side.

I nodded, and Dr. Bingle proceeded. A sharp, invasive pressure exploded inside of me. I would have screamed if the shock hadn't robbed my breath. John finally winced, but it wasn't from the squeeze of my hand. "You're strong, Charlotte. Remember."

I couldn't even say the words. I could hardly think of them.

When the doctor came into view, his mustache was arched. His brows were low on his face. He had to force a smile. "Lily Anne is strong and stubborn. I'm afraid she put her arm right back."

I hunched over and glared at my husband. "Oh, she gets that from you…"

He tried to grin—though I was serious—but his lips trembled. "What can I do for them?"

"I think it's best to give it a little bit of time. She may remove her hand, or our princess may allow it later. For now, be here for your wife."

Very soon, the only thing in this world I was certain of was John's hand holding mine. Time didn't move normally—it ground against my bones and organs. I trembled, cried, screamed, and vomited for hours. We lost daylight between it all.

Everyone began to worry. Paul gathered a crowd to pray at the church. Adam held and rocked Evelyn in a pew, imagining how trying the birth of multiple children would be. Tillie stayed perched on our windowsill while Kachina paced the halls of the manor. Benjamin dutifully watched. They hadn't officially gotten married, but a tiny baby rested in her womb as well. As for Dinah, she stayed in her room. I imagined her mind was whirling with every possibility of what would happen if I didn't survive, and how that would reforge John's mind.

But John wasn't worried. It was difficult to watch me squirm in agony, but he steadily kissed and rubbed the hand that meant to squeeze the life from him.

"Did you truly see my future?" I didn't mean to break, but I was afraid for our baby. I was even afraid for my own life.

John gently brushed thickened curls off my face. "Yes," he whispered with a smile, "and you were glorious."

If Lincoln's visions were only of death, I hadn't the faintest idea how his words could have been true. But I chose to believe it. His conviction was too powerful to deny.

Dr. Bingle examined me again. When he spoke, his voice lost its ease. "We're close to the point of no return. I must attempt to move Lily Anne's arm once more."

I breathed and gripped John's sweaty palm tighter. I knew what was coming, but it was so much worse than before. As the pain deepened and exploded across my body, I made a wish within myself. As my back arched and my eyes reached up to the ceiling, all I could think about was how I wanted to be free.

I clenched my fingers tighter, but I didn't feel John's touch. My back bounced against the bed, with no support from a stack of pillows. The room was darker with no gaslights or candles. It was deathly quiet, besides my screams echoing throughout the room. Most importantly, the hand that had reached inside of me was gone.

I took a breath. As I uncurled and felt the fabric against my face, the room's scenery became clear. My books. My writing desk. Runaway's coat hung in the closet. And for good measure, I reached behind me and felt my initials carved in the headboard. "John?"

He didn't respond.

I was in our home.

In labor.

Alone.

"John!" I screamed, overwhelmed once more. John would have realized what happened instantly. Our home in New York was the first place he should have looked. If I could hold on a little while longer. If I could just wait for him, he'd find me…

But it hurt so badly!

I screamed again, this time from the abrupt and short fall to the ground. My back hit something hard. I was in a field of dirt. The hardened shape underneath me began to register as roots and limbs. I looked up as another contraction began and cried at the sight of a broken and scorched tree.

This was our magnolia tree, in our field, where John promised we'd build a life together.

I wanted to bitterly weep at the violet sky, but something was running down my legs, and my water had already broken. John—or even Dinah—*might* have found me there. But it wouldn't have been their first choice. I didn't think I had long. I already felt the urge to push.

I had to move to someplace safe. I had to find my way back to John!

Another wave of pain came upon me, and I curled again. I was no longer in a field of scorched earth. I was on a harder surface, and the scent of dust was familiar to me. I breathed it in, almost relieved. But I couldn't be certain. It was too dark to be sure of where I was. I hoped I was correct, or else strangers were listening to me scream.

"Charlotte?" A sliver of light illuminated a man's figure. He was short and stocky, just like I remembered. His beard was gone, though. I thought he looked much nicer without it. "Sheryl!" he called. "Come quickly. It's Charlotte!"

I heard the rumbling of her feet before she rushed through the door and down the steps. Richard carried a lantern down to give us light. When Sheryl met me after leaving the Cohens' plantation, I wasn't in good condition either, but she was far more worried than I had ever seen her. "God help us, Charlotte…" She pulled back my gown and examined me. "You're crowning!"

"We have to move the baby's arm—ahhh!"

"We're beyond that, Charlotte. This baby is coming now." She was a tiny woman but had such a fierceness about her. "Richard, we need water and blankets. Right now—and a knife."

They scrambled about while I tried to resist the very natural and overwhelming urge to push her out. I didn't want to risk hurting Lily Anne. I would take all the pain in the world to spare her a drop of it.

"No!" Sheryl grabbed my shoulders as Richard came behind to prop me up. She made me look into her intense eyes. "You cannot hold your breath. You have to push. It's time."

"It can't be—"

"It is!" She didn't have the time to be delicate or stoic, even if I sobbed and trembled. "Charlotte, you are going to have this beautiful baby, and everything is going to be fine. We can get through anything. Remember?" She gave me a good shake. "You are strong."

My lips quivered. I hardly had any breath to give her. "I am strong…"

"Good." She smiled. "Now, you've got to push."

I didn't want to. Everything was wrong. I wanted to squeeze my husband's hand, though I appreciated Richard. Mary Anne should have been watching from the corner, bouncing JoJo to keep him quiet. Cooper should have been waiting outside the room, trying his best not to pick a fight with Dinah. She should have been waiting to tempt John with a congratulatory cigar.

At least I wasn't alone. Praise the Lord, I was among friends who had recently experienced their own labor. Sheryl marvelously cheered and encouraged me. She even pleaded with Lily Anne as she tried to maneuver her arm and head. "Work with me, baby. Work with me!" She mostly kept a bright smile on her face—up until the moment when a ring of fire swept across my nether region, and everything within me was released.

It burned deeper than anything I had ever imagined, like I had been ripped apart at the seams. I collapsed onto Richard's chest as Lily Anne's cries entered the world. I was too weak to lift my head, but her voice was so sweet.

"Richard," Sheryl whispered. "There's so much blood…"

He gently set me down on the cellar floor, propping my head up with a folded blanket. I felt something warm and wet on my chest, and Sheryl guided my arms to wrap around it. I managed to look down at her wailing face. She was so red. Poor thing. I rubbed her slick back and struggled to kiss her tiny hand that gave me such trouble, but I lacked the strength to reach her. My arms were trembling. I didn't know how long I could hold her. My life was pouring out, soaking the floor beneath us.

Oh, how I longed to see John one more time! I finally gave him his beautiful baby girl. I could already tell her hair was going to spiral and flow like Dinah's—our beautiful mulatto baby.

"John…" I imagined his face—lovely and firm like a sculpted stone angel—flooded in light. I imagined him taking us in his arms and surrounding us with warmth. His blue eyes would brighten as he gazed at our Lily Anne for the first time. "John?"

My grip on Lily Anne steadied, and I leaned up against his chest. A sense of safety came over me, and I could breathe again. The light was real. It was the healing power of Zhang! "I told you, Charlotte." He smiled as streams of blood rushed down his nostrils. "I've seen your future."

"John?"

He jolted from a cough, and blood scattered across my face.

I blinked hard, refusing to believe it to be so…

But then he fell to the ground, pale like the dead.

"John…?"

Chapter Twenty-Five

"John!" I held Lily Anne with one arm and shook John with the other. His eyes fluttered, then fell closed. His skin was warm and slick with sweat. A strange, familiar sensation lingered around him—an invisible energy. "How did he get here?"

"He just appeared!" Sheryl yelled as she and her husband rushed to John's side.

"No, that's not how he works…" I rubbed his face. I hardly felt any breath from him. What I did feel were the loosened threads of the world, the ones I escaped when I used my powers.

John must have found a way to search for me in the world between spaces!

I kissed his cheek, hoping my touch and words would pull him back from the brink. "Hold on."

Dinah and Kachina were practically screaming in panic. I think Kachina ran to Dinah's room once John disappeared, desperate for her to help. She must have been in the middle of explaining as I appeared before them, drenched in blood with a baby on my chest. They immediately hollered, but I couldn't make sense of them.

"I need you." I yanked Dinah's wrist, then blinked back to the cellar before she could respond.

She glanced around the space. It should have been familiar, though she had never been. But once she saw Richard lifting John's arms over his head, in an attempt to restore his breathing, she dropped to her knees and screamed as if her whole world had broken in two.

I didn't have to tell her what to do. Dinah stretched forth her arms as they lightened. Her spiraled curls darkened and straightened. She surrendered her feminine curves for the sharper edges of a man. Zhang wasn't much bigger than her, but her shirt and trousers tightened. The soles of her feet were bare. She sobbed miserably as the light of life poured from her body and into John.

I lightly bounced Lily Anne. She hadn't stopped crying since she came out of me. I kissed her shoulder, which appeared to be fine. It was one less thing to pray about.

A very shallow breath entered John's body. Then another. Then again. They became deeper as Dinah hunched over. I hadn't seen Zhang that tired since he failed to save Hotah and Peter. But she wouldn't stop until the color returned to his face, and John finally opened his eyes.

"John!"

He followed my voice and leapt to his feet. I collapsed against that fool's chest, wailing as if he had died. John wiped the blood from his nose before wrapping his nearly all-powerful arms around us. I was relieved—I truly was—but furious that we had almost lost him.

"You can't…" I pulled away from him, so overwhelmed with tears that I could hardly speak. "You can't ever do something like that again—not even for us." I slammed my fist on his chest and whimpered. "You're too important for the world, John."

John's head drew back, and his eyes narrowed as if I had said something offensive. "You are my world." His gaze softened as he looked at our daughter. "You and Lily Anne."

John grabbed the back of my neck and pulled me into a kiss. There was never going to be a world in which he would let me die so that he might live. I could taste it on his lips. He didn't know how to go on without me. We had built so much together—but it was all for my sake.

Dinah remained on the floor, breathing hard, wiping her tears. The strain of healing John clung to Dinah as she returned to her true form. Richard tried to help her stand, but she stared at his hand as if she didn't know what to do with it. She wouldn't rise until John lifted her.

"I owe you a debt of gratitude."

Dinah held her chest, fighting for control. "The pleasure was all mine."

Lily Anne finally stopped crying. I adjusted so Dinah could get a clearer look at her face. Her eyes were the purest of blues.

Dinah almost smiled. "She looks like you, John."

"She looks like her wonderful mother." John kissed my forehead, and the smack of his lips seemed so loud in the sudden quiet. There had been such chaos—and now there was nothing. A baby lay in my arms. I had carried her for nine months…but how was she there? It didn't feel real.

I stretched out my gown and silently gasped. It was soaked in my blood.

"Are you alright?" Sheryl asked.

"I'm fine." I wasn't. I was shaking.

John kissed me again. "I think I'll take a walk with Dinah for a moment." She was trembling as well. "Sheryl, do you mind getting Charlotte cleaned up?"

"Of course. Richard will clean down here."

John led Dinah outside while Sheryl guided me to her bedroom. I wasn't in pain, but I moved slowly, as if I had forgotten how to walk. Her baby slept in a crib. She reached for Lily Anne while I was distracted. I shot her a sharp look—enough to make her stop.

"It's alright, Charlotte." She steadied herself and met my eyes, as if calming something wild. "You're both fine."

My grip loosened, and she took my baby. I didn't move as she washed her. I didn't watch and learn how to swaddle her in a warm blanket. My eyes stayed steady on Sheryl's little baby, but I don't even remember what she looked like.

"Come on, Charlotte. Let's get you clean." I raised my arms, and she pulled the stained gown over my head. I managed to wash, though I moved too slowly for Sheryl's liking. She made sure I was spotless, marveling at how completely my body had been restored. Her clothes were too petite for me, so I put on one of Richard's nightshirts. Then she guided me to her bed, and I hovered over Lily Anne.

Her reddish color deepened into a light brown. Her hair was almost dark enough to be black, and her nose was wide. Perhaps she did look like me.

A tear fell on her cheek. Then another. She was so perfect. How could a being feel and smell that soft? But as perfect as she was, I couldn't shake a terrible thought that kept running through my mind.

She almost killed me.

"Charlotte?" Sheryl came over as I baptized my baby with fresh tears. "What's the matter?" She rubbed my back and sounded the most afraid she had been all day.

I hunched over her and wept. I wept so bitterly that it burned my chest. "I'm a failure of a woman…"

This was something I was meant to do. I was born to do it. It should have been as natural as breathing, yet I was terrified to do it again.

"No, you're not a failure." She wrapped her arm around me. "You've given your husband a beautiful baby girl."

"And he wants nine more…" My wailing disturbed Lily Anne's sleep, and I felt like an even greater failure. How was it possible that Mary Anne could carry JoJo with such grace, and I was nearly the cause of making my child crippled and orphaned?

"Charlotte…" She gently positioned my arms, then placed Lily Anne within my grasp.

I felt unworthy to hold her, but it was foolish to reject her. I was her mother, after all.

Sheryl sat in front of me and offered a solemn smile. "This is our second child. The first was a miscarriage before you met me."

"I'm sorry to hear that…" I felt ungrateful. At least I had a child in my arms. I had yet to suffer such a loss.

"After it happened, Richard tried to comfort me. He said, 'Maybe the Lord didn't think we were ready yet…'"

It was the first flash of anger I had ever seen on her face. "I was ready for my baby." Sheryl's eyes welled, and she held her tightened jaw for a moment. "Even good men—very good men—don't understand women. They can't. They don't carry these burdens. They can mourn with us. They can have their own pain, but they don't know what it's like to have someone they carried die."

Sheryl wiped her face and cleared her throat, but her nose and forehead were bright red. "If you truly don't want to have any more children, John will understand. He loves you."

I wanted to smile, but my lips trembled. John would understand, but I hated disappointing him.

"But just because you had a bad experience, doesn't mean they'll all be like this. Wilma came, and she has eased our hearts."

I rubbed my baby's cheek. I believed she could bring unspeakable joy, as JoJo had for Mary Anne, but I hated how I felt. "Why is it like this at all?"

"We live in a fallen world. I don't have a better answer than that." She shrugged her shoulders and smiled halfheartedly. "But there's still beauty in it."

Sheryl rested her forehead against mine, and we watched Lily Anne whimper until she hollered. I tried to draw on Sheryl's strength and take her words to heart. I was fortunate to have found her.

I thought of Hannah, travailing in the temple for the existence of her son. Was her heart as heavy as mine as she begged God for a child? What if I couldn't give John the son we always dreamed about? I so wanted a little boy who looked like his father…

When Lily Anne wouldn't stop crying, Sheryl suggested she was hungry. She massaged my hardened breasts until my milk flowed out, then helped my baby latch on. It was another maddening thing my body could suddenly do. "The wonder of being a woman…"

"A wonder, indeed."

John returned while our baby was being fed. Sheryl stepped away to give us time alone. Dinah had returned home. I asked if she was alright, and John said she'd recover. I wasn't sure. Seeing someone you love close to death shakes the foundation of everything you are. Even our battles with the zealots had never brought us that close to the end.

There was always a chance I could lose John, Cooper, and the rest of my loved ones.

"What's the matter?" John asked as he held us.

I couldn't stop the tears from flowing, but I could shape their meaning for him. I forced a smile, praying his senses didn't catch my racing heart. "She's just so perfect, John."

He mirrored my smile, and his eyes filled with bright wonder. "All because of you."

When her heavy eyes finally closed, I placed our baby in her father's arms. It eased my heart to watch John stroke her plump cheek and nuzzle her nose. His soft expressions reminded me of when he was a boy, and I saw how she bore his image. The peace on his face was something I wanted to give him another nine times. I wanted to give it another thousand.

But I didn't know if I could stand it.

Before we said our goodbyes to Richard and Sheryl, John asked how he could repay them. They were modest, generous people and said they needed nothing in return. I had mentioned before that Richard dreamed of opening his own tavern, so John insisted on funding it. They were flattered but refused. John wouldn't accept their refusal and said he had more money than he knew what to do with. He even offered shelter in New Seneca. As an essential worker, Richard hadn't been drafted yet, but the fear of war loomed over them.

They eventually agreed to consider his offer. They needed time to decide whether they should leave their home, move up North, or live in our brave new world. "Be careful," Sheryl said, giving me one last hug. "You're not safe in the South."

John's fingers slid down my wrist before wrapping around my hand. "Don't worry," his tone darkened. "The Overseers aren't safe anywhere."

I wanted to visit Mary Anne before returning to New Seneca. She was more than happy to be awakened from her sleep by our arrival, but JoJo was not pleased with his mother's shrieks of joy. I tried to settle him, but he would only accept her. Once he was fed and put to rest again, she held Lily Anne. She constantly remarked on her beauty.

John kept glancing at JoJo's crib as if intrigued. It was their first meeting. "Wouldn't it be wonderful if our children married?"

"Thank you!" Mary Anne beamed. "Yes. I accept."

I shook my head and made myself comfortable on her bed. "You two are ridiculous…"

I might have been healed, but I was exhausted. I let the two of them talk as I drifted to sleep. That was the longest time they had been together since he conned her into loving him for Lady Cohen's games. There had been tension between them before, but I hoped they could be good friends. I also hoped he would answer the hard questions about my labor. I didn't want to speak of it.

We returned early in the morning, and everyone was overjoyed and eager to meet Lily Anne. John wanted to parade her as if it were coronation day. I dressed and bore a smile for our friends, the children, and other citizens who came to congratulate us. I thanked Paul for his prayers and told him I looked forward to my daughter's baptism. The people brought food and gifts. It was a wonderful day…

Yet I was suffocating.

John was surprised when I asked if we could return to our home in New York for a while, but he agreed. I thought I needed quiet, but even silence felt thick. I loved Lily Anne's cooing as my husband kissed her belly, but every glance was tainted by the memory of when I could barely hold her.

She almost killed me, yet she was worth my life.

She was worth my life, yet being unable to mother her made all I had ever done feel meaningless.

I didn't know how to make sense of it, and I didn't want to dim John's joy.

I thought I was hiding it well, but when I heard her cries in the middle of the night, the sting from the ring of fire gripped me once again. The scent of dust filled my lungs, and the night darkened. I was suddenly back in Sheryl's cellar. I clutched my chest and fought not to scream. If I hurried, I could return without anyone noticing.

"I'm…strong. I am…strong."

I took a deep breath and returned home to Lily Anne's ferocious cries.

Her father was holding onto her, his eyes brimming with terror—perhaps even anger. "What was that?"

I thought to make an excuse, but the truth escaped in wild sobs. I doubled over and hid my face in a pillow. John's hand rested on my back. I had to tell him the truth. My fears wouldn't stop spilling out.

John didn't insist on more children, nor did he relinquish his dream. He listened and assured me that everything would be alright—with time.

We spent a few days in isolation. John gathered food and even cooked for me. When Lily Anne cried in the middle of the night, he rushed to soothe her. If she wanted to stay awake after feeding, he stayed up with her. He was so kind, and he never complained.

Eventually, I forced myself to cook my husband breakfast. He brought me flowers and a soft bear for Lily Anne. He didn't speak. He only hugged me from behind as I stirred the porridge. It was too cold to train outside, but I ran in place and boxed with John. Once we were finished, we sat in the bath until it turned cold. I teased John about smelling like a woman.

He smiled and kissed my shoulder. "No, I'll smell like *my* woman."

I tried to be grateful for those small moments. I didn't feel as happy as I ought to be, but sometimes, you have to force yourself to be happy.

For supper, I cooked salmon, potatoes, and peas—I had grown accustomed to eating them. The bread came out perfect, and I nearly ate the whole loaf myself. I appreciated my husband's cooking, but that was not one of his gifts.

John smiled as I reached for the final piece. "I'm glad to see your appetite return."

I grinned at Lily Anne, who was peacefully observing me from a bassinet next to me. "Mary Anne says nursing a child makes you hungrier than pregnancy."

"Hmm…" I was disappointed. I expected a quip about my former eating habits or a joke about Lily Anne making me plump. He was distracted, tapping a glass of milk.

"John, what's the matter?"

His knee bounced, and he took a very long breath. John held it in for too long, then deflated. "I need to train and get stronger."

I raised my brow before finishing the last of my peas. "You train every day."

He tapped his glass again, then raised his eyes. John meant to be stern, but he was pleading. "I need to travel to the world in between spaces."

My body went cold. The image of blood flowing over his smiling lips was still fresh in my mind.

"No."

"Charlotte—"

"No!" I didn't mean to yell, but my heart immediately spiked. My hands were shaking, and I was taken back to the day I could barely hold Lily Anne. I was so cold as my very life drained from me. "I won't allow it. I won't help you do it."

"You're the only one who can."

"Good! It's an insane idea!" How dare he sit there and suggest such a terrible thing? I wanted to hit him. I probably would have if he weren't across the table. "I almost lost you."

"It's a weakness."

"Not being able to do everything doesn't make you weak!" Was it his arrogance that drove him into such a reckless decision? "You weren't made to do what I can."

His eyes sharpened, along with his tone. "Maybe I'll never be good at it. Maybe there will always be a cost, but my body can adjust—learn to handle it better. There may come a day when your life is on the line again. I need to be able to find you."

I laughed—bitterly and hysterically. John had always been mad for me. The house we sat in was proof enough. But this was beyond it all. What he asked of me was too cruel. I would not participate in his preplanned sacrifice.

"I can't..." I picked up my baby and began to leave before I acted regrettably.

"Charlotte—"

"Don't touch me!" I blinked a few feet back once he reached for me, clutching my baby for dear life. "I don't want to be around you right now."

His eyes were wounded and angry, but my rage and wounds were far deeper. He didn't chase or call after me.

I sat in Lily Anne's room, so John wouldn't see me shaking. I bounced her as I struggled to steady my breathing. I couldn't think of my husband's request. I needed some kind of distraction.

I found Asha's doll in Lily Anne's chest. Its face was darker than hers, and it was expertly sewn by Asha's mother. When my daughter was old enough, we could have tea parties with her soft friends. I couldn't wait until she was old enough to appreciate what we had given her and what we had lost…

I sighed and set the doll down. It was difficult not to think of John almost dying while I rocked the cause back and forth. The fact that it happened would never go away, but I believed my love for her would ease the sting.

She almost killed me, but she was worth my life.

Her father felt the same way.

If I didn't help him improve the odds of when he inevitably risked his life, then he would knowingly lay it down. That might have been the duty of a Messiah, but John was just a man with one life to live.

I didn't want to apologize yet, so I waited a few hours before he finally checked up on me. I was in the middle of reading to Lily Anne. "That does not sound appropriate for an infant."

I suppose *Frankenstein* was rather dark. "She's mature."

John took that as a sign that my mood had improved and cautiously entered. He sat on the floor, folded his legs, and waited.

I put the book down and stroked Lily Anne's tiny fist. I wondered how powerful she'd become and what sort of abilities she held within her. Perhaps I could find the strength to raise her alone, if need be, but she wouldn't be all that she could be without her father.

None of us could.

"If I'm going to help you, we have to do this right."

John lifted his head higher, then smiled, intrigued. "What do you have in mind?"

Chapter Twenty-Six

"This is the way I can best explain it." A glass of water sat on my kitchen table, filled to the brim. My husband stood in front of it, pointing at one spot on the rim, and then directly across. "Imagine this water is frozen solid—a block of ice. I want to travel between these two points. What would I do?"

I was already amused. "Walk across…?"

"Precisely." John's inquisitive grin was quite handsome. "But you, dear Charlotte, operate with an entirely different set of rules. You don't have to walk through space itself. For you, the world between is…fluid." He trailed his finger across the surface, leaving ripples behind.

"Even if I travel through water, it's the same distance. How do I get there…instantaneously?"

"Because the world between spaces can bend for you." John rotated the glass, causing it to spill over on my kitchen table. He wanted me to see the waves rise and fall, but I mostly paid attention to the mess it created. I grabbed a cloth and handed it to him. Instead of wiping it down, he stretched it from two points on opposite ends. "Perhaps this is a better illustration. If a human wanted to reach these two points of distance, they would have to walk. You, on the other hand…" He brought the two endpoints together, folding the cloth in half. "…can bend space."

John's smile widened, as if he had been waiting to say those words his whole life. "And the most interesting part…" He weaved and locked his fingers together. "…is that space and time are intertwined."

I wanted to share John's excitement, but I kept glancing at the mess he made. "This seems dangerous. If I can…" I chuckled. It all seemed too extraordinary. "…fold space and time, can it be broken?"

"I doubt you're powerful enough to damage it, but users without your immunity could be destroyed."

His words hung heavily in the air. When John and I saved a group of orphans from a fire, I pushed myself beyond my limits at the time. I felt the world between spaces, even witnessed beautiful, streaming lights that bound all things together. I could feel its threads on my skin, just as I felt them on John when he arrived in the cellar. The binding force was powerful—but I could slip through it all. "How am I doing this?"

"It's instinctive. When you imagine a place that you've been to, your mind accurately estimates how to fold the space between two endpoints. It's much more difficult to go to a place you've never been to. It may be impossible."

I looked at my baby to see if she was just as bewildered as her momma, but she was beginning to rest her eyes. "What about you?"

"When I travel, I can only go as far as I see. It's like punching through a wall; I'm not moving like you do. It's dangerous for people who aren't biologically conditioned for it."

I chuckled. "So, you're like a child who needs to stay in the shallow end of a river or else you'll get swept away?"

His head lowered to meet my eyes. "It feels worse than that…"

It was easy for me to travel, especially alone. When I saved the 151 soldiers, I put my body through torment. I suppose it was a little like swimming uphill with a load on my back. I kept that to myself. I didn't need to remind John of my recklessness. "How can you sometimes tell where I'm teleporting from?"

John pursed his lips. "I thought you hated that word."

"It is what it is." I was sore about it, but it wasn't an awful name.

"It's…" His head swayed as he searched for the words. "…like a disturbance. It's natural for you, but *it isn't natural*. My senses are fine-tuned to pick it up."

"And how did you find me in the stream? Did you sniff me out?"

He shrugged. "It's a combination of my senses, knowing you so keenly, perhaps even recognizing your signature—thanks to Mary Anne. Your powers help, of course."

That meant searching for someone in the stream or going to a place unknown was out of the question for me. If it were like a current, I could also get swept up and spat out somewhere unreturnable. "So, Dinah couldn't learn to search in the stream in my form?"

John shook his head. "Dinah doesn't change. Once she copies a power, it will remain what she mimicked at the point of contact. You're far more powerful than you were last year."

More than a year ago, I thought John was my enemy. So much had changed. Our turnaround began when he showed me our house and explained his powers. He also spouted interesting theories about me. "If space and time are knitted together, and I can bend and move freely through its stream, could I…"

I raised the glass and watched the water ripple again. It seemed too astronomically powerful to be real. "Can I go to the past or future?"

John turned his face away and struggled to shrug it off nonchalantly. "It's not impossible, but that's not within your skill set yet." The curve on his lips was almost mischievous.

I set the glass down. "What is that face for?"

The smirk grew wider, but his lips remained sealed.

I placed my hands on my hips and gave him the same tone I gave the children when they misbehaved. "John Cohen, what do you know?"

He raised his hands and took a step back, laughing almost maniacally. "If I knew anything, I couldn't tell you."

My mouth dropped, absolutely flabbergasted. "And why not?"

"Because that's how it must work!"

"Who on God's earth taught you about time travel?"

"That is a very interesting question." John folded his arms. His eyes saw past me and deep into his secrets. "You have instincts. I do as well. I always have insight when I see a power, but I can't hold enough memory to copy more than five at a time. My mind isn't quite that powerful. If I were Dinah—"

"You'd be insane."

He chuckled, and I felt a little guilty. I didn't mean to say that out loud. "Dinah is tragically the sanest person I've ever met. It's this world that's mad…"

"She is trouble…" I glanced at Lily Anne. Dinah was the reason my child had a present father. "…but she's been useful."

John had not successfully changed the subject. I was curious about his behavior for some time, but I probably hadn't been suspicious for long enough. He suggested time travel last year when we reconnected.

But if he couldn't tell me—yet—what else could I do? "I don't want you to be hurt."

"That can't be helped." He sighed, knowing he was disappointing me. "I need to build up an immunity—teach my body to quickly repair the strain. It will probably always hurt me, until…"

"I die?"

He nodded slowly. Out of all the things we discussed, that was perhaps the most unbelievable thing to him. "If you die, I will become a more powerful version of you."

I didn't plan on dying anytime soon, but I also didn't plan the recent scare. However…

Maybe he truly had seen my future. And if that were the case, I didn't need to worry about leaving my child motherless anytime soon.

I smiled and wrapped my arms around my husband's waist. "We have to do this gradually. Baby steps."

"Hmm…" His fingers grazed my shoulders, then rested on my arms. "I don't like baby steps."

"Then don't ask for my help!"

He leaned in and playfully glared. "Fine. Baby steps."

We returned to New Seneca. It was difficult to relinquish control to Agnes and Martha, but they were eager and willing to care for my daughter. I needed to be near or return for feedings, but John's training took me far distances.

If John's goal was to follow me in the world between spaces, he needed to get better at tracking. We swept across the land nonstop. It was important for John to get used to the air's subtle rupture as I slipped into the stream, and what it felt like when I slipped out. He had a talent for it, but it needed to be refined.

The next step was to blindfold John, and that hindered him. He hadn't practiced teleporting blind. His vision acted like the point of a needle poking through the fabric of our world. It was difficult for him to break through without that point of force.

I rested in the mountains while he sat with his legs folded and concentrated. I indulged in a ham sandwich as his body got more and more tense. "You know, I did this as a novice."

He pulled his blindfold and glared. He meant to be mean, but he reminded me so much of a rebellious child making an empty threat.

"Sorry…" I laughed into my food before taking another bite. It was important to keep our energy up.

John huffed through his nostrils and covered his eyes once more. I was too cold to wait all day for him. I brought him home to focus in our room. A few hours later, I heard a thud while I was playing with Lily Anne.

When I looked out the window, he was on his back in a rosebush. His blindfold was still on, but he gave me a salute. I shook my head and told Lily Anne, "That's your father."

After a few bumps, falls, and collisions with citizens, we deemed it wasn't a good thing for John to blindly teleport. He still couldn't travel to a place by memory, and the furthest he jumped blindly was about his line of sight anyway. We didn't want him falling off a cliff or even getting trapped within a wall.

He kept his blindfold on, and I blinked small distances in front of him. He was eventually able to follow the small jumps. Once he had grown accustomed to it, I blinked further than what he might immediately hear or smell. He needed to sharpen a different sense. We spent days developing his ability to sense the disruptions until he could blink blindly toward them. And after he accomplished his goal, we spent time improving his ability.

Everyone knew John was training to be stronger, but the reason was a secret. Of course, Kachina and Dinah knew. Kachina was more than supportive and had the utmost faith in John. Dinah didn't object, but she was still shaken by John's near-death experience. She needed a distraction, so she kept her hands busy by squeezing them around the throats of zealots.

Paranoia reached a heightened level in the South. Their fear of the Gifted led to witch-hunts, false accusations, and mob violence. Dinah, Tillie, and Tony followed leads, but they didn't find potential recruits. Confederates were so full of hate that innocent people were trampled and stoned to death. The mob wasn't connected to the inner workings of the zealots—only swept up in the same hatred.

We lightened our training as Christmas approached. In the South, it was a somber time filled with grief, fear, and resentment. Fathers were dead, boys were on the battlefield, and mothers had to scrounge resources for their little ones. The North felt the absence of their loved ones, but women like Mary Anne made the most of it. Elijah was kind enough to let her and JoJo stay with them. Isaiah wasn't home, but his wife and daughters came over and offered her much needed affection.

New Seneca was bustling about. Everyone wanted to decorate Christmas trees like Queen Victoria, so families carved and painted ornaments. They also hung ribbons and other trinkets. I spent much of my time purchasing gifts. I wanted every woman to have a treasured piece of jewelry, and every man a fine watch. We also brought many toys into the community. We handed them off on Christmas Eve at the mansion while children sang carols. Individuals and families were more than welcome to exchange gifts in the morning, but John and I wanted to make certain everyone had something of value.

On Christmas morning, we dressed Lily Anne in a white bonnet, made by her dear Aunt Mary Anne, and went to church. She would have to make her own decision about what to believe when she was older, but in the meantime, her father and I were blessed to have her in our lives. Despite the tragedies that plagued John's life, he always believed in God. He wanted divine judgment for the people who had wronged him and to believe his parents were at peace. Mercy and forgiveness did not come easily to him, but my husband surprised me occasionally. Overall, he had come a long way. I never thought he'd allow a human to pour holy water on our daughter's head. When Paul placed his hand on Lily Anne's stomach and prayed, John had the most darling smile.

Afterward, John played in the snow with Alfie and the other children while Martha, Agnes, and I prepared a Christmas feast for our close friends and their partners. Emma was happy to watch over Lily Anne as she slept. When she woke up, Emma fetched me. She was allowed to let Lily Anne hold her finger, but I wanted Lily Anne to be a little less fragile before Emma held her.

We had a hearty feast with turkey, potatoes, beans, bread, fruit, and pies. After we were good and stuffed, we sat by the fire and exchanged gifts. John told me to close my eyes, then slipped a bracelet on my wrist. It was made with care and a little unrefined—like my signet ring—but the infinity loop was quite elegant.

"I've always loved you, Charlotte. There's never been a moment of existence when I haven't—nor shall there ever be." He was so handsome, kneeling before me like a valiant knight. I traced the infinite loop with my thumb, contemplating the dangerous training that would resume tomorrow. We were running out of baby steps. It was time to take a few leaps.

It's not as though I expected John to die. I expected him to master his training, then take me out to celebrate. That's why I secretly commissioned Cooper's expert tailor in New York to produce an ensemble for him. The frock was black, cut from fine wool, lined with silk, and had a smooth finish on the lapel. The shoulders were structured, the torso was fitted, and there was a slight flare at the bottom. The waistcoat was made of finely woven brocade, with a subtle pattern of olive leaves that became more visible in direct light. I also purchased trousers, a new white shirt, a white pocket square, and a black cravat.

Once I presented him with gold cufflinks and a new pocket watch, Adam laughed and patted John on the shoulder. "You were severely outmatched, my friend."

"This is for her as much as it is for me. Charlotte obviously wants me to be ravishing for a night on the town."

"That is a sharp outfit," Dinah chimed with covetous eyes. "If you don't want it, I'll take it."

"Oh, no!" I shook a finger at her. "We are in the era of femininity." Since Dinah wore a dress to the festival, I thought it was an appropriate time to embrace her true form. I purchased four outfits for her. One was a dark red velvet frock with puffy shoulders and a matching skirt.

Dinah tried to hide her smile as she rubbed the fabric between her fingers. "I did get you something as well, Charlotte…" She reached inside her pocket and pulled out a small velvet pouch. She could hardly look at me when she placed it in my hand.

I pulled the ribbon, and the fabric opened like a flower blooming. In my palm rested a golden locket. "How sweet."

She still wouldn't look at me. "Open it…"

Inside, there were two detailed hand-drawn pictures. One was of my beloved, John, and the other was my heart, Lily Anne. "This is so thoughtful." I knew her well enough to know she didn't want a hug, but she knew me well enough to brace herself for it anyway. "Thank you. Truly."

Dinah tensed and grumbled, but much of it was an act. After we finished with all our presents, John took Nathaniel, Zhang, Adam, and Benjamin to his parlor to smoke cigars and have a little wine. When Dinah asked if she wanted to join them, she paused and looked at Evelyn and me, gabbing over hot tea and cake. Goldie, Tillie, and Kachina were engaged in their own conversation. "No. I think I'll stay here."

John smiled. "That's perfectly fine."

Eventually, John pulled Zhang aside and asked for his assistance with training. I also told my ladies that they would be coming with me to New York. Kachina was informed, so she knew where to find us. Dinah looked so worried. I touched her shoulder and told her to trust John. She nodded, but when it was time to say goodnight, she took the initiative to hug me. She only did it so it wouldn't be so strange when she hugged John goodbye.

I understood her fear, but John was correct. He needed to be stronger. He was going to risk his life for mine. He needed better odds.

In the morning, I took Zhang, Martha, Agnes, and Lily Anne to our home in New York. Then, I took John back to our bedroom in the mansion. I believed it was best to switch between two familiar spaces.

As I held his hands in mine, the strength in his fingertips gave me courage. "Are you ready for this?"

He nodded without the slightest hesitation.

"Then come home to me." I slipped from his grasp, then teleported home to our Odysseus tree. Zhang was waiting in a chair in case John arrived too fatigued. Martha and Agnes were downstairs with Lily Anne. I waited patiently for a few seconds, then anxiously for another thirty. Once a minute had passed, I was pacing across the room. Another minute passed, and I wondered if John had even left. I returned to New Seneca, but he was nowhere to be seen.

My chest ached, and I couldn't breathe. Over and over again, I heard the soft thud of John's body landing behind me in Sheryl's cellar. We had made a terrible mistake, and he wasn't going to get to Zhang in time. Lily Anne was going to be fatherless…

No! Those were intrusive doubts. I had to rebuke them. John would find a way back to me. Of course, he would. I had to breathe, bring peace to my heart, and return home.

John had not arrived by the time I returned. Before I could give myself permission to panic, Zhang's hand pulled my wrist. "John is strong." His gentle smile arrested my anxiety. "He will return to you."

I believed in John, but I also chose to believe God knew that I couldn't handle him dying. I had been through enough trauma as of late, and God would have mercy on me. I clung to the locket Dinah gave me and prayed with my face to the bed—until there was word.

"Lady Charlotte!" Martha called from downstairs, two hours later.

I leapt off the bed but couldn't stand to wait long enough for my feet to touch the ground. I teleported to the foyer, where

John wearily stood. "John!" His face was freezing, and his clothes had frost on them. "What happened?"

"That wasn't..." He paused to catch his breath. "That wasn't a baby step."

I helped him into a chair. We gave him water, bread, and time to gather his bearings. I did my best not to make a scene, especially in front of my ladies. "Was it too far a distance to track?"

"It's more accurate to say it was too great to fold." He held his chest and took another breath, bewildered by his fatigue. "I couldn't follow you, and I had to leave the world between spaces. It spat me out over the Great Lakes. I managed to heal myself a little bit, but I floated in the water a little while before I had the strength to fly."

"You naturally heal instantly. Why are you struggling so much?"

"Because it's a catastrophic injury. If I didn't have my abilities, I'd be dead."

That was a harrowing thought. No one but John could track me then. "We'll get some more food in you and try from a closer location."

John's brows rose, but he nodded. I was a little surprised with myself as well, but I took it as a good sign that he survived at all. John didn't jump to Sheryl's cellar from New Seneca. He followed my path, folding space through thousands of miles and shredding his body to do it. It made his feat more infuriating...and romantic. But given that John lived to tell the tale, he was much further along than we originally thought.

John felt normal after an hour of rest. Though Mary Anne was still in Chicago with family, we figured she wouldn't mind if we used her office at the Crimson Hotel as a starting point. After I returned to my bedroom, John dropped to his knees with a bloody nose about two minutes later. Zhang healed him the first few times, but then John said his body needed to get used to repairing itself.

For the next few days, we gradually expanded. We travelled to Philadelphia, to Ripley, then Detroit. He arrived fatigued, but he didn't need Zhang's power to recover. After that, we took more leaps from New Seneca. He could manage the jumps, but they were tiring. He needed Zhang again, but it was also tiring to heal such extreme injuries.

On New Year's Eve, I was at my husband's bedside, watching him shake in agony. John had obtained rare spices and sauces as a Christmas present for Zhang, so he used them to make a rice dish with vegetables and pork. I helped John eat and drink to build his strength. I had hoped we'd be home for New Year's Day, but he was determined to suffer through the night. I stroked his hair, and John managed to crack a smile. "Thank you for doing this. I know this isn't easy for you."

"No, but it's about more than Lily Anne and me. Everyone in New Seneca depends on your power, so you have to get stronger." I kissed his cheek. He was still warm. I didn't want to bother Agnes and Martha, so I stepped away to fetch more water.

From the balcony, I saw Tillie standing in the foyer, wrapped in nothing but a blanket that she clung to for dear life. "Tillie?"

When she glanced up at me, I saw the same sense of dread that I had once seen in her friend's eyes. She swallowed hard to fight back tears. "It's Dinah."

Chapter Twenty-Seven

The South learned to fear Ghost stories again.

On New Year's Day, John donned his infamous Ghost ensemble and plagued any suspected lair of the Overseers. One such place was a church in Alabama. Locals said crackling and popping preceded the attacks. Then screams followed. The scent of burnt hair and cloth lingered in the air. The authorities found very little blood. The bodies had lines of discoloration, as if they were cut with a blade of fire and seared shut. One man had a burn from his groin to the top of his head. His robe had split open and slipped off. The two pieces of his body fused unevenly, like two halves pressed together by unsteady hands. Twenty people were lying across broken pews and a burning altar. It must have been terrifying to see Ghost suddenly appear under the colored light of glass-stained windows, slinging a screaming blue sword.

Journalists remarked they hadn't seen something that brutal since Ghost's killing spree on a train. Due to the burns, people wondered if it was the Blue Devil. Washington thoroughly denied that Archangel had anything to do with it, but Lincoln knew better. I'm certain he would have tried to reel John in if the situation weren't so dire.

Shortly before midnight on New Year's Eve, I teleported home to Dinah's room. She passed out on her bed. Dr. Bingle was by her bedside. He had stitched her wound, where she had been stabbed. Her lovely color lost its vibrancy, and her breathing was faint.

Tony apologized a million miles a minute. He had gotten separated from Dinah. When Tillie found her, she was unconscious and bleeding out. He was so panicked that he teleported them home, including Mr. Pike. It was the first time an outsider set foot inside our walls, so Kachina was furious. Tony didn't know how to teleport to our home, but he had been to Manhattan. Tillie flew from there.

Even after Zhang's healing light closed Dinah's wound, she didn't wake up immediately. The doctor said her mind was distressed. When John touched her cheek, he understood why. "They took her powers."

Mr. Pike said it was routine. They were following another lead to a zealot hideout. Someone tried to escape, and Dinah transformed into Henry to go after them. The next time they saw her, she was on the ground as herself.

John was especially furious that Mr. Pike was now aware that something could take away our powers. It was information John didn't want the government to know. Mr. Pike insisted on staying until Dinah woke up. My husband trusted Nathaniel to give him a small tour and keep him occupied.

Dinah woke up in about an hour, immediately sobbing and profusely apologizing to John. He insisted it was all right, but he was quietly furious with the situation. "How'd the zealots get the drop on you?"

She could hardly speak. I had to give her a tissue to wipe the snot from her mouth. "It was the Burning Man…"

My heart stood still, and my veins turned to ice. I looked at John, but his eyes were steady on Dinah. "You found him?"

She clutched her chest and trembled. For a few seconds, all she could manage was a nod. "I was overwhelmed by the visions and the memories. There was so much death at once…" It was difficult to see her moan and even scream from anguish. John was trying to be patient, but fury rested on his body like the brocade waistcoat I purchased for Christmas, becoming more detailed the longer she stared.

I had to take Dinah's hand and keep her eyes on me. It was the only way to stop her from muttering hysterically.

The Burning Man used to be a normal man named Gideon—Dr. Gideon Mercer. His family was affiliated with God's Overseers, but he was not devoted to their cause. He felt called elsewhere and traveled to a war-torn village in Africa. He noticed dizzy spells and weakness began to plague the people, followed by confusion. Children collapsed in the middle of the road due to exhaustion, and women were lethargic and confused. The men were off waging war.

Dr. Mercer tirelessly investigated the cause of the sickness. Some thought it was divine judgment for the brutality of their warriors on the battlefield. He thought it might be the water or a parasite in the local food, but he hadn't gotten sick, and neither had a pregnant woman. She worked with Dr. Mercer to tend to the village, but she was very far along.

When warriors returned to many graves, they found their culprit. It must have been the outsider—a white demon.

He ran for his life, fearing that he'd be hacked to pieces or skinned alive. His heart elevated, but it somehow found a way to climb even higher when arrows and spears flew toward him. An arrow struck his shoulder, and the doctor fell to the ground. As he pushed himself up, he observed discoloration on his skin and a warm glow.

The next round of arrows was pushed away by his force and disintegrated midair. The men who fired them didn't even have time to scream. All that was left of them were impressions of ash, like shadows frozen in time.

Gideon walked to the village in a daze as the faces of every child, poisoned by his body, came to mind. He felt power rising from his core and seeping through his skin. The doctor told himself that living with such impurity was impossible. He only kept going to see if the pregnant woman had survived. Then, he would purge the world from such evil by taking his own life. Much of the village was blown apart by the force of the explosion, and a thick debris cloud stretched on for miles. He could barely see, but he heard a woman crying for help. The warriors feared she might be cursed, so they put her in a well to be dealt with later.

Gideon managed to get her out, but her leg was wounded. He cared for her in the rubble and delivered her baby in two days. As he held the newborn in his arms, the constant sensation ceased. The boy appeared unremarkable as he cried for his mother, and Gideon found comfort in finally feeling unremarkable himself. Fresh tears rolled down his cheeks—tears that would have evaporated without the child's gentle skin.

The mother reached for her son, but he was more than just a boy. He was a cure. If Gideon took his own life, one impurity would be cleansed. If he took the boy and wielded his power, the impure didn't have to be burned alive.

But the mother wouldn't understand. She was a heathen who worshipped a strange god. She would not grasp the boy's significance, nor could she protect him.

His eyes fell on the makeshift splint around her leg. She reached desperately, sensing something was wrong. He eased away. "I'm sorry."

She screamed and threw a fistful of dirt at Gideon's back. She crawled on her hands and elbows, dragging herself until he was beyond her vision. Then, she sobbed in the poisonous dirt, already feeling the aftereffects of Gideon's power. She was going to die there.

Childless.

Gideon sobbed in shame until the mother's screams faded into the background. Once they were gone, his heart hardened. He was sent to that village to see the devastation of the cursed. Now, he could live the rest of his life devoted to a righteous path.

He sent word to the Overseers while he cared for and experimented on the child. The Overseers wanted the boy, but they were appalled by Gideon's curse. Gideon promised to keep his powers at bay with the boy's blood, but if there ever came a day that their enemies grew too powerful and resisted purification, his power would be necessary to bring them to heel.

There were pockets of cursed people around the world. Thousands had been burned by their organization. Great discussions were held to decide where Gideon and the boy would go. After a faction of Overseers was destroyed in Virginia by a handful of cursed, Gideon believed he was called to the United States of America.

Gideon kept quiet and hidden in the organization. He injected himself with the boy's blood, but it worked better on others. He had to inject himself more frequently, and he kept the boy by his side for good measure. He reluctantly lent the boy out to destroy Ghost and his crew. Due to the damage Ghost had done to their organization, it was necessary.

Of course, we successfully rescued and hid the boy.

The Overseers were weaker than ever, the boy was lost in the wind, the Union labeled them as enemies of the nation, and Lincoln openly flaunted one of the cursed and used him to claim Atlanta. The Overseers had to change their strategy.

Evangelism.

Instead of living in the shadows, they would tell their most faithful to come out of hiding and make their righteous path known. The Southerners were determined people, but they were also desperate. The more loss they suffered, the more devoted they became.

At first, Gideon was devastated that his blood supply was running low. But if he were destined to be a plague upon mankind, he would make certain it was aimed in the right direction.

As to where his target might be, Gideon didn't know, but the White House was on his mind, and so was Grant's army in Virginia.

Once Dinah finished telling Gideon's life story, John breathed through his flared nostrils. His knee bounced a few times, and then he got up and walked out the door. After it slammed shut, Dinah exploded in another fit of tears. "I've disappointed him again…"

"No, Dinah, that's not true. He's angry at everything else." He might have been furious that his best warrior was powerless, but that fury wasn't directed at her. Gideon came to the US after Lady Cohen, Mary Anne, and I rescued John from the zealots. John killed most of that group by himself and only grew more powerful. He must have felt untouchable, like God had blessed his violence…

They used our victories as opportunities to spread fear and hatred. John always knew something like that would happen, yet I pushed him toward hope. John didn't have it in him to be seriously angry with me, but the thought must have crossed his mind.

After John calmed down, we told Mr. Pike about Gideon's plan, minus everything about Moses. He asked if we would take him to Washington, D.C., and we agreed. Lincoln was already knee-deep in politics, fighting to get the House to pass the Thirteenth Amendment. The news of Gideon could not come at a worse time.

Lincoln's long limbs stretched across the fireplace mantle of the Red Room. His head was low as he watched the flames. Then he spoke, lower than his normal pitch. "Will you wash your hands of this, too, Mr. Cohen?"

John's eyes narrowed. "I beg your pardon?"

Lincoln's arms fell as his posture straightened. It was always alarming how tall the president was, and he never looked more like a giant than when he turned to face John. "Will you leave this demon to run amok and take thousands of lives?"

John resisted the urge to match the president's volume, but the tone was gravelly like a mean dog. "You knew the price for my cooperation, and there's still a debt to be paid."

"What good is power if it's not used for the betterment of mankind?"

His eyes widened as if a nerve was struck with a chisel and hammer. "I have never been considered as 'mankind!'" My husband exploded, as if all the rage he had directed at the nation was fired at one man. "Neither has my wife, and neither are you!"

"And neither is this Burning Man!" Lincoln had seen the eyes of many young and rebellious men. His son was about John's age. He respected his struggles and heartaches, but he could not allow John to stray toward a darker path. "Mankind has failed, yes, Mr. Cohen. That is the case. But we must not fail!"

John threw his head back, chuckling harshly as he recalled me pleading with him to end the Draft Riots. We didn't know then that the price for bringing peace would be Asha's blood. "I've heard this song and dance before…"

"Then listen this time!" Lincoln was bold enough to place his hand on my husband's shoulder and grip him firmly. "This is our burden to bear, you and I together."

John removed Lincoln's hand and stared in defiance, but Lincoln would not cower—even to golden eyes.

"This is the responsibility of having power. It is God-ordained for a purpose." He held out his hands, as if he could feel Fate gathering in them. "This is our purpose!"

Mr. Pike didn't strike me as a man easily surprised, but his brows were raised. It was quite a sight to see.

I didn't know what I wanted. Of course, I wanted the killing to stop, the zealots defeated, and Gideon to be put down, but I also didn't want my husband to be in danger. If the Burning Man could turn people into ash in seconds, John couldn't survive that.

But he was our sworn enemy, whether we knew it or not. If he wasn't dealt with before coming to Virginia or the White House, who was to say he didn't eventually find his way to New Seneca?

John understood that, and his posture softened. "Gideon renounced his right to life once he became a zealot." His eyes were still fierce and golden. "I kill zealots."

Lincoln's arms and shoulders relaxed. He even took a breath. "Then you agree to stop Gideon?"

"I'll hunt him down, but I don't want to hear even a whisper about my methods."

Lincoln almost smiled. "You won't hear a word from me."

John looked at me for final approval. I held my chest, remembering the blood on his pale face. It took everything within me to nod.

"If you find him first, tell me immediately," John said. "I will not allow Gideon to destroy what I've built for the people of New Seneca."

"And I will not fail the people of New Seneca either." Lincoln held onto John's shoulder again and spoke with all the sincerity in the world. "Hold fast, Mr. Cohen."

My husband became cold and focused after that night. Without Dinah's ability to absorb knowledge, he had to resort to crueler means of obtaining information. Sometimes, it was brute force. Other times, he dropped zealots from high distances and listened to their screams. If he had two or more, he would let one smash against the ground for the others to witness. They were ready to talk by then. Even Mr. Pike had a particular toolkit filled with many means of making men talk. Those leads led to more zealots, but Gideon was well-hidden.

One important name was given to John—Mr. Voss. He was a close associate of Jefferson Davis, the President of the Confederacy. My husband did not consult with Mr. Pike before chain-teleporting to Richmond. The White House of the Confederacy was guarded, but their bullets were no match for John's speed. They should have counted themselves lucky that he never drew his blue sword. Instead, John stretched forth his hand and froze their hands and feet in place. Once he kicked down the front door, he was met with a barrage of bullets. He waved his hand, and a thick wall of ice shielded him. The soldiers paused in shock, then screamed as the ice shattered into shards. John teleported amongst his enemies—punching, kicking, and smashing their heads against walls. They were incapacitated. Some were seriously injured, but there were no casualties. He teleported up the winding staircase on the hunt for his prey.

Jefferson Davis was in his office, crouching under his desk while four of his personal guards aimed their guns at the door. Curtains blocked the windows. The room was tense but silent in hopes that Ghost would pass over them. Mr. Voss was in the corner with his pistol ready in hand, sweating profusely. Everyone believed Ghost was there to martyr their president—everyone except Mr. Voss.

They heard heavy thuds, gunfire, and men hollering from the other side of the door. When the commotion ended, heavy footsteps and the gentle jingle of spurs unsettled their nerves. Then, it was quiet—too quiet for too long. They pointed their guns at the door until their arms trembled and beads of sweat dripped in their eyes.

A crackling sound came from behind, but by the time they could turn their heads, a blue light slashed four burning strokes into the wall, and then a hooded figure smashed through brick and plaster. He breathed, and a chilling blast coated the room in frost, fog, and snow. Everything happened so fast; Jefferson Davis could not see. But he heard their screams. His vision did not become clear until his back was up against the wall, and Ghost's fingers were gripped around his jaw.

"Did you know?"

His guards were incapacitated. He didn't see any mortal wounds, but when he turned his head, he saw Mr. Voss pinned against the wall and gagging from an ice spear to the chest.

"Did you know Mr. Voss was an Overseer?"

President Davis was a stubborn man who had seen the face of Death many times, but nothing was like the golden sheen in that man's eyes. "No."

"Because if you did, I'll gut you right now." John's grip tightened a bit, and Davis hollered. He didn't sense that the president was insincere. Even a man of great stature was left defenseless as he watched the spear in Voss's chest expand until his breathing ceased. Ghost's eyes had turned bright blue, so Davis understood who had real power and control in that room.

"I didn't know." A cold and bitter pain swept his jaw as it frosted.

Ghost's eyes narrowed, but he released Davis and let him fall. "I believe you."

Davis rubbed flakes of snow off his sore face, contemplating how close he was to death. A paper drifted from above and landed in his lap. It was a folded drawing of a man.

"This is a zealot with horrific power. He's going to use it to kill thousands, and they may be Southerners."

Jefferson Davis was amazed. Based on the rolling, musical cadence of his voice, he assumed Ghost was from the Deep South. "What would you have me do?"

"I'm hunting him." John turned his gaze toward the hole in the wall. "You should as well."

Then he disappeared…just like a ghost.

The papers went insane after John's antics. The South didn't need to exaggerate Ghost's brutality, but it did. The Northern papers mostly stuck to the facts, but the facts were gruesome. Worst of all, a soldier working in the Confederate White House also survived an attack in Georgia from Archangel, and he swore they had the same yellow eyes.

Lincoln had to deny any connection to Ghost or the attack on Jefferson Davis. The Conservative faction of the Republican Party wanted peace with the South, and meaningful steps toward that goal became a bargaining chip for their votes on the Thirteenth Amendment. He was such a trustworthy man that most took his word for it. The Democrats, however, were incredibly suspicious.

Lincoln almost scolded John for his lack of restraint, but one look silenced him forever. They made an agreement, and lives were on the line. Mr. Pike did warn John that if the public were to discover Ghost and Archangel were both the identities of the federal agent appointed by Lincoln, Congress would be more difficult to reason with. John knew that to be true, but he had tunnel vision. Killing Gideon was a priority above all.

Dinah's sketch of Gideon was posted in every general store, church, and government building in the North. Even in the South, a bounty was placed on Gideon's head. He was wanted alive for a mere five thousand dollars, but at least Jefferson Davis did something. The Union Army was informed of a shoot-to-kill order, but in case he slipped by, John hovered over the Capitol. He stayed close to Lincoln when he wasn't on the prowl, shaking hands with elected officials and dining with donors.

I barely got to see my husband. He forbade me from searching for Gideon, and I didn't argue. I wanted to be home with my daughter. Her movements were more fluid, and her neck was stronger. She was engaged with the world and smiled often. I found myself smiling more as well.

I did make a trip to New York to warn Mary Anne about the Burning Man. I begged her to join us in New Seneca. If Gideon wanted to destroy a civilian population, New York was a devastating target. For the first time, Mary Anne seemed shaken, but she quickly regained her composure. "I couldn't leave all of these people here to die, Charlotte. They wouldn't all join New Seneca, nor would John invite anyone who didn't pledge loyalty to him. I don't blame him. He must defend and preserve what he's building."

Her eyes fell on JoJo, who had finished a crawl across the floor to his mother. She set him in her lap and waved his hand toward me. He smiled infectiously. Cooper's son was old enough to start recognizing faces, yet he had never seen his father. "This war won't go on for much longer. Joseph will be home soon to watch over us."

"And if the Burning Man comes?"

Her eyes sharpened, and her motherly, baby voice disappeared. "I would blow his head off."

I can't say I ever stopped worrying about Mary Anne's safety, but I was definitely more concerned for anyone who stood against her. If someone as unique as the Burning Man came close to the city, I assumed she'd be able to sense him.

"You know, they're going to vote on abolition tomorrow."

"I heard…" Mary Anne kissed JoJo's cheek and cuddled the boy. "I'm glad Joseph will live to see it. He's made a better world for his son."

"And my daughter…" The hardest part of the war was knowing Cooper was hauled up in Petersburg in a nonstop siege. It had been 230 days of gunfire and trenches. Surely, he wouldn't be the same man as before.

Danny and Steve were under General Sherman and had completed the March to the Sea with the capture of Savannah. The Carolinas would be next. I was grateful they were both well and alive. At least they had each other to stay in good spirits. Cooper's letters seemed very lonely. He made friends easily, but many had died in battle.

I prayed for my friend every night. I prayed that he could kiss his wife, hold his son, and know that I appreciated all that he had done for my daughter before she was even born.

The next day was intense. I tried to keep busy taking care of Lily Anne and reading to the children, but my mind was constantly whirling. Tony was to teleport home once the final decision was made. Final whipping occurred in the morning, followed by passionate debates. The final vote began in mid-to-late afternoon.

I was in the kitchen baking a pie when Tony emerged from a shadow, his curly hair nearly covering his eyes. I think he wanted to play a game with me by his hesitation, but his smile was irresistible. "It's done, ma'am. It passed."

The pie dropped to the floor, and the filling broke through my carefully woven lattice. "Truly?"

"Yes, ma'am. It's true."

I was glad Tony was the one who told me. He got to experience a tight and hysterical hug, and I hadn't shown him nearly enough affection for all he did on our behalf. It was also wonderful to see such joy in his ethereal eyes.

I rushed through the mansion, hugging every brown face I saw and telling them the news. Martha had to stop herself from falling with Lily Anne in her arms, but Agnes dropped to her knees and sobbed. I ran out into the snow, teleporting and shouting tearfully. "The Thirteenth Amendment has passed! Slavery has been abolished in the Union!"

I pushed the double doors of the church open, and Reverend Paul stopped mid-sermon. Once he saw my tears, he reached deep within his soul and shouted a mighty praise to God. "Hallelujah!" I teleported to the pulpit and wrapped my arms around him. We cried together in victory, as the congregation danced and shook tambourines.

It was a happy day for everyone. Our community wasn't segregated. Freedmen were friends and lovers to Native and Gifted alike. Our joys and terrors belonged to everyone, and we rejoiced together.

The only brown face I hadn't spoken to was Dinah. I wiped my face clean and returned to the mansion. It was rude of me to burst into her room, but I thought she might forgive me. "Did you hear? They passed—"

"The Thirteenth Amendment. Yes. It needs to be ratified by the states now." She didn't even look up at me. She hovered over her desk, meticulously drawing. "You're the fifth person who's disturbed me."

The immense excitement stripped away. Cold and exhaustion settled into my bones while I stood in silence. "It's a momentous occasion."

Dinah shrugged her shoulders and buried her nose closer to the paper.

"I thought since you were a former slave, you would…"

I stopped when I heard her chuckle harshly. It was quiet and brief, but I did not imagine it. Then she had the audacity to mumble, "It won't change anything…"

I thought of Sam, Dave, and Cooper celebrating the small wonders of life with a glass of bourbon while I danced with Steve, Mick, and Danny. Sam and Dave were gone. It was a miracle every day that Cooper survived. The blood they spilt wasn't for nothing. It could never be for nothing!

I huffed and marched over to that woman, grabbed her shoulders, and forced her to look at me. "I know you've been down, and with good reason, but we've been waiting for this day our whole lives. It changes everything!"

"Humans still want to kill us!"

"Not all of them!" Where would I be without the kindness of my friends in New York, or Sheryl, or even the slaves on the Cohens' plantation, willing to put themselves in harm's way after I fell out of favor? She knew all of that. She had seen my memories, so how could Dinah be so ungrateful?

I glanced around the room. The bed wasn't made, clothes were on the floor, and it reeked of smoke. She was back to wearing men's trousers and shirts, even though she couldn't transform. "You can't give up, Dinah. Now is the time to dig deep and focus! We're so close to the future we've always dreamed about."

"I am focused." Dinah shook herself loose and turned back to her drawings. "More focused than I've ever been…"

She was so infuriating! I was tempted to snatch them right from under her pencil…until…

"What is this?" I stepped closer to get a better look. It was a map. Precisely, she was drawing a map of Europe, but there was a stack of others. There were stars, circles, and notes on them. Beside her was a stack of lists with detailed reports of possible sightings. It took time for Dinah to sort out memories that were that detailed. Since she lost her powers after touching Gideon, we assumed we had learned all that we could from her. "Is this what I think it is?"

Though her eyes were dark and tired, she managed to grin. “It’s a map to John’s army.”

It truly was a glorious day. Once President Lincoln legitimized New Seneca, and John felt we were strong enough to handle possible threats, he could set off on a new adventure. We’d be more than a small town of powerful settlers. We’d truly be a nation.

John was delighted by the news, and he had his own to share. Lincoln was going to host a ceremony to commemorate the passage of the Thirteenth Amendment. He didn’t legally need to sign anything, but he wanted to. It was mostly to be made up of politicians and cabinet members who pushed for the bill, but we were also invited. I was surprised John bothered to tell me, considering the danger, but he must have thought it was worth jumping on him and kissing him.

I suggested John wear his Christmas suit, but he said it wasn’t that fancy of an occasion. He told me not to fuss about my dress all night. It wasn’t a ball.

In the morning, my ladies helped me into a lovely blue checkered dress, and I was reminded of when I first arrived in Ripley after crossing the Ohio River to freedom. It was modest with a high-neck collar. The bodice hugged my form well. My stomach was flat, but my body had changed from pregnancy. My hips were wider, and my breasts were larger. As my ladies set my skirt, so all the folds and pleats fell correctly, John watched me with a smile. “Why are you staring at me like it’s for the very first time?”

“Perhaps it is the first time.” He motioned for Martha and Agnes to step away, then hugged me from behind. “Perhaps this is the way I’m always meant to remember you.”

I glanced at the infinity bracelet on my wrist. It paired nicely with my heart locket and signet ring. “Are we about to get everything we’ve ever wanted?”

“I’ve already received all I’ve ever wanted.” John managed to find a piece of uncovered skin and kissed my neck. “Now, everything else is for you.”

As we walked inside the White House, we were nearly run over by Lincoln’s boy, who was dressed in a small Union uniform. Mr. Slade was chasing after him, but he stopped to breathlessly greet us. "Welcome."

I don't believe I let go of John from the moment we arrived. We had small chats with politicians. Some, I recalled from the White House party. They certainly remembered me. John had also made great relationships with Congressmen. His financial contributions were much appreciated.

I was disappointed that none of my activist friends were present. Perhaps they were a little too radical for the Congressmen, but I was grateful to be present in the Blue Room, standing behind the president's desk. His remarks were short. History didn't record them, but I recall—before he paused and steadied his hand—that he spoke softly and resolutely. "This is a constitutional cure to the evil of slavery."

He had a row of pens that he used for different parts of his signature. While the crowd clapped and cheered, he handed them to key supporters. When he touched the last pen, he smiled and raised it to me. "For you, Mrs. Cohen."

I held my breath and trembled, squeezing John's hand. Outwardly, I thought I had made a scene, but all the witnesses saw was a brief pause before I took hold of history. "It's Lady Cohen, actually. Thank you."

He bowed his head humbly, then rose to his feet. "Gentleman—and Lady Cohen—let this day be known as the end of tyranny in the United States of America."

A roar of applause and cheers followed. John and I were the only ones not clapping because I still had a hold of his hand. But he was happy, perhaps even relieved. If Lincoln could keep this monumental promise, he could keep one more.

"President Lincoln!" A panicked cry echoed across the White House until it drowned out the hushing applause. A few soldiers marched into the building, but one rushed through a doorway to the Blue Room, squeezing past Congressmen too slow to move. "Trouble, Mr. President. Terrible news!"

I felt John's eyes on me, and I turned to face him. He knew, and I did as well. There was such a terrible pit in my stomach. If the Burning Man wasn't in DC, he might have been in Virginia. I had been bracing myself for terrible news about Cooper. My body tensed, already suffocating.

Lincoln glanced around the room. It was far too late to make it a private report. "Go on, son."

"Atlanta..." There was great bewilderment in his voice, as if he didn't believe the words he was about to say.

But the panic in his heart was all too real. "...Atlanta is gone."

Chapter Twenty-Eight

The echo of the soldier's voice quieted, and a hush rested upon us.

Confederate civilians hadn't returned to Atlanta. The Union made use of the railroads and turned it into a supply and intelligence hub. General Sherman moved on and secured other victories since Archangel conquered the city, but there must have been between fifteen and twenty thousand soldiers stationed there.

"Gone?" A thunderous boom escaped from a congressman. "What do you mean, 'Gone?'"

An inaudible eruption filled the space as panicked men bombarded the young soldier. He looked barely old enough to enlist and shrank in the presence of elected leaders shouting and pawing at him.

Lincoln searched for Mr. Pike. He was in one of the doorways with a very stern expression and uncharacteristic panic in his eyes. He nodded slowly, so the president would know the boy's words were true.

"In God's name, settle down!" Lincoln banged on the desk, and the room fell quiet. I wondered if it was his position of authority that gave him power over men, or if he was the type of man who demanded such authority. Perhaps both were woven together in Lincoln's soul. He knew, even better than John and me, what happened to his troops. I saw it in his dark eyes. "Speak, officer."

He gulped before addressing his Commander-in-Chief. "Reports say there was a bright flash of light, and a powerful, piercing sound swept the land…" He winced and held his chest, as if he expected to vomit. "The city appears to be destroyed, sir."

Lincoln's face tensed. The light of day lit the Blue Room well, but the shadow of death loomed heavily on him. "Is there word of any survivors?"

"We don't know. The air is too hot…"

It was unsettlingly quiet for a room full of men who professionally argued all the time. They must have understood no human artillery could do such a thing. The most powerful men in the country drowned in the revelation that this war was beyond them.

Then, the damn broke.

"How could this happen?"

"It was that Archangel fellow!"

"He is a demon!"

"No!" I didn't mean to yell. It was like God pressed it out of me with a hot poker. With all their sudden bickering, I was surprised so many eyes came upon me, and they certainly gazed at me like a woman who didn't belong. "It wasn't Archangel, and I won't let you spread that terrible lie."

"Who else has that kind of power?"

"The zealots!" Mr. Pike's low voice exploded across the room, his frustration mounting. "Have you all been blind this entire time?"

"This is the work of the Overseers," Lincoln assured, careful to resist the temptation of looking in our direction. "Our enemies must be swiftly defeated."

"Our enemy is the Confederacy!" One man was bright red, pointing at Lincoln as globs of spit leaped from his mouth. "You made this war with the zealots over freaks while our nation was already broken!"

John's grip on my hand tightened, and his nostrils flared. I put my head down, not wanting to see the fine gentlemen who had abolished slavery devolve into wild beasts.

"Where has Archangel gone?" Another one asked and received curious grumbling in return. "We haven't seen him since Atlanta. He could have gone rogue."

"No."

I raised my head upon hearing my husband's voice. It was loud enough to gain most of the room's attention. His face was tense, but his eyes were heavy from the uneven burden of the world…like Cooper's.

"John…"

He didn't glance at Lincoln for his permission, nor consult Mr. Pike. He raised our woven fingers to his lips and kissed my hand. "It's time."

He took a small step forward into the future, still holding onto me. "I'm the Archangel."

The room hushed again. Representative Thaddeus Stevens pushed up on his cane, and the wrinkles around his eyes lifted. Other men were far more confused than intrigued. Lincoln folded his arms and pressed his lips. That was proof enough for the doubters. Rage followed. There was hand-waving and shouting, genuine questions about why the war hadn't ended months ago.

John tired of it quickly. "I owe you nothing!"

His words cut like a sword, and they hushed again. If they doubted his words, his golden eyes were the final piece of evidence. They must have been frightened to provoke him, like animals running into a predator. He might not have shared Lady Cohen's blood, but he was made in her image.

"Mr. Cohen…" Lincoln's voice accompanied John's furious, quiet breaths. "The time has come for you to wield what God fashioned you for."

John took a final look around the room. Those giants suddenly seemed so small to me. "I'll slay the zealot myself, Mr. President."

Lincoln gave a final nod before I clung to my husband's arm and took him home. "Godspeed."

We passed through the world between spaces, unbound to the threads of time and space that held all of Creation in place. In that realm, I was granted an unspeakable power by the Almighty to bend the world to my will. But the tighter I clutched onto my husband, the more he slipped through my fingers.

"Charlotte…" John immediately took notice of our Odysseus tree—the bed he fashioned for us. He probably expected I'd take him to New Seneca, but it wouldn't have been quiet enough.

"Please, don't go…" I latched onto his sleeves and collapsed on his chest, shaking and heaving. I had thought of Gideon's ash shadows a dozen times. I had even imagined them dragging innocents down like Tony's ability. I didn't want to lose him. I couldn't!

"Charlotte…" His voice was stern, then softer. "I have to."

"No! We can find Moses, and we…" I felt so guilty even bringing it up. "…we can turn Gideon's powers off. You don't have to fight him."

"And risk the boy's life? Risk all of our lives?" John's pitch rose, just in tone, in surprise. "I have to fight him myself."

"I know! I know you do…" I was being selfish. I had risked my life for the Union, for strangers, and my friends. It was an easy decision to make, as if it weren't one at all.

Allowing him to die for them was a different matter.

"You've talked about seeing my future, but you didn't say you saw your own." I raised my head and touched my darling husband's face. He always had the look of an angel, yet I was overwhelmed with hopelessness. "Tell me that you know you'll survive."

John tried to remain a statue, but his lips trembled after mine did.

I fell back into his chest, aching. He whimpered once he received Lincoln's reaper sight. Was this the moment we would be separated forever? What about Lily Anne? What about New Seneca? It wasn't fair that he had to die to put Gideon down.

"Charlotte, none of that is important right now." He raised my head and wiped my tears. His hand smelled of lavender, and

I wanted him to hold me forever. "I know I've disappointed you in the past, and you've overlooked much of the pain I've caused because of what I could be in the future. But…"

John pressed his head to mine as his eyes mirrored my grief. "I need to know if you believe in me today—in the man I am in the here and now."

It wasn't even a question worthy of his lips. "Of course, I do."

I kissed my husband for what could have been the final time, and the world fell away, as it did the very first time he kissed me on the Cohens' plantation. It was before the lashes and before the scars. It was before I ran away and before I abandoned him to his demons. It was before Cooper, the riots, and before the war touched our loved ones. There was only that moment, and I felt whole.

"Then I'll come home to you," John spoke softly, like a prayer. "I promise, I always will."

I nodded and wiped my face. We didn't have more time to spare. John chose me because I had the strength to be his queen, and leaders didn't get the luxury of crying in the bedroom while the world burned.

I took his hand again, and we appeared in Lily Anne's nursery in New Seneca. Martha was watching our daughter with a warm and peaceful smile, as if there were no troubles in our world. How quickly it faded once she saw our faces.

Martha handed Lily Anne to her father as she rushed to spread the word. We didn't have time for lengthy goodbyes and sentiments. John hugged and kissed our daughter only long enough for Agnes to fetch his tattered cape. Dinah rushed to find us, but we had already handed Lily Anne off by the time I teleported to the park.

Alfie was standing on the turtle statue with a pile of snowballs behind him, reaming the other children mercilessly. Margaret tried to hide behind Emma, who was unbothered as she rolled a mound of snow as large as John's torso, but she was a little too tall.

"Don't you dare throw that!" I said to Emma, and her shoulders dropped in defeat.

"Master Cohen!" Alfie ceased his attack and rushed his beloved mentor. "Are you here to play?"

"No, Alfie." John patted the boy's head. He was always cool, whether during the blazing summer or freezing winter. "I'm here because you're going to help me save the world."

His eyes were pale like a blue sky, and they brightened. "The whole world?" he asked with a chilling breath.

John did the same. "The whole world."

"We're fighting zealots?" Margaret said with a smirk that reminded me entirely too much of John. "When do we leave?"

"*I'm* fighting zealots." His heavy hand roughed up her raven hair. "But you'll be with me in spirit."

If we explained more, they would have begged him not to go or at least not fight alone. I was still tempted to convince him to stay home, but where could we hide from a man who exploded? Congress knew John's identity. It was all a matter of time before the world found out about New Seneca.

"I'll tell you all about my battle later. It will be my greatest tale yet."

I latched onto John's arm, recalling when I was building my reputation as Runaway. I hadn't raided any major plantations yet, and I heard of farms and scattered households where people were enslaved. I came to the peak of Kennesaw Mountain to expand my vision. Up there, I saw rail lines and the smoke of a locomotive. Sunlight shone on top of a few buildings, and a few steeples reached toward the heavens.

When my feet landed on Kennesaw Mountain again, a blast of warm air hit my face. John turned his back toward the city to shield me. We must have been twenty miles away from Atlanta, yet a black cloud of smoke and an ominous glow flickered for me.

"Don't stay here. Go to Lincoln until the battle is over."

"I can't, John. I have to stay here with you."

The winds began to whirl behind John and lifted him off his feet. They robbed me of his touch. "Go on, woman. I'm serious. Lily Anne needs you."

The harsh air got into my lungs, and I coughed into my hands. If it were bad there, the center of the blast must have been hell on earth. I wanted to defy my husband as he rose into the sky, but I couldn't bear the thought of risking us both. Lily Anne needed her mother, and her father was mad enough to fight through Hades to find us again.

I returned to the White House, but Lincoln was not there. I was escorted by Mr. Pike next door to the War Department Telegraph Office. He spent more time there than any other place, listening to reports about the war late into the night. I informed the president that John had entered the blast zone and was about to engage in battle.

All lines from Atlanta were gone. Updates slowly came from Marietta, while surrounding troops marched to mount a rescue team for survivors. Based on the burden pulling on Lincoln's shoulders, I don't believe he expected to find many.

The history books aren't very detailed with this particular story. Witness accounts were scarce, and Americans would rather idealize their own heroes. But this story has been told dozens of times. Children of New Seneca grew up on it and passed it on to their children. It's the story of their founding, and what it took to keep us safe.

Thick storm clouds unnaturally formed over Georgia. A caped man rose high into the grayish skies, above the air's unnatural heat and poison. The atmosphere tightened and loosened according to his will, until a burst of thunder roared across the land, followed by the sound of abundant rain.

The heart of the city was so hot that the droplets sizzled and evaporated before hitting the ground, but it did ease the heat and breathing for the survivors.

John's eyes brightened and ceased the wind from underneath him. While rapidly descending to the ground, he focused on the moisture in the air. A chilled breath escaped as John braced himself and spoke the mantra drilled into our bones. "I am strong."

A burst of snow exploded across the city like an avalanche. The bright snow blinded him for a moment, and then his vision blurred from exhaustion. He had to push himself—long enough to heal and long enough for the wind to catch him before he smashed into the ground!

John wavered as he landed on his feet, his knees practically buckling. In the center of the blast, the snow never reached the ground; it collapsed into warm rain midair, drenching John before it flashed into steam at his feet. John had a natural heat resistance, thanks to a trait inherited from his father, but this heat was different—harsher than normal fire. He summoned Alfie's power to cool down, but something sick lingered in the air and clung to his lungs.

John fell to his knees, coughing as a glowing figure took shape in the smoke. John's body struggled to adapt. His vision came into focus, and dozens of ash shadows darkened. Buildings were destroyed as if part of them had disappeared without notice. Not all bodies vanished, though; some were charred corpses. In the distance, a woman with bloodied and blistering skin screamed over half of a small, blackened body. The other half had collapsed into dust against a broken wall.

"You came…"

John's senses flared like a warning siren in his skull. Every nerve in his body commanded him to run. He teleported to the screaming woman, just as a flash of light and heat swallowed the street. Instinct took over. He ripped himself backward through space, again and again, through the afterimage of the blast. He didn't stop until his back collided with a tree. A heartbeat later, the blast hit—debris and sound tore through the air where he had just been.

John stretched forth a hand, as if he could push back the heat. He felt it beginning to sear patches of his skin, so what hope did the woman in his arms have?

That small, blackened body was likely her child. What would it look like for his wife to weep over Lily Anne? If he didn't stop this menace, they could be the next to burn!

John grunted and focused on the surrounding moisture. The temperature wrestled within his hands. He focused on the molecules in motion, feeling them like Mary Anne could. But it was John who forced them into stillness with Alfie's borrowed gift.

John's lungs felt a chill, then his hands. He hollered and pushed, with all he had, until it expanded into a great wall of ice!

The blowback pressed cracks into his shelter, and John pushed his body harder. The wall thickened and hardened, refreezing the edges as they tried to melt. He would not stop pushing until the force stopped.

He fell to his knees, letting the ice cool his face. Slowly, his mother's power began to knit what was torn. He could breathe and see again. He was a survivor. Lillian taught him how to be.

Once his breath was restored, he looked down beside him. The woman's body had more severe burns, and she no longer breathed. He reminded himself that she was only a human…

But he had failed to save her, and that filled him with fury.

He rose to his feet and paused. Getting close to Gideon was too dangerous if he could explode at will. John's instincts warned that full combustion was a very bad idea…but a smaller, more controlled explosion might be enough.

But he would have to get close to concentrate.

John took another deep breath. It came easier this time. His powers were extraordinary, but he was not without limitations.

The same had to be true for Gideon.

John looked at the sky, thinking of his dear wife, and warped space to rise into the clouds. The winds caught and held him aloft. He shifted the atmosphere again, more violently than before. Rain broke apart in midair, torn into ice crystals and vapor by the instability of the storm column. A flash of light danced across the black clouds, followed by a crack loud enough to sound like Heaven screaming for justice.

On the outer perimeter, rainfall struck the ground hot enough to hiss into steam, briefly cooling the air for survivors. But closer in, moisture never settled. It was dragged upward before it could complete its fall.

At the center, it was too hot to be hell. Flames could not hold. Heat could not spread. It stayed steady and accumulated. All life—even the buildings—returned to dust in Gideon's presence.

But John would not relent.

He focused on dropping the temperature and pelting the city with waves of icicles. As he pushed himself beyond what he believed his limits to be, he thought of Margaret, Alfie, and the rest of the children he trained and cared for. They were too young to grasp the depth of their potential, but John was tapping on the door of it. New Seneca was going to be well cared for, even if he didn't survive.

But John didn't plan to die!

Gideon was hidden in dark smoke, but John could sense him—like placing your hand over a boiling pot of water. But it was only bubbling then. John had a moment to breathe and prepare.

John could feel it now: not just the wind, but direction. Not just a storm, but a path. A tightness in the sky. That's where the bolts of light threaded across the clouds and screamed.

If John could feel the path, like the nozzle of a gun, surely, he could make it discharge.

One survivor would later write that the flash of light was so bright, he thought the sky was splitting open for Christ's return. The thunder that followed sounded like an army of archangels, blowing their trumpet across the horizon.

But his awe did not last. When the second strike came, and lightning tore across the ground like a sweeping barrage of burning arrows, the illusion of divinity shattered. It was not mercy. It was not a judgment. It was an indiscriminate force.

The superheated atmosphere bent and guided the strikes away from Gideon, but they were close. The air around him was defiant. Every bolt searched for an endpoint yet found none that would hold. They split, scattered, and reformed elsewhere.

John's jaw tightened. His body quivered, but his resolve strengthened. The storm did not know where Gideon ended and the world began—so John would define it!

He gritted his teeth and focused on a line of air. He felt its heat and thought of Alfie as he clenched frost-bitten fingers in a tight fist. He drew a slow, chilled breath to steady himself, then hollered as he pulled the heat from a narrow column of air, easing its turbulence until it aligned into a single continuous path.

For a moment, the storm held. It recognized the path. A blast of light and destruction followed, striking beneath Gideon's feet.

Gideon might have been an exploding man—but he was still just a man. The force knocked him off his feet and shot him through a cloud of black smoke. He was in John's sightline now, flat on his back and gathering his bearings. The heat around him shifted—subtly, but unmistakably.

John was able to feel the source of Gideon's instability. It gathered in his chest and spilled outward. The thought of combusting it sent shivers down his spine. Gideon must have been exhausted, but another blast—hot enough to strip John's bones clean—was still possible.

Even still, he needed to get close.

John closed his eyes and steadied himself, thinking about his place of refuge—home. When the love of his life abandoned him, he persisted. Fueled by devotion and hope, he cut and lined every plank of wood and hammered every nail. He carved the bed where his future daughter was conceived and painted her bedroom, well before her mother could stand to let him hold her.

His body became cold, so cold that it began to ache. Alfie might have been completely impervious, but John was not. His teeth chattered, so he clenched them tight. He had to keep pushing and focus cold moisture into his hands…

He found comfort in the memory of the first time he made love to his beloved, and the certainty it gave him. The smell of her cooking, morning flowers, lavender in her bath. He cherished every smile. Every laugh. Even the fire in her when she lost a fight. He could picture her—rising into the sky, drawing back her fist—so certain she would win.

Of course, he caught her hand when she teleported. His senses and reflexes were too sharp.

The same could not be said about Gideon, who struggled to rise on his feet again.

John hollered, shaping his fury into a spear. He hung too high in the air for Gideon to track clearly, but the man below braced for impact. Another large blast was out of the question, but once the Blue Devil was close enough to Gideon to see the white in his eyes, John would be dust.

Gideon held his glowing chest, and it flickered.

Seventeen thousand. That's how many lives were taken because John smashed in the heads of zealots with a shovel, after they had nearly burned him and his beloved alive. They put a bullet in Lillian's head, just like his father. He killed them all terribly for it, and it was justified.

And in Gideon's eyes, that was enough to justify seventeen thousand more deaths.

John didn't want to be the reason for tiny husks of ash. He just wanted to go home and hold his daughter.

With one final yell, he drew back his spear and committed to strike. As he moved forward, his eyes caught the ground behind Gideon. The air subtly snapped as John folded space and closed the distance in an instant. Gideon blinked, foolishly believing he still had time.

A spear of ice came into his vision as it burst from his chest.

Gideon's breath caught. If he had been granted a final wish, it would have been to purge the "curse" before him—but even his wishes were not protected from John.

Blood burst from his eyes, mouth, and ears. A rupture in his brain was the cause. John thought it best to be thorough.

Then heat surged reflexively through Gideon's chest, one final time.

John gripped the spear of ice and froze it in place as the air around them blistered. He grimaced as his cheeks, nose, and knuckles singed, but he held tight to the spear, even as his lungs began to burn.

Expand. Freeze. Expand.

John closed his eyes and fought against the heat surging through the field, forcing it to compress where it spread and collapse where it tried to build. If he didn't contain Gideon, Lily Anne wouldn't have a father—and he would be condemned to the afterlife without his beloved.

He could not allow it.

The violent force threw John off his heels, but he held the line, pushing streams of cold into the unstable core until his arms and hands darkened to blue.

Chapter Twenty-Nine

John was found passed out on a pile of snow, shivering. Adam carried my husband on his back and flew him to us. Nathaniel gathered a small fire in his palm, and warmth slowly returned to John. Zhang followed with healing light until he winced and opened his eyes.

I was the first thing he saw. "Hi, John."

A slow smile crept on his face…until he recognized the tree behind me on Kennesaw Mountain. Then he sprang to his feet, spitting mad. "I told you to go to Lincoln!"

"I did, John! But I couldn't stand by and do nothing!" I glanced around at the crowd of onlookers. "I wanted to get Zhang, in case you needed healing. Everyone else wanted to come. They demanded it."

He paused, taking them all in at once. "You brought Margaret? She's thirteen!"

"It's only search and recovery," Kachina said, arms folded. Tillie was perched on her shoulder. "You've trained her for worse."

Margaret lifted the hood of her oilcloth cape. "I can handle this."

John grunted lowly, sensing the weight of them all. "Wait..." His voice dropped. "You moved fifty people by yourself?"

John held my face. There was still blood under my nose. I wiped it again with my checkered sleeve. "I had to."

My beloved's chest began to swell. He tried to mask his brimming pride with a headshake, but the smile was too strong. "You're impossible."

"And you love me for it." I was grateful to taste John's lips, to have him hold me in his arms. He was, indeed, the most powerful man in the world, and that came with heavy crosses to bear. But I would always be willing to stand beside him and carry the load.

John pulled away from my lips and let the happiness linger for a moment more before straightening up. "Let's get to work. Search and rescue only."

Margaret took to the sky. Her control was still unrefined, but her talent bent the storm, cooling pockets of lingering heat. Nathaniel calmed fires with his will. Kachina walked barefoot through the rubble, sensing survivors beneath it. Mr. Clark smelled charred flesh and heard the faint breathing of soldiers. He directed James, Christopher, and Benjamin to them, and they led men in digging through collapsed streets. Adam, Caroline, and Arthur ferried survivors out by air, while Henry ran them to safety.

Kachina carved a shelter in the earth, something to keep the wounded out of the rain. Zhang and John moved from body to body, healing all they could, while Edith eased their suffering with illusions. Dr. Bingle and Hoshi's copies treated wounds with herbs and salves from Evelyn's garden. When we were overwhelmed, I transferred patients to Manhattan, Jacksonville, and other hospitals I had visited. Tony rode in Tillie's shadow as she searched for marching troops from Marietta. He then transported them to the devastation.

They witnessed all of us using our God-given gifts to heal a broken world that had firmly rejected us. We pushed until we couldn't lift ourselves into the sky, our knees buckled, and we fell over from exhaustion. Even Henry ran so much that his pants caught fire.

Only John had the stamina to keep going until the end.

As John rubbed the soot-covered hand of a whimpering child, his eyes softened. Men, women, children—hand after hand, he tried to ease their suffering. Even with all our gifts, many died. Some even faded in his arms.

I think he lost his taste for war that day. Even his most ardent supporters were shaken by the piles of bodies. I couldn't imagine all those families mourning, and many would have no body left to bury.

As terrible as it all was, I was grateful to be by John's side. Cooper had to suffer through the horrors of war alone.

The newspapers didn't know the fine details of the battle, but they had plenty to say. Southern papers, matter-of-factly, reported that John stopped Gideon. Their editorial spin was that Gideon was also Gifted, and this was a deadly gang war between a violent species. John was also exposed as a deserter of the Confederate Army, and being the husband to the most wanted woman in the South did him no favors.

The North reported *Archangel Defeats the Man Who Burned Atlanta.* Their story wasn't as detailed as the tales John told the children, but they did write about the rescue. A thirteen-year-old girl controlling the weather certainly sold papers.

Now that it was public that John was Archangel, the nation wanted to know more about us. The papers speculated that John was also Ghost. Congressmen had questions, and since Lincoln appointed John as the federal agent of the reserved lands in the Dakota Territories, they expected answers.

John appeased them in private, meeting with Republicans. He denied nothing about his history as Ghost and was completely unapologetic. He was far less patient and charming than his land baron performance. His prickly demeanor was fine for Congressman Thaddeus Stevens, who was also a frank and impatient man.

Stevens despised the zealots' ideology. He wanted them hanged and special protections for Gifted as a condition for joining the Union. John liked that, so he extended a hand of trust toward him.

A handful of Senate Republicans were invited to New Seneca for dinner and a tour. A few members of Lincoln's cabinet came on another occasion. John wanted us all to appear harmless, except for one arranged nonchalant display of power—Caroline and Margaret chasing each other across the sky, and Emma carrying a cart full of equipment overhead. They needed to understand John wasn't the only one who could crush them if they stood against us.

Dinah told John she didn't want to dress up to entertain humans, and he let her be. She did watch Lincoln's men from the balcony of the manor when they arrived. She told Tillie that Secretary Seward's eyes were too busy, like he was taking inventory. Then, she returned to isolation.

The politicians marveled at our diverse community. They witnessed children of all colors playing together at the park, Paul leading a Bible study of women at the church, Kachina working with freedmen as they broke ground for the future library, and Natives working with white farmers to harvest Evelyn's crops. They were comforted by how much Agnes and Martha admired me and by the respect I showed in return.

During dinner, many questions and comments were directed toward me. They wanted to hear how Runaway saved 151 colored men and many of my other adventures. John stood back with a smile as I charmed the very men who held the power to solidify our agreements with Lincoln.

Afterward, I visited Dinah in her room. I thought our progress might brighten her mood, but she hardly smiled after her powers were taken. Her cynicism was entirely intact, though. "The humans are probably taking stock of our powers. What happens if they find out about the boy? Mr. Pike would certainly procure him for a contingency. You don't make a god without learning how to kill it."

I couldn't disagree. I had to assure Dinah of what I already knew. "John would find a way to stop them. We all would."

Beyond our resolve, I did have faith in our Republican allies. I forced Dinah to accompany John and me to a debate, so she might witness how passionately they fought for our rights. Before we were escorted to the gallery, Mr. Pike took us to a temporary exhibition room where beautiful pieces of art were displayed. In the center stood the finished work of Lincoln reading the Emancipation Proclamation with his Cabinet.

"Is it what you hoped for?" John asked quietly in my ear.

The colors were a bit darker and washed out than they ought to be. After meeting Lincoln's Cabinet, I didn't believe the artist quite captured their likeness. Lincoln was much warmer in person. "I recognize them."

Dinah laughed, hard and brief. "That's a polite way to put it…"

History is difficult to preserve because it evolves in the present. Personal perceptions are a lens through which artists and journalists use to paint the world. Our story was told by men who despised, feared, and even worshipped us. I suppose that's why I finally decided to write all of this down, so the world would know history through the eyes of a woman who loved and was well-loved in return.

The gallery was crowded, but Mr. Pike had three seats reserved. I sat between the two of them to watch their faces as the men below stirred with restless energy. Their voices were like rising tides, whispering to one another over their desks, then shouting across the room.

"Slavery may have been struck down by law, but what is freedom without safety to enjoy it in? We cannot abandon them to violence."

"It is not only the slave who has suffered under the heel of persecution. For far too long, America has turned a blind eye to the cries of her children!"

"All people of these United States must be protected by law. For what other purpose does the government exist than to ensure our God-given rights?"

John smiled every so often. A grin even broke through Dinah's sour face, but she hid it once I had noticed. I leaned over and patted her hand. "It's alright to have hope. Everything eventually changes. This is America's moment."

The room fell quiet as the Gentleman from New York was called to the podium. His face was refined by time rather than diminished. He wore his suit well and walked as if he knew it. The Democrats straightened in their chairs, expecting a show.

"Gentlemen, we have long-debated equality—its meaning and its purpose—in this chamber." His eyes, sharp and polished, turned toward Thaddeus Stevens. "When our Founders declared 'all men are created equal,' did they speak a poetic truth for a civilized people…or a literal statement of Creation?"

The Gentleman from New York almost smiled as he turned about the room. "Not all men can fly. Not all men can call lightning from the heavens. Not all men can reduce an entire city to ash at will."

John's face firmed as his fingers pressed together. Our fellow gallery members struggled not to look our way.

"No, God did not create all men to be equal, so what does it mean to be equal under the law?" The Congressman pointed toward Stevens, whose face wrinkled more than usual. "My Republican colleagues have confessed that liberty is not secure in a world where safety is not guaranteed. How can *we* be safe in a world where little girls can rip bank vaults from their hinges? Where men could stab you to death faster than you could ever feel the pain? Where the ground could swallow you up at a woman's whim?"

His Democratic colleagues loudly interjected with cheers, which fueled him with enough audacity to point his wicked finger toward John. "That man could scatter our brains across this chamber with a thought!"

I was remarkably surprised by my husband's restraint. I was also surprised that Dinah stayed silent, besides her heavy breaths.

"And yet he hasn't." A Republican spoke.

Then another. "He defeated the Burning Man and saved thousands of lives!"

"If they possess such power, why has this war not already been ended?" He asked the Republicans. "None of these so-called 'Gifted' have offered to fight for the Union's cause. Are they not loyal to this nation?"

It wasn't only the Democrats who cheered the Gentleman from New York. A ripple of resentful muttering moved through the Unionists. Several Republicans remained seated and were too quiet.

"They have not risked their lives, yet they are so eager to claim protection of our laws. Why should they be entitled to equal rights or special privileges granted by President Lincoln?"

My breath steadied, then held.

Righteous indignation burned in the Congressman's chest and spread throughout the room. "Twenty thousand acres in the Dakota Territories have been designated to a federal agent through Lincoln's war powers, which he has abused time and time again. A person granted such authority by the Union should be loyal to it, without question!"

A roar erupted in the Chamber, and each voice pulled at the threads that made up Dinah's armor.

The Congressman continued, shouting over their cheers. "How can we be safe if such beings are left with unrestrained and unsupervised power? We are the ones who need protection under the law from the men created to be unequal."

Each word struck at what Dinah had lost. The zealots took her power, but at least she had New Seneca. The humans were coming for that as well. We watched John, expecting him to rise and make men cower with a word or look.

But he did not move.

Dinah whimpered and rushed out as the gavel struck.

"Go after her," John commanded with his eyes focused on the men below him.

Dinah was in the hall, holding her chest. She turned away from me as I approached. "Take me home."

"Dinah…"

"Charlotte, please!" She reached for me but kept her face hidden. I wanted to drag her back inside, but I also hated the idea of Democrats seeing her cry.

I took Dinah home, and she composed herself in the privacy of her room. By the time her light skin lost its redness, Congressman Stevens had finished his reply to Congressman Wood. He reminded the Chamber of his Southern sympathies and that Mr. West, the assassin who meant to take the life of the beloved Runaway, was under his employ. Stevens said there was no need to be envious of the Gifteds' power when men like the Gentleman from New York squandered the little they had.

He easily won back the room by reminding everyone of the zealots' brutality and their level of infiltration. He didn't call Wood a traitor, but he questioned why traitors found comfort around him. Stevens used Wood as evidence that the Gifted needed self-determination.

John was pleased.

Dinah apologized for her outburst.

John promised that he'd never allow the humans to take their land, and he also assured that talks with Senate Republicans were going well.

Later that night, John went for a flight to think. Lily Anne and I watched him from a balcony. I asked Agnes to bring me tea. Instead, Dinah brought me a cup.

"I miss flying."

I moved Lily Anne to one arm and grabbed the cup with the other. "You'll be able to do it again real soon. You may have to fly around the world and bring more Gifted home."

Dinah pressed a hard grin to her face and leaned against the iron railing. She looked so lovely under the moonlight as she longed to join John amongst the stars. "Thank you."

I blew into my hot tea and braced for something strange. "For what?"

Dinah shrugged and kept her eyes focused on the ripples in her tea. "…for trying to change me." She laughed, so I must have looked as surprised as I felt. "I wish I could share your optimism. It's touched everyone here."

"Everyone except for you…"

"I'm not untouched, but…" She shrugged again, her eyes glittering with pain. "I've seen too much of this world." She wiped away a tear as soon as it escaped. "Some things aren't meant to change. Humans don't. I don't. Fate doesn't. Atlanta was always meant to burn…"

The Reaper's Sight was a heavy burden on her. At times, a shadow of darkness loomed on her face as it did to Lincoln. I thought she'd get peaceful sleep with no powers, but Dinah had yet to find rest.

"Even if we can't change Fate, we can stand in defiance of it. We were there to save who we could."

"*You* were there…" Dinah's voice faltered, and she wiped away another tear. I expected she felt guilt for staying behind. She collapsed and sobbed once we teleported everyone home.

"Don't misunderstand me. I'm committed to our people. I love them. I love John. I love…" She turned her head away from me, embarrassed. "…I love you…"

I smiled bashfully, but kept quiet.

"I appreciate all that's being done here—I'll fight to protect it—but I just can't trust the humans." She spoke as if such a thought would pull her apart at the seams. "The only peace we can have is through power."

The old Charlotte, the one who ran away from John years ago, would have argued with her. I understood the world better now. The Union was created by force, and the Union was preserved by force. The difference between General Grant and his predecessors was his commitment to keep advancing, no matter the cost. Even then, the Siege of Petersburg raged on. Men like Cooper refused to retreat and refused to hold.

He kept pushing forward.

The Union forces were stretched around Confederate supply lines, leading to starvation and desertion. Grant was going to win by outlasting his enemy. There were other ways to win a war—overwhelming force, manipulating the enemy until they tore themselves apart, strategic alliances—but they all required force to maintain peace.

"Well," I raised my cup, "it's a good thing we have John."

Dinah paused as her eyes glimmered, as if I had reassured something in her. A smile crept across her face, then she clinked her cup against mine. "Amen to that."

We scorched our tongues for the pleasure of filling our bellies, as we watched John master the night sky. Dinah didn't have to stay on the ground for long. By the end of March, her powers returned.

I asked her if she still had visions of rushing ships. "No. The ship has finally found the shore."

I assumed the Civil War was finally coming to an end.

Chapter Thirty

On April 2, John chain-teleported to Petersburg during the Union's final siege. Once the tremors began, General Robert E. Lee fled. John didn't immediately chase after him. Cooper never got close enough to talk to John, but he saw him on the front lines, healing soldiers.

One soldier wrote in his journals that John spoke after flooding him with warm light. "It would be a shame to die so close to the end."

General Grant continued the pursuit. On April 9, stone walls were erected around Appomattox Court House. General Lee had no choice but to surrender. Grant was kind enough to allow Lee's men to keep their horses, so they could return home and resume civilian life, likely as farmers. He knew what it was like to have to work for a living and thought they should be afforded the dignity of providing for their families. Lincoln was also strongly against retribution. He wanted the nation to heal.

Grant wrote in his autobiography that he gave John a cigar as they watched the defeated general ride away. Grant never quite trusted my husband, but he was intrigued by the young man. "After all this time, why now?"

"Why join you now?"

Grant nodded. He never believed John was necessary, but more lives could have been saved if he had intervened. Or…so he thought. Death still visited Union soldiers in Atlanta and reaped thousands.

John took a long inhale of the cigar. Lee was approaching the horizon then. "There's a man under your command by the name of Joseph Cooper. Do you remember him?"

Grant had hundreds of thousands under his command, but he couldn't forget one introduced to him by the president. "Sergeant Cooper? Yes."

"He's a friend of my wife. He's married to her best friend, and he's never had the chance to see his boy." John tapped the cigar, and ash fell to the ground. "I wanted Charlotte to stop crying about it."

Grant placed a fist on his hip and stared, bewildered. "You ended a war for a woman?"

"What other reason is there to end a war?"

It was a remarkable answer, and one Grant understood. He always did like me. "I'll make the arrangements."

On April 10, Mary Anne put on a white dress with pink flowers and took her son to Central Park. They sat on a blanket and ate together, ignoring the judgmental eyes of strangers. JoJo still enjoyed his mother's milk, but he was a big boy with a growing appetite. Mary Anne was tempted to put him in trousers early. He was a masterful crawler but had yet to take a step without Mary Anne's hand. His legs were strong enough. He just needed a little bit more courage!

"Come on, JoJo!" She bent over and walked with him. "Come on, JoJo. You can—"

"Mary Anne!"

She stopped. Mary Anne pulled back her hair and caught her breath. She clutched her chest, overwhelmed by a sudden wave of loneliness. She needed time to gather her courage. If she turned and did not see her husband, she was going to collapse and never get back up.

Mary Anne took one final breath and turned around. "Joseph!"

Cooper ran to his wife and allowed her to soak him with fresh tears. "I missed you, sweetheart."

"I knew you'd come back to me. I knew it!"

JoJo was left standing on his own. He was disturbed by his mother's tears and began to cry.

"Oh, no…" Mary Anne picked up the boy, and he hid in her chest. "It's alright, JoJo. This is your daddy."

Cooper took a hard swallow before touching the back of his son's head. He marveled at how accurately he dreamed of him, but he mostly attributed that to Mary Anne's drawings. "He's beautiful…"

Cooper couldn't say much more than that for a while. He held them both until JoJo realized he was safe and his mother was happy.

I wrapped my arms around my husband's waist. "Thank you."

"It was no trouble at all, my dear. No trouble at all." Without John's interference, Cooper likely wouldn't have been home for another year. The United States Colored Troops were assigned by the federal government to guard the Texas-Mexico Border from the French-backed forces of Napoleon III. They were also stationed along the South to protect colored folks and enforce Reconstruction policies. Cooper didn't want special treatment, but he was extremely grateful for it.

I planned to make up for lost time with my friends. On April 14, I was getting ready to take Lily Anne to play with JoJo. Dinah offered to fetch Asha's doll for me in New York. She returned and transformed back into herself just as John entered our room, out of breath.

He and Grant had a meeting with Lincoln. While they waited, Grant asked if I cared for plays. John said yes. Grant was invited to see *Our American Cousin* with the president, but he sadly had to decline because of his wife.

"Does your wife not care for plays, General?"

"My wife does not care for Mrs. Lincoln."

John chuckled but understood. "If the President will have us, we would love to attend."

Lincoln thought it was a wonderful suggestion from Grant. After the meeting, Grant decided to leave Washington to visit relatives in New Jersey, and John flew home quickly to deliver the good news.

"That's wonderful!" I hugged John tight, then remembered Lily Anne in my arms. "But what about Lily Anne's visit with JoJo? He was looking forward to it."

Dinah laughed. "Cooper survived a war, but he can't look after two babies? You can't miss this opportunity."

John didn't say anything, but his eyebrows certainly agreed with her.

"I suppose Mary Anne knows how to take care of a baby…" It's not as though I hadn't left Lily Anne alone before, but I was uneasy about it.

"Come on," Dinah gently punched my arm. "You can wear a nice dress. John can finally wear that fancy suit from Christmas." She boldly rubbed John's chin. "He can shave…"

"I was thinking about growing out my beard."

I didn't say a word, but my eyebrows agreed with Dinah. I didn't mind how he looked with some hair on his face, but I preferred it to be smooth.

"Fine. I'll shave, but we had best hurry."

John quickly washed and sent for a barber. He was so handsome, and the cut of his waistcoat was perfect. I loved how the olive leaves shone in the light. "You look divine."

"Oh?" He pulled me into his chest. "I'm finally 'divine' enough for you?"

"Well…"

He tickled my neck with kisses as punishment. It was the first time since I had been burned by the zealots that I went out with my neck completely bare. It was still an ugly scar, but I didn't have to hide it anymore. The only thing around my neck was the locket Dinah gave me.

John held Lily Anne in his arms and rubbed her belly. Her laughter was soothing. I couldn't remember the last time I looked at her and thought of our near-death experience. "Are you ready, Mrs. Cohen?"

I touched my husband's arm and smiled. "Of course, Mr. Cohen."

We took Lily Anne to the Crimson Hotel. Mary Anne was understanding and encouraged us to go. When I lingered a little too long, holding my daughter's finger, Mary Anne nudged me away. "Go. Everything will be fine."

"We promise," Cooper said with JoJo resting on his father's shoulders, growling like a little monster.

"Don't teach her how to do that…" I warned. "I'm raising a proper lady."

"Unlike her mother," John muttered.

I elbowed my husband in the chest and teleported us both to the White House. "You had better behave if you want to tear this corset off later…"

"Yes, ma'am…" The low timbre of his voice sent a shiver down my back. I found myself hoping the play didn't last too long.

Mrs. Lincoln was already waiting in the carriage when we arrived. Her husband was detained, telling funny stories with friends up until the last possible second. He wanted to stay, but the newspapers had already announced that he and General Grant would be at the theater. He didn't want to disappoint the people.

We waited patiently for a few minutes. Mr. Slade eventually went to fetch him. "Apologies." He looked larger than life in his top hat.

"No need," I told him. "I thank you for the invitation."

"We all have cause for celebration." I assumed Lincoln meant the end of the war until his smile deepened.

An amazed curve spread across John's lips. "We have the votes?"

"Indeed, we do."

I'm embarrassed to say I lost all decorum and threw myself at the president. "The Senate will ratify our agreement? And they agree for us to run New Seneca?"

He gently laughed at my shameful display. "Just the agriculture you'll provide to the West is more than worth their cooperation."

John would never express gratitude as openly as I did, but he did offer his hand for a firm shake. "Thank you, Mr. President…for everything."

Lincoln's other wrinkled hand took hold of John. "Don't give up hope, young man." The president's grip was tight, and he shook my husband. "There's more light in this world than you realize."

John paused and breathed in Lincoln's words as if they were oxygen. His eyes met mine, and I finally believed my husband had learned to have genuine hope without bloodshed. "I'll try to remember that, sir."

I was happy, even honored, to have that time with the president and my husband, but something heavy lingered in the air that I couldn't shake.

I tried to resolve the uneasiness with conversation as we walked to the carriage. "You've done so much for the country. I hope you'll consider resting for a while. Perhaps you should take Mrs. Lincoln on a trip."

"Don't worry, Lady Cohen," Lincoln took my hand and helped me onto the carriage, "I'm meeting with an old friend soon."

My stomach dropped, but I masked it with a smile. "That sounds nice."

Mrs. Lincoln was in an irritable mood. She hardly wanted to look at her husband and fanned herself practically the entire way to Ford Theater. The rest of Washington was festive. Though Jefferson Davis had not surrendered and had not been captured, everyone knew the war was over. The Confederates had no more fight left in them, and hardly any men if they did.

As I watched families on strolls through the street, I took hold of John's hand. What happened to Atlanta was devastating, but I was grateful that none of his other targets were destroyed.

We had the honor of sitting in the presidential box. The play was about an awkward, naïve American cousin visiting aristocratic English relatives. My husband rarely laughed out loud, but as a former circus performer forced to adjust to high Southern society, he found it hilarious.

After the curtain fell at the close of the second act, Lincoln's bodyguard, Mr. Parker, came up from behind and whispered to John. I heard something about New Seneca, and John nodded.

My chest tightened. "What is it?"

"There's some kind of situation."

"With Lily Anne?"

"No," he chuckled. "Calm down. She's safe with Mary Anne. I have to go to the telegraph office in the War Department."

"I should come with you."

John pushed me back into my seat. "If I need you, I promise, I will send for you." His eyes were stern before he kissed my forehead. "Enjoy the play."

John placed his hand on Lincoln's shoulder and spoke quietly in his ear. Lincoln patted John's hand, soft like an understanding father, and nodded. "It's fine. Go."

John left out, and Mr. Parker slipped out as well. He did not return.

I wished John had let me follow him. I had a terrible pit in my stomach, and it had been there all day.

I looked at Lincoln, since he had visions of the future. He seemed peaceful. The unnatural shadows that loomed around him were gone. Even Mrs. Lincoln had relaxed and conversed with him. She was slighted by the Grants' backing out (even though she didn't care for Mrs. Grant either). She appeared to have given in to her husband's joyous mood.

I tried to surrender to the joy in the room. President Lincoln deserved his victory, and so did the woman forced to worry about him and her own son at war. So did all those people in the audience, laughing at a play about cultures clashing. We all deserved that small moment of relief after so much bloodshed. I cherished the love the people had for their leader, and the content on his face from a job well done.

John came through the curtain, just as we were all caught in a roar of laughter, but…

The bottom of his frock didn't flare quite the right way, and the subtle olive leaf detailing was absent from the brocade. I looked up at John's clean-shaven face, and it was a bit younger than it ought to be. It was the face of the man I had run away from years ago…

A pistol emerged from his pocket, and my body felt as though it had sunk into the floor. I wanted to warp time and space to knock John's hand away, but I had never felt so fixed in place, as if Fate had taken hold. It was only a moment's hesitation, but that was enough to alter the course of our world.

Even though she wore my husband's face and spoke in his voice, I couldn't unsee Dinah. I knew John too well, and I certainly knew her well enough.

"Bygones."

A burst of flame. A blast of smoke. A snap of Lincoln's head.

The crowd didn't hear the gunfire over the roar of laughter, but they certainly heard Mrs. Lincoln's shrieking scream.

I sprang from my seat, determined to stop her. She was powerless while in John's form!

Then she drew a knife, stained with fresh blood, and I froze.

My worst fear was that she had found a way to get the jump on John and wound him. The second was that she found Moses.

Dinah smirked, then jumped from the balcony and landed on the stage. The actors had run away, and much of the crowd was still too shocked to strike her down. But even if they weren't, who would be crazed enough to fight who they believed to be the Archangel…

Ghost…

Blue Devil…

"Sic semper tyrannis!" Dinah raised her bloodied knife into the air. She wasn't declaring victory—not just yet. She was declaring war and judgment upon the land. "Long live New Seneca."

AUTHOR CHRISTINA L. BARR

NINJADUSTPUBLISHING.COM

Dear Reader,

Thank you for joining Charlotte, John, Cooper, and Mary Anne on another remarkable adventure. They will return.

To check out my other titles and to join my email list for updates, visit **NinjaDustPublishing.com**.

If you enjoyed this book and this series, I ask that you leave a review on Amazon and other book websites, social media, and spread the word to your bookish family and friends. It does help to grow my business.

Charlotte has always had a special place in my heart, and it means the world to me that I've been able to share her with you. She has a winding path ahead of her that will be quite different than the history we know.

I look forward to continuing her journey with you.

www.ingramcontent.com/pod-product-compliance
Lightning Source LLC
LaVergne TN
LVHW100502110826
845146LV00002B/484

* 9 7 9 8 9 8 8 1 2 7 3 5 2 *